Prime Suspect
The sensational thriller behind the h... Jane Tennison fights for the right to... boys will do anything to stop her.

A Face in the Crowd
The coroner's report identifies a body as young, black, female and impossibly anonymous. DCI Jane Tennison is up against a brutal killer in a city where racial tensions are running high.

Silent Victims
DCI Tennison is now head of the Vice Squad. On her first day in the new job, a high-profile case, one that might threaten to destroy everything she has worked for.

Above Suspicion
The first instalment in the bestselling Anna Travis series. Anna tackles her first murder case, one that might bring down a much-loved actor.

The Red Dahlia
Anna Travis and James Langton return, and must work together to capture one of the most terrifying killers they have ever encountered.

Clean Cut
For DI Anna Travis, this time it's personal, as DCI James Langton is almost fatally injured by a suspect and Anna must keep them both alive.

Deadly Intent
DI Anna Travis is pulled onto a case that has already claimed the life of an ex-police officer. As the body count rises, the police wonder if this is the work of a killer from the past.

Silent Scream
Young British film star Amanda Delany had the world at her feet, until she's found murdered. As DI Anna Travis strives for promotion, this might be the case that breaks her career.

Blind Fury

The body of an unidentifiable young woman is discovered. And then DI Anna Travis receives a letter from an imprisoned murderer: he knows the killer.

Blood Line

Under the watchful eye of DCS James Langton, Anna Travis is given her first case. But is it a full-blown murder investigation or purely a missing person case?

Backlash

The police arrest a murder suspect, but then the man tells them this is his third victim. Cold cases will come back to haunt DCS James Langton and DCI Anna Travis.

Wrongful Death

A suicide case suddenly starts to look like a murder, as DCI Anna Travis is torn between her London team and a new opportunity with the FBI in America.

Cold Shoulder

The first novel in the thrilling Lorraine Page series. Lieutenant Page was thrown out of the homicide squad, but as they search for a serial killer, she is the witness they need.

Cold Blood

A movie star's daughter vanishes in New Orleans. Lorraine Page tackles her first case as a private eye, which threatens to drag her back to the world she fought to escape.

Cold Heart

A movie mogul is found dead in Beverly Hills and his wife is charged with murder. Private investigator Lorraine Page is the only one who believes she is innocent.

The Legacy

From the poverty of the Welsh pit valleys to the glories of the prize ring, from the dangers of prohibition America to the terror of Britain at war, this is the story of a remarkable family and its fortunes, and the curse that forged their name ...

The Talisman
Sequel to *The Legacy*. For each new generation, the talisman is the key to a fortune. It should have been buried with Freedom Stubbs, but his spirit is restless in his grave.

Entwined
No matter how cruelly twins are separated, their lives will always be entwined. In the newly liberated streets of modern Berlin, two extraordinary women are drawn together.

Sleeping Cruelty
Sir William Benedict has always desired acceptance from society's elite. But after a political scandal erupts around him, he turns to his sisters to help him get revenge.

Royal Flush
A wealthy race horse owner has set high hopes on a magnificent colt, Royal Flush. Afraid he will lose everything, he pursues a diamond worth dying for.

Twisted
Marcus and Lena Fulford are the envy of their friends. But when their daughter Amy goes missing, the perfect facade starts to slip.

Tennison
From the creator of the award-winning ITV series *Prime Suspect*, starring Helen Mirren, comes the fascinating back story of the iconic DCI Jane Tennison.

Hidden Killers
Newly promoted Jane Tennison is conflicted as she becomes inextricably involved in a multiple rape case, and must put her life at risk in her search for answers.

Good Friday
When rookie detective constable Jane Tennison survives a deadly explosion, the race is on to unmask the terrorists. Before the Metropolitan Police's Good Friday dinner, Jane must convince her senior officers that her instincts are right before there's another bloodbath.

Murder Mile

Jane Tennison, now a Detective Sergeant, has been posted to Peckham CID, one of London's toughest areas. As the rubbish on the streets begins to pile up, so does the murder count: two bodies in as many days. With press headlines claiming police incompetence, Jane is under immense pressure to catch the killer - before they strike again . . .

The Dirty Dozen

Jane Tennison has worked hard to become the first female detective ever posted to the infamous Flying Squad. But the Dirty Dozen is a notorious boys' club. Determined to prove she's as good as the men, Jane discovers from a reliable witness that a gang is going to carry out a massive robbery.

Blunt Force

After being kicked off the Flying Squad, Jane Tennison soon discovers the most brutal murder she has ever seen.

Widows

A security van heist goes disastrously wrong and three women are left widowed. When Dolly Rawlins discovers her gang boss husband's plans for the failed hijack, an idea starts to form. Could she and the other wives finish the job their husbands started?

She's Out

The thrilling sequel to bestselling *Widows*. After serving a lengthy prison sentence for the murder of her husband, Dolly Rawlins is set free with only one thing on her mind – the six million in diamonds she stashed prior to her imprisonment

Widows' Revenge

Against all the odds, Dolly Rawlins and her gangland widows managed the impossible: a heist their husbands had failed to pull off. But then Dolly discovers that Harry Rawlins isn't dead. He knows where the four women are and he wants them to pay.

Buried

The gripping first book in the new DC Jack Warr thriller series.

Lynda La Plante

COLD SHOULDER

SIMON & SCHUSTER

London · New York · Sydney · Toronto · New Delhi

First published in Great Britain by Macmillan, 1994
First published by Simon & Schuster UK Ltd, 2010
This edition published by Simon & Schuster UK Ltd, 2020

1 3 5 7 9 10 8 6 4 2

Simon & Schuster UK Ltd
1st Floor
222 Gray's Inn Road
London WC1X 8HB

Simon & Schuster Australia, Sydney
Simon & Schuster India, New Delhi

www.simonandschuster.co.uk
www.simonandschuster.com.au
www.simonandschuster.co.in

A CIP catalogue record for this book is available from the British Library

Paperback ISBN: 978-1-4711-9861-8
Trade paperback ISBN: 978-1-4711-9919-6
eBook ISBN: 978-1-8498-3263-2

Printed and bound in Great Britain by
CPI Group (UK) Ltd, Croydon, CR0 4YY

COLD SHOULDER

LOS ANGELES, CALIFORNIA, 12 April 1988

I T WAS dark, the alley lit only by neon flashes from the main street; not a single bulb above the many exit doors leading into it remained intact. The boy was running. He wore a black bomber jacket, a bright yellow Superman stripe zigzagging down its back, shiny black elastic knee-length pants, and sneakers, flapping their tongues and trailing their laces.

'Police officer – freeze.'

The boy continued to run.

'Police officer – freeze.'

Half-way along the alley, the boy sidestepped a trash-can like a dancer. The flash of a pink neon light gave an eerie outline to his young body, and the Superman stripe appeared like a streak of lightning.

'Police officer. *Freeze!*'

The boy turned, in his right hand the stiff, flat metal of a 9mm pistol, and Lieutenant Page unloaded six rounds from the long-barrelled .38. Bam-bam-bam-bam-bam-bam. The boy keeled over to his right, in a half spin, his head jerked back, his arms spread, his midriff folded, and he fell face forward. His long dark floppy hair spread over his gun arm, his body shuddering and jerking before he was still.

Lieutenant Page approached him, automatically reloading the .38. The hoarse voice of Sergeant William Rooney barked out to back off, to put the gun in the holster.

Pushing past, his wide ass hid the body as he squatted down on his haunches.

'Get back in the patrol car, Lieutenant.'

Page did as requested, snapping the shoulder holster closed. The car doors were open. A crowd of people, hearing the gunshots, had started to press forwards. Two uniformed officers barred the entrance to the alley.

Sergeant Rooney was sweating as he carefully wrapped the weapon before easing it away from the boy's bloody fingers. He stared at the young dead face, and then walked slowly to the patrol car. Leaning inside, he displayed the weapon, cushioned in his snot-stained handkerchief. 'This the weapon, Lieutenant?'

The 9mm pistol was a square, flat silver Sony Walkman. Inside was an old Guns 'N Roses tape. Axl Rose had been blasting out 'Knock on heaven's dooowarrr . . .'

Page turned away. Rooney's fat face was too close, sniffing like an animal, because he knew, and he could smell it. 'Get back to base – and fucking sober up.'

The locker room was empty, stinking of feet and stale sweat; the vodka was stashed under a tote-bag. Just feeling the coldness of the bottle gave Lieutenant Page's jangling nerves instant relief. Page leaned on the sink, not even attempting to hide the bottle, drinking it like a man in a desert until it was empty. Suddenly the sink was slippery and the floor uneven, moving, shifting, and the long bench against the nearest wall was a good, safe, secure place to hide beneath.

Fifteen minutes later, Sergeant Rooney kicked open the door. 'Lieutenant? You in here?' His fat feet plodded down towards the washbasins. 'Captain wants you in his office. Now!'

*

She was hunched against the wall beneath the bench, her skirt drawn up, one shoe on, one off, knee poking through laddered tights. Her head rested on one arm, the fine blonde hair hiding her face. The other arm was spread wide across the floor. Rooney tapped her upturned hand with the toe of his black crêpe-soled shoes. 'Lieutenant!'

He bent down slowly, and yanked her hair roughly away from her face. She was unconscious, her lips slightly parted, her breathing deep and laboured. A beautiful face, the fine blonde eyelashes like a child's, the wide flattish cheekbones, and perfect straight nose almost enhanced by her flushed pink cheeks. Out cold, Lieutenant Lorraine Page was still a class act.

Rooney stood up, then with his foot pushed her arm closer to her body. She moaned and curled up tighter. He wandered over to the washbasin, picked up the empty bottle, then returned to Captain Mallory's office.

'You find her?'

'Yep! She's out cold on the floor, bottle must have been in her locker.'

Rooney stood it on the Captain's desk and just shrugged his shoulders. 'She's a lush, been coming down for a while. I reckoned she was in control, I've talked to her . . . She always had an excuse – you know, marital problems, et cetera, et cetera . . .'

Captain Mallory stared out of the window, then sighed. 'Get her out of here, will you? Get her badge, her gun, and tell her to stay out of my sight.'

Lorraine didn't even empty her locker: it was done for her, everything stuffed into the regulation tote-bag. The key was taken, her weapon and badge signed out. She was helped from the station, too drunk to comprehend what was happening. Rooney had gripped her by the elbow, pushing her roughly through the corridors. The zipper on her skirt

3

was half undone, her slip showing, and if Rooney hadn't held her tightly she would have fallen more than twice. He even banged her head, as if she were a prisoner, warning her to dip low to get into the rear of the car. She had laughed, and he had slammed the patrol car door so hard the vehicle rocked.

'You think it's funny? I hope you can sleep tonight, Lieutenant. Sleep as deeply as that kid you took out. Now get her the hell out of here . . .'

As the car drove out of the station yard, the mother of the dead boy, weeping hysterically, was being brought in. All she had been told was her son had been shot while escaping from a drug bust.

Two weeks later, Lieutenant Lorraine Page was officially out of the precinct. No disciplinary action was taken. She lost her pension, her career, but her forced resignation was quietly glossed over and it never reached the press. Tommy Lee Judd's family never knew the name of the officer who shot their fourteen-year-old son six times. At the inquest it was stated that the boy had ignored three police warnings to stop. He had been charged with crack dealing two years previously but the statements from his probation officer that he had been clean for the past six months were glossed over. His death was recorded, and the record filed away. No one mentioned that he had had no weapon, and had been mistaken for another suspect – or that the officer who opened fire had subsequently been released from all duties and was no longer attached to the force.

In fact, Lieutenant Page might never have existed, and, as word passed, no one who had worked alongside her spoke to her again. She was given the cold shoulder. She had betrayed their badge, her rank and position: she had been drunk on duty, and a fourteen-year-old boy had died.

They closed ranks – not to protect Lorraine, but to protect themselves.

Twelve years' service, two commendations, and a service record that any officer, male or female, would have been proud of, was over. No one cared to find out what would become of ex-Lieutenant Lorraine Page.

After the shooting, when she had been unceremoniously dumped outside her apartment, she had stumbled inside and collapsed onto her bed. Mike, her husband, knew she was on night duty and had already dressed, fed their two daughters, and driven them to the school. Their babysitter, Rita, collected them and took them home where she checked the details of Lorraine's duty times. According to the rota, she was due for two days' leave. Rita would have stayed to make the girls their lunch, but little Julia, only six years old, was calling, 'Mommy, Mommy,' as four-year-old Sally began collecting her toys to play with her mother.

'Is your mommy home?' Rita asked, surprised.

'Yes, in bed,' piped Julia.

Rita tapped on the bedroom door and peeked into the room. Lorraine was lying face down, her head beneath a pillow. 'Mrs Page? Is it okay if I shoot off now?'

Lorraine eased away the pillow. 'Yeah, yeah, thanks, Rita.'

Julia climbed up on the bed. She had already delved into her toy box, bringing out puzzles and something that made a pinging sound that cut like a knife through Lorraine's blistering headache.

'Mommy, can we go to see the puppets?'

'Mommy, I want pee-pee.' Sally pulled at the duvet.

'*Mommy*, can we go to see the puppets?' Julia repeated, as Lorraine slowly sat up.

'Mummy, I want pee-pee *now*.'

Lorraine had to hold onto the edge of the bedside table

5

to stand upright. She took her younger daughter into the bathroom and helped her up onto the toilet. 'I not got my panties down,' the little girl howled.

After a good belt of vodka she found in the freezer, she was not so jumpy and strung out. Once she'd settled the girls in front of the TV, Lorraine had another few nips of vodka with three aspirin so she could bathe and clean herself up. By the time Mike returned from his office, the kitchen was in order, their bed remade and Lorraine, with her face made up, looked presentable. Wearing a long cotton wrap, she was checking the fridge for what she could cook for dinner when she heard the front door slam and Mike's usual, 'Hi, honey, I'm home.' He dumped his briefcase and, smiling, came to stand behind her, slipping his arms around her and cupping her breasts in his hands.

'We got time for a quick one before they come?'

Lorraine eased away from him. 'Who?'

He returned to the table and picked up his briefcase. 'Donny and Tina Patterson. I said we'd eat here and then go to the movie. Rita said she could babysit.'

She closed her eyes.

'You haven't forgotten, have you? I wrote it down, it's on the board.'

'Fine, yeah. Did you get groceries in?'

Mike pursed his lips. 'You said you'd pick up dinner on the way back from work this morning.'

'I'm sorry, I forgot, I'll go get something now.'

'Don't bother,' he snapped, and went into the bedroom. She followed.

'It's no bother, for chrissakes, it'll take me two minutes. I'll get dressed and—'

He began to loosen his tie. 'Send out for something. There's a list by the phone of takeouts, they'll deliver.'

She rubbed her arm. 'Anything you don't make a list of, Mike?'

He glared. 'Yeah, and you know what that is. I haven't

6

slept with you for a month – you want me to start putting that down? Like, when it suits you?'

She walked out, not wanting to get into an argument as the two little girls hurtled into the bedroom to fling themselves at Mike. He swung them round, tickled them on the king-sized bed to their delight. Then he showered and changed, bathed each girl, combed their hair and put them into their pyjamas. They were tucked up in bed, each with their own special toy, when he returned to the kitchen. Lorraine was sitting with a mug of black coffee.

'You want to say goodnight to them?'

'Sure.' She got up and bumped into the edge of the table, and gave a little smile. As soon as she was out, he checked the freezer. One look at the bottle was enough.

'Did you call for some takeouts?'

Lorraine was cuddling Sally. He repeated the question and she sighed. 'Yeah, yeah, there's some pizzas coming any minute.'

'Pizzas?' he said flatly. Donny Patterson was his superior in the law firm, so Mike had wanted something more special but he went to lay the dining table. He could hear Lorraine reading to the girls, who were giggling loudly – she was good at funny voices. He took out the best cut glasses and the best mats and even gave the cutlery a quick polish. Then he went into the kitchen and began to make a salad. He was neat and methodical as usual, carefully slicing each tomato, washing the lettuce and the celery.

'You going to get dressed?' he called out, one eye on the clock.

Lorraine was lying on their bed, eyes closed. He opened the wardrobe and began to choose a shirt, a pair of slacks. He took great pride in his clothes, which were expensive, stylish, proof of his new-found success. He was hoping to be made a partner in the firm, and knew it was on the cards.

'What you working on?' she asked, stretching her arms above her head and yawning.

7

'It's the Coleridge case. It looks like he'll divorce his wife without too much aggravation, and it's more than likely he'll get custody of the children.'

'Really?' she said, without any interest, as she watched him holding up a shirt against himself.

'Do you like this shirt?'

'Yeah.'

'What are you going to put on?'

She swung her legs over the side of the bed. She didn't feel like seeing anyone, let alone going to a movie or having dinner with two self-important, wannabe-wealthy middle-class snobs. 'Oh, maybe the Chanel or the Armani. I dunno, Mike, and I've got a headache.'

'You want an aspirin?'

'Nope, maybe I'll take another shower.'

He held her close. 'The Pattersons are important to me, sweetheart, okay?'

She kissed him and rested her head against his shoulder. 'I'll be a good girl, promise.'

He touched her cheek. It never ceased to amaze him that she could arouse such passion in him. He loved the way she looked, her tall slender body. 'You okay? Did you have a bad night?'

She pressed her face into his neck. Did she have a bad night? The painful blurred memory physically hurt, and she moaned softly, a half sob which he took to be confirmation that she wanted him. He began to slide her robe off her perfect shoulders, kissing the side of her neck.

'I better change.' She stepped away from him.

'What's the matter, Lorraine?'

She sighed, shaking her head. 'Nothing, Mike. I guess I'm just tired.'

He heard the shower running and slowly got dressed. As he reached for his cufflinks, he saw the photograph of Lorraine and her former partner, a dark, tousle-haired, moody-looking guy. Lorraine always referred to him as Lubrinski. Since his death, she had been different, unapproachable. Mike had tried unsuccessfully to get her to talk about it but she seemed loath even to hear Lubrinski's name. Mike had not said a word when the silver-framed photograph appeared after the man had been shot. He had tried to persuade Lorraine to take a few weeks' leave but she refused. Instead, he knew, she had asked for more overtime and specifically night duty.

Lubrinski's laconic half-smile seemed to mock him yet he was sure there had been nothing between them. She had admired him, Mike knew that. He had seemed shy, hardly speaking on the few occasions Mike had met him.

Lorraine came out of the shower, wrapped in a towel with another round her wet hair. 'You want some aspirin, sweetheart?'

'Yeah, yeah, thanks.'

The hair-dryer felt leaden in her hands. All she wanted was to lie down and sleep. Mike handed her a glass of water and two aspirins. He kissed the top of her head; her hair fell in a soft pageboy style, flattering her heart-shaped face. 'I'll maybe get a partnership soon,' he said, as he sat on the edge of the bed. 'It'll mean a lot more money and you not having to work.'

She slowly rubbed foundation cream over her cheeks, a small dop on her nose. 'When will you know?'

'Well, this Coleridge case is good for me. He's an influential guy – he's even said he'd recommend me to his friends.'

'All getting divorces, are they?' He laughed as, dipping the thick brush into the face powder, she dabbed it over her face. 'I thought you wanted to specialize in criminal law.'

'Yeah, I did – maybe I still do but it's good to get a grounding in all aspects. Besides—'

'Divorce pays better, doesn't it?'

Mike's expression was sharp. 'Is that such a bad thing? Do you like this place?'

'Yes, of course I do.'

'Well, I'll be making a lot more soon. Next we'll have a house in Santa Monica, right on the beach.'

'Oh, business is that good, is it?'

He laughed again. 'It'll take a few years but Donny seems to think I'll go places. When I look around here, it's hard to believe what we came from.' He slipped his arms around her. 'And I'll never forget how I got it. If it wasn't for you . . .'

She smiled, now brushing on a light blusher. Those days when he was studying day and night, when he worked at any odd job he could get, those days were a long, long time ago.

'We'd have more time together as well.'

Lorraine put down the brush. 'If I was at home with an apron on and a casserole in the oven?'

'I doubt if you'd ever be that, sweetheart, but you know we should think about it and also, maybe, about a holiday. When will you know about your next vacation so I can work it out with Donny?'

She carefully outlined her lips, her pale blue eyes staring back at herself. 'I'll talk it over with Rooney.'

The doorbell rang and Mike charged out. It was the pizza delivery. She should get a move on. She heard him on the phone, confirming with Rita what time she was to come over. Mike the methodical! Upwardly mobile Mike was so different nowadays, she seemed to be losing him.

Lorraine stared at the blurred picture of Lubrinski. She touched his face with the tip of her forefinger. His face seemed to crease into a smile – but that was impossible, he'd never smile at her again. Lubrinski was dead; he had died in her arms. Sometimes she felt as if *she* was dead. Nothing seemed real any more; this apartment, all the new-fangled equipment Mike filled it with, all the new furniture.

Mike had organized the move down to the curtains. She'd liked their old place even if you did have to lug the strollers up and down three flights of stairs. She missed the neighbours. Sometimes Mike's energy drained her and lately she was always tired. She never spoke to anyone in the building and didn't even know who lived on her floor.

The doorbell rang again and she could hear Mike welcoming the guests. Still she sat, unable to muster enough energy to join them. She pulled out the bottle from the bottom drawer of the dressing table. Just a few nips, that's all she needed.

Donny and Tina were chattering in the kitchen while Mike uncorked the wine. Tina Patterson looked as if she was heading out to a premiere rather than the local cinema. She kissed Lorraine on both cheeks and Donny gripped her tightly in a firm 'trust me' handshake. Mike ushered everyone into the dining area and proceeded to pour the wine. He was doing everything – seating his guests, bringing in big platters of pizza, apologizing for the informal dinner, explaining that Lorraine had only just got home from duty.

She sat sipping her wine. She couldn't look at the pizza: its bright colours made her feel like vomiting. They discussed the Coleridge case. Donny constantly gripped Mike's shoulder in another 'trust me' gesture that irritated Lorraine, just as she found Tina's delicate hands with their red-painted nails annoying. They made clicking noises on the plate as she picked up a minuscule slice of pizza, popping it into her collagen-enhanced lips. 'To look at you, Lorraine, you'd never know you were a cop, it's just amazing.'

Lorraine forced a smile as Mike reached over and held her hand. 'I'm so proud of my wife. You know, she's been commended for bravery twice.'

He sprang up from the table, went to the side cabinet and returned with two framed photographs. Lorraine in

11

uniform with President Reagan and in a group picture of the year's most decorated officers. 'Lorraine caught the killer of that little girl, you remember the one that was found in a drainpipe? The caretaker had done it, she was the one that caught him.'

Tina made the right noises, shaking her head and rolling her eyes – with admiration, Lorraine supposed. She drained her glass; she needed another drink. 'I'll put some coffee on,' she said, leaving the table. She took out the vodka from the freezer and drank from the bottle. She had only just slipped it back when Tina appeared carrying the dirty dishes. 'Men's talk in there. Can I help?'

Lorraine laughed. She was feeling better, eased by the vodka and wine. Tina began to stack dishes in the dishwasher.

'Do you get involved?'

'Pardon?'

'When you have to do these murder investigations, do you get involved?'

'Yep.' Lorraine was fixing the coffee percolator.

'Does it affect you?' Tina enquired, running her hand under the tap. 'I always know when Donny's on a tough case – he's so moody. He works out at a gym to get rid of the anxiety, you know, but . . . that case of the little girl . . . That must have been terrible.'

Lorraine fetched a tray. 'She was only six, her name was Laura Bradley. She'd been raped, tortured, and she had a face like a little angel. Yeah, it hurt me.'

Tina hunched her shoulders. Lorraine set the tray, placing each cup in its saucer with deliberate precision. 'For a while afterwards, I got possessive about the girls, scared they'd be picked up. It never leaves you. You think it'll go away but it never does.'

Tina had left the kitchen. Lorraine could hear her next door.

'Okay, you guys, no more business, this is movie night. We're just gonna enjoy ourselves.'

The movie programme had so many previews that Lorraine excused herself, saying she wanted to go to the ladies. She needed another drink. She reckoned if she just slipped out to the nearest bar and had a quick one, she'd be back before the film had started.

When she hadn't returned half-way through the movie, Mike went to look for her. He called Rita to see if she had gone home; she hadn't. Back in the cinema, he told the Pattersons that Lorraine sent her apologies but had felt ill, and rather than spoil their evening had gone home. It was after eleven when Mike got back. He checked Lorraine's duty periods; as he'd known, she was on a two-day break but he called the station in case he'd got it wrong. He was put through to Bill Rooney.

After the call, Mike paced the apartment, sat in the kitchen, then in the living room flicking the TV from channel to channel, waiting. He checked the girls. He waited until he fell asleep on the sofa. He was woken by shrieking laughter. He got up and crossed to the window.

Lorraine was standing on the pavement outside, paying off a taxi. Two people were inside it. He watched her drop her purse and fall against the wall before she reeled into their building.

The front door was open as she walked from the elevator. She took a deep breath and, with a fixed smile, peered inside. Mike grasped her by the elbow and drew her into the kitchen. He kicked the door closed. 'Where've you been?'

'Oh, I hadda do something.'

'What?'

'Just interview somebody.' She was trying to keep her

voice from slurring; her eyes were unfocused. He pushed a cup of coffee towards her. 'I'm tired.'

'Drink it and sober up.'

She rested her head in her hands. Mike drew out a chair and sat opposite her. 'I know, Lorraine.'

'Know what?'

Mike told her he had spoken to Rooney. She sighed, looking away, and shrugged. He leaned over and gripped her hand. 'I know about the shooting. Why didn't you tell me?'

She tried to pull away her hand. He wouldn't let go. 'Why won't you talk to me?'

She pushed him off and hunched up, clasped her hands together. He had to lean further forward to hear her. 'There's nothing to say, Mike.'

He got up and paced the kitchen. 'What do you mean, nothing to say?' He wanted to slap her. 'You were drunk on duty and you're telling me that you have nothing to say about that?'

She gave a soft laugh. 'No complaints.'

He gripped her hair and drew her head back. 'You killed a boy, Lorraine.' She made no effort to release herself and he shoved her forwards, disgusted. 'You shot him.'

She nodded.

It was impossible for Mike to know what she was thinking; her eyes were glazed, and she seemed to be half smiling.

'You're out, don't you understand? You're out of the force. *They've kicked you out!* Rooney told me they took your badge.'

She shrugged again. 'Well, that'll make you happy, I'll get some nail extensions and some Carmen rollers and make myself into a Tina clone. That what you want, Mike? *Is that what you want?*' Her face was ugly with rage. She had no shame – and worse, no remorse.

'Go to bed, Lorraine.'

She stumbled against the doorframe, and fell face down on the bed. Mike didn't bother to undress her. He was almost out of the room when she said something, muffled by the pillows. She was repeating it, over and over. 'I don't remember, I don't remember, he's dead, he's dead.'

Mike never heard the plaintively whispered, 'Don't go.' Instead, he sat in his study until dawn, compiling notes for his case.

The next morning, glass of whisky in her hand, Lorraine sat at the kitchen table. Nothing meant anything any more.

Mike joined her and sat opposite. She held up the glass. 'Hair of the dog.'

'What are you going to do?'

'You mean work?' she asked.

'No. Will you be on trial or what?'

'I don't know.'

'I blame Lubrinski. You've not been the same since you started working alongside him.'

'Lubrinski's dead, for chrissakes.'

Mike watched as she refilled her glass. Suddenly he sprang to his feet and yanked away the bottle. 'That's enough.'

She held out the glass like a dirty diaper. He snatched it. 'It's nine thirty in the morning. How long has this been going on?'

'What going on, Mike?'

Holding the bottle, he almost felt in need of a drink himself.

'I just wanted something to ease me up a bit. I've been kind of tense lately.'

He was speechless.

'I don't have a problem, Mike. It's just . . . lately things have got to me.'

He felt as if someone had punched the air out of his

lungs. Lorraine looked at her bare feet. 'I feel all strung out and I can't remember what happened the other night.'

He swallowed. 'You killed a kid, Lorraine. They've taken your badge, you're out, don't you understand?'

'Oh.' She said it lightly, still staring at her feet.

'I'm gonna talk to Rooney again. I don't know if they're pressing charges.'

'Have you talked to Rooney, then?' she asked.

'Yes,' he snapped. 'I told you last night. How the hell do you think I know about it? And what do you think Donny is gonna say about this if it gets into the press?'

'Donny?' she said, confused. 'What's he got to do with me?'

'He's got a lot to do with *me*. I'm in the middle of a big case right now. How do you think it's gonna look if they find out my wife not only opened fire on a kid but was drunk on duty as well?'

She rubbed at her neck. 'It's none of their business.'

Mike closed his eyes. 'No? You think the press won't have a field day with this?'

She took out a cigarette, hands shaking. He watched as she tried to light it. She inhaled deeply. 'You remember that day, Mike?' He sighed. She looked at him, tilting her head to one side. 'Best day of my life. You'd just qualified and . . . what happened, Mike? I feel like I don't know you, like I'm drifting in some kind of sea. I hate what you're becoming and I've gone along with it, never felt I could say anything to you but it's all changing between us. You want success more than you want me.'

Mike poured himself two fingers in the tumbler she had used and drained it. It was as if someone was pulling the rug from beneath his feet. Suddenly everything he had been striving for was ragged at the edge. He sat down, cradling the glass in his hands. 'Nothing has changed between you and me, nothing. I love you. I always *have* loved you. Okay, maybe I've had to put in more hours lately, but then so

16

have you. You know I wanted you to give up work, you think I didn't notice the strain you were under, but you'll never talk to me.'

She knelt down at his feet and wrapped her arms around him. 'I want things to be the way they were when we both had nothing.'

'You had your career. It was me that had nothing,' he said petulantly.

'But you know why? I worked hard so we'd have a home and you'd have your chance.'

He kissed her forehead. 'Maybe you haven't noticed that I'm earning good money now – you haven't needed to work for years and you're missing the girls growing up.' She leaned against him and he slipped his arm around her. 'Whatever happens, we'll come through this together.'

They went to bed and made love for the first time in ages. That evening, Lorraine began to prepare dinner, even putting candles on the table. Then it started, the panic. It swamped inside her, beginning, as always, with fast flashes of faces. Lubrinski, then Laura Bradley, and now the boy? A boy running with a yellow stripe down his sweater. All she could think of was to get just one drink; then the panic would stop and the pictures would blur into oblivion. She wouldn't feel so uncomfortable, so trapped. Just one drink would do it and she'd be all right. She went on with the dinner, having just one more, then another and another.

Mike didn't come home until after midnight. He saw that the table had been laid for some special occasion; the candlewax had melted over the cloth. In the kitchen he found two wine bottles and the Scotch bottle, all empty in the trashcan with the remains of dinner.

Lorraine was asleep, still in her dress. He didn't wake her, not even to tell her that Donny had offered him a partnership. He pulled the quilt from beneath her and laid it gently over her. He went round the apartment and threw every liquor bottle he could find into the garbage chute.

Not until he slid into bed next to her did he see that Lorraine was cradling the picture of Lubrinski in her arms. When he tried to take it from her she moaned and turned over. Maybe there had been a lot more to their partnership than he had realized.

Next morning, Lorraine was up early, cooking breakfast for the girls. Mike could hear her laughing and talking. By the time he went into the kitchen, they were ready for school.

'I'll drive them,' she said. 'You haven't had breakfast yet!'

He snatched up his car keys. 'I'll drive them, okay?'

'When will you be home?'

'I'm in court today so I'll be late.' He walked out without kissing her goodbye, slamming the front door.

She was making the bed when he called. He'd booked her a doctor's appointment.

'You did what?'

'Listen to me, sweetheart, he's somebody you can talk to, friend of Donny's—'

Lorraine interrupted, 'I don't need a god-damned shrink, especially not some asshole friend of Donny's. There's nothing wrong with me that a few days' rest—'

Mike was adamant, not wanting to sound angry but unable not to. 'Yes, you do, Lorraine, listen, don't hang up—'

Her voice was icy, calm and controlled. 'No, Mike, I don't need anybody, I am not sick, okay? That's final. I'll see you tonight.'

Lorraine made no contact with the station. She checked the newspapers for articles on the case, but was afraid to read about herself. She was afraid, too, to be seen on the street and for the next few weeks she led a double life. When Mike left in the morning she did some housework and ordered in groceries. When Rita brought the girls home, she played with them, read to them and cooked dinner for Mike. He knew she was drinking but she denied it and he never saw her with a glass of alcohol in her hand. He had no idea that she spent her days sitting in front of the television with a bottle of vodka. She appeared sober, keeping herself at a sustained level, and every night he would look for empty bottles. Mike hid from himself that she was drinking consistently, partly because it meant less tension between them. He asked Rita to tell him if she ever saw Lorraine drinking, especially in front of the girls.

It was only a few weeks later that Rita called him. 'You'd better come home, Mr Page. I don't know where she is – she left the girls by themselves – anything could have happened.'

Mike drove like a madman back to the apartment. The children had been alone for most of the day. After Mike had calmed them, he asked Rita to stay with them, and went out in a blind fury to find his wife. After searching in vain for three hours, he called home. Rita was in tears: Lorraine was back, she was drunk, unable to stand upright. A cigarette in her hand, she apologized, telling him that she had had an important meeting. She seemed barely to hear him when he talked to her, and if he touched her she screamed abuse at him. Then, as if terrified of something or someone, she begged him to hold her tightly.

Next morning, shame-faced, she promised him he would never see her like that again. Never again would she touch a drop.

Mike coped as best he could. He instructed Rita never to leave Lorraine alone with the girls until he was at home. But the situation grew worse. Time and again he confronted her with empty bottles he found hidden around the apartment. She would swear she hadn't had a drink and even accused Rita of planting the bottles.

Mike was at breaking point. He tried to understand Lorraine's frame of mind by putting himself in her position – she had shot an innocent boy and had lost the job she had always been so proud of – but all he felt was shame and guilt, of which she showed none. She seemed more intent on blaming his success for her failure.

'You spoiled it. You wanted us to move up and we were happy where we were.' The continual goading made him feel she was pushing him physically to hurt her. 'You were the housewife, but I was out on the streets. You were the mother, but I had to earn for both of us, out on the streets with my breasts still full of milk for my babies.'

No matter what he said she twisted it against him. If he had any guilt about those years when she had kept him and the children, it was soon dispersed by her venomous onslaughts. She exhausted him; night after night he would come home in dread to find her ready for a row. At other times, she would kneel at his feet and beg his forgiveness, pleading for him to carry her to bed. And yet she seemed incapable of tears.

In the end Mike went to Donny's doctor friend. He needed to talk it over with someone. The doctor warned him that unless Lorraine sought help Mike would be dragged down with her. He encouraged him to leave her and thus force her into taking medical help. But Mike's own guilt and his awareness of how much Lorraine had done for him, held him back. When his daughters became scared of their mother, though, Mike made one last attempt.

Lorraine finally agreed and he accompanied her, quiet and sober, to the doctor. She spent two hours with him, talking first with Mike present and then alone. After the appointment she had appeared almost triumphant, admonishing Mike for wasting money. There was, as she had said to him over and over again, nothing wrong with her.

Mike returned the following day and was told that Lorraine had insisted that she was perfectly all right and able to cope with no longer working. She had refused to give a blood test.

But the drinking carried on and the rift between them grew deeper. Lorraine adamantly refused to admit anything was wrong: she had her drinking under control. She was becoming sly; apparently sober, she continued to dress well but rarely left the apartment. Mike continued to find empty bottles hidden away.

Only six months after Lorraine had left the force, he filed for divorce. He refused to make her leave the apartment, and signed it over to her with the contents. She protested when he insisted on custody of the girls but otherwise seemed not to care. He gave her five thousand dollars and promised three thousand a month in alimony. She was strangely elated when he brought the papers for her signature, which made him suspect that she didn't believe he would go through with it. But she signed with a flourish and smiled.

'You do understand what you've signed, don't you, Lorraine?' Mike asked quietly.

'Yes.'

He gripped her tightly. 'I'm leaving and taking the girls but call me if you need me, and I'll do whatever I can to help. You need help, Lorraine, all I want is for you to acknowledge it.' He felt wretched. She helped him pack, kneeling to lock the suitcase. She was wearing a pale blue denim shirt and her feet were bare. Her hair shone as she bent over the cases. Mike wanted to hold her, to make love to her. This was madness.

The Pattersons came to help with the cases. The girls, clasping Tina's hands, thought they were going on holiday. It had taken only the afternoon to get everything packed and out, such a short time after all the years they had been together.

'Tina's going to take the girls in their car. Do you want to say goodbye to them?' Mike asked.

21

'No. I don't want to upset them.' She heard her daughters asking if they were going to see their granny and why was Mommy staying behind? She heard Tina reassuring them that Mommy would be coming to see them. She heard Donny call out that everything was in the car. She heard Mike say he would be out in a few minutes. She heard Rita saying goodbye, her voice breaking as if she was crying.

Mike walked into the kitchen. Lorraine turned and held up the glass. 'Just milk.'

He leaned on the table. 'I don't want to go, Lorraine.'

'Doesn't look that way to me.'

'I love you.'

She tossed her hair away from her eyes. 'I love you too, Mike.'

There seemed nothing left to say. He crossed to her, reached out and held her in his arms. She rested her head against his shoulder, the way she always used to. He could smell lemons, a clean, sweet smell of freshly washed hair, and he tilted up her face and kissed her. She had the most beautiful clear blue eyes he had ever seen. She seemed to look straight through him, yet her lips had a soft sweet smile.

'Promise me you'll get help?'

'I'll be okay. Don't worry about me, Mike.'

Donny Patterson sat in the car. He watched Mike walk slowly down the path, looking as if he was crying.

'You okay, partner?'

Mike got into the car and blew his nose. 'I feel like such a prick. She doesn't seem to understand what's just happened.'

Donny put his arm round his friend. 'Look, buddy, I been through this three times. It's not easy, but, Jesus, now it's over you're gonna feel such relief. She's got problems. You tried every way to help her, Mike.'

'Maybe we'll get back together,' Mike said.

Donny gripped Mike's knee. 'Christ almighty. When are you gonna face facts? She's a drunk and she was dragging you down with her. If she won't get help, you're gonna have to forget her, act like she's dead. Believe me, it's the best way. Say to yourself she's dead, be a hell of a lot easier.'

Mike nodded. His heart felt like lead. He closed his eyes. 'I loved her,' he said softly.

Lorraine sat on the sofa, flicking the TV from channel to channel. There was no need now to hide the half-bottle of vodka that lay beside her. She could do what she liked, she was on her own. She didn't deserve anyone's love or respect, she knew that. She was deeply ashamed that she didn't have the guts to slit her wrists. Or was it because she didn't deserve to die so easily? She was her own judge, her own jury. She had to be punished.

Lorraine finished the vodka and went in search of more. She looked around the bedroom, seeing the open wardrobe doors, the empty hangers where Mike's clothes had hung, and backed out of the room. She discovered another bottle hidden in the kitchen and had drunk most of that before she wandered into the children's room. She was humming tunelessly. She got into Sally's tiny bed, holding the bottle to her chest. She could smell her daughter on the pillow; it was as if the little girl was kissing her face, she felt so close. She reached over to the other bed for Julia's pillow and held it to her cheek. She snuggled down clasping the pillows. 'My babies,' she whispered, 'my babies.' She looked drunkenly at the wallpaper, with its pink and blue ribbons threaded round children's nursery rhymes. 'Run rabbit, run rabbit, run, run, run . . .'

She could feel a lovely warm blanket begin slowly to cover her body, a soft pink baby blanket, like the one tucked round her when she was a little girl, like the one she had wrapped round the dead child's body. She felt her chest tighten with panic, her body tense. She could hear him now. Lubrinski.

'Eh, how ya doin', Page?'

'I'm doin' okay, Lubrinski,' she said aloud, startled to hear her own voice. 'I'm doin' fine, partner.' She frowned. Who was screaming? Somebody was screaming, the terrifying sound going on and on and on, driving her nuts. She rolled out of bed and ran from the room. She tripped and fell to her knees until she was crawling on all fours into the bedroom. The screaming continued. She heaved herself up and caught sight of a figure reflected in the dressing-table mirror. She clapped her hands over her mouth, biting her fingers to stop the screams. *She* was the woman, it was *her* screaming. The terrible sweating panic swamped her.

It was Lubrinski's smiling face that calmed her, looking up at her from the dressing table. She snatched up the photograph. 'Help me, Lubrinski, for chrissakes help me.'

'Sure, honey, take a shot of this, then what say you and me go and rip up the town? You wanna hit the bars?'

'Yeah, why not, you son-of-a-bitch?' Lorraine gave a tough, bitter laugh, and felt herself straightening out as the panic subsided and she was back in control.

That was the first night Lorraine went out to drink alone in one of the old downtown bars. She never knew who she ended up with, she didn't give a damn, and they didn't mind when she called them Lubrinski. A lot of Lubrinski lookalikes came and went, and there were many more drunken nights when she didn't care if Lubrinski was with her or not. All she cared about was getting another drink to keep her away from the terrified woman who screamed.

The downward spiral began the night after Mike left her. It was a long road she travelled, searching for oblivion. It was frighteningly easy. People were real friendly in the bars but they used and stole from her. When the money had gone she sold the furniture, and then the apartment. It was good to have a big stash of money, never to worry where the next bottle came from, and still she kept running from the woman in blue whose terrible screams frightened her so much and dragged her down so far. She could take the fights, and the taunts of prostitutes and pimps. Hell, she had arrested many of them. They pushed her around and spiked her drinks but drunk, she didn't care. Drunk, the screams were obliterated. Drunk, the men who pawed her meant nothing. Drunk, she could hide, feel some comfort in slobbering embraces, in strange rooms, in beds where the little rabbits didn't creep into her mind and she didn't hear the children singing, a high-pitched shrill voice that turned into a scream.

'Run, rabbit, run rabbit, run, run, run . . . RUN.'

CHAPTER 1

CALIFORNIA, 11 April 1994

S HE HAD almost died that night. The hit-and-run driver had probably not even seen her, and Lorraine could remember little. She had been taken to hospital with head injuries. The following weeks were a blur, as she was moved from one charitable organization to another; she had no money and no medical insurance left. Eventually she was institutionalized and preliminarily diagnosed as schizophrenic. To begin with, she was not thought to be an alcoholic as so much else was wrong with her. She had severe abscesses, a minor venereal disease plus genital herpes, skin disorders, and poor physical condition from lack of decent food. Eighty cigarettes a day had left her with a persistent heavy cough. She contracted pneumonia, and for a few days it was doubtful that she would live. When she pulled through, the hallucinations, screaming fits and vomiting made the doctors suspect severe alcohol withdrawal symptoms.

A string of psychiatrists and doctors interviewed her and prescribed various medication. After two months she was transferred to the nightmare of Ward C, Watts City Mental Hospital where LA County sent only their worst cases, the drop-outs and no hopers. Drug-crazed kids, deranged old ladies, suicidal middle-aged women – every fucked-up female soul who walked the earth seemed to be marooned with Lorraine. They added chronic alcoholism to Lorraine's list of ailments. Her liver was shot, and she was warned that if she did not give up drinking she would be dead within the year. Eventually she was transferred to the White Garden rehabilitation centre.

Rosie Hurst was working as a cook at the centre, one of those women who gave their free time as part of a rehabilitation programme. Rosie, a big, plump, sturdy woman, with short, frizzy permed hair, was a recovering alcoholic with six months' sobriety. She worked hard and was as friendly as she could be with the inmates, a there-but-for-the-grace-of-God attitude never far from her thoughts. Some of the saner inmates were allocated menial jobs in the kitchen and that was how Rosie got to know Lorraine Page.

Lorraine didn't want to live. She had been waiting to die, wondering hazily why she wasn't already dead, and then musing that, perhaps, she was. And this was hell. It wasn't such a bad hell – the drugs made her more relaxed – but she wanted a drink. It was the only thought that occupied her dulled senses. Her mouth was thick and dry, her tongue felt too big, and she drank water all day, bending down to the small fountain in the corridor, hogging it, mouth open, hand pressed down on the lever for the water to spurt directly into her swollen mouth. Nothing dulled her thirst.

'How long you been an alcoholic?'

Rosie had been watching her in the corridor. Lorraine couldn't say because she had never admitted it to herself. She just liked to drink.

'What work did you do?'

Lorraine could not recall what she'd been up to for the past few years. All the weeks and months had merged into a blur, and she could hardly remember one year from another. Or the bars, dens, seedy, run-down clubs where she had been drunk alongside girls she had once picked up and locked away. They had liked that. And the pimps she had hassled and booked in her days as a vice squad trainee, liked being able to sell her so cheaply. She was known to go with anyone, as long as they kept her supplied with a steady flow of booze. Hotels, bars, dives, private parties . . . Lorraine would be cleaned up and sent out. It didn't matter how many or who they were, just as long as she made enough money for booze. She had been arrested, not just for hooking but for vagrancy, and released, pending charges, but had never made her court appearance. She had simply moved on to another bar, another town.

At the time of the hit-and-run accident, Lorraine had reached rock bottom. So far down in the gutter she couldn't even get a trick, and no pimp wanted her attached to his stable. So many truckers, so many different states, she was unaware she was back in LA. She owned only what she stood up in, had even sold her wedding ring. She was such a wreck that the prostitutes didn't want her hanging around them. She was even out in the cold from the street winos, because she stole from them. She had become incapable of caring for herself or earning a few cents for food.

No one remembered her as Lieutenant Page, it was all so long ago. The human flesh trade moves on and changes fast. Many of the young vice-patrol cops who saw her falling down in the streets had no idea who she was. Sergeant Rooney had been promoted to captain. He didn't know if she was alive or dead, and he didn't care.

No one cared, not even Mike or her children. Mike had tried often, over the years, to help her. He heard from her occasionally on the girls' birthdays and at Christmas, but she was incoherent on the phone and lapsed into strange silences apart from asking him for money. The calls stopped when Mike moved house. He remarried, and the children settled into a new school, a new life. They no longer asked about their mother; they had a new, better one. Lorraine made no attempt to contact Mike again. She seemed almost satisfied that she had at last severed every tie.

Only Rosie, because of her own problems and her open friendly nature, wanted to help Lorraine, so thin and pale, with that strange waif-like blonde hair that hung in badly cut, jagged edges. Her fingers were stained dark brown with nicotine, and she had lost a front tooth. She also had a strange way of looking at people, her head tilted as if she were short-sighted, an odd, nervous squint, made more obvious because of a nasty scar running from her left eye to just above her cheekbone. The shapeless regulation blue hospital gown hung loosely on Lorraine's skinny frame. She wore overlarge brown shoes – like a ballet dancer's; someone had passed them on to her and they flopped at her heels as she walked.

Rosie and Lorraine worked side by side, helping to dish out food and make up trays. As the weeks passed, Rosie realized there was more to Lorraine than appeared on the surface. She never had to be told twice which inmates required a special diet but passed out the food to the right women.

'You must have had a job once. How old are you?' Rosie was trying to make conversation.

'I guess I must be around thirty-six. D'you have a cigarette?'

Rosie shook her head. She'd given up smoking when she gave up booze. 'I used to work on computers. What sort of jobs did you do?'

Lorraine was delving among the food scraps in the trashcan, looking for a butt end. She gave up and dried her hands. 'Rosie, you wouldn't believe me if I told you . . . I'll go an' see if I can steal one.'

Rosie watched as she shuffled over to Mad Mona, who really was out-to-lunch, but always had a guarded packet of cigarettes. She watched Lorraine searching Mona's pockets, pretending to tickle her, and then the screaming started as she caught Lorraine with her precious packet. But Lorraine got one, because she came back puffing like an asthmatic on an inhaler.

'Do you have any family?' Rosie enquired, as Lorraine leaned against the door, eyes closed.

'Nope.'

Rosie remarked that she had a son somewhere, but hadn't seen him or his father for years. She busied herself at the sink, and was about to resume her conversation but she saw Lorraine had gone. Rosie took off her overall and went to collect her wages, a pittance, considering the number of hours she put in, but she was only part-time, and most of the staff were Mexican. Probably they were paid even less. She smiled at the receptionist as she buttoned up her baggy cardigan. 'I'll see you in a couple of days.'

The receptionist nodded. 'It's hot out. You won't need that on.'

Rosie shrugged – she had arrived so early that there'd been a chill in the air. She asked how long Lorraine was being kept on the ward.

The receptionist checked on the clipboard behind her. 'Oh, she's due to be released. May not be here when you come back Thursday. The doctors haven't signed her out yet, but she's down to leave. Has she been okay in the kitchen? You know the way they are – steal anything . . .'

Rosie's shopping bag suddenly felt heavy: the chops, the half-chicken she had removed along with the sugar, potatoes and carrots meant she'd be fired if she were caught. She hurried off, saying she wanted to catch her bus.

Lorraine, however, was still resident when Rosie returned two days later. She looked even paler, and coughed continually. According to the receptionist, she had developed a fever, so they were keeping her in for observation. Rosie was concerned, but did not have time to talk as she had to prepare lunch.

It was not until later, when they were washing up, that she could ask Lorraine how she was. She seemed reluctant to talk and didn't bother helping Rosie with the trays, more intent on guarding her position at the water fountain. Her need for alcohol was becoming more desperate each day; she craved sweets and nicotine, stealing treasured hoards of chocolate bars and cigarette packs from the unwary.

With no money and no place to live, she decided she'd have to turn to Rosie who might have somewhere she could stay – and something worth stealing. That was her sole motive for talking to Rosie. Lorraine wanted a drink, wanted money, wanted out of the crazies' ward. All Rosie wanted was a friend.

'You know, I could help you – if you want to help yourself. If you tell me, say, "Rosie, I want to help myself", then I will do everything in my power to help you. I'll take you to my meetings . . . We have counsellors, people you can really talk to, and . . . they'll help you get work. You're an intelligent woman, there must be something you can find . . .'

Lorraine had given her that odd squinting look, smoking a cigarette down to its cork tip. 'Yeah. Maybe I could get my old job back.'

'What did you do?'

'I was a cop.'

Rosie chuckled, rolling out pastry. She jumped when Lorraine stood close behind her, so close and so tall she had to lean over.

'I am arresting you on the charge of molesting that pastry, Rosie. Anything you say may be taken down and used in evidence against you . . .'

Rosie laughed, and Lorraine tickled her, just like she tickled Mad Mona. Far from stupid, Rosie was beginning to suspect that Lorraine was after something. She wondered what it was. She dropped heavy hints that she was broke just in case Lorraine had thought otherwise and was after money . . .

Three weeks later Lorraine was given her marching orders. While she waited for Rosie to arrive, she cleaned the kitchen. Then she helped Rosie all morning, but it was quite late before she mentioned that she was leaving. To her surprise, Rosie told her she already knew. 'I've been thinking about all the things you've been telling me, Rosie. And, well – you're on. I'll come to one of these meetings 'cos I want my life back.' Her voice was hardly audible. 'I'll tell you a secret. I really was a cop, a lieutenant.'

Rosie looked up into the pale face. 'Is that the truth?'

Lorraine nodded. 'Yeah. Look, can I crash on your floor until I get a place of my own?' She reckoned if Rosie knew she had been a cop she would trust her. It worked.

Rosie gave a wide grin, concealing her hesitancy. 'Sure you can, but it's not much of a place. Do you have a lot of gear?'

Lorraine lied, telling Rosie that her belongings were with a friend she didn't want to see because she was another drinker – and she wanted to stay clean.

Rosie understood, knowing it was a mistake for a drinker to return to old friends and old habits.

'Okay. You can stay at my place.'

At the end of the day, Rosie waited for her outside the hospital. Lorraine was wearing an odd assortment of clothes. Nothing fitted – sleeves too short, the skirt waist-band hanging around her hips. She carried a clean set of underwear in a brown paper bag, and seemed even taller, thinner and stranger-looking than she had in the safety of the rehabilitation clinic. Someone had given her a pair of pink-framed sunglasses, the lenses so dark they hid her eyes. Seeing her in the bright sunshine, Rosie had severe doubts about taking her in. She wished she had not been so friendly.

Lorraine was silent on the long journey, as they changed buses four times. She didn't like going back to her home territory, Pasadena, but then she didn't really know any place any more. She was glad to have Rosie – even felt a strange desire to hold her hand, afraid she would lose sight of her.

Eventually they were walking along a wide road with small dilapidated bungalows, past a four-storey apartment block. Rosie pointed to a grocery store. 'I shop there and live above that garage just a few yards along. It's very convenient.'

Lorraine nodded. Even from this distance she had seen the liquor section in the store. Her body broke out in a sweat, her mouth felt rancid, and she licked her lips. As she stood at the counter next to Rosie, who was buying bread and salads and coffee, she felt like screaming. Her eyes constantly strayed to the bottles: she wanted a drink so badly she felt faint.

'Here we are, now, you go up ahead. It's so narrow, this staircase, I'm always tripping down . . . watch how you go, the fifth step is loose . . .'

They climbed up the wooden stairway and Rosie unlocked the screen door, then her front door. As she pushed it open a cat screeched and dived out between Lorraine's legs.

'That's Walter. Go in, you first.'

Rosie's tiny apartment was stiflingly hot, even with the blinds down. She turned on the air conditioning, which whirred noisily. There was a living room and one cramped bedroom with a tiny shower room attached. The kitchen was a messy corner of the living room. Rosie busied herself unloading the groceries, pointing out the couch for Lorraine to sleep on, bringing sheets and pillows.

'Now, do you want some tea, or coffee, or something cold? I think I've got chilled Coke – or lemonade?'

Lorraine rested back on the sofa, rolling an ice-cold Coke can across her forehead. She was still desperate for a real drink. She gulped at the Coke, draining the can quickly.

Rosie held up a packet of cigarettes. 'I thought you'd be needing one, so here.' She tossed it over. 'Now you clean up and run a comb through your hair, and then we should go, the meeting's due to start in about an hour.'

Lorraine closed her eyes and sighed. 'Maybe I'm a bit too tired today.'

Rosie loomed over her. 'Today is when you really need to go, and I can arrange that you go every day for the first few weeks.' Lorraine managed a weak smile and hauled herself to her feet, crossing through Rosie's dusty bedroom into the small bathroom, which was crammed with jars of creams, tubes, and a vast array of worn toothbrushes and half-squeezed toothpaste tubes. Old tights were hung up to dry, large faded panties and a greyish bra pinned on a piece of string, so large Lorraine stared in disbelief.

She ran the water and bent down to drink it, gulping it down, then she splashed her face and reached for a thread-bare towel. She looked at herself then, really studied herself, no drugs and stone-cold sober for the first time in years. The image that stared back was of a stranger. Her eyes were puffy, washed-out, red-rimmed, and her nose had small, white-headed spots at each side. She caught sight of her yellowish, stained teeth, the gap in the front. The scar stretched her cheek slightly, an ugly reminder of a past she wanted to obliterate. She traced the outline of her cracked, swollen lips and then ran her hand through her thin hair, strands of it coming away. It looked as if someone had hacked it haphazardly, any way but straight. Maybe she'd even done it herself, she couldn't remember. There were not just days or weeks or months she couldn't remember but whole years.

Rosie rapped on the door. 'What are you doing in there?'

Lorraine took a deep breath. 'Just washing. Won't be long . . .' As she dried her hands she gazed at the stains along her fingers, the nails jagged, bitten and dirty. Everything about her was hideous: she was revolting, she disgusted herself, she *was* disgusting. And deeply angry. She didn't know this person. Who was she?

Rosie looked up from the sofa and smiled. 'You ready?'

Lorraine looked around for the pink-framed sunglasses. She pushed them on, as if to hide behind them. 'Thank you for taking me in like this. It's very good of you.'

Rosie, searching for her keys, wafted her hand. 'I made a vow, because somebody helped me out when I was down. I promised that I'd help someone else if I could. I guess that person is you.'

Lorraine sat at the back of the meeting, hands clenched, face hidden behind the sunglasses. The other people there had greeted her with such warmth that she had wanted to run out of the building. Gripping her hand, Rosie had found her a seat. She was introduced only as Lorraine. Nobody gave their last name unless they wanted to. As the meeting began, Lorraine was able to look at the others. None looked in bad shape though a few had a lost air about them, as they sat with their heads bowed, or stared into space. Slowly she began to pay attention to those who told their stories.

One woman recalled how she had not known who she was for fifteen years, because those years had merged into one long, blurred binge. Now she was smart, and positive, and proud that she had been dry for four years. She had met someone who had given her love and stability. Soon, she hoped, she would have the confidence to tell him that she was an alcoholic. He had been so embarrassed for her when, sober, she had tripped over a paving stone and fallen flat on her face. She laughed then, saying that she hadn't had the heart to tell him she had been face down on the floor more often than she had been upright. She grew emotional, lifting up her arms as if she were at some Baptist church meeting. Lorraine sighed with boredom. 'I'm standing upright now, and I intend to remain this way, just as, when I get a little stronger, I will tell him that I am an alcoholic. Hopefully he will come to one of our meetings so he can fully understand my illness and that I believe, at long last, I am in recovery. I want to recover – just as I know I will always be an alcoholic. I am an alcoholic. Thank you for listening to me, thank you for being here. God bless you all . . .' She burst into tears and many people clustered around her, hugging her, congratulating her.

Lorraine remained at the back of the hall, embarrassed by the show of emotion. She was glad when the meeting ended, refusing to hold other members' hands as they prayed together for strength and guidance. Rosie, on the other hand, was very into it all, her eyes closed, clutching the hands of two elderly women.

Later, back at the apartment, Rosie was full of enthusiasm and energy. 'Those meetings saved my life. Some people have been going for ten or fifteen years. When you face what you are it doesn't stop. You will always be an alcoholic. One drink, and you're back at square one. What you've got to understand is that you have an illness, and it kills you. If I hadn't stopped drinking I'd be dead now, as would most of those people there tonight.'

She set the table, splashed water into glasses, clanking ice cubes. She was sweating even more than usual from the heat of the stove. Even at seven in the evening, the air conditioning was so half-hearted that the temperature in the apartment was nearly eighty degrees.

Lorraine played with her food, drank three or four glasses of water. Rosie reached over and scraped the remains of her meal onto her own plate, ploughing through the leftovers as if she were starving. Her mouth bulging with food, she waved her fork in the air: 'Now, what are we going to do about finding you some work? You've no money, right? As soon as we've finished supper, we can catch a bus, go to another meeting across town, see if maybe anyone has any work, just to tide you over, nothing too strenuous . . .'

Lorraine couldn't face another meeting, let alone another bus ride. 'Maybe I could just sleep now? I'm really tired.'

Rosie nodded – perhaps they were pushing it. Instead, she chatted incessantly, about her job as a computer clerk in a banking firm. She took out her family albums, displaying her parents' home, her ex-husband, the son she hadn't seen for five years. She talked until her eyes drooped from tiredness. 'I lost so much, Lorraine, but I'm hoping to see my son soon. My ex said that I could have a day out with him. I want him to get to know me as I am now. The most important thing is that I take every day on its own, I count every day as precious, because it's a new day without a drink.' Lorraine smiled, but inside she wished Rosie would leave her alone. She yawned in the hope that Rosie would take the hint and go to bed but she went on for another hour, delving into the pages of her beloved AA manual as if it was a Bible, reading snatches aloud.

At last she stood up and wagged her fat finger at Lorraine. 'I am responsible,' she said. 'Keep on telling that to yourself: *I am responsible*.' She went into her bedroom and closed the door.

Lorraine flopped onto the couch with relief. She lay there for about fifteen minutes, listening to the air conditioner, the cat lapping its milk . . . and all she could think about was how she could get a drink without Rosie finding out. Eventually she drifted into sleep. She slept without pills, without alcohol, a deep, dreamless sleep.

*

Lorraine was awake before Rosie, and started brewing coffee. It was only five, and still reasonably cool. She felt hungry, too, and ate some bread and cheese, followed by a bowl of muesli. She'd had four cups of coffee and five cigarettes before Rosie appeared.

'Good morning, coffee's made . . .'

Rosie grunted, poured some and returned to her room. Lorraine sat by the window, smoking. A new day. Would she make it without a drink? Could she make it? Most important, did she *want* to make it? She didn't answer the question – she was too aware of the rich smell of coffee, and that it was a beautiful day.

Rosie was not at her best in the morning. She remained grumpy, uttering low, growling complaints as Lorraine took a shower. She was in the small bathroom for a long time, scrutinizing herself. Scars covered her thighs: small round marks like cigarette burns dotted all over her white-bluish skin. Her feet shocked her: they looked like an old woman's, reddish toes and heels all blisters and corns, with hideously long toenails – she was surprised they hadn't been cut at the hospital. She scrubbed herself almost raw, using up all the hot water. She oiled and massaged herself with Rosie's lotions, cleaned her teeth gently, and creamed round her mouth so her cracked lips felt less painful. Finally she used Rosie's shampoo and hair conditioner, searching the cabinet for nail scissors and a manicure set.

Rosie was seething. Lorraine had been in her bathroom since half past seven and it was now almost nine. When she emerged, swathed in Rosie's towels, Rosie pushed past her and banged the bathroom door shut.

'Well, thanks a bundle!' She stormed out. 'You've taken all the hot water! Now I gotta wait an hour, maybe more. I always have a shower in the morning.'

'Sorry,' Lorraine muttered. The floor shook as Rosie thudded into the sitting room.

'Would you come in here a minute, please!' Rosie boomed.

Lorraine sighed with irritation and followed the voice. Rosie, like some irate sergeant-major, stood with her hands on her hips.

'Okay. This is not a hotel, not the goddamned hospital. When you get up in the morning, put your bedclothes away and it'd be a nice gesture if you tried washin' a dish when you used it. This is my home. It may not look much but it's all I got an' I work my butt off to keep it.'

Lorraine watched as Rosie dragged her sheets and pillow from the couch and hurled them towards her. They landed at her feet. She was picking them up when the floor shook again and Rosie thrust a dirty ashtray under her nose. 'And all this smoking – it's not good for me. Please try and cut down or at least open the window and wash out the ashtray.'

Lorraine couldn't get a word in edgeways. Rosie slammed into her bedroom and two seconds later charged out again demanding that Lorraine go back in and clean the bathroom.

'It was a shit-hole when I went in there!' Lorraine screeched. 'You like it so fucking much, *you clean it*!'

Rosie glared. 'No fucking way! Get the vacuum from the closet, *and clean up in there*!'

Lorraine sat down and rubbed her hair. 'I've just got clean, I don't want to get all dirty again.'

Rosie charged to the closet, yanked open the door and dragged out an old-fashioned vacuum cleaner. Her fat body wobbled under the pink nylon nightdress, and she wore the most extraordinary bedroom slippers, like boats, but with the face of Pluto on one and Mickey Mouse on the other. The faces were old and food-stained – Pluto was minus one ear.

Lorraine watched as the immense beam bent over to fit

in the plug. 'You've not had that out for a while, you should run it over the carpet in here. It's full of cat hairs. Are you working at the hospital today?'

Rosie switched on the hoover and glowered. 'No, I am not. Why? So that you can have a good rummage through my things? I only work part-time, in case your memory fails you. Mondays and Thursdays.'

Lorraine nodded, uncertain what day it was, and fazed by Rosie's personality change. Rosie continued to complain, bellowing above the machine's whirring, which made Lorraine's head ache. Peace came when she departed for her shower, but only for a moment: more thuds emanated from the bedroom as Rosie dressed. Closet doors squeaked, drawers banged open and shut, until Rosie appeared with an armful of clothes which she tossed onto the floor. 'Here, something might fit. If it doesn't, chuck it out. I dunno why I kept that lot, maybe because I hoped I'd shrink . . . Help yourself.'

Lorraine looked through the odd assortment of garments, all in dreadful colours and a mixture of sizes, ranging from a ten to a sixteen. Nothing fitted. A few items were vaguely clean, but there were no shoes or underwear. Finally she chose a print dress three sizes too large and tied a belt around the waist. At least it would be cool. She put on her panties from the day before, turned inside out. She had no bra, no stockings or tights. She looked around for the brown paper parcel she had brought from the hospital, but couldn't remember where she had left it. Her hair was dry now, and she tied it back with an elastic band, then folded the rest of the clothes and put them into a black plastic garbage bag. She tipped the contents of the trashcan into the bag, and carried it outside for collection.

It was such a beautiful morning that she walked to the deli at the end of the street, and stood staring in the window with all the bottles on display. The windows were barred, and Lorraine threaded her fingers through the meshing, longing to go inside. She didn't have so much as a cent so, unless she robbed the place, there was no way of getting a bottle. Reluctantly she walked back to Rosie's, climbed up the wooden staircase, then hesitated. She could hear Rosie talking on the telephone, and she sat on the steps, listening.

'Well, I was hoping as I've got a few days off this weekend if we could make it Saturday? I can get the bus over . . .'

The call went on for a while longer, then Lorraine heard the thudding footsteps, and a door slamming. She went inside and opened the fridge. Rosie appeared dressed in a white blouse and circular cotton flower print skirt. Her frizzy hair was wet, and she tugged a comb through it.

'Water was still cold! And you had the last Coke yesterday. I'm not a charity, you know. Now, we'd better see which meeting you go to . . .?' Rosie began making a series of phone calls and talked at length to someone whom she described as her sponsor. Eventually she hung up.

'Jake figures I shouldn't be your sponsor, but since I've taken you on, I'll give it a try. Any time, day or night, if you feel the need for a drink, or someone to talk to, then you just tell me. Have you wanted a drink this morning?'

'What do you think?'

Rosie sighed irritably, and warned Lorraine that she did not have enough money to ferry them both all over LA. 'Don't you have any money at all?' she barked.

'No, but I'll manage . . .'

Rosie pushed past her, into the tiny kitchen area, took cereal and fruit, and began to munch noisily. Slowly, the warm, friendly Rosie began to surface. She complimented Lorraine on how she looked, and started counting dollars from her purse. Lorraine watched, trying to work out how much money it contained. As soon as she had a chance, she would steal it and get the hell out of the apartment.

'How about social security? Can you claim any benefits?'

41

Lorraine shrugged. Said she couldn't recall any social security numbers, but declined to admit to Rosie why she didn't want to – the skipped bail, court appearances, debts . . . If she tried to apply for financial assistance she'd be arrested. Rosie gulped her coffee and began to make a long list, chewing the end of an already gnarled pencil.

'Okay. We got enough here for a few days, but we'll look around for jobs, see about taking you to the social security to see if they can trace your numbers and maybe you'll get some benefits. Not that you can live on what they dole out, I know, I'm on it—'

'We? I can manage on my own.'

'No, you can't. I can't go off to the hospital and leave you, well, not until I can trust you. So here's some suggestions . . .' She had jotted down waitress, cleaner, mostly menial jobs, and then listed all the addresses of AA meetings. Lorraine wondered idly if all this effort was to help Rosie keep on the wagon, never mind herself.

'I thought you said you were something to do with computers. Can't you get a decent job?' Lorraine enquired.

Rosie looked up. 'Oh, yes. I can get into any bank and they'll make me head cashier! I lost my job, my respect-ability. I've got no references, not even a driver's licence, they took it away. I thought you'd know that – if you were a cop like you said. If you were, why can't *you* get a decent job?'

Lorraine began to chew at her nails. She'd finished the pack of cigarettes; now she craved not only a drink but a cigarette, too. She suddenly felt tired, and yawned. It was as if she had been up for hours, which indeed she had, but it was still only ten o'clock.

'Can I use your toilet?'

'You don't have to fucking ask me to go to the john, for chrissakes!'

When Lorraine didn't show for fifteen minutes, Rosie went to check on her. She was curled up on her bed, deeply

42

asleep, her hands cupped under her chin. Rosie studied Lorraine's sleeping face, and realized that she must once have been beautiful. You could still see glimpses of it: in repose, Lorraine's face lost its hardness. Her mouth was closed, so you couldn't see the missing tooth, and the deep scar was hidden by the pillow. For the first time Rosie really wondered about Lorraine's past, still certain that the cop line was just that – a line.

She crept out, then searched through Lorraine's belongings. Nothing. The brown paper bag was empty of any personal mementoes. No letters or cards, no make-up – and the plastic purse they had given her was empty, she hadn't lied about that. But Rosie was sure she had lied about having no family; a girl who had been as attractive as Lorraine must have had someone – had maybe even been somebody.

Rosie let Lorraine sleep for almost the entire day. She read, made some calls, cooked lunch for herself. Food was one of the few pleasures she had left in life. At four o'clock the phone rang. She snatched it up, afraid it would wake Lorraine.

'Hello, is this you, Mommy?' The high-pitched voice tore at her heart. At last he had called. It was her son.

'Yeah, it's me. How you doin', Joey? We gonna meet up? I kinda thought maybe this weekend?'

'I can't, I got a big game, I'm on the second division basketball team, and so I can't. I gotta go now.'

Rosie started to panic. He was going to put the phone down. She wanted to tell him she would drive across LA to see him play, but she stuttered, 'Wait, Joey, what about you gettin' a bus out here to me? I can meet you at the depot, Joey? You still there, Joey?'

'I'm goin' to Florida. Me and Dad are movin' there, we got a place sorted and everything.'

'Florida?' Rosie screeched.

There was an ominous silence. She could hear Joey whispering. 'Is that woman goin' with you, Joey? Is – put your dad on the phone, Joey, you hear me? I wanna speak to–'

Rosie was shaking, she knew that cheap bitch was there, knew she must be putting her ten cents in. Her hand clenched round the receiver as she heard her son calling his father, and then the phone being put down. 'Hello? Hello?'

Her ex-husband came on the line – she could even hear his intake of breath as if he was preparing himself to speak to her. It always got her so mad, the way he talked to her, all calm and coming on like he was a shrink, or as if she was ten years old. 'Rosie?'

'What's all this about Florida? You never said anythin' to me about Florida, takin' my kid to Florida.'

'Rosie, just calm down.'

'I'm calm, for chrissakes. I'm angry too.'

'When we're settled we'll write. This is a good job for me, a lot more money.' The voice was smooth, saying each word too slowly.

'I wanna see Joey. I'm not interested in what you earn – you never paid a cent to me, anyway.'

There was the sound of heavy breathing and then he repeated slowly and painstakingly that as Rosie had not been awarded visitation rights, never mind custody, she had little say in where her Joey lived. That was up to him and he was making the best decision for his son's welfare and if she didn't like it then she should hire a lawyer.

'Oh, yeah? And where do I get that kind of money?'

'You got it to buy booze, Rosie. Maybe you're stewed right now – you usually have been in the past when you've called. It's been six months since your last call and Joey doesn't wanna know, Rosie. It's not me and don't think it's Barbara either, he–'

'You bastard.'

Again the heavy breathing. 'Rosie, I'm sorry, let's not be like this. We'll write, we'll be in touch and I'm hanging up now because I don't want to get into an argument. I'm hanging up, Rosie.'

She looked at the receiver as she heard the line go dead and replaced it gently on the cradle. She patted the phone with the flat of her hand, wishing it was her boy's head. She didn't even know how big he was now, it had been such a long time . . . One day, she told herself, she'd hold him in her arms and he would forgive her. She felt so empty she wanted to cry, for all the lost years.

Hours later, Lorraine woke up, heart pounding. There had been a violent crash, as if the front door had been knocked down. Music thumped out, the volume on maximum. She sat up, and eased herself off the bed. She didn't recognize the screeching, confused voice, and the sound of breaking glass topped even the music.

Lorraine pushed open the bedroom door, and gasped. Rosie was reeling around the room, falling into furniture, drinking from a quart bottle of bourbon. She leered at Lorraine, and waved the bottle. 'You wanna drink? Come on in, sit down, have a drink with me!'

Lorraine watched, incredulous, as Rosie crashed into the kitchen, smashing glasses as she attempted to get one from the cupboard. She swore and kicked at the jagged pieces. Her eyes were unfocused, her face bright red and sweating. She swayed as she poured and held out a half-full tumbler. 'Have a drink, skinny!'

Lorraine was about to take the glass when the front door opened. She had no idea who the short, squat man was, who knocked the glass out of Rosie's hand, snatched the bottle from her and began pouring the contents down the sink. Rosie screamed and lunged at him with a punch, missed, and fell into the closet. Brushes tumbled around her as she slumped on the floor, weeping. Her sobs came louder as he ran water into the sink, making sure every drop of liquor was gone. Rosie's head fell forward onto her chest and her breath came in terrible, heaving rasps.

'Help me get her into the bathroom and *turn that fucking music off*!' Lorraine did as she was told, and between them they dragged Rosie into the bedroom then the bathroom by both arms, like a beached whale, and inched her into the base of the shower, before the man turned it on full blast. When Rosie finally came to, she began to vomit. The man held her head up, getting soaked himself in the process. He snapped out instructions for Lorraine to pass him towels and a pillow. When the vomiting subsided he stuffed a pillow under Rosie's dripping head, and stood up. 'She'll sleep it off now.'

Lorraine followed him into the sitting room. He was attempting to dry himself with one of the kitchen towels. 'You started her on this binge, huh?'

Lorraine shook her head. He began to brew coffee, and fetched cups, treading warily over the broken glass. 'What brought it on, then?'

'I dunno.' She folded her arms. The smell of the bourbon hanging in the air made her swallow because it smelt so good. 'You got a cigarette?'

He tossed over a squashed packet, and rubbed his shoulder. 'She must weigh a ton. I'm getting too old for this – she's put my shoulder out before now, and my back. Once she knocked me out stone cold . . . So, if you didn't bring the bottle in, did she get it herself?'

Lorraine lit the cigarette and pocketed the packet. 'I dunno. I was asleep.'

'Oh, yeah?' he sneered. 'Sleeping one off, were you?'

Lorraine was annoyed by his aggressive, punchy manner. His neck was short, his greasy black hair thinning, even his hands were podgy. 'You her boyfriend or something?' she asked.

46

'Her what? You kiddin'? Need a bigger man than me to take that rhino on. I'm her sponsor, but I dunno for how long. They called me from the liquor store – little arrangement we have, saves them from one of her visits. You get her started, did you? Then she went for a bottle? After she's finished one bottle she's only after the next, and those bars they got up may have kept them safe from the riots but they wouldn't from Rosie.' He helped himself to coffee, and poured some for Lorraine. 'I'm Jake Valsack.'

'Lorraine.'

Jake eased his square backside onto the sofa. 'Well, you made it through a night, then? And . . .' He looked at his watch and smiled. When he smiled, his face changed from something that resembled a chimpanzee into a cute pixie. 'You been dry almost a whole day. We'll go to the meeting – she won't be round for a while yet.'

Lorraine had no desire to go to another meeting, so she said she'd stay with Rosie. Jake hooted with laughter. Once again she grew increasingly irritated with him.

'So, Lorraine, what kind of work did you do before drinking?'

She crossed to the kitchen and poured more coffee. 'I was a secretary.'

He swivelled round. 'So you can type, huh? You got a job? Rosie said you'd need one.'

'You going to give me one?'

Jake hooted again. 'What you think I am – nuts?'

Lorraine sat on the sofa arm. 'So what did *you* do before drinking, Jake?' she inquired sarcastically. He looked up at her from round, dark eyes – he was a dead ringer for a chimpanzee.

'I was a doctor. Still am a doctor only I can't practise any more. Now I help run a clinic for junkies and alkies and anybody who needs help, like Rosie.'

Lorraine looked away for she could read the pain in those animal eyes. Maybe Jake could see something similar

47

in her own because he seemed to relent. He opened his wallet and passed over a card. 'You can call me on that line. I know somebody who needs a bit of clerical work done, be a few bucks in hand – or you can work for me. I'm a glutton for punishment. We need as many helping hands as possible, but there's no money in it.'

As she pocketed the card, she felt Jake's cigarettes. She didn't dare bring one out in case he asked for them back. He stood up and glanced at the broken screen door. 'Tell Rosie I'm around.'

Lorraine watched his stocky figure strut off down the road. Then she searched for Rosie's handbag. She was opening the purse when she heard moaning from the bathroom. Rosie was trying in vain to stand up. Lorraine looked at her, in no way disgusted by the spectacle: she'd seen and been in a lot worse states herself. 'I guess I just tied another one on, didn't I?'

Lorraine laughed. 'Yep, you sure did. Your pal was here – Jake.'

'Was he? Well, are you gonna stand there gloating or are you gonna help me get up off the fucking floor?'

Lorraine tried to pull her up but fell forward on top of her. Rosie felt like a mammoth blanket. Eventually, after much tugging and heaving, she managed to get into a sitting position, where she held her head in her hands and groaned. Lorraine fetched a glass of water and held it out. Rosie gulped it down, and then demanded another. She drank four full glasses before she rested back against the shower. 'Did you say Jake was here?'

Lorraine nodded, and Rosie began to cry, guilty and morose. She sobbed and sobbed, a jumbled, incoherent stream of adoring phrases about the chimpanzee man, blowing her nose and wiping her eyes.

'I'm off to see if I can find a job, Rosie. Did you hear me?'

Rosie hauled herself slowly to her feet. 'Sure. Do what you like.'

'Can I take a few dollars?' she called from the sitting room.

'Sure, honey, if there's any left. I dunno how much I spent . . .' Rosie dragged herself unsteadily to the chair by the telephone and sat down. 'I'll wait a while, then call him. I need to talk to him. I'm sorry, but I guess you'll do better without me. I knew I'd make a lousy sponsor. Jake was right about that.' She leaned back with her eyes closed. 'You must be proud of yourself. You didn't have a drink with me, did you?'

'Nope, guess I didn't.' Lorraine emptied Rosie's purse, and walked out.

She had no intention of seeing Rosie again. She felt almost lighthearted, a strange new confidence in herself: she had not taken a drink. She might have finished the bottle if Jake hadn't walked in when he did but, as it was, she had not had a drink.

The late-afternoon sun was brilliant, blistering down, and she could feel the pavement scorching through her cheap second-hand shoes. The feeling of being in control of something as simple as her own feet, of walking in a straight line, made her confidence jump a tiny notch higher. She took off the elastic band from her hair, and shook it loose. It smelt of lemons, just like the old shampoo she used, how long ago? Lorraine reached the corner, and stopped to light a cigarette. Tossing the match aside, she inhaled deeply and let the smoke drift slowly out of her mouth. She sucked again at the cigarette, watching the lit rim of tobacco move up the white paper before she exhaled. She didn't want to think about the past, about what or who she had been.

A car crawled to a stop just ahead of her. She'd seen it

out of the corner of her eye even before it passed: a dark blue Sedan. She could even describe the driver – linen jacket, blue open-necked shirt, cropped blond thinning hair, round, rimless glasses, and a wide, wet mouth. That was all she focused on as he leaned out of the window. He smiled, running his thumb around his shiny wet lips as he asked if she needed a lift any place. Lorraine stepped closer, inclining her head, making sure the jagged scar couldn't be seen, keeping her lips half closed. She didn't want to scare him off, didn't want him to see too much of her teeth – or lack of them. She was an old hand at this and knew that if he was a cop he would try to get her to name a price. She bent lower, down to his level.

'You lost?' She said it softly, her hand reaching out to the door handle. 'You need me?'

He stared at her as if sizing her up, then looked past her both ways before he jerked his head. 'Get in.'

Lorraine went round to the passenger side and climbed in beside him. He drove off fast like they always did, acting flash. Acting stupid. He said quickly, licking his wet lips all the time, that he wanted oral, he wanted it public. Did she understand? Lorraine leaned her arm along the back of the seats, but as she touched his neck, he jerked away. He didn't want to be touched, he said, he hated being touched. He kept on driving, passing every car on the highway until he wheeled into a supermarket car park. The ground level was almost full, people staggering to and from the store with bulging bags of groceries, their hatchbacks open wide as they loaded up.

He bypassed the first level, then the second, tyres screeching as he drove round and up the narrow entrance lane. In the fourth-storey parking area, he pulled into a space. He had hardly switched off the engine before he unzipped his trousers. Lorraine put her hand out. He swiped it aside. 'I told you, I don't want you to touch me!'

'Okay, chill out, man, want me to talk dirty, you like that? That what you want?'

His body was tense, his hands clenching and unclenching.

'No, I reckon you want to be sucked off, right here, like with maybe someone close enough to catch you at it, that's exciting, isn't it, bad boy? You're a very bad boy, aren't you? Well, you got lucky because that's my speciality. I give the best head. Come on, you want to ask me for it, yes? That's what you want, isn't it?' His lips twitched, his eyes darting round the gloomy parking lot. She kept her voice low, whispering, making sucking sounds, and he closed his eyes. 'Like I said, I'll make you feel good, real good, and this is a real public place, but we got to sort out my dough. Can we sort that out? Yeah?'

He looked out of the window, getting more excited as a few customers stashed away their groceries, their voices echoing in the concrete building. He loosened his belt, as if he hadn't heard her, pulling at his pants. 'Just do it, bitch.'

Lorraine's back pressed against the passenger door and her left hand felt for the door handle. If he played games, she was out. 'Twenty dollars.'

A woman with her husband and two kids parked directly next to them. As they headed towards the elevators, Lorraine's john started to jerk himself off, his mouth stretched in a weird wet smile of pleasure. His erect pink penis burst up from his crumpled flies and he began to pant, leaning his head back, as his left hand flicked the switch for his seat to recline.

Lorraine tried again. 'Twenty dollars.'

He lost his erection and gave a half sob. She swore, realizing he was one of those half-a-minute stand-up-for-America and then the weeping impotent syndrome.

Fumbling in his wallet, he took out a thick wedge of bills, peeled off a twenty and tossed it at her. 'See what you can do for it, bitch!' He reached over and grabbed her by the hair, forcing her face onto his pink flaccid worm. Lorraine could smell him, smell his trousers, even the cotton of his blue striped boxer shorts. His hand on the back of her neck was holding a strand of her hair as he pressed her further down onto his crotch.

Was it the sweet lemon smell of her freshly washed hair? Or that she was stone-cold sober? She knew exactly what she was being paid to do, she'd done it too many times before. But never sober. Face down between a john's legs, having just been paid twenty dollars for a blow-job in a shopping precinct car park, the ghost of Lieutenant Lorraine Page resurfaced and fought back for a tiny fraction of respectability. She couldn't suck him off.

'I'm sorry. You can have your twenty dollars.'

He held onto the back of her head, forcing her down. She pushed up with her hands trying to free herself. He was much stronger than she was now and, leaning over the seat towards him, she was vulnerable, incapable of getting away. He was able to hold her down with only one hand, and her head was stuck under the steering wheel. She heard the click of the glove compartment being opened but couldn't see what he had taken out. She forced herself to relax, to try to get into a better position so she could move off him, but he still held onto her hair.

The first blow stunned her for a second – it glanced off the back of her scalp – but he had hit her with such force that he had automatically released his hold. She pushed upward with all her strength, propelling herself against his chest. He slipped back in his reclining seat, and it was then she saw the claw hammer. As he tried to raise it to strike her again, she knew he could kill her if he wanted.

Lorraine twisted her face towards his, and bit into his neck. She held on ferociously, her teeth breaking the flesh. He screamed, now more intent on getting her off than on using the hammer, but she wouldn't release her bite.

52

The family loading their groceries looked over to the Sedan parked next to them. Its windows were steamed up, but the screaming made the woman push her kids inside their car. She even shouted for her husband not to go across, but he took no notice, and as he reached the driver's door, he called out: 'You all right in there?' He turned back to his wife, who gestured for him to walk away, but he bent down, his hand tentatively reaching for the handle on the driver's door. 'You all right in there?' he repeated.

As he opened the door, Lorraine fell out, face forward onto the cement floor, almost knocking him off his feet. The family started to shriek as they saw the back of her head covered in blood, and blood streaming from her mouth.

The Sedan jolted backwards, dragging Lorraine with it – her dress was still caught on the reclining seat lever. The man who had come to her assistance made a grab, almost had the driver by his sleeve, but he too fell, as the car swerved to make a turn. The door slammed shut, and with burning rubber tyres the blue Sedan shot down the exit ramp.

The woman was bending over Lorraine as she struggled to stand. At her feet was the wallet: it must have fallen from the john's jacket in the struggle. She snatched it up. 'He tried to rob me, he stole my bag and—'

The woman shouted for her husband to call the police, but Lorraine shook her head. 'No, no, it's okay – I've got my wallet. I'm fine really—'

'But you've been injured, look at you.'

Lorraine backed away from their concerned faces. She touched her head. 'It's nothing, I'll report it to security. Thank you very much.'

By now the woman's husband had run back to them, red-faced and shaking with nerves. 'I'll get the police. Are you okay?' The woman suddenly became suspicious of Lorraine, and caught her husband's arm. 'Get in the car, just leave her. She said she doesn't want any help. *Get back to the children!*'

He looked from his wife back to Lorraine, who managed a half-smile. 'I'm okay, thanks for your help.'

Still he hesitated, but his wife called him again, and as he hurried across to her, Lorraine could hear the shrill voice. 'Can't you see what she is? Didn't you see her face? She's a whore, she was probably trying to steal from him. Just get in the car!' They continued to argue, even as they drove out and he stared back at Lorraine, confused and shocked.

In the ladies' room Lorraine soaked a handful of toilet tissue, and held it to the back of her head. She had lost a shoe, her dress was bloodstained and she couldn't stop the flow of blood from the back of her scalp. Her mouth, too, was bloody, and she panicked. Had he hit her in the mouth? But it wasn't her blood, it was his, from the bite she had given him. She was shaking now, her legs jerky, and she had to sit down on the toilet seat to stop herself fainting.

With trembling hands she opened the wallet. A driving licence plus a photograph – but not of the man inside the car. There were odd ticket stubs and dry cleaning receipts, and more than three hundred and fifty dollars. She folded the money, and stuck it into her panties. Then she stuffed the wallet into the trashcan.

She remained at the washbasin for another fifteen minutes, using more tissue soaked in cold water as a pad. When she had recovered enough to make her way slowly outside, she still felt dizzy and faint, so she hailed a passing cab and gave him Rosie's address.

Lorraine hardly had the strength to get out of the cab and the driver was blazing when he found his seat was bloodstained. Jake, who had returned to check on Rosie, was watching the display from the apartment window.

Thinking her as drunk as Rosie had been, he nevertheless helped Rosie to carry her upstairs. When he spotted the wound on her head he insisted Lorraine go to the hospital. She refused. She didn't want any hospital or police reports – she was fine. And she had not had a drink.

The wound was still bleeding freely, so reluctantly Lorraine agreed to go with Jake to his clinic to have it stitched. By the time they arrived she was subdued. She lay on the couch as Jake examined the gash. He doubted her claim that the wound had been caused by her falling on a loose paving stone. It looked to him as if someone had struck her from behind; if the blow had landed an inch further up, her skull could have been shattered. She'd been lucky.

Lorraine returned home with Rosie and Jake, her head bandaged and with a cropped haircut. Rosie put her in her own bed, and gave her the sedatives and antibiotics Jake had prescribed. Once she was asleep, Jake began to quiz Rosie. 'What did she tell you that you think is lies, then, Rosie?'

Rosie shrugged. 'Oh . . . just that she used to be a police officer.'

Jake smiled, his eyes concentrating on unscrewing the hinges of the damaged screen door. 'Well, that may be fantasy, of course. *I* think she's a whore and that's why she didn't want to go to the police. Someone nearly killed her today, though. But my worry is you – because you are my main concern, Rosie dear, and you were doing so well before she came on the scene.'

'I don't think she had anything to do with me tying on a load, Jake. That was down to my husband.'

Jake squinted at the hinge. 'Maybe, but you're vulnerable right now, sweetheart, and it won't take much to make you fall off the wagon. How long has she been dry? Not long. Right?'

Rosie knew he was right and that he meant well, but she

couldn't keep calling him just for social reasons – even though she had every right to call him when she was in trouble. 'I get lonely, Jake. I need a friend.'

Jake held up the new hinges. 'Who am I to say what you should or shouldn't do? I'll have to come back and fix this tomorrow. These aren't the right screws.'

Rosie sighed and looked to the bedroom. 'I think we'll be okay, for tonight anyway. It'll take my mind off things looking after her.'

Jake put on his jacket. 'Up to you, but keep your eye on her. I don't trust her.'

He had made no mention of Lorraine's reaction when he had seen the thick wad of notes fall out from under her skirt. Her expression was angry and when he asked about the money she had told him to mind his own business; it was just her savings. Jake was sure she had a police record, he could tell by her face: that hardness. She must be as tough as any man to have taken such a crack and still be able to walk around.

Rosie started to make some chicken soup, even though it was eighty degrees outside. She was feeling a bit wobbly and had almost eaten the entire pot before taking a small bowl in to Lorraine. She had been awake for quite a while, but kept her eyes closed, wincing as Rosie collapsed onto the bed. Her head ached, a sharp nagging pain that pressed into her eyes.

'Soup,' barked Rosie, holding up the bowl and a large spoon. Lorraine smiled. It was the last thing she would have thought of asking for on a warm clammy evening but when she tasted the first spoonful, it hit the right spot – as her mother always used to say. She took the spoon from Rosie, and fed herself, dunking the fresh white bread into the remains, and finally wiping the bowl clean.

'I'd offer you some more but I made a pig of myself,' Rosie admitted as she took away the bowl.

Lorraine snuggled down. 'I'm full and it tasted so good

. . . and I don't mind you sleeping with me – you'll never fit on that sofa out there.'

Rosie laughed. 'Well, thank you very much! I thought I'd take the cushions off and put them on the floor. I'd kick you out, but Jake said you should watch it, you know, not roll about or bang your head. I'll manage out on the sofa – but only for one night.'

Lorraine listened to the plodding feet moving around. Her hand had slipped up her panties to feel the money, afraid that maybe Jake had mentioned it to Rosie. It was still there, and it acted as a comforter. She had more than three hundred dollars, enough to get away from Rosie.

The bedroom floor shook as Rosie reappeared with some hot chocolate, slipped the mug onto the bedside table, turned on the night light, and straightened the duvet. It was the caring that did it, simply being tucked in like when she was a little girl, that made Lorraine's heart ache.

'Rosie . . . you still there?' Lorraine whispered.

'Yep, hovering like a hot-air balloon. Don't forget to take your antibiotics.'

Rosie watched Lorraine slowly raise herself on her elbow, her face twisted. 'You want an aspirin?'

Lorraine nodded, and Rosie fetched two tablets and held the mug of hot chocolate to her lips. Lorraine felt the thick sweet liquid slip down her throat.

'I'll be right outside if you need me.'

Lorraine flushed. 'Rosie, I, er . . . well, I guess I do want my life back and if it means going to those meetings, well, then we'll go together.'

Rosie nodded. 'I should fuckin' hope so. G'night, sleep tight. Tomorrow you're back on the sofa.'

Lorraine gave a soft laugh, and nestled down. She hadn't heard the sound of her own laugh for so long that it warmed her now, and made her feel good, as did the soft duvet and big, squashy pillows. Nearly four months, she calculated, and she had not had one drink. Could she – did she really *want* to stay on the wagon? The money was a hard lump in her panties. She eased it out and tucked it under the pillow, keeping her hand on it, feeling drowsy, wondering vaguely why the driving licence had a different picture from the guy who had picked her up. The car was probably stolen, she told herself, the wallet must have belonged to its real owner. She sighed deeply as she recalled the incident. The claw hammer kept in the glove compartment. Very convenient. The position he had forced her into on his lap, the reclining angle of the seat . . . as if he had done it before? Jake had said she was lucky to be alive, another fraction of an inch higher and he would have cracked her skull open. If she hadn't bitten his neck she'd be dead. She knew she had marked him – the bite was deep. Should she call the LAPD in the morning, give them an anonymous tip-off? Describe the attacker? She yawned, maybe. Maybe she should just get some sleep, take it all day by day as Rosie said.

Rosie pulled the cushions off the sofa, turned the TV set down low and, from her reasonably comfortable position on the floor, propped herself on her elbow to see if there were any more game shows scheduled. She used the remote control to move from channel to channel, paying only a moment's attention to the local news item that showed the photograph of Norman Hastings, whose body had been discovered in the trunk of his dark blue Sedan. He had been beaten to death with some kind of hammer. His wallet was missing. Anyone with any information regarding the dead man was asked to contact the local police, and a number was flashed onto the screen. Fifteen minutes later, she switched off the TV and settled down, with a regretful sigh. Tomorrow was another day, another meeting when she would have to admit she had slipped. She began to recite

58

the twelve AA traditions. She rarely got beyond the sixth or seventh and tonight was no exception. By the third she was soundly asleep. 'The only requirement for AA membership is a desire to stop drinking.'

CHAPTER 2

THE NEWS bulletins about the discovery of Norman Hastings's body were repeated on the early-morning television shows, but now included footage of the abandoned blue Sedan and a further request for anyone who had seen him or his vehicle to come forward. The officer heading the murder enquiry at the Pasadena Homicide Division was Captain William 'Bill' Rooney.

Directly after the morning shows, Rooney's department received a phone call from a Don Summers. He was not a hundred per cent certain, but he thought he had seen the blue Sedan in a Pasadena shopping mall car park the previous afternoon.

Rooney did not get around to questioning Summers until the following day. He doubted if Summers's evidence could help, since he could not be positive that he had seen the exact car, and had not made a note of the registration number. Neither had he had a clear view of the driver, only the woman who had been in the vehicle with him. Rooney was able to ascertain that at the time of Summers's possible sighting of the blue Sedan, Hastings, according to the autopsy report, was already dead. Rooney also had details of the dead man's missing wallet, and knew that it contained a few hundred dollars which Hastings had withdrawn from his bank on the morning of his death. He suspected that robbery was the murder motive as they had failed to come up with any other reason. Hastings appeared to be a happily married man, well liked at his work and without enemies or anyone with a grudge against him.

Rooney did not review Summers's call-in statement until he had further evidence from Forensic and the full autopsy report. Although the interior of the Sedan had been cleaned and no prints found – not even those of the dead man – Forensic had discovered two further blood samples, one on the driver's seat, the other on the inside of the glove compartment. What prompted Rooney to question Summers personally was the woman's shoe found rammed beneath the front seat. It did not belong to Hastings's wife.

Rooney sat with Mr and Mrs Summers, as Summers repeated his statement of how he had seen the blue Sedan parked, heard the man screaming and gone to investigate. He was now more sure that it was the one in the photographs shown to him by Rooney. His wife was convinced that if it was not the same car, it was the identical model and colour.

'Okay, now, can you tell me about the woman? The one you stated was in the car?'

Summers gave a good description. Tall and thin, she was wearing a bloodstained flower-print dress. She was injured, her mouth was bleeding, and he thought she had a head wound. She was also clutching a purse. She had told him the man had tried to rob her. Summers's wife interjected that she had thought it was a lie, because when they offered to call the police or for some assistance the woman had refused, insisting that she was all right.

Rooney asked for a more detailed description of the woman. Summers was hesitant, but his wife wasn't, recalling the thin, wispy, badly cut blonde hair, that the woman was about five feet eight inches tall, but exceptionally thin and sickly-looking. She remembered remarking to her husband that the woman might be a prostitute.

'What made you think that?' Rooney asked.

Mrs Summers bit her lip. 'I don't know, just something

about her, a toughness. She was very rough-looking, sort of desperate – and, of course, she was covered in blood.'

'That doesn't mean she's a whore,' said Rooney.

Don Summers glanced at his wife. 'Maybe she wasn't. All I can say, and I got a closer look than my wife, was that the woman was terrified – and she was really hurt, blood all over her dress.'

Rooney showed them the shoe found in Hastings's car and they confirmed that the woman had been wearing only one.

'We need to find our Cinderella,' Rooney joked, but the Summerses didn't find his comment amusing. They were overawed by the massive new Pasadena police station, a high-tech palace, the holding cells below computerized.

The building was so spacious that Rooney himself felt uncomfortable. He wasn't used to so many corridors, rooms and sections, so many clerks. The old days, when a guy could pass a pal in the narrow, paint-peeling corridors, have a chat, smoke a cigarette, were over. Nearly every office had no-smoking signs; some officers had even stuck them on their computers. Only Captain Rooney continued to work in a haze of cigarette or cigar smoke. If the truth was told, he didn't quite fit the new high flyers who surrounded him, but retirement was looming shortly. He reckoned the Hastings murder would be his last case and he hoped to crack it fast, get a good retirement bonus and then be put out to pasture. The prospect made him uneasy, but then so did the new station. He was unsure about life outside the police, which had been the only world he had known since he was eighteen.

By the time Rooney returned to his office there had been another call in connection with the Hastings homicide. This time the caller was anonymous and refused repeated requests to divulge her name. She did, however, give a detailed description of the man she thought was driving the car belonging to the deceased: around a hundred and eighty pounds, possibly about five feet ten, though she wasn't sure, blue eyes, rimless gold-framed pink-toned glasses, a straight nose, thick-lipped mouth, wearing a linen jacket and shirt. She described a bite wound in his neck that would be visible above shirt collar level, close to his jugular. It would be deeply inflamed as the teeth had broken the skin and drawn blood. Furthermore, the man was in possession of a claw hammer, which he kept in the glove compartment.

Rooney looked at the duty sergeant's notes. 'She said all this over the fucking phone?'

'Yes, Captain. Then she hung up.'

'So, you get a trace on it? Shouldn't take more'n a second with all this new-fangled equipment.'

The call had not been traced, partly because it was felt to be a 'joke' call, and when it had been deemed genuine, she had already hung up. Rooney plodded back into his office. He waved the anonymous statement at his lieutenant, Josh Bean. 'You fuckin' read this? Whoever she is she wants him caught – she's even described the weapon. What's odd, though, is that the only thing she seems unsure of is the guy's exact height. Everything else, clothes, hair, glasses, mouth, even his weight, she gives it all. But not her name! And the stupid sons-of-bitches didn't trace the call.'

Bean took a look at the statement. She hadn't given the car registration number, he mused, as Rooney deposited his overweight frame behind his desk in his precious old leather swivel chair.

'I reckon that Summers woman was right – she was a whore, that's why she doesn't know how tall the guy is. Maybe he never got out of the vehicle, just picked her up on the sidewalk . . .'

Bean nodded agreement. 'Unless both the Summerses and this caller got the wrong guy. Maybe he just drives a blue Sedan.'

Rooney leaned on his elbows. 'Possibly, but it's the

hammer, a claw hammer. If you read Forensic on the type of weapon used to kill Norman Hastings, they say: "A blunt-edged hammer-type head, one inch in diameter, with a claw section one and a quarter inches long".' He sifted through his files until he found the Forensic photographs of the dead man, close-ups of the blows inflicted to his skull, cheeks, and chin. If the anonymous caller was right, they were looking for a killer with a big bite taken out of his neck.

Rooney looked at Bean and grinned. 'This shouldn't take long then, should it? We got Dracula out there now – but at least we can check all Hastings's associates. No bite, we'll eliminate them.'

Lieutenant Bean frowned, unsure if Rooney was joking. Suddenly he barked at Bean to get cracking.

'I thought you were joking, for chrissakes!'

Rooney picked at his bulbous nose. 'Fuck off. We got to take that call seriously, it's too detailed not to. Go on, move it! And, by the way, the shoe we got could also be the whore's. The Summerses sort of thought she only had one shoe on *but* they weren't certain.'

'Right. I'll take the shoe with me – get everyone to try it on, maybe find the owner.' Bean was joking but Rooney looked as amused as the Summerses had been by his Cinderella crack. He carried on, working through the file, yawning. Something was nagging at him – the description? Was it too pat? Some kind of hoax? But the fact that they had found bloodstains in the glove compartment where the anonymous caller claimed the man kept the hammer was just too close a coincidence. Rooney guessed the caller was the woman the Summers couple witnessed leaving the car – and that Mrs Summers had been correct. She probably was a whore.

*

Lorraine had the worst headache she had ever known. No hangover had been this painful. She was dizzy if she stood up, if she moved she felt sick – and she had vomited the first time she sat up. Thanks to the antibiotics and the aspirin, however, the splitting pain behind her eyes eased a fraction. She had made the phone call then, while Rosie was out getting ice from the grocery store. She had been brief intentionally as she didn't want a trace made, and she was back in bed when Rosie returned.

The torn old sheet crammed with ice was soothing, but there was no way she could get up and go to the AA meeting. Rosie was uneasy at leaving her alone, but needed to go to the meeting herself. Lorraine just wanted to be left alone. Her whole body ached, but the pain across her eyes was torture, so bad she couldn't even think of a drink, let alone getting up to pour one. All she wanted was for the pain to go away.

She remained in Rosie's bed for more than a week, had to be helped to the toilet, for even that small amount of exercise exhausted her. She found any noise unbearable – no TV, no radio. She could eat, and Rosie waited on her hand and foot. She enjoyed being needed; it occupied her mind and, like Lorraine, she didn't give a thought to booze.

Two weeks went by. Jake never got round to contacting his friend at the clinic to ask about Lorraine. In fact, like Rosie, he had grown quite fond of her because, sick as she was, she didn't complain, and often made him laugh. Her pain was obvious, however, and he had told Rosie that if Lorraine's condition did not improve she should be taken to hospital.

Almost half-way through the third week, the headache subsided and Lorraine was able to shower by herself. That afternoon, Jake took out the clamp stitches. The wound had healed well, but he was doubtful about his prowess as a hairdresser. Lorraine had almost a crew-cut at the back of her head and crown while the front was long and jagged. It gave her an almost boyish look, and she made them laugh when she tied a ribbon around the front strands to keep them from flopping in her eyes. She read a lot, magazines at first, because even flicking through the newspapers gave her a headache but gradually she began to plough her way through Rosie's spartan collection of bodice-ripping blockbusters.

She kept the money stashed beneath the mattress. Sometimes she had qualms of guilt when Rosie paid for everything, but didn't know how she could hand out money if Rosie believed she was broke. Afraid of being questioned too closely about its source, she decided against mentioning it. And Jake made no reference to it either.

Four days later, she saw a way round it. When Rosie returned from work, Lorraine presented her with fifty dollars. 'You can be proud of me, Rosie. I went over to my friend, then to a pawnbroker's. Here, this is for you. I sold off my things.' Rosie had no idea that Lorraine had never left the apartment, but she did remark that it was time they discussed the sleeping arrangements. She assured Lorraine she didn't want her to leave, it was just that Rosie needed a good night's sleep in her own bed. That night, Lorraine moved back onto the sofa.

Months had passed since Lorraine had last touched alcohol, had been stone cold sober; it was six weeks since the attack. Curled up on the uncomfortable sofa, she began to plan what she should do next. On the positive side, she was sober. She had no craving, yet, but would it develop as she regained her strength?

Money she had, almost three hundred dollars. It seemed like a fortune, but she knew it wouldn't last long. She wanted to move on, but the question was, where to? And what would she do? Two more days and it became obvious, not just to Rosie but to herself, that she could no longer hide out in the small apartment. Rosie was already hinting that the fifty dollars had been swallowed up in groceries.

Lorraine felt incapable of making major plans for her future; it was the immediate that occupied her. Marooned in the apartment she watched a lot of TV and could follow the murder inquiry. The news showed an artist's impression of the woman seen in the blue Sedan, which she found almost amusing; it bore no resemblance to herself, and Lorraine felt no guilt in not making further contact. The police were making inquiries in all the cab ranks, trying to trace if anyone answering the blonde woman's description had hired a cab that afternoon. They had drawn a blank at all the hospital emergency departments. It seemed no one had seen either the woman or the deceased's blue Sedan on the day of his murder. Lorraine's phone call was becoming more and more important to the investigation.

Jake, now a frequent visitor, was disturbed by her inertia. In an attempt to motivate her, he suggested that, if she was interested, his friend could do something for her teeth. They needed treatment badly, and the missing tooth didn't help her looks. If she could find thirty dollars or so, he said, she could get it capped.

'Know a laid-off dentist, too, do you, Jake?'

Jake laughed, but she was right – his friend was AA and only just starting to rebuild his practice.

Lorraine spent four days in agony, but the end result was two front teeth capped, all her cavities filled, her gums cleaned and the rest of her teeth bleached. Her mouth was swollen and sore, but the exercise had been a success. She used the lie about selling off her belongings again, and paid the thirty dollars. She also gave Rosie another twenty, adding that now she had nothing more to sell or pawn. Rosie believed her: Lorraine was a good liar.

She went to the local hair salon to have her hair streaked, cut and blown dry. Jake's pitiful attempt at styling limited her choice – the back was so short where the scar was still visible – but the salon made a reasonable job, taking the back and sides even shorter and the front into a low fringe, like a twenties crop, which accentuated her cheekbones, while the highlights gave body to her thin hair. She was by no means transformed into a beauty: her nose was crooked, flattish from where it must have been broken, and the white jagged scar on the left side of her face remained. Nevertheless a new, more confident, Lorraine was emerging.

Rosie was astonished and full of admiration as Lorraine presented herself, and Jake was equally complimentary in a back-handed way. He had whistled, then said, 'Honey, you must have been a cracker!'

Rosie became a little envious. Nothing she could do to her frizzy mop would ever change her much – and it rankled that Lorraine could have an expensive haircut, yet not pay a cent towards the rent. Money was short, and Rosie's salary plus her benefits was hardly enough to keep herself, never mind two.

It also irritated Rosie that although she went to AA regularly, Lorraine made excuses to stay in the apartment and read. Eventually she made it clear that she was not a charity, and it was time Lorraine got off her ass . . .

But Lorraine was scared to leave the safety of the apartment. Even Jake's presence was comforting. He was always so dependable and calming. She still made no mention of her hidden stash: it was her only security and it meant that she could, if she wanted, go on a whopper of a binge. The idea of drinking remained an avenue of escape for her but she no longer woke up with booze on her mind. Far from it: some days she relished the simple pleasure of waking up and knowing where she was. But that was soon replaced by fear – fear of being let loose and alone.

Lorraine never hinted at her inner turmoil. To Rosie and Jake she appeared confident and composed. She was meticulously clean, often taking two or three showers a day,

68

scrubbing her body until it felt raw. She examined her teeth and gazed at her face in the mirror, studied her scars, as if she was trying to find out who she was, where she had been the past six years.

She drank bottled water all day and ate so well that her skin took on a freshness and her fingernails grew. She sat for hours polishing and filing them, totally preoccupied with herself. She never did any housework, looking on as Rosie changed sheets and went alone to the laundromat. Not once did Lorraine cook or wash up; she ate whatever Rosie banged down in front of her, and ignored the heavy hints about outstaying her welcome.

Finally, Rosie turned to Jake. She wanted him to ask Lorraine to leave.

'I thought you liked her?' he mused.

'I did, I do, but she just *takes* from me, Jake. And I'm not just talking about money. She uses all my hot water, all my things, and now she doesn't even talk to me, never says thank-you, just sits looking at herself, cleaning herself. Sometimes she reminds me of my goddamned cat. She's got to leave, she's driving me nuts!'

Jake came round when he knew Rosie was out. He tapped on the screen door and let himself in. Lorraine was sitting by the window, reading. She looked up, acknowledged him, then returned to her book. 'We got to have a little chat,' Jake said, sitting on the sofa. Lorraine didn't look up. He crossed his fat legs. 'I know you're maybe scared of leaving here, you feel safe, feel like you're getting back to some kind of normality. But it's an unreal normality, Lorraine. This is Rosie's home, and she's broke – caring for you and herself . . .'

Lorraine snapped the book shut. 'Okay. I'll leave.'

'You don't have to do that – but you got to get a job, put some money into the housekeeping, help out around the place. Then, when you've found your feet, maybe you can get a place of your own.'

69

Lorraine stared at her manicured fingers and looked out of the window. 'I dunno about that . . .' She turned to him. Her eyes were washed-out blue, wide apart, without expression. He couldn't tell what she was thinking. 'It's been a long time since I worked, Jake. You know – with sane people . . .' She half smiled. 'Maybe I'm not ready to take on any responsibility. I'm kind of living day to day, but I hear what you're saying, and I'll leave.'

'Where will you go?' Jake asked.

She shrugged. 'I dunno. I'll make out. What do you care?'

'I care a lot – especially after all that dental work you got done! Hate to see you go and start the rot again, because if you walk out of here with no purpose you'll be back on Skid Row pretty soon.'

She sighed; she felt tired and it hurt to think. She ran a finger along the scar at the back of her head. 'Skid Row. That where we met, huh? Joke, it was just a joke . . . Look, Jake, I'm real tired, so if you don't mind leaving . . .'

He got up and went to the kitchen. 'I'll make us some coffee.' He saw the way her face tightened. She wanted him to leave, he knew, but he hadn't finished. 'Let's talk some more, Lorraine, throw a few ideas around. Like I said, you got to find a purpose.'

She picked up the book again. Jake walked over and snatched it away. 'You can fuck around with Rosie, Lorraine, because she's weak and desperate. She needed you in some sick kind of way – it took her mind off her own problems. But now you got to put a bit back, understand me?'

She smirked at him. 'Why don't *you* put it back, Jake? Give her a screwing, she needs that more than anything else! She hasn't been laid in five years.'

He could have slapped her sullen face, but he didn't. He just held the steady gaze of her washed-out eyes. 'You been screwed lately, then, do you? Remember it?'

70

'I've had enough to last me a lifetime.'

'I bet you did. A lot of drunks whore for booze – that what you did?'

'Fuck off.'

Jake gripped her skinny wrist. 'I fuck off – and you're fucked. You need Rosie, you need this place, because it's all you've got – but you've used her. I'm just trying to help. You're already helping yourself.'

'Am I?' she snapped.

'Yes. You look a hell of a lot better than when you first arrived – and you can keep on looking and feeling better – but you have to want a future!'

Jake had to hand it to Lorraine: she still didn't give an inch, still showed no sign of what she was feeling. She did, however, drink the coffee he made and even though she didn't speak to him again, she seemed to listen, chain-smoking his cigarettes, staring at the wall. Eventually he could think of nothing more to say. He wrote down a few contact addresses for jobs and went away, feeling depressed and disappointed. She didn't say goodbye or thank him for the extra pack of smokes he had left.

By the time Rosie returned, however, the apartment was tidier, and Lorraine had vacuumed and cleaned the kitchen. Rosie's bed was made, the shower room was clean. Even the cat had been fed.

Rosie muttered thanks and put down a grocery bag full of cans of Coke, oven-ready french fries, and a cooked chicken. She began cooking dinner as Lorraine watched television, shrugging in reply to anything Rosie said. They ate in silence, Rosie glancing at Lorraine as she sucked each chicken bone, eating with her hands, polishing the plate clean with her bread. Rosie shifted onto the sofa for a better view of the TV as Lorraine cleared the table and washed up. Not until she had dried all the dishes and put them away did Lorraine begin a conversation.

'Jake was here.'

'Yeah, I know.'

'I'll go an' see if I can get a job tomorrow, start payin' some rent.'

Rosie nodded. 'Okay. You want to come to AA tonight?'

Lorraine hesitated. 'Okay.'

As before, Lorraine sat at the back, playing no part in the proceedings. As she checked over the list of jobs she'd try for in the morning, her head throbbed. Then, without any warning, the sweating began, and she slipped out into the corridor where she found the water fountain. She had gulped down several cupfuls before she was steadier and her mouth stopped feeling like sandpaper. The fountain was close to a large bulletin board: there were lists of contacts, jobs, AA meetings, white elephant and garage sales. Lorraine noted down an address for second-hand clothes.

Rosie appeared, looking concerned, but seeing Lorraine squinting up at the bulletin board in that odd way she had, writing down information, she relaxed.

Lorraine looked over to her. 'I guess I'll need some clothes for work. There's a yard sale on. You want to come?'

It wasn't until they got there and Lorraine began to stack up suits, shirts, shoes, that Rosie wondered how she was going to pay. When she asked how much they'd cost, Lorraine told her fifteen dollars for the bunch – the woman wanted to get rid of the stuff quickly as she was moving. She had actually paid a hundred and fifty and was now down to less than a hundred bucks in her stash. The fact that she had broken into it for something other than booze, was – even though she didn't realize it – another step forward.

Rosie sat draining a can of Coke as Lorraine inspected her new clothes, trying them all on, mixing and matching. Her face wore a studied, concentrated expression. She muttered and nodded, running her hand through her hair. 'Mmmm, nice, not bad . . . yes, I like it.'

She felt jealous as she watched Lorraine parade up and down like a model on a catwalk. The clothes were good, anyone could see that, tailored skirts and jackets, a particularly nice cream silk shirt, and a black crêpe one, tasteful walking shoes and a pair of brown slingbacks that had never been worn. 'I doubt if you'll need that gear for the jobs Jake's got lined up for you,' Rosie pointed out, burping from the Coke.

Lorraine was looking at herself in the long wardrobe mirror. 'Maybe I'm gonna try for a real job. There were quite a few listed at the meeting.'

Rosie pouted. 'Like what?'

Lorraine turned round. 'Receptionist – got to look smart for that – nice and easy, sittin' down all day. I might get lucky.'

Rosie sniffed. 'You might not.'

Lorraine hardly slept. The sofa was uncomfortable at the best of times, but constant worrying about the next day made her toss and turn. Four times she had to walk through the bedroom to the toilet, but she didn't disturb Rosie, who slept as always like a beached whale, snoring loudly. Lorraine's thirst seemed unquenchable. She finished all the Coke, all the bottled water, sweating and shaking, flopping up and down on the old sofa. Then it started – the craving. She badly wanted a beer. Would it be so bad to have just one?

She slipped into Rosie's old dress, and inched open the screen door. The need consumed her; she could think of nothing else. She got as far as the bottom step before she saw the patrol car moving slowly up the road, the two officers inside staring at the buildings as they cruised along. She watched for a few moments before returning to the apartment, where she looked out from the window as they passed on down the road. By the time they had disappeared she didn't feel so desperate. Still fully dressed, she got back on the sofa.

She had been expecting them. They must have contacted the cab ranks by now, but because she had seen no sign of police interest, she had been too wrapped up in herself to give it a second thought. Now she remembered . . . but instead of focusing on the present, Lorraine recalled her own days in uniform.

The only female in the precinct, she hadn't even had a place to piss in privacy until they designated a toilet for her. She would do anything rather than go into the john and even when she had her own there was always a cop leering, presenting his dick for her appraisal. Her partner would throw fits because she was always asking him to pull over at public conveniences. It got so she wouldn't drink during the day so she didn't have to piss. They nicknamed her the Golden Camel, because no matter what temperature blistered the paint off the car, rookie Lorraine Page never accepted a drink. Later, she sure as hell made up for it, and when she had moved on, and upwards, she could drink most of her colleagues under the table. It had started as an act of bravado, to show she was as good as any man on or off duty. She could hold it. And then she got a new nickname: 'Hollow Legs Page'.

Half dreaming, half awake, Lorraine recollected times she had not thought of for years. In these sequences she was always in uniform, and what hit her hardest was the persistent humiliation to which she had been subjected. A woman in a man's world, a woman none of them wanted or encouraged to become part of their close-knit group. She had clawed every inch up the ladder – she had always had to prove herself tougher than any man. She was not better educated, she had no special qualifications, and if her father had not been a police officer she doubted that she would ever have joined up. She'd enrolled almost as an act of perversity.

Lorraine had hated her father because he had no time for her while he had doted on her brother, Kit. Whatever Kit had wanted Daddy made sure his precious son got. Kit was the pride of the family.

Lorraine's mother had been an alcoholic, a frightened, pathetic woman who drank in secret, who remained inside the house, afraid of her own shadow until she had drunk enough confidence to go out. To everyone's embarrassment, she would be picked up and brought home in a squad car by one of her husband's colleagues. She was never charged with being drunk and disorderly, whatever she did. If she stole money or became abusive, it was quietly glossed over, and she would be locked in her bedroom to get over yet another binge. Poor Ellen Page, sober and regretful, apologetic and weepy. Lorraine used to hide from the sound of her sobs by covering her ears with her pillow. When her mother was sober, the house would return to order and routine – until the next time.

Lately Lorraine had not given her mother much thought. Now, she could picture her pale face, her white hands always twisting the thin gold wedding ring. Her red-rimmed eyes, her lank blonde hair. Lorraine was the image of her mother: perhaps that was why her father had so little time or love left for her.

She never discovered what had started her mother's drinking. She used to search for the hidden bottles and, under instruction from her father, pour the contents down the sink. At first she always told him when she found the tell-tale bottles, but it seemed to Lorraine that the awful fights that followed were always directed at her – as if the blame was somehow partly hers. In the end, the pale, thin look-alike daughter protected her mother, and simply poured away the booze without saying anything.

Lorraine's mother died quietly in her sleep. She was only

forty-two, and Lorraine thirteen, but from then Lorraine ran the house. She cooked and cleaned up, waited on her father and brother. She would watch them leave for ball games, always together, like pals rather than father and son.

Kit was killed in a car accident. Two kids joy-riding in a stolen car mounted the pavement and ran him down. She could see him clearly, it was strange, she hadn't given him a thought in she couldn't remember how many years. Now she could even hear his voice, the way he always called out when he came into the house: 'Hi, I'm home, anythin' to eat?' He had never talked about their mother's 'problem' – if anything he refused to acknowledge there was one. When Lorraine was forced to clear up her vomit, wash her like a child, he shut himself in his room and played his records. Loud, louder than ever if Ellen was weeping, or if she was stumbling around the kitchen trying to get supper ready.

That night Kit hadn't come home for supper, and her father got the phone call, just as she was about to serve him steak. She could smell it, all these years later, the steak, the mashed potatoes, and the mint peas. She knew it was something terrible because of her father's expression and the way he let the phone slip from his hand as he pressed his face into the old flowered wallpaper. Then he punched the wall twice before he walked back and collected his jacket.

'There's been an accident. It's Kit.'

Lorraine was left alone with a father who never came to terms with his grief. He hadn't been affectionate before the accident, but afterwards he showed her no warmth whatsoever. If he felt any pride in her being accepted into the police academy, he kept it to himself, and he was dead three weeks before she graduated.

Lorraine sold the house and prepared to move into an apartment. It had been while sorting through his belongings that she had found pictures of her mother. She had once been so beautiful, with a fragility that took Lorraine's breath away, but the sweet smile, even in her youth, was a little frightened. She also found albums of photographs of her brother, every achievement recorded for posterity. But there were few pictures of herself, and those she did find had been left in an envelope.

Lorraine burned most of the memorabilia, and sold all the furniture along with the house. She kept a photograph of her brother and one of her parents on their wedding day. She would have liked one of them all together, as a family, but there hadn't been one – there hadn't really been a family. Now she had nothing – not even a photograph of Mike or the girls. She pictured them in her mind, little Julia and sweet-faced Sally . . . and Mike. The feeling of loss swamped her. She forced their faces from her mind and found solace in counting the specks of dirt on the wallpaper – anything rather than think of the past.

She woke up as Rosie thumped into the kitchen. She felt stiff from the cramped position in which she'd finally fallen asleep.

'I'm going to be late,' Rosie muttered, in her usual bad-tempered early-morning mood. She stood to shovel in her cereal, milk trickling down her chin. Lorraine stretched.

'Will you feed the cat?' Rosie barked.

Lorraine joined her in the kitchen. 'Do you think alcoholism is hereditary?'

Rosie rammed her cereal bowl into the sink. 'If you came to a few more meetings you'd know, wouldn't you? But they say it is. Why don't you read the leaflets I gave you?' She continued spouting as she returned to the bedroom, and Lorraine uttered a silent prayer that she had not gone out for that beer. Another day over, sober.

Rosie plodded down the road and turned the corner, just as the squad car drew up. Two officers checked the address and glanced up the rickety wooden stairs. The cab driver had not been sure of the number he had driven the woman to, but he had known the street and the date his fare had flagged him down. His description of her matched that of the other two witnesses, and he had picked up the fare a short distance from the shopping mall car park. He was able to add one more detail: the woman had a front tooth missing.

Lorraine examined herself: the suit jacket was a fraction too large, the skirt band a couple of inches too wide, but she bloused up the jacket, a safari-style fawn cotton, and with the cream silk shirt beneath, it looked good. She borrowed a pair of pearl stud earrings from Rosie's jewel box, and used her mascara, a little rouge and powder and, as the lipsticks were all a violent orange, rubbed on lip balm instead. When she heard a rap on the door she hesitated: maybe she should have asked Rosie about the earrings. If she was back, she might get into one of her moods. She heard a second rap; knew it couldn't be Rosie, who would have used her key, and assumed it was Jake.

She stepped back in shock as the two officers lolled at the door. One remained outside while the second came in to 'ask a few questions . . .' She lit a cigarette and sat on the edge of the sofa, thankful she had cleared away the blankets and pillows.

'Do you live here?'

'Yes, I do.'

'What's your name?'

'Laura Bradley. Actually I'm just staying here, I don't own this apartment.'

'Who does?'

Lorraine gave Rosie's name. He asked for a description, and she said Rosie was dark-haired and in her late thirties.

'Is she fat?'

Lorraine half smiled. 'No. Why? Has something happened to her?'

'No. Were you here early evening on the seventeenth of last month?'

Lorraine nodded.

'Did someone else come here? Did a taxi cab bring someone else to these premises?'

'No. Not that I can recall . . .'

The officer stood up, walked towards the bedroom, and pushed open the door.

'Just the two of you live here? Nobody else? Short, dark-haired man?'

Lorraine laughed. 'No. It's a small place. Why are you so interested?'

The photograph was not the same as the one in the wallet but much larger. Yet Lorraine knew at a glance that it was the owner of the vehicle licence – the owner of the wallet.

'Do you know this man?'

'No, I'm sorry. What has he done?'

'He was murdered, ma'am. Haven't you read about it? Local man.'

Lorraine looked suitably shocked, then stood up. 'Maybe he lived here before I came to stay – I can ask my friend.'

The officer slipped the photograph back into his jacket. 'Thanks. Truth is, we're only interested in tracing the woman – cabbie reckoned she was dropped off around here.' He relaxed, smiled at Lorraine. 'As you don't fit the description we must have got the wrong place, but thanks for your help, been nice talkin' to you.'

Lorraine followed the young officer to the door. 'Was she murdered as well?' she asked innocently.

'No, but we think she may have known the man driving the deceased's vehicle. We have two witnesses.'

'They saw her coming here?' asked Lorraine.

'No. In the local shopping mall car park, and we were told she may have been brought here by cab. We're asking everyone in the street if they saw her. She must have been hard to miss – she was covered in blood.'

Lorraine opened the front door. 'I'll ask Rosie when she comes home if she saw her. Do you have a number? Somebody I can call?'

The officer told her to contact her local station or sheriff's office and they would pass on any information to the department handling the homicide.

After they had gone, Lorraine leaned against the door. Her heart was beating so rapidly that she felt dizzy. She began to talk herself down for being so stupid. She was not involved in any murder. All she had done was tip off the cops with the description of the man who picked her up. There was nothing to be afraid of – except that she had taken the wallet. But she'd got rid of it and nearly all the money was gone. They had not been new notes so she doubted they could be traced. Why was she worrying about something so inconsequential when the officers hadn't even recognized her as the woman they wanted for questioning? She ran her tongue over her newly capped teeth. She had come a long way since that attack, physically and mentally, and she congratulated herself on the way she had handled the cop.

She even mentally castigated the police for being so slow in finding the cab driver who had driven her home that afternoon. If she had been on the case it would have been the first thing she'd have checked.

Self-satisfied, she left the apartment, her pace quickening as she walked towards the bus stop. Nothing in her appearance resembled the woman the police had described: her hair was well cut. She looked elegant, though the shoes were a bit tight and she was without a purse, but she was more confident than she had been for years. She caught a glimpse of her reflection in the grocery store window as she

80

passed and didn't even notice the rows of liquor bottles, so intent was she on admiring herself. It was another day, and she had moved on faster than she could ever have anticipated or believed possible.

CHAPTER 3

APTAIN ROONEY looked over the reports and statements from the various officers. They were, as he had half expected, of little use. The cab driver had given them a bum address and nobody had located the bloodstained woman with only one shoe. She had disappeared – could even be dead. The Summerses had been questioned again to see if they could match the description from the anonymous caller. He was similar, they said, but they were not too clear about the driver of the vehicle. When shown a photograph of Norman Hastings, they were sure that it was not him. Rooney doodled over his notebook.

He wondered again if they were looking for two killers, the man and the blonde woman working together. They had killed Hastings and then had an argument – maybe they had come to blows inside the car at the shopping mall. The woman subsequently made the anonymous phone call describing her partner, husband or lover . . . But if that was so, she would have known the killer's height and could even have given his name, although that might have incriminated her, too. Rooney concluded that the woman was probably not involved in the murder and did not know the killer's name or height because she was, as he had first thought, a prostitute the driver had picked up.

The missing blonde woman had become a vital witness to the murder of Norman Hastings. Somebody out there knew who she was. A man and a woman had helped her out of the cab; the man had even paid her fare. Rooney instructed his officers to step up the search for her, and called in the two officers Lorraine had met earlier.

He checked over all the statements they had taken. They were convinced that no one had lied. They thought the cab driver might have been mistaken. 'We saw only one blonde woman, Captain – but she'd got all her teeth, her hair was short and she was real smart, just staying with her friend. She didn't look like a whore or the type to know one.'

Rooney told them to question everybody once more. Seeing them exchange covert, bored looks, Rooney snapped, 'Get the cab driver to go with you, if needs be. Go on, get moving!'

The two men had just reached the office door when Josh Bean walked in. 'You better look at this, Captain.'

Rooney reached out his podgy hand for the internal fax sheet. Bean gave the nod for the two men to leave the room, but to wait outside. Rooney looked up. 'We'd better check this out. Looks like our missing girl.'

He snatched up his jacket, told the two officers they could go off duty. If the new information panned out, they had just found their star witness.

The run-down apartment block was a graffiti jungle. Burned-out cars littered the disused yard and every window was smashed. The Paradise Apartments billboard, showing palm trees and a semi-naked girl sunbathing, was peeling and covered in daubed slogans.

Rooney stepped under the obligatory yellow tape to join the group gathered round the covered corpse. There were five patrol cars, lights blinking, and a horde of officers assembled to protect the men in this notorious down-town area. Groups of kids were hanging around watching avidly. This wasn't unusual in the middle of the day as most of them never bothered to attend school for more than one or two days a week, if that. This was crack-dealer territory. The kids on their BMX bikes more than likely had shooters stuck up their fashionable jackets.

'Who found her?' Rooney asked as he neared the corpse.

'That kid over there, one with the red hat on, but he must have had help to drag her from the trunk of the car. That's been there for weeks, by the way, the car not the body.'

Rooney stared at the kid, who was no more than six or seven and laughing as he pointed to the dead body, nudging his pals.

'She was in the wrecked car, nearest the tapes. He dragged her out here, said he thought she was alive – but if she had any jewellery on her, she ain't got it now.'

As he crouched down, Rooney took out his handkerchief to cover his face – the stench was of a body at least two days old. So much for the kid's story about thinking she was still alive. She was wearing a floral patterned dress, with a belt and flat black shoes. Rooney noted they were the same size as the one they had found in Hastings's car. Her thin legs were bare, and one stretched out at an odd angle. Her arms were by her sides, the back of her dress undone. The thin blonde hair was matted with dark congealed blood; a wound gaped at the base of her skull, so deep, he could see white bone. Slowly they turned over the unwieldy corpse. Her face had been hammered out of all recognition. Blood obliterated the brightly coloured flowers that had once patterned the front of her dress.

There was nothing Rooney could do; he couldn't tell if it was their witness or not. His only option was to wait for the report to come in, and for her to be cleaned up so he could see her face.

'Any of her teeth missing?' he asked as an afterthought.

An officer peered down into the mass of blood hiding her face. 'I can't tell, her nose has been flattened so bad . . .'

Rooney returned to his office with Bean. They opened a bottle of Scotch, and both had a heavy hit. No matter how many you see, it's always the smell that gets to you, stays in your nostrils. The sweet, sticky, cloying smell of rotting flesh.

'I think it's our witness. Cinderella,' Rooney said flatly. 'Fuck it! Really needed to talk to her.' He sighed.

'Yeah.' Bean knocked back his drink.

Rooney looked up as his secretary peered in. A message had come through from the city morgue: the corpse wouldn't be ready for viewing until at least the following day, maybe longer. Did he want to speak to the scene-of-crime officers? Rooney jerked his head for Bean to go and do the leg-work; he had some paperwork to finish. Bean raised his eyebrow, knowing Rooney always said that when he wanted to take himself off home. But he was wrong this time: Rooney spent the next hour making phone calls to different precincts. It was something one of the officers had said – or he might even have said it himself. She had been hammered in the face and at the back of the head. He wanted to know if anyone else had a similar homicide – weapon used probably some kind of hammer, that was all . . . In reality he passed more time chatting to old buddies, in no hurry for the facts. He knew he wouldn't get them straight away, if at all. Old files would have to be sifted through, and checked out on computer. Probably wasting everybody's time, but he caught up on gossip, arranged a game of billiards and agreed to have a drink with Colin Sparks, an old poker-playing pal he'd not seen for six months.

Sitting on a bar stool in Joe's Diner, his fat ass bulging over the red plastic stool top, Rooney had downed two beers and a chaser by the time Sparks walked in, but promptly ordered another round and a fresh bowl of peanuts.

Sparks whacked him on the back, then produced a dog-eared file. 'I'm late because I got interested in that! It happened before I got transferred – it's been around for four years. Dead hooker. Go on, read it.'

Rooney grinned at the young, fresh-faced lieutenant, and cuffed him like a father would his son. 'Looking sharper than ever, Colin. How you keeping?'

'Fine, new baby on the way – everythin's good.'

Rooney opened the file. He looked at the prostitute's face, her dyed blonde hair scraped back from her head showing at least an inch of dark hair growth. Half Mexican. Maria Valez, aged thirty-two. The next page had a photograph of her body when it was discovered in the trunk of a wrecked Buick. Like the dead woman that afternoon, Maria's face had been virtually obliterated by heavy blows. There was an enlarged shot of the back of her scalp, showing the deep wound. Type of weapon, possibly a claw-sided hammer. No witness, no arrest, no charges, case closed for lack of evidence, but authorized to remain open on file.

Rooney closed the file and tossed a handful of peanuts into his mouth. 'Can I keep this? There's a few details on blood groups I'd like to check out with my case.'

'Go ahead.'

'Thanks,' smiled Rooney, as he waved at the waitress for another round. 'An' I'm gonna treat you to the best curry in Pasadena!'

Rooney, well toasted, and Sparks, soberish, left Joe's Diner to head for the Star of Asia curry house. Rooney's crumpled alpaca coat flapped. The file was stuffed under his arm and he was sweating in the early-evening heat. He upped his flat-footed pace to get into the air-conditioned restaurant.

*

Lorraine emerged from the health club Fit as a Fiddle feeling like a washed-out rag. Her heels were blistered, her silk blouse creased, tears of sweat dripped from her fringe, and her hair was wet at the nape of her neck. So far she had applied for ten different jobs to discover either that the position had been filled, or that she didn't have the required experience. At Fit as a Fiddle she had snapped back at the Cher-with-muscles lookalike: 'How much fucking experience do you want to pick up a phone and book an appointment?'

'Cher' had wafted a hand adorned with fake nails. 'Maybe I was just bein' polite. You look like death warmed up for starters – and you're too old, okay? That real enough for you?'

Lorraine had slammed out and was about to throw in the towel and go home, when she realized she was standing outside Seller Sales, the next job prospect she had noted down. She pulled at her jacket, using the sleeve to wipe the sweat from her face, and walked into the run-down office. A moment later and she would have faced Captain Rooney as he and Sparks went into the restaurant three doors down the street. As it was, she almost walked straight out of Seller Sales: no one was in what she supposed passed for reception – a counter, a bowl of wilting flowers, two posters for Gay Liberation, and a faded breakfast cereal ad. She opened the door, which buzzed, and a man shot round from a room at the back. 'Thank God! Come on, come on, hurry up. I'm Art Mathews. I've been getting desperate.'

Lorraine hesitated and closed the door, following Art round the screen and into the back room. He was about five foot four, tight, muscular little body, shown off by a close-fitting white T-shirt, skintight white jeans, white sneakers and white socks. His dark eyes were too large for his face behind huge glasses – round, thin, red-framed bifocals – and made even more striking by his complete baldness.

The room was cluttered with paints, trestle tables, stacks of canvases, ladders and rolls of carpet. Art walked in small, mincing steps, side-stepping all the paraphernalia with a dancer's precision.

'Now the phone is somewhere, and the lists. Oh, Jesus, where did I put the lists? I'm so behind – and they said you'd be here hours ago . . .'

Lorraine looked around. 'I think there's a misunderstanding.'

Art stood, hands on hips, his little rosebud mouth pursed. 'Seller thingy closed down months ago, I've taken the shop lease over. I'm opening an art and photographic gallery here tomorrow, would you believe it? My God, if you knew what I've been through . . . WHERE'S THE FUCK-ING PHONE!'

Lorraine spotted it beneath a table. Art dragged it out, swore because it was off the hook and sat cross-legged on the floor. Lorraine watched as he arched his body to enable him to drag out a card from his jeans pocket, and punched out some digits.

'What are you here for?'

She coughed. 'Receptionist.'

He looked at the card, then back to Lorraine, his eyes darting like a demented frog's. He pursed his lips as his call was connected. 'This is Mr Art Mathews and I was prom-ised a . . . hello? FUCKING ANSWER MACHINE!'

He sprang to his feet. 'I need someone to call my guest list, there's over a hundred people, and I need it done by tonight. I need someone here to help me open this up. I've got to get that paint on the walls, hang those canvases and photos—'

Lorraine unbuttoned her jacket. 'I'll do it. How much you paying?'

Art clapped his hands. 'Ten bucks an hour – I love you. What's your name, darling?' She told him. 'Right, Lorraine, here's the phone, grab a seat, I'll find the list and you start

88

with the calls. I need to know how many are coming so I can order the wine . . .'

'Have they been invited already?' Lorraine asked.

'They have, dear, but not to this address. I had a problem with my last place. Now if I don't open and show all the canvases and the photographs then I'll be fucked – I'll lose my credibility and it's hanging on a thread as it is . . .'

He alighted on a bulging Filofax. 'Right, darling, here you go. Be charming, be distant, but get an answer.'

Lorraine put down her cigarettes and lighter, and studied the guest list, detailed in a neat fine scrawl, in pinks, greens and blues with red stars drawn against some names. 'Does the red star mean they're important?'

'No – just a good lay!' Art shrieked with laughter. He almost did a triple spinning turn as the buzzer sounded in reception.

Lorraine could hear a lot of shrieking and raised voices, then Art returned with a massive floral display – and two extraordinary-looking transsexuals, carrying a basket of food, a crate of distilled water, and two more floral displays. 'These are my dearest friends, Nula and Didi, they're going to help me. This is – what's your name again, dear? She's going to make all the phone calls, and be Girl Friday.'

Nula and Didi began to put down their goods as Art moved to clear the back of the room. Lorraine pulled out a clean page from the Filofax, and started making calls. She looked up gratefully as Nula placed a paper cup and a bottle of spring water by her side. Didi was inspecting some tapes, then crossed to a ghetto blaster and slipped in a tape. Lorraine expected some ear-shattering music to interrupt her call, but she was surprised by Mahler's Symphony No.9, the volume almost restful. Didi laid out a neat row of tapes, choosing each with studied concentration. She turned to Lorraine, her husky voice half whispering: 'Do you like opera?'

She nodded as Didi selected the next tape. She had never listened to opera in her life.

The pace at which Art and his two friends worked was astonishing. They had painted all the walls with a quick-dry rough white, swept the floors, stacked the rubbish, torn down the screen partitioning at the front of the shop, and were now painting that area, using big roller brushes on sticks.

Lorraine remained at the table, making calls and listing acceptances and refusals. She now had her spiel down to a bare minimum: 'Good evening, I am calling on behalf of Art Mathews's new gallery, Art's Place . . .' She gave the address, time of the show and mentioned that wine and canapés would be served from seven o'clock. Most said they would try to make it, but only twenty would definitely be there.

The strains of Puccini floated into the room, and Lorraine downed two bottles of water as she continued her calls. Nula slipped her some home-made banana cake wrapped in a napkin, a little bowl of fruit salad, and some crispbread with home-made pâté. Her big hands were rough from scrubbing, her overall covered in white paint splashes but she had the sweetest of smiles. Didi paid Lorraine hardly any attention as she was intent on finishing the work. When they did take a short break the three huddled together, admiring the gallery, discussing where the paintings and photographs would look best.

Art occasionally leaned over her to see the list, but on the whole behaved as if she weren't there. It was almost ten o'clock when Lorraine made the last call to a Craig Lyall. The deep, rather camp voice enquired if it could speak to Art. She covered the mouthpiece. 'Art, it's a Craig Lyall, he wants to speak to you.'

Art passed his brush to Nula. His whiter-than-white outfit was filthy, his round glasses speckled with paint. 'This is he,' he lisped into the phone.

Lorraine got up and stretched. Her back ached, and her mouth was dry again. She wandered towards the main room where Nula and Didi were unwrapping canvases and stacking them against the walls.

Art rang off, came across and put his arm around Lorraine. 'Well that, my dear, was good news. Craig Lyall, sweethearts, is coming.' He peered up into her face. 'You can go now but I insist you're here tomorrow. What on earth did you do to yourself? Car crash?'

Lorraine stepped away from him, her hand automatically moving to her scarred face. 'Yes.'

'You should have it fixed, dear. I know the best surgeon if you want his name . . .' Art put his arm back around her waist and gave her a little hug, beamed, then released her to dig deep into his pants and took out a thin leather wallet.

Lorraine felt embarrassed as he counted out thirty dollars in ten-dollar bills, but she took the money and pocketed it fast. 'See you tomorrow, then,' she said, hovering at the doorway. All three smiled and Art accompanied her to the main exit. He unlocked the door, which buzzed as she stood on the mat. He tutted, 'I'll have to get this fixed.'

Lorraine turned back to see him inspecting the faulty buzzer, his bald head shining in the street lights. She intended to get a bus and was heading towards the bus stop, when a car travelling in the opposite direction tooted its horn. Lorraine looked over, and was relieved to see Jake at the wheel. 'You want a lift?' he called. By the time she had crossed the road, Art had closed the door and returned to Nula and Didi.

Nula looked at Didi and nodded. 'Tell him.'

'Tell me what?' Art asked, his attention focused on the paintings.

'I think I've seen her before though I can't put my finger

on where. I've been trying to remember all evening. How did you find her?'

'She just walked in off the street. I thought she was from that agency I use, but she was looking for work at Sellers Sales.'

Nula studied her nails. 'That's been shut for months.'

Art said, 'Didn't you like her?'

Didi shrugged. 'I've just got this funny feeling about her.'

Art wished they would pack up and leave as he liked to hang the paintings alone, taking his time to choose where each would go. 'Isn't it time you two left?'

Nula gave a camp, 'Well, thank you . . .' and started to put her stuff together.

Didi was almost ready, giving a last look around. 'It looks good – be even better when I bring some more knick-knacks tomorrow.'

Art kissed them both, almost tearful with gratitude. 'You'll be here in the afternoon, won't you? Are you working tonight?'

They both chorused 'yes' and he watched them walk off, arm in arm, high heels, tight skirts, only their rather broad shoulders giving any indication of their former masculinity.

As soon as they were out of earshot, Nula snapped, 'I think you should have told him.'

Didi pouted. 'Why didn't *you*? It's always me. We'll have to sort it out between us. If he finds out he'll go ape-shit, so we'll sort it.'

Art watched them hail a cab then closed and bolted the door. He took out a tiny square envelope from his jeans pocket and carefully laid out a half-inch line of ice. This would see him through his all-night session. He snorted, blinked back tears as the ice burned his nostrils, then took a few deep breaths. No rush, nothing immediate like cocaine . . . he'd given that up. It would be a while before he felt any real benefit, so he placed the canvases around the room, then sat cross-legged in the centre of his little white gallery to appraise each painting. They were awful and he knew it.

Nula had showered and changed. She wore an overtly sexy outfit: stacked heels, tight leather mini skirt and, as she was well endowed, showed off her tits with an outrageous low cut bodice. She heard the door opening and turned from her make-up table. Didi dangled the car keys. 'Ready, sweets? You'd better go and get on the pitch, I've got to change.'

'Well, another night, dear. I'm ready and I'll be waiting.'

The prettier of the two, Nula pouted at herself and dipped her fingers into thick moisturizing cream. She hated her big hands which, even with nail extensions, looked too large and mannish. 'Funny the way I keep on thinking about her, that Lorraine. Do you think she's a prostitute?'

Didi teased her hair. 'I suppose you could always ask her. She said she'd be there tomorrow. You look lovely, now go on, get out or I'll never be ready.'

Half an hour later Nula was on their patch, hustlin' her tricks, duckin' and divin' down to the cars that cruised past. Most drivers knew she and Didi were trannies – the area was known for it. Both had their own regular customers and both paid off a regular lookout. Curtis wasn't actually a pimp, more of a minder, but he took a cut of every trick and seemed to know how many johns came and went. But Nula and Didi paid up without argument. It wasn't worth the aggravation to protest. Besides, at times they were glad of his tips as he seemed to know in advance when the Vice Squad were in their area.

Tony de Savoy – nicknamed Curtis because he had an old-fashioned haircut like Tony Curtis used to have – strolled up smiling warmly. He kissed Holly, his special sweetheart, tapped her tight little ass for her to get moving, then turned to Nula.

'Hi, how you doin'?'

Nula shrugged. 'Bit quiet tonight. Tony, you know a broad called – oh, I can't remember her name – Lorraine Page. Big tall blonde with a sort of beat-up face?'

'She's not one of mine, why?'

'I just met her tonight, remembered her from some place.'

Holly folded a piece of chewing gum into her tiny mouth and chewed hard. Curtis looked at the wrapper. 'Put it in the trash-can, slut.'

Holly pouted and bent down exaggeratedly to retrieve it, sashayed past and flicked it into a bin.

Curtis nudged Nula. 'She's a looker, isn't she? And with a figure to match. Eh, Holly! Shake that tight ass.'

Holly giggled and twisted, showing off her tits, then flounced off, teetering on her high heels, swinging her ass.

Nula saw a car cruising and took off as Curtis slipped a comb through his slicked-back hair. 'See you later. You just missed a trick – nothing gets by my sweet Holly.'

He laughed as she started to cross the road towards the john. 'I'll be at the Bar Q,' he called out as she sidestepped an oncoming car and gave the finger to the driver.

Nula watched him stroll on down his territory, stopping to chat to his girls. It still needled her that she couldn't remember where she knew Lorraine Page from. Holly was starting to get into the john's car and Nula hurried across the road after her, giving a quick look back to see if Curtis was still watching. But he was chatting up two black chicks, laughing and still flicking his comb through his grease-mop hair.

'This is mine, Nula baby. He wants a real woman, see ya.' Holly laughed as she got into the passenger seat.

Lorraine sat in Rosie's bedroom, telling her about Art and the gallery. She even gave her ten dollars towards the rent.

94

'Will you go back for the show, then?' Rosie asked.

Lorraine pulled off her creased shirt. 'Well, he wanted my phone number in case he has some more work, so I think I'll go.'

Rosie bashed the pillow. 'Put my earrings back in the box! And ask next time – they happen to be real pearls. About the only thing my ex-husband ever gave me . . .'

Lorraine made a show of removing them and replacing them. Rosie watched her every move, irritated yet again by Lorraine's confidence. She seemed to be getting herself back together, but instead of feeling pleased, Rosie felt jealous.

'Maybe I'll come with you.'

Lorraine switched on the shower. 'Don't force yourself. What's the matter with you?'

Rosie sat up. 'Nothing – but didn't you think I'd be worried? Jake was, too.'

Lorraine unzipped her skirt. 'Did you send him out to look for me?'

'Of course I did. I didn't know where the fuck you were – no note, nothin' to tell me what you were doing.'

Lorraine stepped out of her skirt, and Rosie turned away, not out of embarrassment but with the shock of seeing just how thin and scarred Lorraine was. 'What the hell happened to you?' she asked softly. 'All those scars . . .'

Lorraine wrapped a towel around herself. 'I got them when I was too drunk to feel I was getting them. Some of them are cigarette burns – maybe I did them myself . . .'

Rosie sighed as she heard the shower running. She'd meant to tell Lorraine, and Jake for that matter, that she'd lost her job at the hospital. It was nothing she'd done: they were cutting back on part-time staff.

By the time Lorraine emerged from the shower, however, Rosie was fast asleep. Lorraine turned off the light and went into the lounge to make up the sofa bed. She sat, still wrapped in her towel, with the TV turned down low, smoking a cigarette. Another day without a drink – and a day when she felt she had done something positive. But what did it all mean, anyway? She closed her eyes as she leaned back. Was every day going to be like this? Tramping from one place to another looking for work? She got to thinking of how much Art and his two helpers had achieved in one evening. They had transformed that shitty little place, not into anything fantastic, but he was going to be able to open a gallery – maybe even make some decent money. What was *she* cut out to do? She wondered what Nula and Didi did. Maybe they worked in another gallery or a night club. She'd liked them, Art, too, and the music – maybe things *could* get better . . . Maybe the key was to do as Rosie and Jake said and take each day as it came, not try to think of any long-term future, just another day – and one without a drink. She was so tired she fell asleep almost immediately before any pictures of her past had time to squeeze across her mind. She had no reason to think that her past would catch up with her the longer she remained sober. Old memories long forgotten would resurface to haunt her, like her dead brother's face. She had been able to deal with Kit, but there would be more, much more and she was not ready for it. The closer the past inched towards the present, the sooner she would have to face what she had obliterated by drinking.

Nula met up with Curtis for breakfast. She hadn't seen Didi for hours so presumed she had scored either a hotel john or an all-nighter. Curtis was edgy. He'd been looking for Holly and kept asking everyone who came and went if they'd seen her. Nula said she'd seen her score but not since. She could tell he was pretty coked up so she downed her coffee, paid what she owed him and took herself off. It was almost five thirty and she was feeling strung out, worried that Didi hadn't turned up.

Didi was at home, lying prone with an ice pack on her head. Nula leaned over her, concerned. 'You okay?'

Didi removed the ice pack to show a bruised eye. 'What do you think? Look at me, I got a black fuckin' eye and my foot, I twisted my ankle when I got out of the car, it's all swollen up.' Nula brought more ice and wrapped it in a tea towel to place on Didi's foot. She was concerned: the bruised face could always be taken care of but if Didi couldn't walk, that blew it for picking up customers and people would start asking questions.

Didi sighed, shifting the ice pack on her head. 'Oh, I remembered where I saw that Lorraine . . .'

Nula was creaming her face. 'Where?'

'AA meeting, we were both there, few days back.'

'So, that's that, then.' Nula wiped the tissue over her chin, looking at the blur of grease and make-up removed from her stubble-free face. She touched the soft skin lovingly. Odd that she hadn't remembered Lorraine from the AA meeting. She was usually good with faces.

'I'm gonna look terrible for the opening,' Didi moaned. 'Art won't let me in, I'll look so bad – you know the way he is.'

Nula looked at her. 'I wondered where you'd got to. I was worried, then I thought you might have scored. Curtis was strung out, lookin' everywhere for Holly.'

'I couldn't walk, could I? And my face, Jesus Christ, look at my face. Be hard pushed to score anything looking like this.'

'You'll be fine. I'll cover those bruises and your foot'll go down. I remember once I had a john punched me straight in the nose. I thought I was gonna die, two black eyes, but I got a real cute nose afterwards.'

Didi stared at her as if she was crazed and then eased the ice pack over her face. She started to cry but Nula said nothing. She put Didi's discarded clothes in the wardrobe with distaste. They were stained, and would have to be laundered. Suddenly she saw the car keys on the dressing table and whipped round. She began to panic. Why had she brought the car keys back?

'Where's the car?' she asked and Didi slowly removed the ice pack. 'What did you do with the car?'

'I just had to leave it outside, I couldn't walk back.'

Nula swore. She could have slapped Didi but instead she snatched up the keys and walked out slamming the door. Didi flopped back onto the pillows. Sometimes Nula really freaked her – she had no feelings. She cuddled down under the sheets, feeling sorry for herself. Then she felt beneath the pillow for the big topaz ring and slipped it on her finger. It made her feel better, more secure. At least she'd kept that safe.

The morning was bright and clear with the sun bringing a deep low orange glow that seemed to pinpoint the beige, highly polished metal of the Lincoln. A police car drew alongside it, as the two officers noted it had been left in a no-parking zone. That was the only reason they stopped. One officer got out and looked at the front of the car: he noted down the licence plate and returned to his car. He glanced back, which was when he noticed the pink material sticking out from the trunk.

The car had not been reported stolen but both officers walked over to it. One tried the doors. They were unlocked. He peered inside as the second officer pressed open the trunk.

She lay curled up on her side. One glance was enough. Her face was grotesque, beaten so badly that hardly a feature remained intact, and there was a gaping wound at the back of her skull. No one could have recognized her easily, but the tiny anklet she wore with a name engraved in gold letters made them think she was possibly called Holly.

CHAPTER 4

L ORRAINE WAS up and cleaning the apartment before Rosie was awake. She put some coffee on to brew while she stacked and folded her sheets and bed linen. She had a plastic bag full of laundry ready to take to the laundromat, and was mentally compiling a list of groceries.

Rosie eventually surfaced, glowered and established her usual early-morning gloom. Lorraine's hyperactivity served only to increase it.

'You want any laundry done?'

'Jesus! I don't know at this hour, do I?' Rosie banged open the cupboards as Lorraine started up the vacuum.

'Can you just *leave* that until I had my breakfast?'

Lorraine picked up the laundry and walked out. She had it spinning when she took off for the nearest grocery store, the same shopping mall where the attack had occurred. She didn't give it a second thought – all that seemed far in the distance and, in any case, she wasn't anywhere near the parking lot.

It had been a very long time since Lorraine had shopped or bothered to choose food. She wandered up and down the avenues of goods, and the effort of concentrating on what she wanted to buy became more and more difficult as the Muzak attacked her in one ear while a bubble-gum voice belted out 'sales of the day' in the other, enhanced by the high-pitched *ping* of computer cash registers, a clicking she couldn't identify, bells ringing from check-out assistant to floor manager as prices were asked, or assistants screamed conversation and the *peep-peep* of each article as it was passed over the automatic price scanner.

It seemed to Lorraine that only she was aware of the sounds. She noticed all the other shoppers were moving like lightning – it seemed that their sole intention was to get from A to B at the fastest possible rate. Carts collided, there was heavy breathing from a customer if she took too long weighing food. Not until she got to the freezer side did it occur to her that maybe the customers were moving so fast in the grocery section because they had just suffered frostbite in arctic temperatures. Nothing was familiar; had it really been so long since she had done something as ordinary as going to a grocery store?

No matter how hard she tried, Lorraine could not get the polythene roller bag open. Her tomatoes were still on the scales as she battled with her bag that – she felt sure – was only a single strip of plastic. 'Excuse me, could you show me how to get this open?'

The pink-gingham-clad shelf filler didn't look up from her task of stamping the canned peas, with what looked like a small Sten gun. Now Lorraine knew what the *click-click-click* noise was and she waited until the gun had ceased firing before she wafted her unopened bag. 'Is there a trick to this?'

The assistant stuffed her gun into her pocket, and without uttering a word took the bag, licked her forefinger and thumb, rubbed them over the serrated edge, shook it open and returned it to Lorraine.

'Very hygienic. Thank you!' Lorraine turned back to her scales with the waiting pound of tomatoes only to discover someone else had tipped them out.

She bought salad, yoghurt, fresh fruit, oranges for juice, some wholewheat bread, cereal and nuts. She was picking up some cherries when it started. She steadied herself, and pushed her cart over to the freezer section. Her whole body began to shake and she could feel perspiration breaking out all over. As she opened the ice-cream freezer, the gust of chilled air reminded her of the morgue and the first time she had had to take prints from a corpse. She had not shown any disgust, or emotion, but had clung to the fingerprints card, the black ink roller.

'Get the prints, Page, and bring 'em up to records.'

Lorraine had lifted the stiffened hand. She was a black woman, about fifty years of age. Lorraine didn't look at her face, but forced herself to concentrate on taking the prints. No sooner had she uncurled one dead finger than it recurled, the woman's hands tightening like fists. Lorraine was unaware that the team were all watching her, giggling like schoolboys as they saw her struggle. Eventually she had forced the woman's hand to lie flat, palm upwards, but just as she began to roll on the black ink, it had taken on a life of its own, curling so tightly around Lorraine's fingers that she could not release them. The watching men broke up, and only one of them had the decency to feel sorry for her. He was not much older than she was, but the team had shown him the ropes – unlike Rookie Lorraine: she was to be their entertainment. She watched as he hit the elbow of the deceased, which opened up the fist long enough for prints to be taken. She had laughed, treating it all as a big joke. But she'd had nightmares for weeks of being trapped by the dead in that hideous vice-like cold grip.

'Please shut the freezer doors,' snapped a gingham-garbed floor manager as she marched past. Lorraine rested her head against the fridge door, as the sweating subsided, but her hands were shaking. She didn't understand why she had suddenly remembered that incident.

When Lorraine got home, Rosie was sorting through the help-wanted ads, checking the possibles. By mid afternoon, she had made a few calls, but found no work. She sat watching television, and eating the nuts Lorraine had brought home. She paid scant attention to the announcement that a seventeen-year-old girl, Angela Hollow, nicknamed Holly, had been found brutally murdered.

Lorraine blew dry her hair, then rubbed moisturizer over her face and neck, and into her hands. She was sitting on Rosie's bed, smoothing cream into her fingertips when Rookie Lorraine Page appeared again. The rubber gloves she wore to examine a corpse always made her hands dry, and she kept lotion in her locker. The others teased her about it, but it wasn't just the dryness – it was the stench. No matter how fresh the corpse, there was a sickly sweet smell to it. Lorraine never wore perfume, so the moisturizer not only felt good, but smelt clean and fresh. As she massaged her hands, it started again. She was powerless to stop the memories.

They say your first homicide is the one you remember most clearly. Lorraine had been summoned to a domestic and her car had been first on the scene. The small house had looked so neat from the outside, so normal, so quiet that she and her partner had radioed back to base to double-check the address. A neighbour had called to say they had heard screaming and gunfire.

Lorraine tried the front door. It was open. The woman's throat had been slashed, as had her arms and chest. She was wearing a cotton shift, nothing else, and there was so much blood that the material was a bright vermilion red. They found her husband in the front bedroom with his head blown apart, the gun still in his hand. Blood had sprayed over the walls and soaked into the blanket on the bed where he was lying. The third body, that of a twelve-year-old girl, was in the back bedroom. She had been killed by a single knife wound to the heart. She was tucked up in the bed, the covers up to her chin, one arm around a doll, as if peacefully asleep. Subsequently they discovered pornographic material and videos of the child and the dead man. Lorraine never forgot viewing those wretched home-made films, just as she never forgot how innocent the little girl had looked with her doll. She learnt from that incident never to judge by appearances: the family with no previous criminal record, the suburban couple with their respectable jobs, played out in secret a despicable game of perversion on their own child. It was a hard and brutal lesson for a twenty-year-old rookie cop. Worse followed, but sitting in front of Rosie's dressing table, the memory of that first suicide came back. Lorraine felt icy cold, as if she was standing in the morgue, as if the child's murder had just happened, as if the little girl was calling out to her.

Rooney stared at the body, moving around the stretcher, pulling at his nose. The hammer blows to her face had broken both cheeks, her nose, and the right side of her jaw. The wound to the back of her head would have killed her, as it had cracked open her skull. She had no other body scars, no new skin abrasions or bruising, and her fingernails were intact, but there was evidence of previous beatings. At seventeen years old, Angela Hollow, blonde, about five feet seven, with a good figure, had three previous arrests for prostitution.

Rooney thanked the morgue attendant and returned to his office. Bean was waiting. He had interviewed Holly's pimp and four other girls who had seen her on the evening of her death. No one had seen the man who had picked her up, but one witness remembered the metallic beige car. They had not glimpsed the driver as he had been on the far side of the road. All they remembered was seeing Holly cross the road at about nine thirty. She had not been seen since.

Rooney looked through the statements and tossed over the file he had been given by Colin Sparks. 'Have a look at that, Josh. I want the blood group checked out against that girl we got and on the Hastings guy.'

Bean left the office, but returned immediately with a lengthy internal fax. 'You better look over this, it just came in.'

Rooney nodded. 'Angela Hollow. It's a fucking hammer again.'

As he went out, Bean heard Rooney swearing. The fax sheets were the result of his previous evening's calls. Three more girls, in different areas over a period of seven years, had all been killed by hammer blows to the back of the head, and suffered severe facial injuries. All were hookers of different ages, their bodies left in the trunk of a stolen vehicle. No witnesses. Each case left open on file. Three murders, Angela Hollow made it four and Maria Valez five, the woman from the wreck, still unidentified, six, and if the killer had also murdered Norman Hastings it was now seven. If they had all been killed by the same man, as Rooney began to suspect, he had better start gathering the evidence to link them together. He was now about to launch a multiple murder inquiry.

Later that afternoon he got the first verification. The blood found inside the stolen Hastings car matched the retained blood sample from the murder case handed to him by Sparks. The killer of Maria Valez had left no other incriminating evidence behind, but Rooney made a note that she had, like the woman in Hastings's car, put up a struggle. According to the autopsy reports, she had clawed and scratched her assailant: blood samples had been taken from beneath her fingernails. None of the other women had struggled: they had been killed by the blow to the back of their heads.

Rooney summoned Mr and Mrs Summers again, hoping they would be unable to identify the corpse from Paradise Apartments as the woman they had seen in the mall car park. If it were not her, then what they had witnessed in the car park, the woman in Norman Hastings's car, was a failed murder attempt, possibly by the same killer. It also meant that Cinderella was still alive and, once again, a vital witness – or accomplice.

As they had been throughout, Mr and Mrs Summers were eager to give every assistance. They had never been to a morgue before or played a part in any criminal investigation let alone a murder inquiry. Rooney decided they should see the body together, and he accompanied them into the viewing room.

'Okay, she's behind the curtain. We can turn her around, get any side you want to see, right or left. You just take your time . . .'

He pressed the buzzer for the curtain to move away from the screen window.

The dead woman had been cleaned up, her hair washed and combed, and they had also had her face repaired, covered and filled in by a qualified cosmetic mortician. A little trace of make-up served only to enhance the deathly pallor and her eyes were closed.

Mrs Summers let out a gasp. She stepped closer, but her husband remained where he was, staring through the window. It was the husband Rooney concentrated on; he had been close to the woman for longer and had spoken to her.

'Yes,' said Mrs Summers.

'I don't know . . .' said her husband.

'It's her – look at her hair, it's the same hair.'

'Maybe.'

Mrs Summers turned to Rooney. 'I'm sure it's her.'

Rooney nodded, then looked at Mr Summers. 'What do you think? We can turn her round if you like?'

'No, no, I think my wife is right. She's the woman I saw.'

Rooney asked if he was positive that it was the woman he had tried to help in the parking lot that afternoon.

'Yes,' Mr Summers said firmly.

Rooney returned to his office. Bean was waiting for him: he had received confirmation via police records, and they now had an ID of the victim. The dead woman Mr and Mrs Summers had just identified was Helen Murphy, aged thirty-nine, a prostitute, mother of three children, all in care. Murphy had been reported missing three weeks before she was found.

The Summerses' mistaken identification left Lorraine in the clear yet unaware of how valuable a witness she was, just as it meant that Rooney and his team were no longer looking for her. Instead they focused on trying to find a link between the dead women and Norman Hastings.

But Rooney was still not satisfied. He looked over the report and asked if dental records were available, remembering that the cab driver had said the woman had a front tooth missing. Helen Murphy had false teeth. Rooney was anxious to bring the cab driver in to view the body. He was not as positive as the Summerses: she was similar and had the same colouring, he said. Eventually he agreed that it was probably the woman he had picked up. Rooney conceded that Helen Murphy was the woman from the car park, which meant there would be no further visits to Rosie's address. That line of inquiry was now closed.

It was five o'clock when Rooney faced his team. He had requested extra officers and an incident room. They waited patiently as he shuffled his papers. 'Okay, this is Helen Murphy,' he began. 'Prostitute, blonde, aged thirty-nine, body found in the vicinity of the derelict Paradise Apartments in the trunk of a wrecked car, she had been there for approximately two to three days.'

The men stared at the blow-up pictures. Next to appear were Angela Hollow and the stolen vehicle, then Maria

Valez, and three more unidentified females. Lastly there was a photograph of Norman Hastings and his car.

Rooney paused as the men murmured and made notes. 'Okay. Obviously the Norman Hastings killing is different because he's male. Maybe the car was stolen and Hastings managed to see or catch the thief. Either way, he was killed with a similar weapon to that used on each of the others: a claw hammer. We know it's not the same weapon – some of the impressions taken from the women are of different dimensions, but all of them have been hammered in the face, and the claw section used for one blow at the back of the skull, near the base. When the victim is face downwards, the claw hammer strikes and gets drawn upwards, leaving – as you can see – one hell of an open wound.'

Rooney waited as they took it all in, then began again. 'The women are all prostitutes, all with records, obviously all blonde. No witnesses. Nobody has ever come forward with any motive, and so far we haven't found a link between the women, apart from their line of business and the fact they were tall, blonde and – apart from the last girl, Angela Hollow, nicknamed Holly – all dogs.'

Rooney continued for another hour, explaining the Summerses' part in the inquiry and Hastings's missing wallet. He concluded with the description of the man driving Hastings's stolen car. The man they were hunting, he pointed out, would have a bad bite mark on his neck, close to the jugular, according to Helen Murphy.

'Our first hammer killing comes in 1986, the next 1987, then 1988, 1991, which was Maria Valez, and the last two, Helen Murphy and Angela Hollow, plus Hastings, are all within months, if not days of each other. We've got a gap between '88 and '91, unless more come to light. Let's hope to God they don't – and let's give this all we've got.'

One young, eager-faced officer asked where they were going to start and Rooney, unsure himself, snapped that as the victims were hookers, they should start by asking on the streets, in the brothels. To begin with he wanted it kept low key and, until they had more evidence, he wanted the press kept out for as long as possible.

Rooney returned to his office feeling worn out and hungry. Bean looked up as he barked out, 'You feel like some curry?'

Bean didn't, but agreed to accompany Rooney, because he didn't think they should keep it from the press.

As they got into the car, Rooney gave him a sidelong look. 'What's the problem?'

'Well, I don't think we should keep this quiet. We could have a multiple killer on the loose! Those gaps between the murders, what if our man was in prison?'

'Whoever the fuck he is, he's on the loose now.'

'That's my point, Bill. He killed Norman Hastings, Helen Murphy, Angela Hollow within weeks of each other. Even if it's hookers he's taking out, the street girls should be warned.'

As Bean expected, Rooney dismissed this. 'We get the fuckin' press on this, they'll blow it up out of all proportion. This way it's giving us time to make some headway, because we have fuck all but—'

'A pretty tight description. Somebody somewhere knows a guy with a fucking bite out of his neck.'

Rooney started the engine. '*That* we never put out, else we'll have Dracula and his uncle wastin' our time . . . The guys on the street can put the word out to the whores but, you know as well as me, nothin' stops them. They'll keep on trading no matter who we say is out there.' He turned the car and prepared to drive out of the police pound.

'Who do you think is out there, Bill?'

'Someone with a hatred of tall skinny blonde whores – how the fuck do I know? You got his description, what do you think?'

'I dunno.'

'Right, you don't know, nobody knows. They may give us all the psychological profiles from so-called professors, why he kills, what he gets out of it. But when you say: "Okay, where do I find the guy?" they don't fuckin' know. The truth is, Josh, they can pinpoint or direct us to a psycho, because he's obvious. But our man, he's not obvious. He's cool, it looks like he's been getting away with it for years. It don't even run to a pattern because of Norman Hastings, who was a straight, decent guy.'

They drove out of the yard in silence. Then Bean sighed. 'Killer obviously has a thing about hookers . . .'

Rooney snorted. 'So maybe his mother or his wife was one. Then you can say he's killing *her*. Bullshit. I hated my mother but that don't make me want to kill every square-faced, red-haired tyrant, now, does it?'

He drew up outside the Star of Asia and switched off the engine. He was beginning to wish he'd not asked Bean along. 'That means he's just taking out his hammer whenever he feels like it. Now shut up, I'm hungry and I don't wanna talk about it.' Rooney got out, locked the car, and caught sight of Art's Gallery. 'Christ, how did that spring up? It was an old real estate agency yesterday.'

He wandered over to look: inside were a lot of people rapping and drinking, arty types, not his sort. A cab drew up and more guests began heading inside. A good-looking coiffured man in a pale blue denim outfit paid off the driver, adjusted his shades, and followed his two tanned friends into the gallery as Rooney walked into his favourite curry restaurant. Art screamed out a welcome to his friend Craig Lyall and drew him into the throng.

Some time later Jake arrived with Rosie and Lorraine. They drew up and parked behind Rooney's car. Jake was wearing a cheap suit with a nylon shirt and wide flowered tie, Rosie a tent-type dress that accentuated rather than hid her bulk, various bead necklaces that clicked as she walked, and a pair of leather sandals. Lorraine had on the same fawn skirt now pressed, the black crêpe blouse, and the safari-style jacket draped around her shoulders. This evening she wore sling-back high heels, and appeared taller and thinner. Her make-up was as sparse as ever, and, as Rosie had refused to let her borrow the pearl studs, she had no jewellery. Art made a great fuss of her when she walked in, telling her she looked simply wonderful, and that her friends were more than welcome.

A camp young man was drifting around with a tray of wine. Lorraine was about to accept a glass when Jake asked loudly for mineral water and she quickly withdrew her hand. The three of them stood a little self-consciously at the doorway to the main room which was crowded with guests.

'Do you want to see the paintings?' asked Lorraine.

'Are there any?' Rosie couldn't see a single canvas as they edged further inside.

Nula beckoned Lorraine and took hold of her hand. 'I remembered where I had seen you – at a meeting!'

Lorraine was puzzled, then she understood. She looked at her glass of water, noting that Nula had one too. She asked about Didi and Nula told her about the twisted ankle.

'Oh, I'm sorry, after all her hard work, too. Have many pictures been sold?'

Nula shrugged. 'I hope so. Art is broke, but then, aren't we all?'

Lorraine looked across at Rosie and Jake standing exactly where she had left them. 'Come and meet my friends?'

Jake was polite, but Rosie stared, looking at Nula with such obvious fascination that Lorraine felt uncomfortable, but Nula didn't seem to mind. She chatted on about the gallery, how much work she and Didi had done and how marvellous Lorraine had been. 'Were you an actress?' she asked Lorraine suddenly.

Lorraine smiled. 'No, I wasn't.'

'What do you do?' asked Rosie bluntly.

110

Nula cocked her head on one side and smiled. 'Anyone who hires me, dear.'

Rosie wasn't sure what she meant and didn't care, she was hot and her feet hurt. She caught Jake's eye. 'Look, I don't think this was such a good idea, why don't we leave?'

Jake looked at Lorraine. 'Okay by me. Lorraine?'

They were about to walk out when Art caught Lorraine's hand and drew her towards some of his friends. Rosie and Jake waited for ten minutes beside the car before Lorraine appeared. 'You two go on, I'll stay for a while longer. Art needs me to help out a bit.'

Jake opened the driver's door, and was about to get into the car when a big pot-bellied man walked out of the Star of Asia, accompanied by a fresh-faced, square-jawed younger man. The older man was deep in conversation while searching in his pockets for his car keys. Yet he couldn't help but see Lorraine, who was only yards ahead of him. Jake saw the way Rooney looked, then looked again. He stopped talking in mid-sentence, as if surprised, or shocked. Jake couldn't make out which.

'Lorraine?' Rooney said loudly.

She half turned and took a sharp involuntary step back, bumping into Rosie.

'It is Lorraine, isn't it?' Rooney stepped closer.

Jake noticed the way she straightened her shoulders, clenched her fists.

'Lorraine,' Rooney repeated again. He couldn't stop staring – it was like seeing a ghost. Was it her? Or was he mistaken? Then she tilted her head, gave that sidelong look and he knew for sure. He said emphatically, but flatly, 'It's Lorraine Page.' She gave a barely detectable nod and hurried back inside the gallery. Rooney watched her go, then stared directly at Jake and Rosie. 'Evening.'

Rosie heaved herself into the car. Jake slammed his door, still observing Rooney as he walked around to his own car.

'What was that all about?' Rosie asked.

Jake shrugged as Rooney drove away. 'He's a cop, so is the guy with him. That Indian diner's a known hangout for 'em. But that's Bill Rooney, a real mean shit.'

Rosie was astonished. 'My, I have never heard you talk like that!'

'Well, maybe there's a lot about me you don't know. I guess there is about your room-mate, too. That fat prick busted me, maybe he arrested her too. Looked like he knew Lorraine from some place she didn't want to be remembered bein' in.'

He drove a few yards, then stopped. 'Maybe I should go back, see if she's okay. She looked a bit shook up.' He was about to reverse when Lorraine walked out of the gallery with Nula and hailed a cab.

Jake set off again. 'You know any more about her? She ever mention some money she had? Remember that night she came back, when she said she'd fallen? She had a lot of money on her then.'

Rosie looked out of the window. 'She told me she sold off some things a friend was keeping for her. Jake, I think I'm gonna ask her to leave. There's something about her – I dunno, but she's . . .'

'Tough?' said Jake.

'Yes, with a selfish streak, too. I mean, I kind of admire the way she's getting herself together but I know as much about her now as I did when I first met her. Sometimes I get the feeling she doesn't want anyone to know her.'

'That cop knew her. He knew her very well.'

Rooney pulled on the handbrake outside Bean's apartment. 'She was picked up for prostitution. Last they put her in a straitjacket, she was that crazy.'

Bean had his hand on the door handle. 'She looked straightened out tonight.'

Rooney nodded. 'Yeah, she sure as hell did. Mind you, I

112

didn't get that close a view, but she was one hell of a looker back then – never fooled around, well, not that I knew of. I think she even had a couple of kids, married a lawyer, but whatever she was, she blew it. That lady sure as hell hit the skids.'

Bean opened the door. He was barely interested in ex-Lieutenant Lorraine Page, but Rooney seemed eager to continue. 'Killed an unarmed kid.' He shook his head. 'Six bullets, emptied the fucking .38 into him – and you know what sickened me? She was laughing, no kidding, meant fuck all to her. She was pissed – she was a lush. I kinda thought she must be dead by now . . .'

'Goodnight,' said Bean, stepping out of the car.

Rooney remained deep in thought. He could still picture her curled up on the washroom floor, skirt up round her thighs. That was the last time he'd seen her, so drunk she couldn't even stand. That half-smile on her face had been the same half-smile she had given him tonight.

Lorraine looked round Nula's strange apartment with its outrageously theatrical living room: drapes and frills, mock leopardskin sofa and chairs, fur rugs, and huge paintings of nude female couples with male genitals displayed in semi-grotesque poses. Just as she was wondering idly if Nula and Didi had been totally transformed or if they still had their cocks, Nula came out of the bedroom. 'Something terrible happened to a friend of ours.'

A limping, red-eyed Didi appeared, dressed in a scarlet silk kimono, a clutch of tissues in her hand. 'She was a friend, only seventeen. They found her locked in the trunk of a car. She'd been hammered to death, not a feature left intact, dear . . . Now what pig-shit bastard could do a thing like that?'

Nula sobbed loudly. 'We saw her last night – I was standing talking to her. Holly was so cute, so nice . . .'

Lorraine listened as they wept and wailed. She didn't know who they were talking about. She tried twice to interject and ask if they'd like her to leave, but they seemed unaware she was in the apartment. Of the two Didi seemed more upset, and it was Nula who eventually turned to Lorraine. 'I'm glad you're here, help take our minds off it, she was only a kid . . . Didi, we gotta keep busy. Let's feed this babe – come on, get that apron on.'

Didi scurried into the kitchen, and Nula sighed. 'She'll be okay now. She's really upset, but I can always cheer her up.'

They cooked a delicious dinner, and the initial shock of Holly's death subsided. Their conversation centred on their friend Art: that he was a genius photographer, his boy-friends, his bankruptcy, his inability to stay in business.

Nula gestured to their apartment. 'This was his, then he made a stack of bread and he *gave* this to us and even when he's been broke and desperate, he has *never* asked us to leave.'

Lorraine nodded. The place was a nightmare, but that was just her taste, and she was enjoying the outrageousness of the pair, swapping stories, jokes, about old times when they'd been dancers. They didn't speak of the present, but out came albums and programmes. Eventually they seemed to talk themselves into silence. The subtle music, playing throughout, was switched off, and Lorraine took her cue to leave. She stood up, smiling her thanks.

'How long have you been dry?' asked Nula.

''Bout four and a half months.' Nula laughed and told Lorraine that she had been dry eight years, Didi four. She looked at Didi, and then pursed her lips. 'I suppose we should tell you we're whores – you've probably put two and two together anyway. It's just that we'd prefer you to hear it from us rather than anyone else – and we'd like to see you again.'

Lorraine was taken aback when Nula, sitting close, slipped an arm around her shoulders. She was wearing a heavy scent and, close to, it was overpowering.

'Listen, I got contacts who could put some work your way, straight decent johns, all you gotta do is ask.'

Lorraine did a neat sidestep, saying that she had some work lined up, thanked them again, and they insisted she take a cab home. She hadn't meant to sound so cool, be so distant, but they were touching on that hazy part of her life that remained unreal, which she hadn't yet faced up to. At the same time, she couldn't help but feel angry that they seemed to know she'd been a hooker. Somehow she had felt that no one could or would suspect that.

Nula kissed her cheeks. 'You come by any time and, keep it in mind, if you need cash to tide you over, we can always get you a few clients.'

'I'll think about it.'

Lorraine was relieved to get away from them, from the cloying perfume. Yet they had, unknowingly, helped her over a hurdle she had dreaded. Seeing Bill Rooney again had been like a punch in the stomach, so totally unexpected that she had been unable to speak, or even acknowledge him. The humiliation of the meeting made her feel physically sick. The cab fare took the last of her earnings from the gallery but she didn't care. One thing she knew for certain, she couldn't turn tricks again.

Each step up to Rosie's apartment was an effort, and the last person she wanted to be confronted by was Rosie sitting like a Buddha watching a mind-numbing game show. Lorraine shut the door and headed for the bathroom. The television was clicked off, ominously.

'We got to talk.'

Lorraine hesitated. 'Yes, I know, but I need a shower first.' The television clicked back on. When she returned to the sitting room, wrapped in just a towel, off went the television. 'Just let me get a drink.' Lorraine slammed the fridge shut. It was empty. 'Thanks! Thanks a fuckin' bundle!'

Rosie smirked. 'Now you know what it feels like!'

'So you did it on purpose? You great fat pig, I bought enough to last days—'

'Oh, yeah!' Rosie sniggered. 'Well, who the hell do you think has been filling up that fucking fridge since you arrived?'

Lorraine turned on her. 'Jesus Christ, I've *given* you money!'

Rosie pulled herself up. 'An' I gave you a roof over your head, and my bed when you were sick. I fed you, washed you – and not once did you have the decency to say thank you!'

'So now you want me out of here, is that it?' Lorraine sighed.

'Why don't you get off your high horse and be real?' Rosie retaliated. 'I'm honest with you, when are you going to level with me?'

'Level with you about what?'

'Who you are for starters!' Rosie shouted.

Lorraine lifted her arms in exasperation. 'You know who I am! I've fucking told you who I am! *I am Lorraine Page!*'

'That's not enough. I knew your name at the hospital. It's like I live with somebody I don't know and I can't take it.'

Lorraine lit a cigarette and closed her eyes. She sat on the edge of the easy chair. 'Rosie, I can't tell you much because I don't *know* who I am. I am trying to find out who the fuck I am so if *I* don't know, how am I supposed to tell you?' She got up and paced the room, taking long drags on her cigarette. 'I look in the mirror and I don't know if this is the way I always looked. I see scars all over my body, and I don't know who inflicted them. I don't even know how I got *this*!' She pulled her hair away from the jagged scar on

116

her face. 'I got marks all over my body. I can see them, you can see them – but what about the ones inside my brain? There are whole years of my life missing, and sometimes I just don't know if I *want* to find out everything.'

Rosie nodded, suddenly concerned. 'How about tonight? You seemed pretty shook up.' Rosie waited but there was no reply. 'That man this evening, the fat guy, he said your name three times. Do you know who he was?'

'Yeah.'

'So why don't you start telling me? No? Okay, I'll make it easier. He's a cop, Jake knew him. Now if you've been in prison, it doesn't worry me – just tell me, 'cos I'd like to know.'

Lorraine gave a soft, humourless laugh. 'You see, you didn't believe me. I told you back at the hospital, Rosie. I told you what I was.'

Rosie stared as Lorraine sat down, rested her head against the chair and closed her eyes. 'I was a cop, Rosie. In fact, I was a lieutenant, and that fat man you saw tonight used to be my sergeant. His name is William – Bill – Rooney. He looked surprised, huh? Seeing me? Maybe because he thought I was dead, probably hoped I was . . .'

'Why did you leave?' Rosie asked.

'I was kicked out, Rosie. Because I was a drunk.' In a low, expressionless voice she began to tell Rosie about her husband, her two daughters, Sally and Julia, the divorce, her husband's remarriage, his custody of the girls whom she had not seen for almost six years. 'After the divorce I went on a binge. It kind of lasted until you found me, Rosie. I sold everything – apartment, furniture. The car was taken because I was caught drunk-driving. I got off with a fine. I got away with a lot of things, I guess, for the next few years. I don't remember much of it, just that eventually all the money ran out and when I had nothing left to sell . . .' She coughed, a heavy smoker's cough that made her body shake and her eyes run.

Rosie waited, watching as Lorraine lit another cigarette from the stub. 'So, go on, when you had nothing else to sell, then what?'

Lorraine gave her that odd, tilted, squint look. 'I sold myself, Rosie – to anyone, anything, any place, just so long as I got a drink. I worked for the pimps I'd arrested, and got drunk with the whores I'd booked. I ended up in shit-holes, bars, and flop houses. And I don't remember hardly a day of it. I got arrested for whoring, I got picked up for vagrancy. Sometimes the craving for drink drove me into a kind of deranged madness. By the time I was hit by the truck – when I was taken to the hospital – I think I had reached a sort of dead end hell. That's it. That's who I am, Rosie. Now you're as up-to-date as I am.'

Rosie began to make Lorraine's bed. It was a sickening story, but not one that she hadn't heard before: everyone she knew at the meetings, including herself, had a similar story of loss and desperation. What was different about Lorraine, however, was her complete lack of emotion when relating it.

Lorraine slipped into the freshly made bed and sighed contentedly, laying her head on her arm. 'I'm thinking . . .' she said softly.

'What about?' asked Rosie.

'Well, I'm not sure about bothering to get myself back together. Who am I doing it for? Be okay if I felt good, or if I felt I was doing it for a reason. But there's no reason.'

Rosie stood, elephantine, in the bedroom doorway. 'Maybe because it's your life. Or perhaps it's those two little girls.' Lorraine said nothing, so Rosie continued: 'My mother died when I was ten and there's a hell of a lot I would have liked to ask her – like who the fuck in my family did I inherit this fat from? My dad was skin and bone. And I'd like to know if she loved me. She took an overdose, you see, killed herself.'

Lorraine propped herself up on her elbow. 'You know, Rosie, sometimes I sort of loathe you, especially in the mornings, but if I forget to say thank you, then I'm sorry. I've no one else who gives a shit about me, no other place to go. So thank you for being my friend.'

Rosie flushed. 'Goodnight, Lorraine.'

Lorraine heard her move heavily into the bedroom, and then lay back staring up at the ceiling. Her daughters had had a new mother for five years, and they probably weren't even little any more. They probably wouldn't want to see her. She didn't even know where they lived.

It hurt to remember, physically hurt, as if each memory was so tightly stored away she had to squeeze it out. It was strange, because instead of being able to conjure up her own daughters' faces, she saw only the little girl she had been assigned to trace. Laura Bradley, six years old, who had last been seen waiting outside school for her mother. Lorraine, the officer in charge of searching the school outbuildings and cellars, had found Laura's naked body stuffed into one of the big air-conditioning pipes. Like a rag doll, so tiny, so helpless, yet her body had felt warm and Lorraine had tried mouth-to-mouth resuscitation. But nothing brought her back to life; even when she had felt the small ribcage lifting, it was not Laura breathing, it was Lorraine's own breath.

Lorraine got out of bed and began to pace the room. Why? Why was she suddenly remembering this child? Laura had been brutally sexually abused, her internal organs ripped by a blunt instrument. Not content with having sexual intercourse, the rapist had continued to torture the defenceless child. Laura Bradley's injuries were so horrific that all the officers on the case were sickened; Lorraine recalled seeing even the big, blustering Bill Rooney weeping. Obsessed with catching the killer, she worked day and night and had no time to spare for her own daughters. She

119

had shouted at her husband that the girls were never to be left alone for an instant, and even hired a baby-sitter to collect them from school.

She poured herself a glass of water. She remembered yelling in fury at Mike, 'I'm trying to find Laura Bradley's killer. You may not think that is important, but you didn't hold her dead body in your arms. I did. And I will not sleep until I have that bastard locked away so my daughters and every kid in this neighbourhood can be safe.'

Mike had tried to make her rest but Lorraine had kept up one hell of an investigation and she wouldn't let it go. She visited Laura's parents and swore to them that no matter how long it took, she would bring in their daughter's killer. Her dedication paid off. From day one she had been suspicious of the school janitor and, as this was before the time they had DNA testing to assist them, she kept up the pressure. Intuition told her she had the right man.

Even her chief hinted that perhaps she should back off, but she refused, returning time and again to the scene of the crime and to the janitor's home, until, in yet another confrontation when she had shown him Laura Bradley's clothes, all her photographs, when she had interrogated him for more than six hours, she finally broke him. He admitted his guilt. She had been so proud, and she had been promoted. Laura Bradley could at last rest in peace.

Lorraine felt chilled now, remembering the visit of the young uniformed officer to Rosie's apartment, asking about the night she had returned after the attack in the parking lot, how she had substituted the dead child's name, Laura Bradley, for her own. She had uttered it without a moment's thought. Now she realized just how often in that long distant past she had placed her work above the needs of her own children and husband. Mike had been right. She had become obsessive. She had also become addicted to the adrenalin, the excitement, the tension and the pressure – until she had found it impossible to relax.

She returned to bed and sat for a moment staring at the wall. Maybe Rosie was right, she should try to contact them again. She would like to explain to Sally and Julia, perhaps even ask for their forgiveness. Yes, her life *was* worth bothering about, even if it was just to make peace with her children and Mike. Feeling calmer, she turned off the lamp, snuggled down and was asleep within moments.

This was the first time she had dealt with a section of her past without getting the shakes. She had talked it over in her mind and remained calm. Forced herself to hold on, remain distant from it. She reckoned it was another step forward in rehabilitation.

But she had spoken to Rosie about her past as if she was talking about another person, another Lorraine. She hadn't cried or, to Rosie, appeared to feel remorse or guilt. Instead there was a cold confidence, a control, that seemed to be getting stronger around her, as if she was divorcing herself from the past. What she was not doing, Rosie had surmised, was facing the full reality.

Rosie knew how harsh that reality was. Unlike Lorraine, she couldn't sleep. Instead, she was mulling over what she had been told. At some stage in her own recovery Rosie, like Lorraine, had asked herself if remaining sober, facing what she was and what she had lost, was worth all the trouble and the pain. Sober, she felt, she had nothing to live for. It had been Jake who had said her life was worth fighting for, for the sake of her son. She had tried to contact Joey, and she had felt really positive – but it had been a disaster. Rosie had been, and was still, unable to cope with the emotional strain of seeing Joey, of knowing there was another woman her son called Mother. She could not cope with talking to her ex-husband, or seeing the new home he had made for himself and their boy. As it all swept over her once more, she began to feel guilty about opening up the same terrible emotional road for Lorraine.

She crept out of bed. If Lorraine was awake she would

tell her that she should take more time before she tried to confront her lost family. She was wrong to push her, she wasn't experienced enough, and maybe this wall of control Lorraine was building around herself was good, and safer for her than allowing anybody like Rosie or Jake to break it down. But Lorraine was sleeping, one hand tucked under her chin, only the strange, jagged scar running from her eye to her cheek marring her look of innocence. She seemed peaceful, a half-smile on her lips.

Rosie made a vow. She would not ask Lorraine to leave the apartment: it was important for her to have a sense of security. Lorraine was her friend. That settled, Rosie went back to bed, swiped at her pillow and, within seconds, passed into a deep sleep.

CHAPTER 5

THE FOLLOWING week Lorraine got a job in a florist's shop. It was only short term, replacing an assistant who was on holiday. She also did four nights at Art's gallery, as he remained open until ten in the evening. He was rarely there, and she was often alone waiting for the odd customer. A number of paintings had been sold, but business was not flourishing. Art was out looking for new pictures, but whenever he saw her, he greeted Lorraine with affection.

The week was good because she was occupied, and with the little money she earned she bought two more outfits from a garage sale. Nula and Didi dropped in for chats, and always brought some home-made banana cake with them. Didi was still limping but she refused to see a doctor. The two transsexuals admired Lorraine's taste in clothes and discussed second-hand bargains they'd bought. Because of their size they often found it difficult to get really stylish clothes, and especially shoes. Lorraine was looking better and feeling stronger every day. The sweatings were less frequent and she had put on weight.

Rosie had started doing clerical work at home and had hired a computer and printer so she was always in. They began a routine of sharing the cleaning and laundry. Lorraine contributed towards the rent and groceries. It meant that at the end of the week, after she had bought her cigarettes and clothes, she had little left. But what was left, she saved.

When the florist job finished, Lorraine asked Art if he could use her for a few more hours. As more paintings had been sold, and he had discovered a new artist, he took her on for two full days a week, plus the four evenings. There were few customers, and she didn't know how the gallery paid for itself let alone paid her salary. On her way to and from work she had to pass Fit As A Fiddle, now called Fit 'N' Fast, and decided to join one of their classes. She only managed the first ten minutes of the step aerobic session before she felt her energy give way. However, she began to practise in the empty gallery with a stack of telephone directories and slowly built up her strength, stepping up and down until her legs felt like jelly.

Lorraine used Art's telephone daily to try and trace her ex-husband. She called a number of Mike Pages but so far she had been unsuccessful. He had disappeared. Rosie surprised her by suggesting that she call the Bar Association: if he was still practising, they would know his address.

Mike Page was living in Santa Monica. Lorraine had not spoken to him directly, but to a secretary, who confirmed that he had two daughters, Julia and Sally. Before she could ask any further questions, Lorraine hung up. Then she stacked up the telephone books and stepped until she was exhausted.

It was a Friday evening, two weeks since Lorraine had found Mike's office number. She had put off getting in touch, always making the excuse that she didn't have enough money to get the bus to Santa Monica – and she was still in need of better clothes. She arrived home with a banana cake made by Didi and some fresh fruit. She was flushed from walking. It had been a full day of exercise: she had done a light workout with Hector, the owner of Fit 'N' Fast, who had put together a beginner's programme, starting with small weights, to build up the atrophied muscles in her arms and legs.

Rosie peered up from a mountain of brown envelopes and watched as Lorraine removed from her bag boxes and boxes of vitamins. Hector had taken to giving them to her free because most were samples. He suggested she took vitamins E, C, D and B12, and with her past record of alcohol abuse, he said, zinc. They all knew about Lorraine's drinking problem – Nula had told them – but Lorraine didn't mind. It was easier that everyone knew, and besides, as none of them drank she was never tempted.

'I see we've been to the hairdresser's – or did Hector turn his muscular body to that, too?' Rosie smirked.

'No, I had it done at the local.' She still had the short cropped cut, but she'd had new streaks put in.

Rosie licked a few more envelopes, slapping them down. She didn't say how good Lorraine looked because she was jealous. Lorraine was changing before her eyes. She was lightly tanned from all her walking back and forth to the gallery and whereas before she had seemed to shuffle, head bent forward, shoulders rounded, now she was straight-backed and looking fit.

Lorraine counted her money, putting some aside for Rosie. Then she went into the bedroom and opened the crammed closet. She took out her shoes, and stuffed the money inside with the rest of her savings. She sniffed gingerly: Rosie's clothes stank of body odour. She wished she had her own closet.

'You comin' to a meeting with me tonight?' Rosie asked, lolling at the door. 'Only I got to deliver these so I thought I'd maybe go straight on.'

'I said I'd go over to see the new paintings being hung.'

Rosie pursed her lips. 'Hector helping out, too, is he?'

Lorraine sighed. 'Hector's gay, Rosie, okay?'

'Maybe he swings both ways – some of them do, you know . . .'

'Rosie, don't start. Go mail your letters, I'll make some supper.'

Rosie banged out and Lorraine went into the kitchen. She cleaned up, then sat down by the telephone. She knew it was after office hours, but she just felt like making another of her calls. Mike Page's answering machine was on. This time she heard his voice, which gave an emergency number where he could be reached. Lorraine jotted it down and waited a moment before she dialled.

'Hello.'

The high-pitched voice was obviously a child's.

Lorraine hung up. She lit a cigarette and smoked it before dialling again. This time Mike answered. She had to swallow hard before she could speak.

'Mike, it's Lorraine.'

There was a pause before he spoke.

'Well, long time. How are you?'

'I'd like to see you . . . and the girls.'

Another long pause, and then Mike coughed.

'Yeah, I understand that, and it's fine by me. When do you want to come?'

Lorraine's hands were shaking. She couldn't answer. Mike asked if she was still there. 'Maybe this weekend?' he said.

'You mean tomorrow?' Lorraine could hardly get her breath.

'Or Sunday.' He suggested twelve thirty. They could have lunch, maybe walk on the beach together.

There was another pause. Then Lorraine said, 'Twelve thirty Sunday, then,' and hung up before he could say anything else. She stared at his address. Her mouth was dry. She mentally repeated every word they had said to each other. They had not spoken for so long.

She sat cupping a mug of coffee in her hands. She had

finally done it. Slowly she calmed herself down. She'd be able to cope, she'd coped so far, and she was looking good. More important, she was sober.

Bill Rooney sat opposite his chief, Michael Berillo, leaning forwards, which made his squat backside spread even more. 'Nothin'. We've not got a single witness—'

'But there was a witness, Bill.'

Rooney nodded. 'Yeah, but that was Helen Murphy. We reckoned he must have tracked her down again after the attack, right? And made sure the second time.'

'But before she died, this phone call . . .'

Rooney nodded. 'That's what we've been going on – all we've had – and it was a pretty good description.'

'What about the bite?'

'By now it'll have healed, or scabbed over, I dunno.'

Chief Michael Berillo was a big, glowering man. No matter what hour of the day or night, he always had a dark, five o'clock shadow. As he leaned back in his chair, his expansive chest almost burst the buttons on his sweat-stained shirt. 'Any of this Helen Murphy's associates give you anything?'

'Nope. She was a real old dog, though, hard to believe anyone'd pick her up, let alone screw her, and most of the people we talked to don't have a lot to say about her. Nothin' complimentary – she was trouble with a major T. She's also moved around. We can't trace her husband – he's a trucker, nobody seems to know where he is – and she's got three kids in care.'

'Irish?'

'What?'

The Chief yawned. 'I said, was she Irish? With a name like Murphy . . .'

'No, that's her husband and he's from Detroit. We talked to a woman she roomed with, a real dive, and she said nobody had seen the husband for at least six or seven months. But we got him circulated so as soon as he's traced we'll question him.'

The two men remained silent, each wrapped in his own thoughts.

'Six.'

Rooney nodded. 'Yeah. Six – seven if we attach Norman Hastings. We've interviewed everyone he worked with, everyone he knew. He's got – or had – a real nice wife and two kids, nobody seems to have anything against him. He was a well-liked, ordinary guy, played poker with a few pals, went to ball games, good steady worker, and—'

The Chief banged his elbows on the desk. 'No connection to any of these women. Did he pick up hookers?'

Rooney shook his head. 'If he did, his wife didn't know it, and none of his friends did either. Unless they were lying.'

The Chief thumbed through the massive dossier which represented the hours and hours of interviews and statements, the lists of officers assigned to the investigation. 'Okay, we'll open it up further. Let's see if any other states have anything on record. Reason is, to keep this on the boil I'm going to need more. We got a hell of a lot of men with their thumbs up their asses and we'll have to open it up to the press.'

'Shit! You do that and we'll have our job cut out for us – you know what a circus starts when there's a whiff of a serial killer on the loose.'

'You've had it all to yourself, Bill, and you've drawn a blank. We got a fucking maniac out there and I can't hold this back any longer. We'll get in a psychological profiler.'

Rooney snorted, and the Chief rapped the desk. 'Get all the help you can, Bill, and get it fast. If you and your team don't get a result soon, I can't let you sit on this – and you know it. Bring in that Helen Murphy's husband.

128

So far he looks like the only possible suspect and you need one.'

'What's that supposed to mean?'

'You dumb? I'll have to bring in more than a fucking profiler. Don't you understand? I'm under pressure. That last kid might have been a hooker, but she was only seventeen years old. And Norman Hastings was, as you've laid out thick and clear, an upright citizen. You think his family don't want a result? It's not just old tarts. One dead bitch like the one you dug up from your pal Sparks can be put on ice. Hastings can't. A pretty blue-eyed angel called Holly can't. You with me?'

Rooney felt the carpet being tugged from under his feet. If they wanted a profiler then he'd get one. If they wanted Clint Eastwood they could have him too. Anything, so long as they didn't give him the side-step just before he was due to retire. 'I hear you loud and clear, Chief.'

'Good – and, Bill, any other bright ideas you get, run them by me first. You started the ball rolling, now it's out of control.'

Rooney got out fast.

Unfortunately, Bean was in his office sitting in his chair. It was a bad omen and Rooney yelled at him to shove his butt off. 'Get onto one of those profilers – and by tonight. And *don't* say one word. Then I want every man on this fiasco in the main incident room in one hour. We want Helen Murphy's fuckin' husband found and brought in.'

Bean coughed. 'There's another one.'

'What?' Rooney's face flushed a deep puce.

'I said there's another one come in, from a Brian Johns, Santa Monica, details on your desk.'

Rooney reached over and picked up the fax sheet. Prostitute murdered 1992, found inside the trunk of a Cadillac, face and skull beaten. Mona Skinner, aged forty. Possible murder weapon: a blunt instrument, some kind of hammer.

Bean shut the door as Rooney thudded into his chair. It creaked ominously, the springs taking the strain of his eighteen stone. Mona Skinner was an ugly, square-faced woman with long, frizzy, bleached-blonde hair and her mouth was turned down in a thin scowl. Her mean, aggressive eyes stared back at Rooney with a 'fuck you' expression. She had been charged with soliciting more than nine times over a period of fifteen years. She had also served four years for assault and battery, and receiving stolen property.

Rooney leaned back and swivelled around. He was angry with himself for opening the can: the worms were certainly wriggling out and all over him. He ran a check to see if there were any links between Mona Skinner and the others. He struck lucky: Mona Skinner and Helen Murphy had both served time together at the same women's prison, had once lived in the same motel. Rooney stepped up the order to find Helen Murphy's husband who now became his main suspect for real.

Rosie ate the spaghetti, waded through the garlic bread and, filled to bursting point, heaved herself onto the sofa. Switching on the TV, she paused briefly to watch the news, then flicked on to find a game show.

'They've still not found that guy that bumped off that local fella. You know what always amazes me?'

Lorraine was washing up. 'No?'

'Well, you know when they put all these ads out for people to come forward if they saw anythin'? That murder happened weeks ago. How do they expect anybody to remember? I wouldn't be able to remember if I saw a guy in a metallic blue car this morning, never mind weeks ago.'

'You'd be surprised,' Lorraine said, wiping round the sink. 'I was working on a case once, and we were up shit creek without a paddle, and then this boy was hypnotized

130

and he gave not only the car's registration number, but about four or five others as well.'

Rosie switched channels again. 'I wouldn't have that done, you know why? Because it means they always got you in their power.'

Lorraine sat down beside her, her mind miles away. She thought again about the wallet, the man who had attacked her. She was vaguely surprised that he hadn't been traced yet. She closed her eyes, conjuring up a mental picture of him, the way he had picked her up at the roadside, how he had wanted her to give him a blow-job in a public place. She saw him as clearly as if it had been yesterday. She remembered his hands: long, thin tapering fingers. Had he worn a ring? She concentrated hard, no, she was sure he had no ring, but then she saw his cuff, his jacket sleeve, and the cufflinks. She leaned forward, frowning in concentration, and then shook her head. It was no concern of hers, she had enough to think about, and besides, the further removed she was from it the better.

The following morning Lorraine went off to the gallery, pausing on the way to buy a newspaper. The headlines shrieked in big bold letters: POLICE HUNT SERIAL KILLER. Sitting in the gallery, she read the entire article, then folded the paper. It seemed almost comical that Captain Bill Rooney should be heading the investigation. From her own past experience with press releases, they had trouble on their hands. She could tell they were covering up, the old phrases they all used to churn out about 'making headway', 'confident of an arrest'. But the biggest giveaway was the police request for any member of the public having further information to make contact. It meant they had zilch.

The buzzer sounded and a flushed, excited Art rushed in, carrying a small gym bag ready for his workout next door. 'I think, my dear, I just made a killing. Last night I had a friend over who knows a big dealer out of New York. He saw the new stuff and went ape-shit! He's back tonight and he's not just interested in one or two but the whole show!'

Lorraine was genuinely pleased as it also meant more money for her. Art had promised that as soon as business picked up she would get a better wage. He danced around, checked the mail, and then said he would be next door if anyone wanted him.

She took another look at the canvases hanging on the walls, still not impressed with the daubs of colour and squiggles that the new Art discovery had supplied.

Later, Nula dropped by. She put her arms around Lorraine. 'You know, I think you're looking even better. As soon as your hair grows a bit more, ask Didi to style it – she's an artist. She can colour as well – she does mine, and she does Holly's—' She froze, and covered her mouth. 'Oh, God, I forgot.'

'There's a big article in the paper this morning, and a photograph.'

Nula looked at it. 'She was much more beautiful than that, a real stunner. You know, the cops have been out every night. Terrible for business, but they reckon this maniac only does whores, so everybody's a bit uneasy. First time they came round, hardly any of us out, but you know business is business. And I doubt if he'd come our end of the street, we just have our usuals and a few that have been tipped off.'

Lorraine smoothed her skirt. 'All the same, you two should look after yourselves. Take the vehicle registration of the johns you're wary of – or better still, don't go with them.'

Nula cocked her head to one side. 'That's just what the cops told us.'

Lorraine smiled. 'Well, make sure you do it.'

Nula opened her tapestry bag and took out a packet. 'Give this to Art for me, would you? It's just some more postcards, and our rent. See you soon.'

132

Lorraine put the packet in the desk drawer and was just about to shut it, when she noticed a thick wad of notes secured with just an elastic band. She looked to the door, then back to the open drawer. She took the money out and flicked through it. There was at least two or three thousand dollars. She held it a moment, tapping it in her hand, then replaced it.

About an hour later Art returned, pink from his workout, his bald head gleaming. He dropped his gym bag and fractionally adjusted a canvas.

'You mind if I say something?'

He turned, and smiled. 'Oh, you sounded so stern, why should I?'

'There's a lot of money in the drawer, Art, and it's not locked or anything. Anyone could just walk in and take it.'

Art danced over and banged open the drawer. 'I meant to put it in the bank this morning but I forgot and I didn't want to leave it in the health club.'

Lorraine watched as he tossed the money into his gym bag.

'Right, I have to go. Will you lock up, leave the keys with Hector next door?' Then, pursing his lips, he delved into his pocket, dragged out his wallet, and started counting out ten-dollar bills. 'Whoops . . . I'm a wee bit short. Can I give you the rest on Monday, darling?'

Lorraine flushed. 'I need it all today, Art. I have to go somewhere this weekend.' She couldn't help but flick a look to the gym bag.

'That belongs to a friend.'

She shrugged. 'Monday will have to do.'

'Okay.' Art smiled. 'Is that your paper? Have you finished with it?'

She passed it to him. He glanced at it and then held up Holly's photograph. 'I didn't know her but she was a friend of Nula and Didi's.'

He waltzed out, and the door slammed behind him.

Remembering Nula's package she hurried after him, only to see him driving away in a cab. She felt pissed off: she needed her money to buy a little something for the girls. She put the package away, then opened the drawer again, took it out and looked at it. Nula had said that her rent was in it; maybe she could just take out what she was owed and leave a note.

Lorraine eased open the package, pulling the Scotchtape away, making sure she didn't rip the paper. As well as some postcards wrapped in a sheet of paper, there was a brown manilla envelope. She crossed to the kettle, and turned it on to steam open the flap. Inside was a big pile of notes. She was surprised by the amount – unless they were behind with their rent. She counted out sixty dollars for herself, and was about to replace the rest and reseal the envelope when she wondered if the postcards were meant for the gallery, so she opened the paper.

Lorraine sat down. She felt sick. It wasn't that she hadn't come across pornographic material when she was on Vice, but each of these was especially revolting because they featured Nula and Didi. Maybe if she'd been more together, she would have realized when she visited that they used their apartment for photographic work – there were certainly enough props. She sighed, looking intently at each disgusting picture, sad that Nula and Didi could subject themselves to such degrading acts, displaying their genitals, their heavy breasts. They featured together, just the two of them, on the first few cards, and then they were joined by various animals and masked figures, and on four cards a pretty sweet-faced blonde girl appeared, her face childlike but her breasts over-large and her curved body taut and firm. Her eyes unfocused, she looked as if she had been drugged, but Lorraine recognized her immediately. It was Holly. No wonder Didi and Nula had been so upset. They knew her because both had screwed her. If the cards had been just of Nula and Didi, even with Holly, Lorraine

134

would perhaps have been less upset, but the rest showed obviously under-age boys committing homosexual acts.

Lorraine lit a cigarette and inhaled deeply. She was no innocent – in fact, it was more than likely she herself had taken part in some perverted session in the past to make a buck. She paced the gallery and kept on returning to the postcards, picking them up and putting them down. She was uncertain what, if anything, to do. Her first thought was to send them to the police, let them sort it out – especially as they featured Holly. She asked herself if the girl's murder could be connected to the pictures. She doubted it – it could just be coincidence. But one thing was for sure: Holly was no innocent and already on the game, so she would have been fully aware of what she was doing. Then Lorraine looked again. *Had* Holly been drugged? If so, had she been forced into the pornographic session against her will, or agreed to do it because she was drugged?

'It's not my business,' she said aloud. She was angry with herself for opening the package. It changed everything. If she sent the contents to the police, they would question Nula and Didi. They might come to the gallery, too. Art was involved, so she would also be questioned – by Bill Rooney. So much for feeling safe and secure. The thought of having Rooney barging into her fragile existence made her feel weak. She was caught, trapped first by stealing the wallet from the man who had attacked her, and then because, as it turned out, it wasn't his wallet after all but Norman Hastings's. She even remembered the dead man's name, could picture his face on his driving licence. 'What a fucking mess!'

Lorraine lit another cigarette, sat at the desk propping her head on her hands. She steadied herself. She knew the wallet was of no great importance to the investigation. More to the point, and this she knew, too, was that her attacker had been in possession of it. It was obvious he had to have taken it from Hastings's body. If the newspaper reports could be relied on, and Hastings's body had been discovered in his own car, then it was surely the same vehicle driven by the man who had attacked her. So it meant that all the time she was in the shopping mall car park, the dead man had been in the trunk of the car.

The officers who had come to the apartment had been trying to trace her, but had never returned. Were they still looking for her? She swore, wishing she had kept the newspaper, but she was certain there had been no mention that the police were looking for anyone seen in Hastings's car that afternoon. She had given them a good enough description, they even repeated it in the paper, so they must be taking it seriously. There was nothing else she could do.

'This is all I fucking need!' she said aloud, as she stubbed out her cigarette, immediately lighting another. Her neck felt tense, her whole body was strained. She began taking everything out of the drawer – leaflets, notes, letters – without knowing what she was looking for. There was no diary, and nothing of any particular importance. She flicked through the supposed sales ledgers, noting the prices Art had paid for his canvases. They were all low. According to the sale-or-return memos, most of the paintings she had presumed sold had been returned. She started to replace the papers, and then stared hard at the money and the photographs.

'Shouldn't open people's private property.'

Lorraine gasped. She hadn't heard him return – the buzzer again! Picking up the photographs, Art began to shuffle them, stacking them, clicking them against the desk as he straightened them to stuff back into the envelope. 'I've been watching you sifting through my desk. What were you looking for?'

Lorraine flushed. 'I don't know.'

Art replaced the photographs, folding the envelope into a tight packet. 'Well, Lorraine, did they turn you on?'

'No, no, they didn't.'

'Takes all kinds, dear.'

'I suppose it does . . .'

Art unzipped his bag, tucked the photographs inside. 'I only came back because I felt bad about not giving you your money. Lucky I did. I'd forgotten Nula was delivering these.'

Lorraine moved out from behind the desk, gesturing to the gallery. 'This is all a front, isn't it? A sham.'

Art glanced around. 'Not all sham, dear. Sometimes I sell some, but I've been ripped off so many times, I keep it on as a kind of pastime. Maybe one day when I've made enough dough I'll be able to find some real talent. This stuff is from Venice Beach, I buy it for peanuts.'

Lorraine shook her head. 'The porn sells, does it?'

Art looked at her, his eyes so enlarged by his glasses that they seemed like a gargoyle's. 'How else do you think I've been able to stay open? I have regular customers, you met most of them. In fact, if I recall, you called them.' He picked up the cash and peeled off a fifty-dollar bill. 'Here, it's a bonus.'

Lorraine didn't take it. 'The pictures of Holly, the girl who was murdered . . .'

'What?'

'There are pictures of Holly.

Art shrugged. 'Well, they won't bother her, will they?'

'Maybe the police would be interested, though.'

He pursed his lips. 'I don't see why, she was obviously enjoying herself and nobody forced her. In fact, I didn't even know the girl.'

'Who takes the photographs?'

He sighed, hands on his hips, then looked back at Lorraine. 'None of your fucking business. Now, let's just forget this, shall we?'

She stared at him, forcing herself to keep her voice steady. 'Why don't you make it worthwhile for me to not make it my business?'

'What?'

'You heard me. You've got under-age kids on those pictures – so pay me. And . . . like you said, it's not my business.'

Art hesitated. He picked up the money, seemed to weigh it in his hand before he made the decision. He threw it at Lorraine. 'You know what my big problem in life is? I trust people. I make friends with people, I give them a break, and they always fuck me over it. Take it, you scrawny, ungrateful bitch!'

She picked up the money and stuffed it into her pocket. As she reached over for her cigarettes and lighter, Art gripped her wrist. 'Just one thing, sweetheart. I want you to sign for that cash, just as a safeguard for me. Just in case you want to rap about me and—'

Lorraine released her wrist and rubbed it. He was strong and he had hurt her. 'You'll never see me again, I promise you that.'

Art didn't speak another word. Lorraine signed for the money, walked to the door, opened it, and the buzzer shrilled. She turned, a half-smile on her face. 'You should get this fixed, you know, Art.'

As the door closed quietly behind her, he kicked at the desk. He was – and always would be – a shit-head when it came to sniffing out people.

Lorraine did some shopping. She was feeling quite high and kept on touching the thick wad of notes in her pocket. She bought two dolls for her daughters, some cans of paint, brushes and a small wardrobe. She bought some tights, underwear, a shirt and, finally, a nightdress for Rosie. Laden with goods she caught a taxi home.

Rosie's jaw dropped as Lorraine staggered in. 'Jesus Christ! What did you do? Win a lottery?'

Lorraine laughed. 'We sold four paintings and this is my bonus!'

Rosie peered at the cans of paint. 'Who's gonna do all this, then?'

'You and me!'

Rosie snorted, but by now she was busy unwrapping her gift. She took out the white cotton nightdress. 'Oh, wow! This is pure cotton, *and* it's new!'

She saw two boxes. 'What's this, shoes?' She opened one, and looked at Lorraine. 'Wow! I might act like a mental nine-and-a-half-year-old, but . . .'

Lorraine took back the box, closing the lid. 'They're for my daughters.'

'So you made contact, then?'

Lorraine walked out without answering. She had left more bags piled outside on the steps and yelled for Rosie to lend a hand. Jake arrived, unannounced, and was immediately recruited to carry in the rest of the paint, trays and rollers. He began to wish he hadn't dropped by as he was cajoled into shifting furniture to clear the room ready for painting. He promised to return later in the evening to help out some more. Lorraine didn't say goodbye – she was carefully putting the two doll boxes under a cushion in case they got damaged.

She and Rosie had a snack and then, draped in old nightdresses Rosie was now prepared to throw out, set to work. After seeing the way Art, Didi and Nula had transformed the gallery, Lorraine imagined it would be easy, but she had underestimated the threesome's expertise. By the time Jake reappeared they had covered only one wall.

He and Lorraine finished the main room and by the time they had pushed all the furniture back into place, it was after midnight. Jake promised he'd return in the morning so they could start on the kitchen and maybe get around to the bedroom.

Lorraine showered and combed the flecks of paint out of her hair. It was good to feel so tired – it meant she didn't have to think over what had happened during the day. She felt stiff from painting, and her back ached, but when she flopped onto the sofa she was too tired even to work out what she was going to do the following morning. She had a bus schedule, a street map of Santa Monica; she had even decided what she should wear. The two dolls were packed in a carrier bag: one blonde the other dark-haired. She didn't think about the future, about having to find alternative work. Tomorrow, seeing her daughters, was all that mattered.

CHAPTER 6

ROSIE WOKE up with a start, and then flopped back. Lorraine was in the shower. She squinted at the alarm clock: half past eight. She couldn't go back to sleep, so she got up and went into the freshly painted main room. Lorraine's bedding was neatly folded, and a pot of coffee was on the stove. Rosie toasted some muffins, then went out to see if the Sunday papers had arrived.

Lorraine emerged, made up and in her new blouse and the safari suit. She also wore the high-heeled slingbacks and skin-tone tights. She no longer needed to raid Rosie's make-up or jewellery box, as she had bought her own cosmetics and a pair of fake pearl earrings.

Rosie gaped, and then sniffed. 'My God, you look good and you smell terrific. Are you working today?'

'Yeah, there's a big art dealer coming so I've got to open the gallery early. I'm sorry if I woke you.'

'No problem. You want a muffin . . . coffee?'

'No thanks, I've had breakfast. I'm off now.'

Jake arrived about an hour later. Rosie was still reading the papers. 'Morning. It's baking out already. Where's Lorraine?'

'Gone to the gallery. You want some coffee and muffins?'

'Wouldn't say no.'

Rosie bustled around getting him a cup and plate, then sat and ate another muffin, washing it down with more coffee. She divided up the paper and they sat opposite each other, reading.

'They found another body,' said Jake. 'Prostitute. Reckon she was killed the same way couple months back, this time in Santa Monica.'

Rosie slapped down the paper. She looked at Jake. 'She's lied. She's not gone to that gallery, she's gone to see her kids in Santa Monica. She's so secretive . . . but I know she's traced them 'cos I saw the address on a note by the telephone and I know she's gone because she's taken the dolls she bought. Now why does she lie?'

'That's maybe just the way she is,' said Jake, folding his paper. 'Why don't we surprise her? Let's get the kitchen started.'

Rosie pulled a face. 'I was hopin' you'd forget all about it, I hate painting, it gives me a backache, and then my arms ache from the brushes. Even Walter's done a bunk – paint gets to cats, you know.' She glared at the bedroom door. 'This is bloody Sunday morning, for chrissakes, a day of rest!'

Jake began to clear the kitchen. It was so small it wouldn't take long, and then maybe they could do the bedroom, really surprise Lorraine.

Rooney was sweating. Ten o'clock and it was way up in the seventies. He hated losing his Sunday: there was nothing he liked better than sitting in the yard with the papers. He had them all stuffed under his arm as he plodded along the corridors towards his office. He saw Bean up ahead with a balding man.

'Morning, Captain.'

Rooney glowered, and waited for Bean to join him. 'That's not him, is it?'

'Yep, he's been working from home, seems a nice guy, real low key.'

Rooney snorted, and together they went into his office. Andrew Fellows was younger than Rooney had first thought. Prematurely bald, his rather handsome face was marred by a pair of enormous ears that constantly caught the attention – they moved up and down when he talked. The more animated he became, as Rooney was to discover, the more the ears worked overtime – and Professor Fellows was an animated man. He used his hands like a conductor, and his trim body in its pristine white T-shirt and tight jeans seemed incapable of staying still for a second. Rooney took him into the 'Hammer Killings' incident room. Photographs of all the victims had been posted up on the walls and rows of computers installed. He looked up expectantly at Fellows. 'So, you come up with anything for us?'

Fellows nodded, his ears waved, and he opened a worn leather briefcase. 'I've spent three days studying all the evidence to date, and I've tried to assimilate the most important aspects so we can cut through the dross. Much of the evidence you gave me was of no use, so I concentrated on this detailed description apparently given by an anonymous caller . . .'

He began to pace up and down. 'The caller gave a concise and exceptionally clear picture of the assailant – apart from his actual size . . .' Rooney sighed, looked at Bean and raised his eyes to the ceiling. Fellows flapped his hands. '. . . leading me to believe she had not met the man before. He was in the car when he picked her up, so she may have been a stranger to him. Let's give him a name rather than have to keep calling him the assailant or killer. Why not – for want of better – "the Teacher" . . .' Fellows laughed. 'Sorry, it's just that the description fits an old college professor I had.' Rooney gave a faint grimace that was supposed to be a smile.

Fellows moved to the row of victims' faces. 'Now, we're led to believe that all these women and Norman Hastings were killed by the Teacher – and this woman, Helen Murphy—' Fellows pointed to the wrong picture, and Bean corrected him. 'Ah, sorry, the body of Helen Murphy was found in the trunk of a car, so we are to presume the Teacher first attempted to kill her, failed, then traced her once more, or knew where she lived or the area she worked, whatever, and killed her, using the same method, claw hammer blows. Am I right so far?'

Rooney sighed. 'Yes, but, frankly, you're wasting time. What we need to know – what *I* need to know – is what sort of man is this bastard?'

'That's obvious. You've been given a remarkably clear description, but don't get me off track. Something's wrong, you see. When I went over the information regarding Helen Murphy, I was confused.'

Rooney coughed. 'What *we* got from that description, Professor, was that he's probably got a good income, a good job and—'

'Yes, yes, but let me get round to that. What's bothering me, as it doesn't make any logical sense, is, if a woman is badly beaten – as witnessed by, er, that couple, Mr and Mrs Summers – and, assuming that it was the same woman who subsequently gave you the killer's description – going so far as to report the incident to the police, describing the hammer – would she go with him again? He had to pick her up again, correct? Now, she was found in a car that had been left unattended, a wrecked vehicle, abandoned for possibly two or three months. Not like any of the other vehicles used. All of those were reported stolen shortly before the crime was committed. So that means our Teacher had to pick her up in another vehicle, kill her, and then dump the body. So Helen Murphy's murder does *not* follow the same pattern as the others.'

Rooney frowned. He'd given this a lot of thought himself and was about to say as much when Fellows continued, pointing at Bean. 'Whoever took the call said the woman was precise, articulate, and spoke fast in an almost clipped tone. She refused to give any details about herself, and they were unable even to ask her name because she continued to talk so quickly, but they jotted down almost the entire conversation, and then she hung up. Yes?'

Bean nodded. He felt almost guilty, as if he'd done something wrong, because Fellows was glaring at him.

'You took statements regarding the victim Helen Murphy, correct?'

'Yes,' Bean said, 'but I didn't do them all, a few of the statements were taken by—'

Fellows interrupted, his arms swinging like windmill sails, 'Who was Helen Murphy? Previously Helena, Helena Dubjeck, an alcoholic, drug abuser, persistent brawler, and . . . I can't recall all her previous charges. And she had false teeth. Also, according to the pathologist, a possible malformation of her upper lip, which you can even see on her photograph . . .' He paused. Rooney was rising slowly to his feet, when the windmill arms waved again. 'One moment. Didn't your anonymous caller say that the assailant, our Mr Teacher, was possibly around one hundred and eighty pounds? Odd, don't you think? Not "fat" or "thin, skinny, well-built" – but she gave you his possible weight? Doesn't that strike you as an odd thing for this kind of woman, Helen Murphy, to say? And you make *no* allowance for the fact that she might have had a speech defect, might even have had – and you must ask those who knew her – the trace of a foreign accent. She was not born in America, was she?'

Fellows ran his hand over his bald head then pulled at one of his ears. 'Do you see what I'm getting at? I would say that whoever made that call describing her attacker was someone familiar with police procedure, familiar with short-cutting a description. Am I right? It was *not* made by Helen Murphy.'

Rooney sat back, transfixed by the information that Fellows spouted out like bullets.

Fellows faced the wall lined with photos. 'These women were all prostitutes, but none of them had been penetrated at the time of death. No sexual intercourse took place. So why did he pick them up? What was he wanting them to do? I doubt he wanted intercourse – perhaps he wanted simulated sex, or to be jerked off. Or I would say he has a sexual problem, probably impotence. They get into his car or stolen vehicle, he drives them to some location. If they are bending over his groin, then it's simple for him to strike the back of the head. Again, go back to Mr and Mrs Summers. The woman they saw was bleeding badly, but also bleeding from her mouth. Correct?'

Rooney nodded. 'She also said she'd bitten the man in the neck.'

'But she also said she'd broken the skin, *his* skin, I presume, so the blood on her mouth could easily have been his blood, not her own. She was facing the Summerses who saw no wounds to her face apart from the bloody mouth – but the back of her head was bleeding. Nevertheless she was quite capable of flagging down a cab, giving an address. *Now*, would that woman, just a few days later, go with the same man again? And be caught the same way, yet again, with a hammer blow to the back of her head? Unless she knew him or was an accomplice to the other killings I doubt it. If she was an accomplice and made that call, then she could or would be arrested.'

Rooney felt inadequate. This big-eared windmill of a man, after just a few days' thumbing through their files, was throwing out mind-blowing stuff. He half expected Fellows to have another pull at his ears and then name the killer. But Fellows had become silent, and was sitting staring down at his sneakers.

'He is a sick man, a tormented man, deeply disturbed, and I think he has killed regularly. I don't think he's been

146

put away or locked up. On the contrary, he's walking around confident, *very* confident, because he's gotten away with it for years. Now, with this press coverage, will it make him stop killing? Possibly. I hope so. But it may make him irrational. You see, he'll want to prove, even more, just how clever he is. You won't catch him unless he makes mistakes. On the other hand, the press coverage could also make him stop, for a while anyhow. But he won't be able to stop completely, because, I would say, these murders are the only way he's able to get sexual gratification.'

Fellows got up again and marched up and down the wall of victims, peering at the faces, turning to retrace his footsteps. 'He must be in full employment, possibly some kind of travelling sales executive. He's moving around a lot of areas. He could even be a car salesman – he certainly knows about cars and how to steal them. I would say he might have a garage, or a storage place where these cars can be hidden. I doubt if he has a family – no wife or children. This man has a hatred of older women, a terrible hatred—'

Rooney interjected to ask about Angela Hollow. Fellows took a deep breath. 'Yes. She was young – and the most recent victim? Prostitute, working the streets the night she was killed?' He looked at the picture of Holly. 'Find out if, on the night she was killed, any other girl or woman was next to her. Maybe Holly crossed to him when he was really after another girl close by, it's possible. Because I have to admit she makes my theory wobble, as she's not in the same category as the others. This worries me . . .'

He tapped the picture of Norman Hastings. 'There's something odd about him, too, if we talk it through. He leaves his car, I can't recall the exact location, our Teacher steals it, or is even in the process of stealing it, and is caught red-handed. Hastings calls out, may even try and stop Teacher so, in that case, why the wound to the back of his head like the women? Unless Hastings was actually opening his car, Teacher, ready for the kill, simply walks up and strikes him?'

Rooney hitched up his pants. 'He went to the bank and—'

Fellows wafted his hand. 'That's immaterial – Teacher's not after money, he even left the victims' jewellery on their bodies. No, he's not after something as mundane as that, he's not a robber. He's a sex killer, he wants sexual gratification, nothing more.'

Rooney waited, almost afraid to interrupt. Fellows sighed, and sat down, looking at the picture of Hastings. 'It's possible they knew each other. I could be wrong, and nothing in all the reports gives any indication, other than that Hastings was an unfortunate man who was simply in the wrong place at the wrong time. What is not clear is what was that place? Outside his bank? In a car park? No one has come forward to say they saw Norman Hastings on the day of his death, so where did it happen? We don't know.'

Fellows went silent, chewing at his lower lip before he returned to the photo wall, to the graphs and memos. He stared at the photographs of the vehicles in which the dead women had been found. A Lincoln Continental, a Chrysler Le Baron, a Saab, a Mercedes, an Eldorado Cadillac – the latter the burned-out wreck where Helen Murphy had been found. Then he looked over the charts of the locations. Beverly Center on Melrose, Shopping Mall Van Nuys, West Hollywood, Santa Monica Boulevard, Century City and lastly the Santa Monica shopping centre. He stood for at least three minutes, his eyes roaming the photographs, the locations. There had to be a link between them, a pattern beyond the method of the murder itself. He needed to know as near as possible the times of, one, when Helen Murphy was killed, two, when the attack on the woman in the Van Nuys shopping mall occurred – the one they had wrongly presumed was Helen Murphy – and, three, Holly's murder.

The three were of interest because Holly's was the last, the failed murder attempt would have been between the last two.

'How close are these, time wise?' Fellows flicked his hand to Helen Murphy and Holly.

Bean crossed to the information section and looked up. 'The reported attack on the woman in the Van Nuys shopping mall was on the same day Hastings was killed. This woman, Helen Murphy, was, as close as we can get from the labs, murdered about three days before we found her.'

Fellows nodded. 'But they can't be exactly sure, can they? I mean, it could be a day either side. Her body was pretty high, wasn't it? Already decomposing?'

Bean nodded and then checked the information on Holly. Fellows had taken a small black leather diary from his pocket and was flipping through it, licking his fingers as he pushed the small pages over. 'And, Lieutenant, Holly was killed on what date?'

Bean looked at Rooney. 'Fifteenth of this month.'

Fellows pursed his lips. 'You got dates for all the others? See if it's always around the same time. I know some of them are four to six years old, but I'd like to get a calendar made up. Would you do that for me?'

Bean nodded. Fellows turned to Rooney and gave a glum smile. 'I'm sorry, but that's about it for today. It's not much because I need more time, and I'll hopefully come up with something else. I expect you've already come to the same conclusions yourselves. Basically, a lot of what I do in the end is simply common sense.'

He picked up his briefcase. 'You're not going, are you?' Rooney asked anxiously. 'I mean, all the team is coming in today to talk this over—'

Fellows snapped his case shut. 'I'm sure you can repeat everything, and I have a game of golf waiting. If you just keep me informed of any new developments, I'll get back to you.'

'What did you think of him?' asked Bean when Fellows had gone.

'I take back everything I said. How's that for starters?'

Bean grinned. 'Odd character, wasn't he?'

'Big ears.' Rooney sighed. 'We're almost back at the starting gate, aren't we? From what he's said, we're off by a long way with Murphy's husband. Nobody's found the fucker anyway.'

He flicked at the blind on his office window. 'You know, way back I was on a case, a missing kid – long time ago – but we'd all given up, we just had nothing. You remember that woman I saw that night when we went to the Indian?'

Bean raised an eyebrow.

'Well, she was on the same case, a little girl missing. She found her body at the school. She was such a cute little kid, and . . .' Rooney sighed, seeing the little girl's face again. 'Anyway, Lorraine – that was her name, didn't I tell you about her?'

'Drunk on duty, right?'

'This was before she became a lush, years before, and she was a good cop, dedicated – well, as much as a woman can be. Anyway, she wouldn't let go, she was so sure it was this janitor, but we had nothing on him. He even had a strong alibi for the afternoon the girl went missing. We'd all scrapped him as a suspect – she was even warned off from visiting the school and his place. Did it in her own time. She just wouldn't back off him. And we had not one shred of evidence, it was just her intuition . . .'

Bean yawned and looked at his watch, he could hear all the men starting to arrive outside, and he wondered where the story was leading. Rooney too seemed uncertain, still flicking at the blind with his fat stubby finger. 'She broke him down, I don't know how, none of us did. She brought him back into the station for maybe the tenth time, questioned him over and over, and meanwhile there was the Captain going ape-shit, saying we'd be accused of harassment. Then she walked out, and she had this look on her face like some prize fighter. She lifted up her fist, said he'd admitted it, that he'd just broken down and admitted killing the little girl . . .'

Bean wasn't listening, his attention on the doorway as he looked at the men that passed. 'Everyone's gathered. You want to go in?'

Rooney hitched up his pants. 'Maybe we try again with Hastings's wife, maybe we've been going too softly-softly, maybe he wasn't such a good, upright, honest citizen. And we start trying to trace that missing witness again. We don't back off, but keep on going – okay?'

Bean sighed. 'You know, even if we do find her maybe all she knows is what she told us and that won't help.'

Rooney jabbed at him with his finger. 'Wrong. She never said where he picked her up from. She probably knows a hell of a lot more than she let on. Now, let's get fucking cracking before the entire Sunday's up the spout. We got to trace that bitch and all leave is cancelled as from now . . .'

The cab drew up outside a narrow, three-storey house facing the ocean that didn't look much but, Lorraine knew, would have to be worth outside three million dollars. Mike Page was certainly doing a lot better for himself nowadays. The cab driver, who had been watching the clock, now turned to face Lorraine. 'You want to drive around some more or are you getting out?'

'Drive around a while longer.'

He sighed. 'Okay. Anything you want, lady, this is your ride.'

They did another tour of Santa Monica, then returned and parked in exactly the same place as before.

'This is it, lady. I got an account customer I need to pick up, so, if you don't mind . . .'

He was lying, she knew, he just wanted her out of his cab, probably because it was Sunday and he wanted to get home. She paid the fare, and stepped out. Hardly had the cab door shut behind her before he drove off. She felt marooned, afraid to walk the few yards to Mike's front door, yet unable to turn and walk away. She stood there, frozen.

'Lorraine?' The voice was unmistakable. It was Mike. She turned and shaded her eyes. He was wearing an open neck shirt, white slacks and flip-flops. A big dog with long scruffy hair padded beside him. Her heart was thudding and she knew she must be flushed a bright red and her whole body broke out in a sweat. Mike had a deep sun-tan and his teeth gleamed; his dark brown eyes had lines at the side, crow's feet, but apart from that he didn't seem much older than when she had last seen him.

'Hi!' He stood about a foot away from her. 'I wasn't expecting you until later.'

'I got a taxi.'

He smiled, reached for her bag and she let him take it.

'I got something for the girls, I don't want you to think I'm staying over . . .'

He took her elbow, about to draw her towards the house, then he stopped. 'They're out swimming but they won't be long, so we can have a chat, catch up.'

She followed him towards the front door, but he went down some steps to enter the house through large french windows which opened onto a verandah.

'This is nice,' she said lamely.

'Yep – and it's breaking me financially, but the kids love it.' He paused. 'Oh, maybe you don't know. I've got two sons – they're with the girls and Kathy.'

Lorraine nodded, presuming Kathy to be their step-mother. She stepped into the big open room, where toys and newspapers, even breakfast dishes, had been left on a huge round table facing the ocean window.

'Sorry about the mess but Sundays we just let everything hang out. Now sit down and I'll get some coffee going.'

Lorraine sat on the wide sofa. She looked slowly around the room, at the paintings, the throw rugs, the grains of sand that sparkled on the floor. 'Can I smoke?'

Mike cleared the table, and looked up. 'Sure, I'll find you an ashtray.'

She lit up, her hand shaking so much that she glanced over to see if he'd noticed, but he was carrying a stack of dishes into the kitchen. The door closed and she inhaled deeply, letting the smoke fill her lungs. She got up and stood by the open window, taking deep breaths to calm herself.

Mike held onto the edge of the sink, shaken. Nothing had prepared him for the way she looked. She had aged so much – she was skin and bone, her face scarred so badly she seemed to squint. He shook his head, wishing he had more time to prepare the girls. Then he heard Sissy calling, and before he had time to warn her not to come down, she was in the drawing room. He listened at the door.

Sissy was wrapped in a cotton kimono. She was deeply tanned and had waist-length, ash-blonde hair. She was as tall as Lorraine, but full-breasted, her legs muscular and taut. Her long arms and perfect hands immediately pulled the kimono closer as she had no belt and was naked beneath it. 'I'm sorry, I didn't know anyone was here.'

Lorraine bowed her head. 'I'm, er . . . well, I guess you knew I was coming. I'm Lorraine.'

'Oh, yeah, I'm sorry. Where's Mike?'

Lorraine swallowed. 'He's making me some coffee.'

She wondered who the beauty was, but Sissy seemed totally at ease, striding to the kitchen. 'Darling, you should have said, or yelled up that Lorraine was here. I'll go back up and shower, leave you two to have a chat . . . Mike?'

153

He walked out of the kitchen and slipped his arm around Sissy. 'Well, you've met. This is my wife, Sissy.'

Lorraine forced a smile as Sissy walked out and up the stairs. 'She's very beautiful,' she said quietly.

Mike nodded. 'The girls adore her, and – well, lemme get the coffee.'

Lorraine looked out onto the verandah and lit another cigarette from the stub. Then she started to cough, one of her awful, chesty, phlegmy coughs that made her feel weak and her eyes run. She gasped, tried to control it and Mike appeared with a glass of water.

'You should give that up!'

She shrugged, still coughing, and took the glass. Mike returned to the kitchen, and Lorraine remained outside on the verandah, sitting on one of the wooden bench seats. She drained the glass and set it carefully on the table. At least her hands were no longer shaking.

Mike carried out the tray of coffee and set it down. He poured a cup, and she smiled. It was the first time she even faintly resembled her old self: Mike noticed that she still had the palest of blue eyes.

'So. It's been a long time, hasn't it? I've often wondered how you were, hoped you'd get in touch.'

He waited for her to reply but she stared ahead. He could see the deep scar down her cheek, and her body shaking slightly. He'd sometimes wondered how he would react to seeing her again. He'd expected to feel anger, or perhaps attraction, rather than this deep sadness. He had worried that she might have some custody query, or have become financially secure enough to want the girls to live with her. But the worn, old-fashioned safari suit, the cheap shoes, everything about her looked seedy and worn. Worse still was Lorraine herself. She had always been so positive, arrogant even, now all he could see was a pitiful shell of what she had once been. That was what he felt more than

154

anything: pity, and an overwhelming relief she was no longer part of his life.

'I don't drink any more, Mike.' Her voice was smoky from too many cigarettes, deeper than he remembered.

'Good, that's good . . .' he said, hesitantly.

'But I sure as hell could do with one now!'

CHAPTER 7

LORRAINE SAT on the verandah shading her eyes, waiting for the first glimpse of her daughters. Mike stepped out carrying two photo albums, and came to sit beside her. Momentarily her shoulder rubbed against his.

'These are my boys – Chip, whose real name is Charles, and this is Mike junior.' They were both blond, both as beautiful as their mother. She quickly turned the pages back to the beginning, barely interested in Mike's sons. The first photograph was one she remembered: they were sitting side by side on a piano stool, Sally with a front tooth missing.

Mike looked up, hearing a shout from the beach. 'Here they are . . .'

Lorraine stood up and leaned on the rail. Sissy had one boy by each hand, and behind her walked a dark-haired teenager – but running up ahead were the girls. Sally and Julia, torn jeans, faded T-shirts, as suntanned as Sissy, they shouted and waved. Lorraine was stunned. They were both so tall, so different . . . she would have passed them in the street and not recognized them. 'My God,' she murmured.

Mike laughed. 'Yeah, they grow up fast, don't they?'

Sally was ten, Julia twelve. Six years was a very long time. Their initial exuberance faltered as they reached the verandah, and they turned to Sissy as if they needed her to be with them, but Mike called for them to come on up.

Julia was tall for her age, as slim as Lorraine had been at twelve.

'Hello.'

Lorraine smiled. She would have liked to put her arms around her daughter, but she wasn't sure if that was what she wanted. Sally wouldn't come close; she hung back as if afraid. Sissy slipped her arm around Julia's shoulder. 'Now, why don't you three show Lorraine the photo album, and I'll make some lunch?'

'Okay,' said Julia.

Sally sat beside Lorraine, but Mike followed Sissy into the lounge and pulled the doors half closed behind him. He watched for a moment before joining his wife in the kitchen.

The three sat in uncomfortable silence. Lorraine knew the dolls were a mistake – certainly for Julia, who seemed sophisticated and grown-up. Sally sat with her head bowed.

'I'm sorry not to have kept in touch with you both . . .' Lorraine said haltingly.

Julia gave her a strange, furtive look. 'That's okay. This is me winning a swimming prize at school.' Lorraine leaned forward to look at the photograph, and the tension eased slightly.

Lunch was served inside because it was cooler, and Julia showed Lorraine where the bathroom was so she could wash her hands. Lorraine crept from room to room, peeking in at each door, until she found her daughters' bedroom. It was full of posters and rugs, old teddy bears and a wardrobe bulging with clothes. Untidy comforters lay on their unmade beds, but it was a room any girl would covet. The last door she opened revealed Mike's study, the walls covered with pictures of the family, and some of himself on fishing trips. There was a large modern desk with stacks of files and papers, and Lorraine was just closing the door when she caught sight of a picture of herself, with the girls. It surprised her that he would have it, and she edged into the room, afraid that anyone should hear her creeping around.

She leaned across the desk to get a better view of the photograph and then froze as she inadvertently knocked some papers onto the floor. They were business letters, and as she glanced disinterestedly over them, the letter heading of one document caught her eye. The company was a vintage automobile reconditioning firm, specializing in imported cars. The letter confirmed that leather upholstery had been installed in a Mercedes sports car, circa 1966, and the client had refused to accept the costs. It was not, however, the contents of the letter that caught Lorraine's attention, it was the small black and green oval raised letters of the company logo: S & A. She was almost certain she had seen it before . . . not on a letter . . . It was on a pair of cufflinks.

'Lorraine? *Lorraine?*' Mike was calling her, and she quickly slipped the letter back and hurried out.

At lunch, the conversation – strained at best – turned to the subject of cars.

'What do you drive now?' Lorraine asked.

Mike grunted and prodded one of the boys. 'I have to have a coach for this crowd, it's an old station wagon. Sissy, however, has an MG – it's an English sports car.'

'I do know what an MG is,' Lorraine said.

Sissy flicked a look at Mike and then smiled. 'That was more for my benefit – it's always in the garage, not because I've damaged it, but because of the spares.'

'Is there a good garage near you?' Lorraine asked innocently.

Mike nodded. 'Yeah, there is. It specializes in vintage

and foreign cars, big money in it. They've got Rolls-Royces and Bentleys and Mercedes Benz—'

Lorraine interrupted, 'Is it a big company?'

'Pretty substantial.'

'How many people does it employ?'

Mike looked a little puzzled, but said, 'Maybe sixty, seventy, I don't know. Why?'

Lorraine smiled. 'I'm sure a friend of mine bought a car from a garage around here – maybe S and A?'

Mike nodded. 'Well, that's the company's logo all right – in fact I'm doing some business with them. Have you got your licence back, then?'

Lorraine flushed. 'No, but I can't afford a car.'

'Not from S and A.' Mike laughed.

'Does your friend live around here?' Sissy asked.

'No, I just heard the garage mentioned.'

Julia got up, cupping her hands to whisper in Sissy's ear. She frowned and shook her head. 'No, you can't, now sit down.'

Julia pouted and slumped back at the table. The room grew silent. Sissy shrugged her perfect shoulders. 'She wants to go play tennis.'

Julia snapped, 'I always play tennis on Sunday afternoons.'

Mike wagged his finger. 'Not this Sunday. Now, help your mother clear the table and—'

Lorraine stood up. 'No, that's okay – you go play tennis, Julia. I don't mind, I have to go in a few minutes anyway.'

Mike stacked the dishes, anything to cover his embarrassment. 'Well, it's up to you, but as you've come all this way—'

'I can come again – if you don't mind . . .'

'Where's Rufus?' Sally demanded, and suddenly they were all calling the dog. It seemed they all wanted to find an excuse to leave the room. Lorraine went over to the bag she'd brought, and took out the box with the doll. 'Sally?' She went out to the verandah. 'I brought you this – maybe it's a bit childish for you, I just thought you'd kind of like it.'

Sally opened the box and looked at the doll. 'Does it talk? My friend Angela's got one that talks and sleeps and cries, and you feed it with a bottle and it wets itself.'

Lorraine looked at the moody-faced child. 'This one drinks and then if you press its stomach, it spits in your face.'

Sally's mouth trembled.

'It was just a joke!'

The child ran into the house, past Mike. Lorraine laughed at his worried expression. "Sokay, Mike, I was never very good with them anyway. I got to go.'

Mike sat on the edge of the bench seat. 'I'm sorry. Maybe they'll take a while to get used to you – that is, if you're planning to make this a regular—'

'Would you mind?'

'No – well, maybe . . . I don't know, it's kind of taken us all by surprise. I think they're scared you've come to take them away.' He stared at her. 'You haven't, though, have you?'

Lorraine hugged her arms round herself tightly. 'I wouldn't want to do anything that'd upset them. Besides, I kind of don't know them any more – and you've changed. She's got you domesticated, carrying dishes back and forth.'

Sissy came out, overhearing the last remark.

She put down the coffee pot, and went back into the house.

'Can you call me a taxi?'

Lorraine was relieved when the cab arrived. She kept the doll she had bought for Julia, because she didn't want Julia to know that she had still thought of her as a little girl; she noticed that Sally hadn't even taken hers out of its box. Sally wouldn't kiss Lorraine goodbye, but hung on to Sissy. Mike kissed her cheek, and Sissy shook her hand – she had a strong, firm grip. She stared coldly at Lorraine as she said, without any warmth, 'Do come again.' Seeing them grouped together, waving, Lorraine knew she would never come back.

She asked the cab driver to take her past the S and A garage. Two massive showrooms were filled with vintage cars, but it was closed. Lorraine got out and walked along the showroom window, peering inside, and shaded her eyes to look at the counter. Dinky toy cars and memorabilia were displayed, but she couldn't see any cufflinks. By the time she returned to the cab, she was sweating again. It was three o'clock, the sun was blistering, so she asked the driver to stop at the next grocery store as she needed a can of Coke.

At ten o'clock Rosie called Jake to say that Lorraine still hadn't come home, and she was worried. Perhaps she was staying over, he suggested. If she was really worried, why not call? She had the number. Jake was exhausted: they had decorated the kitchen and the bedroom, and all the furniture was back in place.

Rosie waited until eleven before she called Mike Page, and was told that Lorraine had left around three. She called Jake. Already in bed, he was tetchy at being disturbed again. 'Rosie, what do you expect me to do? I'm not her keeper. I'm not responsible for what she does or does not do. Now lay off me, okay?'

Twelve o'clock, and Rosie went to bed. The smell of fresh paint made her feel sick, and she couldn't get to sleep, so she got up, made herself some iced tea, and sat by the window. Then she watched some late-night television and eventually, at two thirty, went back to bed.

Monday morning and Lorraine had still not returned, so Rosie called Jake again, but he had left for work, and she didn't want to pester him there. She told herself she was overreacting, but when Lorraine had still not appeared at four in the afternoon, she went along to the gallery. It was shut so she squinted through the window and saw that all the canvases had been removed. The place looked deserted, so she went home.

For want of something better to do, and to take her mind off Lorraine, Rosie began to clear her bedroom cupboards and drawers, tossing out junk she had hoarded. A new wardrobe kit had been assembled in a corner of the now tidy bedroom. Rosie pushed it into position and began to fill it with Lorraine's few possessions. Lastly she put in the shoes – and that was when she found the roll of money. She was amazed at the amount, then felt guilty because it would look as if she had been searching through Lorraine's personal belongings. She had, of course, but not with any ulterior motive.

Jake dropped by at seven o'clock. There was still no word from Lorraine. Rosie was upset. Jake took her to a meeting; he had a good idea that Lorraine would eventually come home, and he refused to borrow his friend's car to go on a street search. If she had started out in Santa Monica, God alone knew where she was.

They came back to Rosie's just after ten, and ate some takeaway food. Midway through the meal, they heard a screaming, hoarse voice. Jake gestured for Rosie to stay at the table and crossed to the window, peered out, and sighed. 'She's home. I'd better go and give her a hand.'

Rosie could hear the sound of breaking glass, and went to the window.

Lorraine was standing in the middle of the road, swinging a doll by its arm. Her blouse was torn, her skirt hanging off and she was filthy. She swiped at Jake.

'Fuck off! *Fucking leave me alone, you shit!*'

Jake backed off, arms raised, and Lorraine kicked out at him, swearing. A woman with a shopping cart was passing by and Lorraine caught her stare. 'What you fucking looking at, you cunt? *Fuck off – go on!*'

Jake had to coax and cajole her to come to the stairs leading up to Rosie's apartment. It took him fifteen minutes to get her up them. She took two steps up and fell down three. She screeched with laughter, then slowly crawled up, only to insist on going down again as she had dropped her doll.

At last Jake got her into the apartment. She stood by the door. 'Hi, Rosie. He fucked you yet?'

Rosie went into the kitchen as Jake tried to get Lorraine onto the sofa. Halfway there she pulled out her shirt, stripping it away from her skinny body: she fumbled with his pants. He swiped her hand aside and dragged her to the sofa, she fell, and slithered onto the floor.

'Run the shower, Rosie,' Jake said.

Lorraine stank of booze, vomit and urine. She had no jacket. She refused to release the doll even when they half carried her into the shower, ran the cold water over her, and between them stripped off her clothes, Jake paying no attention to her naked body, apart from glancing at Rosie when he saw the fresh red bruises and the old scars.

Rosie wanted to weep at seeing her friend like this, but she fetched towels and soaped Lorraine clean. Lorraine became subdued and listless, but she would not let go of the doll. Washed, with a clean nightdress on, she lay down on Rosie's bed.

'Best let her sleep it off,' Jake said, and ushered Rosie out of the bedroom. They picked up the filthy clothes and tossed them into the trash-can. Lorraine fell into a deep, coma-like sleep, with no idea where she was.

Rosie checked on her throughout the night, in case she vomited and choked to death. Jake left, depressed, though it was hardly unexpected. He'd seen it all before

163

with Rosie – but at least Lorraine had been easier to get up the stairs.

Rosie slept on the sofa. She was woken by Lorraine stumbling out of the bedroom. Her face looked pale green, and there were deep, dark rings beneath her eyes.

'Coffee,' was about the only word she could squeeze out. Her head felt like someone had attached a chunk of concrete to it, with a bolt hammered into her skull to keep it steady. She needed Rosie to help her back to bed, and she moaned in agony as she lay down. Ice packs were prepared, and gently Rosie rested them on her forehead. Lorraine slept for the remainder of the day, rising in the early evening for a shower. By then she was able to move around more easily. 'What day is it?'

'Wednesday evening.'

'Wake me Friday.' Lorraine gave a wan smile and lay down on the sofa.

Rosie shopped, using Lorraine's hidden savings: she would tell her when the time was right, but she couldn't work with Lorraine as she was, and the rent was due. So Rosie kept dipping in.

It was Friday before Lorraine's hangover lifted. She was quiet, staring into space, unable to hold a conversation. Every time she attempted to explain herself, her voice trailed off mid-sentence. Rosie stroked her head. 'Honey, you don't have to explain, because I've been there. Just get better, then we can talk.'

Lorraine clasped her hand. 'Thanks.'

Rosie smiled, dipped into the savings again and went out to buy some fillet steak: Lorraine needed her strength building up. She also paid the telephone bill, the electricity bill – dip, dip, dip – but she'd admit it when Lorraine was better. It wasn't stealing, she told herself – what was hers was Lorraine's, after all – it was just that, right now, she was short of cash.

At the weekend when Jake came round, Lorraine greeted him warmly.

He cocked his head to one side. 'Back in the land of the living now, are we?'

Lorraine flushed. 'Oh. Were you here?'

'Who do you think carried you up the fuckin' stairs? You really went for it, didn't you?'

Lorraine gave him that odd lopsided, squint-eyed look. 'Christ only knows what I went with – my crotch feels like I been sittin' on hot coals.'

Jake turned away: he was never sure about her, she had a filthy mouth one minute, the next she came on like a real lady. 'If I was you, I'd get down to a clinic and get checked out. You smelt like a sewer.'

She was unable to meet his steady gaze. At least she could still be ashamed, he thought, that was something in her favour. 'Rosie's been taking good care of you so you make sure you say thank you.'

'I don't need you to tell me to do that, Jake.' Her voice was so husky he had to strain to hear what she said.

'What?'

'I said I'd go and have a medical, *okay*?'

'Good. I suggest you come to a meeting, and keep on coming for a few days, unless you got to go to work. You still think you got work at the gallery? Only I passed it two days ago and it looked all shut up.'

She walked into the bedroom. 'Soon as I feel fit enough I'll be out looking for another job.'

Rosie banged open the screen door, her arms bulging with groceries. Jake took the loaded bags from her. 'You've been spending a bit freely lately haven't you?'

'Let's just say I got a bit of a windfall. Now, will you stay for dinner? I got fillet steak and salad and I'll make jacket potatoes.'

Jake put the bags on the kitchen table. 'Sounds good!'

He continued, whispering, 'She should have herself checked out at a clinic.'

'She's only got a hangover, Jake.'

'She could also have HIV, venereal disease and Christ only knows what else, so have her down to a clinic.'

Rosie looked towards the bedroom wondering if Lorraine had heard, then started unpacking the groceries.

Lorraine had heard, and rested back on Rosie's bed. She was sober. She had little or no recollection of what she had done or where she had been. She dimly remembered stopping off in the cab, going to buy a can of Coke and coming out with two litres of vodka. She had a vague impression of having been thrown out of the same taxi, thumbing a lift from a trucker, and then – blank.

She sighed. Maybe it was better this way. She didn't know why she was getting herself straightened out again. Now she knew she didn't have anyone to do it for. She closed her eyes, making a silent decision that as soon as Rosie and Jake left the apartment, she'd pack up what she'd got, get her stash of money and go. Go and get so drunk she would never get sober again. Her resolution to blow it all – blow herself – made her feel light-hearted, and she sat up, wrapped her robe around her and went into the kitchen.

'This smells so good. We having a party?'

Rooney looked round the tastefully furnished room, and at the pictures arrayed on a bookcase. Norman Hastings with his wife, Norman Hastings with his daughters, his dog, his car, Norman Hastings smiling. Norman Hastings the nice, ordinary husband and father. Rooney could smell baking, mixed with polish, or some kind of lavender room spray. He could hear Hastings's dog out in the back yard with the kids, barking as the creaking swing swung backwards and forwards. The little girls were calling to the dog, to each other, and the sound of their voices added to the air of normality. The only thing missing was their father.

Mrs Hastings came in with home-made cookies and a pot of coffee. She was a pretty woman, nice-coloured hair with a sweet-faced smile. She perched rather than sat on the chair opposite Rooney. She had good hands, square-cut nails without any varnish.

'I'm sorry not to have any news,' Rooney said. She bit her lip, trying not to cry. Rooney hated having to do it, but he couldn't put off what he was there for, and she seemed to sense he wanted something.

'Mrs Hastings, I'm sorry if this seems like going over old ground, but I just want to ask a few more questions.'

She began to nibble a cookie.

'Tell me about a normal, everyday week – where your husband went, who he saw, that kind of thing.'

The familiar story unfolded. Norman Hastings got up at the same time every day, even at weekends. He took his kids to school, he went to work, he came home, he had supper with his family. Two nights a week he went bowling or played poker with his friends. Weekends were kept for the family.

'Did he have any other hobbies?'

'Just taking care of the garden, that kind of thing. He did all the decorating and he built the kitchen and the girls' wardrobes.'

'Nothing else?'

She shook her head, then hesitated. 'We did join a country and western club two or three years ago. We went to four or five nights, but he didn't really enjoy it. I did, but he said they weren't his type.'

'Did you continue going?'

'No. You need a partner, you see, for the square dances . . . I'm not being much help, am I?' she asked.

'Was there anyone you didn't like among his friends?'

167

She shook her head.

'Would you show me over the house?'

She seemed surprised, but stood up, and walked to the door. Rooney trailed after her. She was like a tour guide, pointing out what Norman had done – the extensions, the custom-built closets. She was boring him and he began to feel faintly irritated. The last room they went into was Hastings's den. Its walls were painted the identical colour to three other rooms, the pictures indistinguishable from those in the living room. Norman with his wife, his kids, his bowls-playing pals, his poker pals. Four men standing, hands in their pockets, staring at the camera. Rooney moved closer, peering at the photographs, half hoping he would see a man with wide lips, glasses and a bite out of his neck, but they were all pot-bellied, jovial types with just a faint glimmer of enjoyment on their faces. Rooney sighed and turned away, but as he did he noticed a faint mark on the wall where another picture had hung. 'What was there?'

Mrs Hastings blinked. 'I can't remember.'

He knew she was lying, the house was too orderly for her not to know every inch. 'Was it a photograph?' Rooney asked, relaxed and casual.

'I can't remember. Norman must have taken it down.'

'Do you mind looking for it?'

She hesitated, then crossed to the desk. As she opened a drawer, they heard a crash outside, and one of her daughters started to cry loudly. 'I won't be a minute – I think she's fallen off the swing.'

'Can I look through the desk?'

She paused in the doorway. 'I'd prefer it if you didn't.'

He lifted his hands in apology. Stepping back from the desk he sat down in Hastings's chair. 'I'll wait for you.'

As soon as she was out of the room Rooney looked over the contents of the drawers. Tax forms, house insurance, life insurance, dental and medical checks, they were like the rest of the house, orderly. He drummed the desk top with his fingers. There was yet another photograph of Mrs Hastings, a daughter on either side. Rooney picked it up and stared at it, then he turned it over. There was a hook, and a stand. He looked to the space on the wall, then back to the photograph. When he placed it against the faint dust outline, it matched.

He crossed to the window. Mrs Hastings was examining her daughter's leg, so he returned to the desk and picked up the photograph again. He pushed open the small clips at each side, and opened the frame. There was nothing beneath. He swore, replaced the clips, and was about to stand it upright on the desk when she walked back in.

'She's all right, just a grazed knee.' She stared at Rooney, then at the photograph.

'Pretty photograph – in fact they're all very nice.'

She prodded the frame into exactly the same position as before. 'Yes. He's a professional photographer.'

'Ah, just goes to show – you can always tell!' Rooney paused. 'Mrs Hastings, that photograph was the one off the wall, wasn't it? Was someone else's photograph in it? Is that why you took it down?'

She pursed her lips: she didn't seem quite so pretty now – there was a steely quality to her. 'Yes, it was, now I come to think about it.' She folded her arms. 'I'd like you to go, please.'

Rooney remained where he was. 'Mrs Hastings, your husband was found brutally murdered. Now, I have no motive, no reason why anybody should have done that.'

'Robbery. You never found his wallet. It was robbery. That's what the papers have said and the television news.'

'And you can think of no other motive?'

'No. He's buried now anyway. It's all over. I'd like you to leave.' She pointedly held the door open and Rooney walked past her.

He stopped as they reached the front door. 'The photographer. Do you have his name and address?'

169

'No, I'm sorry I don't. Norman always arranged the sittings.'

Rooney scratched his head. 'Was he local?'

She coloured. 'I can't remember.'

'But you had them taken every few years, you told me so yourself. Surely you must remember?'

'I don't.'

She had the front door open when he leaned close. 'Why are you lying?'

'Please leave me alone.'

Rooney shut the door with the flat of his hand. She pushed against him, and then backed down the hallway. '*I don't want to talk about it*.'

Rooney followed her. 'What don't you want to talk about, Mrs Hastings?'

Her hands were flailing, her face bright pink.

'Why don't we go and sit down?'

'No.'

Rooney gazed at the freshly painted ceiling. 'Don't make me get a whole bunch of officers checking out every photographer, Mrs Hastings, don't waste my time . . .' His voice was low, flat and expressionless. 'Seven women have been killed in the same manner as your husband – a blow to the back of the head with a hammer, and their faces battered beyond recognition. If you have anything – *anything* – that will help me find the killer, you had better tell me!'

She stood with her arms wrapped round herself, her whole body shaking. 'I said if I ever caught him doing it again, I would divorce him – I'd tell his parents, his boss, his friends—'

'Doing what, Mrs Hastings?'

She turned round and her face was ashen. 'He was dressed in women's clothes.'

Rooney didn't show a flicker of distaste or surprise.

She had come home from one of the country and western

nights – when Norman had said he didn't like it, she went alone. She started to cry. 'I was only there a few minutes and I felt stupid all dressed up in cowboy boots, and I just thought he was right, it *was* stupid, so I came home. But he didn't hear me coming in. I knew he was in the bedroom because I saw the light on, and I thought I'd surprise him.' She gave a strange, bitter, high-pitched laugh. 'I don't know who was more surprised, him or me. He was all made-up, with a blonde wig, a cheap awful frilled dress, high heels . . . I – I just couldn't believe my eyes.'

She broke down and sobbed, and Rooney remained silent, waiting. 'Anyway . . . a long time after, because I ran into the bathroom and wouldn't come out, he was on his knees outside the bathroom sobbing, and I was scared he'd wake the girls, so I came out. He'd taken everything off, but he still had traces – his face . . .'

Norman Hastings, on his knees before his wife, had sworn on the Bible that no one else knew, that he had never done it before. But she knew he had, because of all the clothes. She found more in the garage, more wigs and shoes. She had burnt everything.

Rooney asked, 'This photographer . . . do you think he might have had the same inclinations?'

'He was homosexual, but after I found Norman, I refused ever to go to him again.'

Rooney took out his notebook. 'What's his name?'

She wrung her hands. 'Dear God, this won't come out, will it? His parents are elderly – all his friends, his daughters – please tell me this will never come out?'

Rooney promised he would do his best to keep it from being disclosed to the press. He was lying. The photographer's name was Craig Lyall; she even supplied his studio and home address.

Rooney walked down the immaculate path from the tidy little house, and crossed to his car. The big-eared wonder had been right – now he had a lot more to go on. He suddenly remembered Lorraine Page again, and the Laura Bradley case. He recalled how shocked she had been at the normality of the house and family of the brutalized, abused child. He looked back at the Hastings house, and suddenly it wasn't so neat or tidy and homely. He felt deeply sorry for the man, trapped in that perfect little prison. For the first time he also felt an odd compassion for Lorraine Page; she had been a crack officer all those years ago. What a terrible waste.

'Lorraine! *Lorraine!* We're leaving, did you hear? *Lorraine!*' Rosie bellowed.

'Okay, I'll see you later.' She was desperate for them both to go, wanting to take her savings and get the hell out. She was so impatient that as soon as the screen door closed she ran to her closet, and wrenched it open, falling to her knees to search for the money. She found the shoes, and then stared in disbelief at the pitiful remains of her hoard. She began hurling things out of the closet, convinced there must be some mistake. Then she sat back on her heels and punched at the door.

'Rosie!' she snarled.

Rosie and Jake were at the bottom of the steps when the screen door flew open. Lorraine hurled herself down the stairs, her hands splayed like claws. She grabbed Rosie by the throat. *'Where is it?'*

Jake tried to haul her off, but she thrust him back so hard that he crashed into the garbage cans. She dived at Rosie again, who was screeching at the top of her voice.

'My money! *You stole my money, you fucking bitch!*'

Rosie reeled back as Lorraine punched her in the face, tripped over a paving stone and fell. Lorraine sprang at her, pulling at her hair. 'You fucking bitch! That was *my money, my money* – you two-faced cunt, you piece of shit . . . *you fucker!*'

People were coming out of the grocery store to watch. Lorraine was on top of Rosie now, hitting her. Jake was trying to drag her off, but nothing he did could stop Lorraine. She swiped and spat like a wild cat, and then she collapsed, kicking and pounding the road with her fists.

Rosie's nose was bleeding, her face was scratched, her dress ripped and she was shaking with terror. She had never seen anyone so crazy, well, not when they were sober.

Jake had handled crazies and drunks, but Lorraine's immense strength surprised him – she'd almost broken his jaw. He now hauled her to her feet and dragged her over to the steps. He turned on two gawping onlookers: 'Show's over, okay?'

Lorraine didn't resist. She let Jake propel her up the stairs, and a trembling Rosie followed slowly, keeping a good distance.

Jake sat Lorraine on the sofa, then squatted back on his heels in front of her. 'What the hell was that all about?'

Lorraine glared at Rosie. 'Tell him!' she shrieked.

Rosie started to cry, dabbing at her face, and Lorraine swung back her fist and caught Rosie another blow, which started her screaming. Jake prised them apart, pushing Lorraine away. Abruptly she raised her hands. 'Okay, okay . . . but if she won't tell you then I will. Every cent I've saved and fuckin' worked my ass off for – she has stolen. I've got no more than twenty, thirty bucks left from over a thousand.'

Jake frowned. 'Where did you get a grand from? Rob a bank, for chrissakes?'

'What is this? An inquisition? It was my dough. *She's* the one who stole it. Why not interrogate her?'

Jake stood up, ran his hand over his thinning head. 'How much is left?'

Lorraine closed her eyes. 'Not enough to drink myself to death, which is what I intended doing.'

'So, you want to die. Fuck you – and your attitude.

173

Anyone that can make a thousand bucks in less than a week gotta have somethin' goin' for them – unless you did pull a heist, but somehow I doubt it . . .'

Lorraine gave her odd squint-eyed look to Jake. 'Okay. You want to know how I made it? Blackmail, I blackmailed a little queer bastard . . .'

Jake grinned. 'Can we all have a go at him – or is it just you that's got the information on him?'

'It was Art, at the gallery, he's into porno – no paintings – porno, with kids.'

Rooney walked into his office and beamed at Bean. 'Guess what? Norman Hastings was a cross-dresser!'

Bean gaped as Rooney displayed the photographs from Craig Lyall's studio. Norman Hastings in a blonde wig, dressed up and in full make-up, smiled with thick, glossy red lips into the camera lens. 'Jesus Christ, I don't believe it!'

Rooney was pleased with his efforts. He told Bean to bring in the pictures of the dead women, and Rooney held up Hastings's photograph.

'What if Teacher picked up Hastings? Maybe thought he was a hooker?'

Bean deflated Rooney by reminding him that Hastings was found in male clothes, so that theory was out of the window.

'Maybe he knew him? Maybe they dressed up together?'

They were going down the maybe road again, but at least they now had a road. All Hastings's friends would be requestioned.

'What was the photographer like?' Bean asked.

Rooney picked at his nose. 'Campy, queer, probably a cross-dresser too. Best get him back in, you have a talk to him. I got so excited when he showed the photos I might have missed something.'

'Fellows was right, wasn't he?' Bean mumbled. They had begun walking towards the exit when he stopped. 'Bill, what if Helen Murphy is or was not the woman who had been attacked? Maybe we should have another interview with that woman Laura Bradley, go over everythin' again.'

'What did you say?' Rooney snapped. 'The last thing, Laura Bradley?'

Bean explained again about the two uniformed guys who had interviewed a woman at the address where the cab driver thought he had dropped off the injured woman.

'Laura Bradley? That her name?' Rooney stood in the corridor, blinking. He could picture that little girl, see rookie Lorraine Page's face. 'Check her out.'

Lorraine told Jake and Rosie the entire Art, Nula and Didi story, and described her visit to Mike. She felt drained, by them, by everything.

Jake gently touched her head, fixing a stray strand of hair. 'You gonna come clean about that time you got a crack over the back of the head? You had money that night, too.'

'You really are grilling me tonight, Jake, what's with you?'

'I just know it helps to talk things over. You still want to slit your wrists?'

She smiled. 'Maybe not quite so much.'

'Good. So, how did you get that crack on the back of your head?'

Lorraine yawned. 'Well, you know the grocery store? At the end of the road? The crossroads just at the side of it? I walked across there, up along the road, and you know the traffic lights at the end of that block?'

'Yes,' Rosie and Jake said together.

'That's where I tripped and fell.'

Their faces made Lorraine giggle and suddenly they

broke into laughter too. They were all laughing when they heard the footsteps coming up the wooden staircase. Rosie looked out of the window.

'It's the cops.'

Jake caught Lorraine's expression. She was drained of any colour.

CHAPTER 8

LORRAINE DIDN'T panic. She calmly picked up her cigarette pack and headed for the bedroom.

'Jake, if they ask for a Laura Bradley, she's not here. She stayed a while and then left.'

'They coming for you?' Rosie asked.

'Yeah, but I swear I've done nothing wrong. I just got a lot of outstanding violations, and—'

Jake took her by the elbow, pushing her even further into the safety of the bedroom. 'Why Laura Bradley?'

'Because they came here, that friend of mine must have told them where they could find me. Please, Jake, get them off my back and I swear I won't kill myself!'

'It's a deal,' Jake said as he closed the door.

Rosie hardly said a word, just gave her name. Jake did the rest, smooth-talking, open and friendly. Sorry he couldn't help them, but Laura Bradley had left. The young uniformed cop smiled, tipped his hat: with his shades and suntan he could have come straight out of a movie. He returned to his partner, waiting below in the car, and Rosie watched them draw away.

The cop car cruised one block up and parked. The cab driver had said a short dark-haired guy and a fat woman had helped the injured woman, so they radioed in for further instructions.

In some ways Lorraine knew they'd be back – even wished she hadn't played games and had come forward, rather than involving Jake and Rosie. They heard the cops returning, and Lorraine gave a long sigh. 'Okay. Remember that night I cracked my head? Just tell them we were all at an AA meeting, agreed? That's what you say and you stick to it.'

'Why do we have to lie?' Rosie gasped, the footsteps almost at the screen door.

'So I don't get arrested for non-appearance in court. I got traffic violations. I also blackmailed Art Mathews, and you, Rosie, spent the dough – you need any more reasons?'

There was a rap on the door and Lorraine opened it. She'd got her jacket and purse and cigarettes, and made a joke of it. 'Okay, guys, I'm Laura Bradley.'

Rosie and Jake were driven off in one squad car, while Lorraine travelled solo with two officers in another. She was taken straight in to see Josh Bean, and admitted straight away that she had lied, that she was Lorraine Page. He seemed to accept her excuse that she didn't want to get involved, because – as she presumed he already knew – she was an ex-cop. As they spoke, from the corner of her eye, she could see her details rolling off the fax machine. But she was relieved that Captain Rooney was not around. Just being inside the station had brought her out in a cold sweat.

Bean elaborated as to why they had asked her to accompany the officers. He told her they were investigating a murder and asked where she was on the night of the seventeenth of last month.

Lorraine said she was at an AA meeting and gave the address. Bean was quiet, almost too friendly and apologetic for any inconvenience they had caused. 'You see we're searching for a witness, a woman we believe is a very valuable witness.'

Even as he spoke she could see him scrutinizing her, and

it was obvious he doubted that she could be the same woman as described – she had all her own teeth, for a start. Lorraine remained in control, smiled and joked. 'Well, we sure get a lot of riff-raff in the street. Only the other night there was some drunken woman out there, screaming the place down.'

Rosie and Jake kept to the AA meeting story. Rosie told how she had met Lorraine in hospital, how long she had been staying. When they were asked if they had assisted a woman from a taxi on the night of the seventeenth, a woman with injuries to her head and face, both repeated that they were not at home that evening. But they kept glancing nervously at each other.

'You ever see a blue Sedan parked in your street, like this one?'

They were shown a photograph of Hastings's car.

'No, not that I can recall.' Rosie peered at the picture. 'This has been on the TV, hasn't it?'

'Do you know or did you know a Mr Norman Hastings?' Rosie shook her head.

'He was the guy that was murdered, right?' Jake asked.

'I didn't know him,' Rosie said, 'but I seen all the papers. What's this got to do with us?'

Rosie and Jake were released, but were told that they should inform the police of any change of address in case they were required for further questioning. Jake asked if Lorraine was also free to go, and was told that she was still being questioned.

'We'll wait.'

They huddled together to review the officers' questions. They were confused. It seemed a lot more serious than traffic violations but they were in too deep and the spacious waiting room made both feel small and conspicuous. It was to be a long wait.

Four hours after Lorraine had entered the station she was led into a line-up. She had remained calm, accepting a tepid coffee and an extra packet of cigarettes. When she heard that her friends were waiting for her, she asked for someone to tell them they could go home unless they were required for the line-up. They were not: to arrange for a line-up with twelve fat women, and twelve short, squat men in one afternoon was too much to hope for. So Rosie and Jake left the station. They had no idea why Lorraine was still being detained. But Jake had been around too many cops, in too many stations not to know that this was something a lot heavier than traffic violations.

Lorraine knew the procedure backwards, and made it clear she was more than willing to co-operate. She waited patiently, knowing what a runaround would be going on behind the scenes. Captain Rooney had still not made an appearance and for that she was grateful.

The line-up corridor annex was like all the others she had dealt with years before, but larger and with better equipment. The more she looked around the Pasadena station the more impressed she was with the massive building. She wondered how Rooney fitted in, his squalid old office, his grimy-walled, smoke-stained room far removed from the white, neon-lit, airy offices with the red 'no smoking' signs on every door.

She chose place number seven, for no particular reason except to avoid being dead centre or at either end, which were not good positions. The other eleven women carried in their cards and lined up on the small, narrow platform. Some were prisoners, and others Lorraine could not imagine where they had been dragged in from. Probably a couple of hookers, housewives or canteen workers, who were always willing to make a few bucks.

When Mr and Mrs Summers arrived, Bean told them to take their time, to look at each subject closely, without making contact. If they recognized the woman they should walk out and give the number. If they wished her to speak they must ask the officer at their side to repeat whatever they wanted the prisoner to say.

Mr Summers walked slowly down the line first, staring at each woman in turn. Then he left the room. Next came his wife. She, too, took her time, but she was confused as she and her husband were sure they had already identified the woman. They also felt slightly guilty. Had they made a mistake earlier? Both had been so certain that the deceased Helen Murphy was the woman they had seen in the parking lot.

'Could they all smile?' Mrs Summers asked nervously. 'I want to see their teeth.'

Captain Rooney walked into the viewing room. There was Lorraine, at number seven, taller than any of the others. It was strange to see her, chin up, holding the card in front of her, her face expressionless. He moved closer to the glass and stared at the deep scar running down her cheek. She looked different, meaner, harder and yet there was still an attractiveness about her. Her clear eyes seemed to stare back at him, through the one-way glass, almost as if she knew he was there.

The third person to be led across the line-up was the cab driver, unshaven, having been ordered out of bed as he was now working night shifts. He was bad-tempered, asking over and over if he was getting paid for all the time they had used up. He had already identified the woman, hadn't he? In some ways he'd half expected a row of corpses.

Rooney turned to Bean. 'Anything?'

'Yeah. The Summerses both said it could be number four – she's from Records! And the cab driver said it was the skinny woman, number two. She's a hooker, but she was banged up on the seventeenth for breaking into a car.'

'Great.' Rooney sighed.

Lorraine was asked to wait in reception. She had stood upright in the line-up – that was another little tip: never slouch, makes you look guilty, always meet their eyes. Never smile, just look. They can't deal with a straight confrontation.

Rooney sat at his desk, swivelling his chair from side to side.

Bean was looking over Lorraine's charge sheet. 'We can hold her if you want. You had a look at this? Vagrancy, prostitution – she's got twenty-five traffic violations, five non-appearances for court hearings . . .'

'Yeah, I know,' muttered Rooney.

'She said she was at an AA meeting, so did her friends. We can check it if you want.'

Rooney shrugged. Lorraine didn't fit their description, she looked to him to be doing okay for herself – and she was sober. 'I can understand why she didn't want to be brought in.' He held out his hand for the sheets. 'I'll talk to her, you can take yourself off home. Get some rest while you can, this is gettin' out of control an' you got no leave until we get results.'

As Lorraine was led along the corridor towards him, Rooney leaned against the wall. He gave a noncommittal nod and held the door wider for her to pass into his office. She sat in the chair opposite his, and waited. Rooney walked slowly round to his chair, sank into it heavily, then rested his elbows on the table.

'Laura Bradley.'

She smiled. 'Yeah. I dunno why I said it, just came into my head. Maybe the little kid's always there, I don't know . . . I'm sorry I wasted your time.'

He stared at her charge sheets.

'I guess whoever you were looking for must have used my address – old ploy. You tried the apartments either side? There's a lot of oddballs live around that street, and then there's the liquor store on the corner—'

Rooney interrupted, 'I know the area. How long have you been sober?'

'A year,' she lied.

Rooney sighed. He hadn't revealed to Bean why he'd not been around when they'd brought in Lorraine. He'd been with Chief Michael Berillo and he'd been hauled over the carpet . . . 'I'm being really pushed on this one. Chief inferred I'd be off it if I didn't get a result soon.'

'What's the case?' Lorraine asked.

'Seven hookers cracked over the skull with a claw hammer. One of 'em's only seventeen, rest are real dogs.' Rooney smirked. 'Maybe some of 'em are your friends. You want to take a look?'

'Cunt.'

'What are you doing now?'

'Work in an art gallery, go see my kids – pretty boring but it keeps me. Can I go?'

'No. I need someone to talk to. What do you think of the new station – well, be about five years old now. It wasn't built when you left, was it?'

She lit a cigarette, and was surprised when he slumped forward, clasping his head in his hands. 'I'm fucking coming up for retirement, and what happens? I get a case that's . . . I keep on going up one blind alley after another. Nothing makes sense.'

He suddenly looked up, and then got to his feet. 'Come on, take a look, maybe you did know one of these whores.'

She glared at him, and he laughed. 'Hey! You be nice to me. I could have you locked up. You know how many violations you got outstanding? Twenty-five, sweetheart, so move your butt.'

Lorraine followed Rooney into the incident room. The officers in there turned and stared. Rooney announced loudly that she was an ex-cop, and there followed a few strange glances and a whispered exchange between two females who knew that she'd been in the line-up. She lit a cigarette from the butt and heard someone say it was a no-smoking zone. She paid no attention.

Rooney took her over the photographs, pointing out each woman in turn, where they were found, the dates. She looked closely at Hastings. Pinned next to it was one of him in drag.

'How about that for a turn-up? Drag artist in his spare time, I found that out,' Rooney said, as if he expected her to applaud.

She remained with Rooney for two more hours. Back in his office, he talked on and on. She knew he was running everything by her, for no other reason than that he wanted to run it all by himself. She let him ramble on with barely an interruption and wondered if at the end of all this he was going to book her. Then came: 'You ever think about that kid? The one you took out?'

She turned away. She didn't think of him, and she suddenly felt guilty. But Rooney continued, 'You were good, you know. I wish I had someone here with your dedication. If you'd not got on the bottle, you'd be somewhere now. A lot go the same way – well, not quite as low as you. You hit the skids, didn't you? Worked the streets?'

'Yes. Look – can I go?' She stood up.

'No, you can't. Fucking sit down.'

She sat down, and then he blew her away. 'I want you to do something for me.'

She stared.

'Make you a deal.' He picked up the charge sheets between finger and thumb and dangled them. 'See what you can come up with for me. Ask around the whorehouses, the—'

'You kidding me?'

He shook his head, his voice suddenly low and unpleasant. 'No, I'm not kidding. The deal is I'll clear these,' he indicated the long list of charges, '*if* you help me out. Somebody's got to know these hookers, somebody's got to know something, maybe where Murphy's hiding out. We're trying to trace Helen Murphy's husband but so far no joy and I doubt if it's him. If you find anything, any link, you got a clean sheet.'

Lorraine laughed. 'I got a job, Bill.'

He leaned closer to her, and she could smell his stale breath. 'This is not a job, sweetheart, this is a deal. You get a clean slate for helping me out or I'll bust you.'

'Then I'll need a car—'

'Fuck off, Lorraine! Look at this. You've been charged on eight counts for driving without a licence, without insurance and under the influence. No way can I get that cleared. The other stuff, yes – the no-show for court appearances, prostitution.'

'What about expenses?'

He laughed, shaking his head. 'You sure try it on.'

'I got to eat, pay rent. I walk out of my job, and—'

He sneered, 'Do what you did before, Lorraine, sell your little ass—'

She leaned over the desk. 'Screw you. Take those charges and shove them up your ass – it's big enough to take the entire filing cabinet.'

He roared with laughter and slapped the desk with his hand. 'Okay. Fifty bucks.'

'A day?'

'A week.'

'Fuck off. I know how much you pay informers, I also know you'll have a nice little stash that you'll divvy out between you and your pals at the end of each month, filling in fictional names and places. I know, Billy. Fifty bucks a day. I can go on the streets, into the bars, the clubs. I'll find someone with information. Like you said, I was good.'

Rooney got up and crossed to his window. He stood playing with the blind. 'How long you been sober?'

'I told you, a year. Call my husband, he'll tell you. Call my room-mate, she'll tell you. I'm straight, Bill.'

He picked at his nose – it was a habit. No wonder it was always so red, Lorraine thought.

'You'll call in every day?'

'I'll call in on the hour, if that's what you want.'

'Yeah, it is,' he said quietly, and opened his wallet.

Lorraine couldn't believe it: he was going to pay her there and then. 'Is there any way I can get copies of the statements you got to date?'

Rooney nodded, counting out a hundred bucks. 'This is it, Lorraine, and believe me when I say I'll have you brought back in here so fast if you mess me around. I need information.'

'I'll also need photographs – everything you got so far.'

Rooney looked at her, suddenly uncertain.

'I got to know what's going on, Bill.'

'Yeah. I guess you do.'

Rooney watched Lorraine walk out of the building and flag down a taxi before he let the blind flip back into place. He told himself he must be nuts, especially as he'd not even got her to sign for the cash. Added to that, he'd handed over copies of the case files. He had a moment of blind panic: if she was to take it to the press he'd be screwed to the floor. Then he relaxed; he was almost nailed there already. He checked the time and put in a call to Andrew Fellows.

'Ah, Captain, I'm so sorry not to have got back to you since you gave me this new stuff on Hastings. Reason is, I've not had too much spare time, I'm on a lecture tour.'

'I'd appreciate your input as soon as possible,' Rooney rumbled.

'I'll get back to you soon as I've got a moment to go over the file, but I'm up to my ears right now.'

Rooney listened to the drawling voice, half smiling at the 'ears' line, waiting for what he suspected was coming. It came.

'I don't suppose there's some way you could finance me, is there? Only it does take up a considerable amount of my time.'

Rooney said he would run it by his chief and dropped the phone back on the hook. The chief would, no doubt, arrange payment – it had been his idea to bring Fellows on board, so let *him* budget for him. Rooney was stretched and he was not about to pay Fellows out of his own pocket, not like Lorraine.

He remembered finding her on the floor in the old precinct, looking into her face in the patrol car when he held that poor kid's Sony Walkman under her nose. She'd given that half-dazed smile. He remembered that moment now. That kid would've been alive if it wasn't for that bitch. He wanted to be deeply angry, but he couldn't, and it confused him. She had to be pretty tough to have survived, to have got herself back together. At least he hoped she was: that she wasn't right that moment walking into a bar with his case file in one hand and his cash in the other. If she was, then he would make sure, no matter what else he did, that she paid a high price.

Lorraine read through the files all night. Her concentration blanked out Rosie and her television shows. When Rosie went to bed, Lorraine continued working, sifting through every statement, studying each photograph, jotting down notes. It was four in the morning when she stretched and got up. She had sat with her legs tightly crossed, just the way she had when she was working in the old days. She massaged her thighs, easing out the cramp, then sat staring into space. Rooney was right, they had nothing: no witnesses but herself. If only he knew! Lorraine had seen the killer – had almost gone down on him, had almost got herself killed. And she also had a clear memory of the killer's cufflinks. She wondered if Norman Hastings had ever bought or owned a reconditioned vintage car. From what she had read so far, she doubted it – but, then, everyone had been wrong about him being the perfect family man.

Lorraine didn't go to bed until almost five, and by then she was so wired up she was unable to fall asleep. The sofa bed was uncomfortable and too soft, her back ached and her legs still felt as if they were going to cramp up. She was in the half-dream state when suddenly she had a vivid image of the boy. She saw him running, saw the flash of the Superman striped jacket.

'Freeze!

She sat up, wide awake now. She didn't want to see him, didn't want to see herself, didn't want to see the boy's jerking body as the bullets tore into him. She flipped over the sheet, got up and drew back the curtains. She forced herself to think about the murderer, remembering exactly where he had picked her up. Was he local? Somehow she doubted it – he was too flashy, too well dressed. Again, Murphy, the only suspect, did not tie in. Lorraine closed her eyes and visualized his face: the rimless, gold-framed glasses, the blue close-set eyes, the sharp nose and the wide, wet, thick-lipped mouth. She conjured up a picture of his hands, went over exactly what he had said, how he had picked her up, how he had reached into the glove compartment. She wasn't scared, she just let the killer move into her mind. And just as she had done with the Laura Bradley murder, she repeated to herself, over and over again, her voice a soft whisper: 'I'll get you.'

CHAPTER 9

ROSIE WAS so immersed in the horror of the statements and pictures she didn't hear Lorraine walking into the bedroom.

'That was private, Rosie, you shouldn't be reading it.'

Rosie looked up and hunched her shoulders apologetically. 'It's those mortuary shots that get me – really close up, aren't they? I didn't know you looked like that when you were dead, how they can clean them up . . .' She held up Helen Murphy's photograph. 'This is her when they found her, and this is her at the morgue and this is her – I mean, she looks like she's sleeping.'

Lorraine walked into the bathroom. 'They had her face fixed up with plaster for an ID. Made-up, that's all. The only suspect they got is her husband, a trucker, but they're way off, he's not the killer.'

Rosie shut the file. 'I doubt if anyone'll grieve over these women, they look like they're all pretty shot up – in fact some of them look happier dead, know what I mean? Well, not the little blonde girl, she's sort of cute.'

Lorraine leaned on the bathroom door. 'Yeah. She doesn't fit in, does she? All the others are older, worn out, hard . . .'

'You know what I think?' Rosie licked her lips. 'I think he picked *you* up. You were hit on the back of the head but somehow you got away from him. The taxi brought you back here and . . . I remembered it was the seventeenth of last month.' Then she shrugged her heavy shoulders. 'It couldn't have been you, though, could it?'

'Why not?'

'Because that was the day Norman Whatcha-call-it was done – they found him in his own car, right? So he wouldn't have been whacking you over the head and killing somebody else, would he?'

'I fell on the pavement, Rosie.'

'Yeah – and I'm Sharon Stone's lookalike.'

Lorraine walked into the shower and pulled the curtain round her. Rosie surprised her – not that she had said anything intelligent, or especially intuitive even: Lorraine had been cracked over the back of the head in exactly the same manner as described not once but eight times in the files. But it was the simple dismissal of the possibility that the man could have killed Hastings and then an hour later attempted to kill again. Lorraine made a mental note to check through the exact times and dates of each murder.

Lorraine felt tired, but a good sort of tired. She'd worked hard last night just assimilating all the evidence and, although she didn't like to admit it, she had liked chatting over it with Rosie. That's what had surprised her: that she had, for a few brief minutes, felt like a player again. 'Marking out the jigsaw' was the way she used to describe it to Mike.

The water jets sprayed into her uptilted face. Mike and she had talked over her cases to begin with, but gradually he'd become uninterested, telling her that he didn't want to hear about the whores or the details of the murders, he had to study. She had no one to talk it out of her system with: she had just bottled it all up inside.

She gasped, turned the taps to cold. She didn't want *him* to come back into her life, not now, please not Lubrinski, she couldn't deal with him. It had been Lubrinski who realized she was bottling up all the horror, anger, disgust. It had been Lubrinski after a particular heavy night when

190

they had found two teenagers in a boarding house, stiff from death, stiff from drugs, stiff and stinking, but they were so beautiful, like frozen angels the pair of them, who had insisted they go to a bar, insisted they get smashed. And drunk she had suddenly broken down and Lubrinski had gripped her tightly, had even cried with her as he said it was okay to let go, to let the poison out, rather than have it seething inside her. Lubrinski.

Rosie was eating muffins with a jam smear across her cheek and also over the file, which Lorraine promptly snatched away from her. 'You don't get it sticky with jam!'

Rosie washed her hands in a great display, and then returned to reading the files and statements. 'This Andrew Fellows is something else, isn't he? You read what he came up with about Helen thingy? The killer really likes them in bad shape, doesn't he?'

Lorraine couldn't help but be drawn in. 'Apart from Holly.'

'Oh, yeah. Well, maybe he just got lucky that night.'

Lorraine dressed and made up her face. When she came back into the room Rosie was still engrossed in the files.

'Could you borrow that car from Jake's friend?'

'What do you need a car for?'

'I need to go to Santa Monica. A bit of investigation work. Maybe you could help me.'

Rosie's face lit up. 'Do I get paid?'

'Yeah, you'll get paid, Rosie.'

They eventually found 'W-rent W-rent Wreckers' where Lorraine had to pay a hundred bucks down in case there were any further dents to the Mustang. The man was not overly interested in the licence Rosie waved at him, but the car cost fifty bucks for a week, plus gas, with the hundred-buck deposit. Rosie drew a diagram of all the dents to avoid them being conned on their return, and in a cloud of exhaust fumes, bangs, and the engine clacking at an alarming rate, they bombed out of the yard.

The roof was down – it could not go up – and as it was a bright clear day, Lorraine rested back on the torn seat and considered how they – she, she corrected herself – would go about interviewing the men working at the vintage car garage in Santa Monica. All she wanted to know was if they sold cufflinks; if so, how many, and how many men they employed. And she needed to know if they had someone fitting the description of the killer. With Rosie at the wheel, Lorraine relaxed for the journey, as much as Rosie's driving style would allow: she was an incurable horn tooter, thrusting an abusive finger up to anyone who cut her up. Yet, and again Lorraine found herself surprised, she was a competent driver, even if she did cut across lanes. But she did it so positively that it didn't make Lorraine nervous.

Rosie sighed as they turned into yet another road, Lorraine shaking her head. She simply could not remember where the place was, or which route the cab driver had taken. She knew they were close, but she didn't want to ask directions. Instead she told Rosie to drive to Mike's address: maybe she would recognize landmarks, and as Mike's house was along the shore, she was confident she'd be able to direct Rosie from there.

With a screech of tyres Rosie did a U-turn and headed for the beach.

'Keep going, we're almost at Mike's house now.' They drove on until she spotted the house. She hadn't meant Rosie to stop, especially not so close, but she jammed on the brakes hard. Lorraine felt the confidence draining from her. 'That's it, just across the street.'

Rosie peered over the road. 'Very nice. Worth a few dollars.'

'Just drive on, Rosie.'

'But you don't know where we're going!'

'Just drive, will you? I don't want him to see me.' As they set off, Lorraine tried to concentrate on the road ahead. But all she could think of was Mike and the girls. She closed her eyes, and then jerked forward as Rosie hit the brakes again.

'You're not even looking, for chrissakes! We carry on at this rate and we'll run out of gas.'

Lorraine yanked open the door and got out of the car.

Rosie sighed heavily. 'We lost again?'

Lorraine didn't answer, but walked over to the railing and stood looking out to the ocean. Rosie sat in the car for a few moments, then joined Lorraine. 'You okay?'

'Not too good, Rosie.'

They stood side by side, like something out of a comedy duo: one so tall and slim, the other so round. A female Laurel and Hardy, but nothing was funny.

'I've lost my girls, Rosie, I know that. It wouldn't be right for me to see them. They're happy, settled, they call her Mom. They've forgotten me – but, then, I wasn't really worth remembering.'

'Don't say that. Everything's worth remembering, the good and the bad, and things *are* gonna get good for you. You never know, maybe next time you see them it won't be so bad.'

'You think so?'

'I know so.'

Lorraine looked down into the plump, concerned face. 'You're the eternal optimist, aren't you?'

'Yep. That's why I got myself so together.'

Lorraine slipped her arms round her, gave her a squeeze. 'I'm glad I found you, Rosie.'

'Me too,' Rosie said.

Lorraine released her and turned to face the road. She remembered the cab took a right at the next junction. 'Okay, let's go. I think I know the way.'

'You sure you want to do this?'

Lorraine threw up her hands in frustration. 'Why do you think we came here? Now get in the car, I've been working out exactly what I want to say. I'll draw a picture of a cufflink and you show it to the salesman. You say your husband has lost one, and you want to replace it – are you listening? Left, take a left here!'

Five miles later they pulled up in the forecourt of the building next to the vintage car showroom. Rosie got out carrying the sketch, and armed with the questions she had repeated four times to Lorraine.

Lorraine watched her disappear as she passed between the cars on display on the forecourt. When she slid up to sit on the back of her seat, she could see Rosie inside the big glass-fronted showroom, waiting at the long mahogany counter. Then she lost her as Rosie accompanied a man to the far end of the showroom. Lorraine dropped back into her seat, and lit a cigarette, never taking her eyes off the showroom entrance. Had she asked too much of Rosie? She was about to go in after her when she appeared.

'Christ, what have you been doing? Do you know how long you were in there?'

'Sorry, but the guy never stopped talkin'. You want the good news?'

'Yeah, yeah. Come on, tell me.'

'Okay. They sell the cufflinks, or they used to. They were originally part of a promotional thing, started in 1990. You know, spend hundred and eighty-five thousand dollars on a vintage car and they'll throw in a set of cufflinks.'

'Shit!' Lorraine hit the dashboard with her fist. But Rosie wasn't through. She had the number of workers, fifty-eight in all, each of whom had been given cufflinks with their Christmas bonus. Around two hundred and fifty sets had been made up – that was the bad news. Further good news was that the first batch had been made in cheap silver, which had proved so popular that they had had a second batch made. These had been handed out last Christmas –

and only to their executives, the difference being that these were made in nine carat gold. Rosie beamed. 'There's a board showing the top salesmen and the directors, listing their offices, so I presumed they'd be the executives, right? Eight in all.' She fished around in her purse and dragged out a dog-eared Mickey Mouse notepad and a felt tip pen. She sucked the end and then scribbled down as many as she could remember. Lorraine watched in astonishment. Rosie chuckled as she underlined the last name: she'd remembered all eight, even their titles.

'I always win every time! Those game shows where they show you a sort of runner thing with articles and you gotta remember each one! Now, were the links you saw gold or silver?'

Lorraine couldn't remember. 'You see anyone with blondish hair, rimless glasses, wide wet mouth?'

'Nope. The guy was short and fat and looked like he got a sack of potatoes in the back of his pants . . .'

Lorraine grinned, and then looked over the list of names, wondering about her next move. Fifty-eight workers, all with cufflinks, eight executives all with gold ones – and a few hundred vintage car owners with God knew how many more.

'He also said that the silver ones were crap and most of them broke after a few outings. He gave me a set for free.'

Rosie revealed the box and Lorraine snatched it from her. She opened it and knew at a glance that the man who attacked her had worn gold cufflinks. She snapped it closed. 'Rosie, you are a fuckin' marvel!'

Eight names, eight men with gold cufflinks. Now she would work on eliminating each one. She knew she had to be careful: if she confronted her attacker she could be in danger. At the same time she had to be sure; if she gave Rooney bum information he could arrest her, charge her, and have her locked up. She wouldn't put it past him because he had brought up the shooting incident. It must still sit heavy on him, maybe he felt the guilt he wanted her to feel. Lorraine knew she couldn't make any mistakes – there was too much at stake.

CHAPTER 10

THE FOLLOWING morning Lorraine could not summon any energy and had no idea how to progress, so at eight o'clock she took herself off to Fit 'N' Fast.

'I just feel so tired all the time,' she complained to Hector.

He shrugged. 'Bound to feel that way, you've punished the hell out of your body for years, right? You can't suddenly force it into feeling fit. Nothing happens overnight, it takes time and dedication.' He agreed to make out a diet and a tough work-out programme for every other day, including weights, a strict high-carb diet, and a high-protein drink. Armed with a boxful of new vitamins, Lorraine went home.

Rosie looked over the array of cans and pills, and the charts Lorraine was pinning up. 'I'd join you, but I've got a built-in resistance to all of this kind of stuff.'

Lorraine laughed. 'Well, you're so full of energy you don't need it. Do you have a camera?'

'It's in the pawn shop – been there about seven months.'

'Can I get it out?'

'I dunno where the ticket is, and it'll cost a few dollars. It's a very expensive model.' Rosie started sifting through her papers and eventually found the pawn ticket: there was a hundred and fifty dollars to pay. Lorraine wondered if she could buy a cheap camera instead.

'Has it got a zoom lens?'

'I dunno, there's all kinds of attachments for it. I never used it so I dunno what it's got.'

'Okay, go get it, I'll wait here for you. You'd better take this – it's the last of my stash.'

Rosie departed, moaning about being used as a gofer but when Lorraine asked if she had anything better to do, she said, 'I guess not but why do you need it?'

'To take photographs.'

Lorraine worked through the telephone directory, matching the names on Rosie's list. She called each one, checked if they worked at the garage, and slowly narrowed down all the wrong numbers. She was still busy when Rosie returned two hours later.

The camera was a professional fast-slide action with zoom lens. Rosie watched in fascination as Lorraine quickly checked over all the accessories, testing out the viewfinder, attaching the different lenses and grinning in triumph because it even had a laser night shutter: she could photograph at night.

'How come you know so much about cameras?' she asked.

'Part of my job. On surveillance we used high-tech equipment and I went on a couple of courses—'

The phone rang. It was Rooney. 'You out on the streets? What you doing?'

'Gimme time, for chrissakes. Like I said, as soon as I have anything, I'll be in touch. One thing, this Fellows guy, can I get in touch with him?'

'Why?'

Lorraine could hear his chesty breathing down the phone. 'Just like to talk to him. I won't if you don't want me to.'

'Maybe stay away from him, okay?' Rooney said flatly. 'Call me. I need anything you can come up with.'

Rooney hung up. Why did she want to talk to Fellows? He remembered how intuitive she was. Perhaps she'd come across something he'd missed – or was she just ripping him off?

Bean reminded him that the second shift team were waiting for the morning's briefing. Rooney slowly stood up. 'Be right with you.'

Bean joined the men in the incident room. When he saw Chief Michael Berillo pass, he hoped he wasn't going to see Rooney, as that meant keeping everyone waiting, but Rooney appeared right behind the Chief.

He snapped out orders to his men to begin spreading their inquiries to drag clubs and transvestite hang-outs. 'I want everyone, and this is priority, to check out Norman Hastings's contacts. Hastings is our main link to the killer because out of all the murders he's the odd man.'

There was a loud guffaw, and when Rooney saw the funny side, he snorted. He also divulged that he now had a reliable informant working on the streets, who he hoped would soon bring in some information.

The Chief hitched up his pants, and jerked his head for Rooney to follow him to his office. 'Who's your informant?'

'She's a hooker, been arrested a number of times, she owes me a favour. She's asking round the street girls, the pimps. Some of them won't talk to us, so she'll be useful.'

The Chief nodded. 'That's it then, is it?'

Rooney attempted to bluff his way out, saying there'd been the breakthrough with Mrs Hastings. 'Not enough, Bill. I can't let this continue, I'm under pressure, I've had the Mayor on to me, City Hall. I need an arrest, Bill. There's seven fucking women dead.'

The desk phone rang. The Chief picked it up. He listened and scribbled on a notepad which he passed to Rooney.

'They just got Brendan Murphy, bringing him across State today.' He underlined the word State three times, his face darkening, and then he repeated the name 'Bickerstaff', and put the phone down.

'Good news, they picked up Murphy, your number one suspect. Bad news is it's now FBI business as they've had to get the documents to bring him back to us. He's in Detroit. Looks like you're gonna have to hand over the entire inquiry to a guy called Ed Bickerstaff, you know him?' Rooney swore under his breath. 'I don't like it but I've no option. I've even been asked if you're capable of controlling the case. I've gone out on a limb for you, especially as I know you'll be retiring soon. Bill, if you don't pull the stops out, you'll be taking retirement even earlier than you anticipated.'

Back in his office, Rooney opened a fresh bottle of bourbon and poured himself six fingers, downing it in one gulp before he repeated the dose. Not until his third hit did he relax and begin to think straight. What possibilities had he missed, or glossed over? The FBI would go through everything with a fine-tooth comb. It pissed him off, even more so as he was sure Brendan Murphy was not their man. He rubbed his chin. This was the most complicated inquiry he had ever been on and he was nowhere. He had so little that he was almost depending on that whore Lorraine Page to come up with something. He reached for the phone to call her again. There was no reply.

Lorraine sat with Rosie in the car outside the address of Suspect One from the S and A garage, a Sydney Field. When he pulled up outside his house, Rosie got out and asked if he was a Mr Sam Field. He shook his head. She carried a clipboard. 'I'm doing some market research, Mr Field. Do you work in computers?'

'No.' He was surly.

'But you are Mr Sam Field, aren't you?'

'No, Sydney Field. I'm a mechanic, you got the wrong man.' Rosie turned to leave and gave an almost imperceptible nod to Lorraine, who took two photographs. They spent the rest of the evening checking five more names listed from the vintage car garage. It had been a long, tedious afternoon and an even longer night. Six down, two more to go, and Lorraine had not yet seen the man who had attacked her.

The cost of the car rental and payment to get the camera out of hock meant she was already out of pocket, so the next morning she called Rooney. 'I need some more money, Bill.'

'Give me something first,' he snapped.

'I'm checking somethin' out. I'll have it by the end of the day.'

'Drop by, I'll give you a hundred bucks but this is out of my pocket and I'll be out of here in forty-eight hours. FBI taking over.'

'I'd prefer if we didn't meet at the station.'

He swore and then agreed to see her near his Indian restaurant.

Lorraine replaced the receiver and turned, knowing Rosie had overheard.

'What's going on?' Rosie asked.

'Just trying to get us some more cash.'

Lorraine chewed her lips. 'I'm doing this work for an old cop friend, that's all.'

'That why we're taking photographs?'

Lorraine had underestimated Rosie's dogged persistence. 'This cop, he wouldn't be the one you saw outside the gallery? Captain Rooney? Only he's on these murders, isn't he?'

Lorraine made no answer. It'd be dark soon and if they

201

were to make the most of what daylight remained they'd better leave.

They drove into the outskirts of Beverly Hills and parked outside a neat row of bungalows on Ashdown Road, a heavily gay area. Men were already parading up and down or gathering on street corners talking. A blonde woman was tap-dancing on a small square piece of cardboard, tap-tapping away, her flowered hat on the pavement beside her.

A car drew up and Rosie got out with her clipboard. Lorraine suddenly felt the adrenalin pumping. She knew he was not the man, which left only one to go. Who had to be the man, if – *if* – she was right.

Rosie returned to the car, smiling. 'This is better than sticking down goddamned envelopes. Where to next?'

The final address was on the other side of town, on Beverly Glen. With a screech of tyres, Rosie took a sharp right, directly across the traffic.

'Bastards, it's my right of way!' Lorraine clung to the side of the car as Rosie swerved across the road, and steered onto Sunset Boulevard. She peered over to Lorraine. 'You sure we're on the guy? This is movie-star territory.'

'Yeah, it's off to the right.'

They drove past the Bel Air Gates and took a left onto Beverly Glen. They headed up the winding road, passing the signposts to the Bel Air Hotel. Rosie veered from one side of the road to the other as she glimpsed the magnificent properties on either side of them.

Eventually she pulled up outside a secluded, three-storey house, surrounded by a high wall, a barred gate, and signs warning of guard dogs and electric fences. It was here that Steven Janklow lived, the last name on the list. Rosie got out and crossed the road to look through the gates. A Buick was parked in the drive, alongside an old Mercedes SL 180. She rang the intercom bell at the side of the huge gate. 'Hi,

202

I am doing market research into computer users and we have a query for a Michael Janklow. Could I please speak to him a moment?'

The phone went dead. Rosie rang again and repeated as much of her rehearsed speech as she could before the phone went dead again. A gardener tending the well-kept lawns walked towards the gates. Rosie smiled and waved at him. 'Can you gimme a minute?'

He didn't speak very good English, so she had to ask two or three times if a Michael Janklow was at home.

'No, no, his name not Michael.'

'Does he work in computers?'

'No, he work in big garage, you have wrong man, go away.'

Rosie returned to the car. 'I think he's the last guy.' She repeated what the gardener had said and gave the car registration numbers.

They waited over an hour but only saw the gardener drive out in an old truck, the gates closing automatically behind him. Then they saw a German shepherd dog sniffing and prowling around inside the gates.

Lorraine told Rosie to go home and that they would come back early next morning. She didn't want Rooney to meet Rosie and it was nearly time for their appointment. She made the excuse that she wanted to work out, so Rosie dropped her off at Fit 'N' Fast.

Fifteen minutes later Rooney arrived. 'What you got for me?' he asked as soon as Lorraine had got into the car.

She hesitated. 'Well, I've been questioning a lot of the hookers. So far nothing much but a couple of them remembered a guy picking them up, real edgy, and I'm trying to find Holly's pimp to see if he can help. You got anything on a vintage car garage, Santa Monica?' She talked about one of the girls seeing the cufflinks, that she, herself, had discovered that fifty odd workers might have a pair. 'What I'm doing is narrowing it all down, taking shots of the workers, taking them round to the girls. It might be your man, then again it might not. It's costing, though, I had to get a good camera and I gotta pay a friend to drive me around, hire a car.'

Rooney took out his wallet. Lorraine leaned closer. 'I'd like to talk to this profiler guy. Can't you swing it for me?'

'Why do you want to see him?'

Lorraine ran her hands through her hair. 'Maybe I just want to talk to him. I was always good at piecing jigsaws together and he sounds like he knows what he's talking about.'

He folded a hundred and fifty dollars and passed it to her. 'Take it, but I want those photographs, and in the meantime I'll do a quiet check on the men who work at this garage, see if there's anyone with a record.'

'Do it quietly, Bill. If your man works there, you don't want to tip him off.'

He grunted.

'I'll call you.' She had her hand on the door handle.

Rooney hesitated, and then muttered grudgingly, 'I'll give this Fellows a call. You can see him if he agrees. I'm up against it. Anything, Lorraine, anything, for chrissakes get it to me fast, you know what snot-nosed bastards those FBI agents are.'

She got out of the car and he watched her walking down the street, long legs, tight ass. All the guys had tried to get into her pants but she had never, to Rooney's knowledge, got it on with anyone of the old team. It pissed them all off that she refused to have a scene with any of them and they had made her life as unpleasant as possible. To her credit she had treated it as a joke, but then she had always been tough.

'You got any complaints?' Rooney had asked.

'No, no complaints,' she had said, quietly and firmly. She never complained or put any man on the line, even when she found out they were having free fucks from the hookers.

204

She was so tough no one would have believed she would plummet out of control. Rooney wondered now just how long she had hidden her drinking. He had liked Lorraine, admired her tenacity. She had proved her guts too. As he drove Rooney remembered how he and his partner had been called out to an affray in a down-town bar. Neither was prepared to confront the young Mexican holding a waitress by the throat. He'd already knifed two men, everyone was hysterical, and crowds were gathering on the pavement outside.

Rooney called for back-up which arrived in the shape of the young rookie Page, and her beer-gut partner, Brian Dullay. Dullay waddled over to Rooney, bellowing for an update. Suddenly there was a single terrible scream from inside the bar. They needed a decoy: someone to go in the front, distract the Mexican, so they could unarm him from behind. No fucking way, Dullay said. Just as Rooney was about to order him inside, Lorraine stepped forward. 'I'll do it. We can't leave that girl in there.'

While Dullay and Rooney's partner headed for the escape at the back, Lorraine opened the door to the bar. The terrified girl was held by the deranged barman, a knife already cutting through her neck, blood streaming down her dress. Her legs were buckled, she had pissed in her pants with terror, and her face was stricken, frozen, her mouth open wide.

Lorraine walked in holding her hands above her head. 'I'm alone, Roberto, just let her go and you and me can talk.'

The man pushed the girl down to the floor and stamped on her head, holding her firm with his foot. He grinned crazily as he lifted the knife. 'It's too late, no talk now, no more talk.'

Lorraine held her gaze, never flinching when he switched the knife from his right to his left hand. Then he snatched a gun from his belt and pointed it at her. She stood still, without taking her eyes off him. 'It's never too late to talk. Why don't you tell me what's been going on?'

'They kick me out my place, they take my kids, they got no right to do that, I work hard, I pay my taxes, they got no right, I been to the right people, weeks I been goin' an' they say it's okay, nobody can take your place, but they—'

Rooney fired first, then Dullay. The bullet blew the back of the Mexican's skull apart, his blood and brains splattering Lorraine, his body falling over the sobbing waitress.

The girl clung to Lorraine. Even when the ambulance came she wouldn't let go, so Lorraine sat with her until the sedatives took effect then slowly stepped out of the ambulance.

Rooney was talking to Dullay as Lorraine approached him. 'There was no need to kill him,' she said flatly.

Rooney had glared at her. 'He would have used this. You got a complaint?' He had shoved the dead Mexican's gun under her nose.

'No,' she said quietly. 'No complaint.'

Rooney was still thinking about her when he let himself into his home an hour later. He remembered Lubrinski. He was sure there had been something going on between them. They were real close, used to drink together after duty. Thinking of the dark, handsome officer Rooney felt sad. He was one of the best he'd ever come across, bit of a loner but a real man's man. When Rooney had partnered Lorraine with him, he had expected fireworks but instead she and Lubrinski had formed one of the strongest teams he'd ever had. He wished he had a twosome like them with him now but they only come once in a blue moon. Page and Lubrinski, chalk and cheese and yet . . .

Lorraine kept on walking after seeing Rooney. Then she took a bus to Sunset and set off towards the hookers' hangouts and on until she got to the gay quarter. She stopped outside a coffee bar with a few tables planted on the dirty street. She was looking for Nula or Didi but couldn't find them so asked around for Curtis and was told he would be in the Bar Q further along the stretch. The bar was dark, with music so loud it was deafening. There were only a few customers dotted around, none Lorraine knew, so she sat at the bar and ordered a Coke.

'How you doing?' smiled the black bartender. 'Not seen you in a long while.'

Lorraine grinned. 'Is Curtis out back?'

'Yeah, he's got a game going.'

Lorraine could see a few men in the small pool room. She strolled in and stood sipping the Coke, watching Curtis play with three other dudes in snazzy suits and flash ties. Printed silk was the rage among pimps, reminiscent of Micky Spillane. She knew better than to interrupt, but Curtis looked up suddenly. 'You want me, sugar?'

'When you got a second.'

Curtis chalked his cue. As she moved away, he asked one of the players, 'Who's that?'

The man couldn't put a name to the face. Curtis continued the game.

Lorraine went back to the bar and ordered another Coke. A few more customers had drifted in and a bleached blonde with heavy breasts was perched on an end stool, talking to a boy in leathers. She was all of forty, her tight leather skirt up round her crotch. He leaned forward as if hanging on her every word but his eyes were focused on her deep cleavage. Her breasts were pushed up by a wired bra and burst through the clinging Lycra. Lorraine was almost amused to watch the old pro at work. Every move was sexual – she didn't even reach for her drink without the carefully orchestrated swing of her hips, or opening her legs further, constantly touching her breasts, and licking her thickly painted lips. The boy moved closer, desperate to touch her, and Lorraine waited, knew Blondie would talk money any second. Sure enough, she saw her whisper, then lean back, resting her elbows on the bar, and the boy was hooked.

He passed some bills and the come-on act dropped. Blondie downed her drink, slid off the stool and, arm in arm, they walked out. Lorraine reckoned she'd have a room in one of the motels close by and that the boy was probably a college kid high on grass and desperate to get his rocks off. Well, he would, but he would probably not have reckoned on it being so fast.

Curtis leaned on the bar next to Lorraine. He ordered a beer.

'You know some friends of mine, Didi and Nula. I'm lookin' for them, but they're not on the strip,' she said.

'Bit early for them. What do you want?'

'I'm a friend of Art's.'

'You want some videos?'

'Maybe.'

Curtis suddenly moved close to Lorraine. 'So you know Didi and Nula.' He stripped her with his eyes, then focused on her crotch. 'But you're not one of them. You want to turn a few tricks?' he asked casually, as if offering her a drink.

'No, I want to see them and I don't like goin' to their place in case I interrupt a session.'

Curtis tilted his head back and laughed. 'Not party to that, girlie, not with kids, not my scene.'

Lorraine smiled back. He was relaxing, trusting her, and even more so when a skinny black hooker, Elsa, breezed in and saw Lorraine.

'Hey, how you doin'?' she screamed across the bar, then wiggled over and slipped her arms around Lorraine. 'Long time no see, an' you cleaned yerself up. Baby, you're lookin' great.'

Lorraine was entwined in strong skinny arms and the thick black curly wig tickled her face as Elsa kissed her on

208

the lips. Curtis looked on, as Elsa, still clasping Lorraine tightly, told him how many good times the two of them had had together. She traced the scar on Lorraine's face with her thumb, its long, hooked, bright-red nail like a claw. 'Oh, Jesus, do I remember that night.'

'More than I do,' said Lorraine.

The barman summoned Curtis to take a call and Elsa perched on a stool next to Lorraine. 'So, what you been doin', sugar? I thought maybe you were dead.'

'No, I'm alive. You want a drink?'

'Sure, Coke an' bourbon, if you're buyin'.'

They carried their drinks to a booth, but Elsa's attention flitted constantly to the entrance, waiting for a customer.

'Did you know Holly?'

'Sure, sweet kid, one of Curtis's. He's been cut up bad about it.'

Lorraine led the conversation round to which was Holly's pitch but Elsa couldn't remember: she moved about because some of the girls could get nasty and they reckoned Holly was hedging in on their territory. Curtis was small fry: he only had a few girls and was too weak to get heavy with any of the other pimps. He mostly had trannies because nobody else wanted them – trannies and a few young chicks that he screwed more than any john. Holly was his girl.

'The night she died, did you see her at all?'

'Nah, I was in the Long Down Motel. I got a room there now.'

Lorraine tried to ask as much as she could about Holly without it sounding suspicious but Elsa would only say that on the night of the murder, it had been real slow for business and any john was picked up fast. 'You get good nights and bad nights.'

'Yeah,' murmured Lorraine, but then Curtis returned and Elsa moved off to a prospective client.

He leaned on the back of the booth. 'You still want

videos? I can maybe get some in a couple of hours, I got business right now. Come back later.' The barman waved him over to take another call. Curtis did his video and drug trade in the bars, just small stuff. His girls made the drops for him. Lorraine gave him an uneasy feeling. He watched her walking out. He didn't believe the line she'd fed him about wanting a porno video.

'Elsa!' She sauntered across and Curtis covered the phone. 'Who was the blonde?'

Elsa looked back to her john, and scratched the front of her wig. 'Hooker, used to hang round the pool halls, did a few tricks with her way back. She was something else, man, a real sleaze lady, but boozed out – Lorraine. We called her Lazy Lorraine. She'd never score a john, just waited until she was so smashed she wouldn't have known if she had one or not. She went with some weirdos, didn't give a fuck.' She hesitated a moment and then leaned closer. 'Maybe don't trust her too much, okay?'

Curtis gripped her wrist. 'What you mean?'

Elsa twisted free, pissed off because he'd hurt her. 'Word was she used to be a cop, that's all.'

Lorraine walked along the strip, stopped at two more bars and then spotted Nula paying off a cab. She called, Nula turned, was puzzled for a moment, and then recognized her.

'You got time for a drink?' Lorraine smiled.

'No, I just come on, I'm late.'

'How's Didi?'

Nula shrugged and they walked down the strip together. 'She's still got problems with her foot but she won't see a doctor – hates them.'

Lorraine asked again if she had time for a drink. Nula looked at her watch and agreed, but only a quickie. They went to a small coffee bar and sat with two espressos. Nula was edgy, constantly looking out at the strip.

'I wanted to ask you about the night Holly was murdered. A friend of mine was picked up by a real creep. He had wet slobbery lips, rimless glasses, quite middle America, not beat up . . . and she was uneasy about him. She figured she'd seen him the night Holly died – maybe it was him picked her up. Anyway, she did the business and got the hell out of his car.'

Nula stirred her coffee. 'Never saw nobody like that the night she got it. I tell you somethin' though. Didi, right, she was duckin' and divin', she sees the guy cruisin' down the road, right, she reckons she's scored but little Holly beat her to the punch.'

'Wait a minute. Are you telling me Didi saw Holly being picked up?'

'She said it was a guy in a sort of beige-coloured car.'

'Have you told anybody this?'

'No, why should I?'

'Because he might have been the guy who killed her.'

'Yeah, he might not. It was early, just after I come on, so . . .' Lorraine didn't like to push too hard. She started asking casual questions about how they worked it, the trannies and the straight chicks, but Nula wasn't interested.

'You think the john that picked up Holly might have been wanting Didi?'

'Jesus, I dunno. Why you askin' all these questions?'

Lorraine lit a cigarette. 'Just curious. Is Didi workin' tonight, then?'

Nula said she was at a motel with a regular, but she'd be around later. 'I gotta go. With Art gone, we're short of cash.' Nula rested her hands on the table. 'I said I'd not talk to you again because of Art. That was a bad thing you did, Art was a decent guy.'

'Come on, Nula, he was getting kids screwed. I saw the photographs, even saw Holly in a few of them.'

Nula leaned in close. 'How come you're so interested in Holly? What's she to you?'

211

'She's dead. Maybe I feel sorry for her – she was only seventeen.'

'So was I once! We had cops around – some fucker gave them a tip-off. We haven't done any photographic work for weeks – that's because of you, isn't it? You know, I been trying to place your face, like Didi says, we was at an AA meeting but . . . I don't trust you. Stay away from us.'

She walked out and Lorraine took the tab to the counter. As she turned to leave, she saw Curtis outside with Nula, who pointed to the coffee bar. Curtis pushed her, they seemed to be arguing, and then he turned to look in at the window. Lorraine saw the sign to the toilets and walked out. Curtis came in, asked for Lorraine and the waitress pointed.

Lorraine stood on the toilet seat. She heard the door creaking open, then footsteps and the other cubicle door pushed open. As there were just the two, she knew he would try the next door, and find her, but just as his footsteps stopped outside her door, the waitress walked in and told him to get out. Lorraine waited fifteen minutes before she eased open the door and peered into the coffee bar. Curtis was standing directly outside and there was no back exit, or none she could see, so she decided to front it out.

He turned fast when she came out. Suddenly his arm shot out and he grabbed her elbow. 'You askin' questions about Holly an' I wanna know why. What you askin' questions about my little baby for?'

She could see in his face he wasn't going to hurt her. He wasn't scared, just upset.

'What's it to you?' she asked.

'She was my girl.'

Lorraine pulled her arm free. 'Maybe for no reason but that I liked her.'

'You knew her?'

'Yeah, not well, but I knew her.' He made to move off.
'Curtis, wait a minute.'

He looked at her. 'I dunno what you want but stay away from here.'

She took a chance. 'Maybe I'm askin' for the cops.'

He stepped back fast, his face altered, his hands tightened into fists. Suddenly she knew that if they were alone he would hurt her, really hurt her.

'Not in the way you think, Curtis – come on, I was a hooker. All I'm doin' is feedin' back a bit of information, they got nothin' on her killer. Don't you want him caught? She was your girl, you just said so, she was beautiful, real beautiful, and—'

'She's dead, right, so fuck off.'

Curtis walked away and Lorraine followed. He turned into an alley and stopped. Now she no longer had the safety of other people around her.

'You got a fuckin' nerve, lady. Back off me.'

She stood four feet from him, far enough to keep out of range of a swinging fist. She held him in a steady gaze, not afraid, showing him she was on the level, letting him look at her.

'I'm bein' paid under the counter, fifty bucks. I'm not paid to do anythin' else, just see if there was anyone who saw her that night, saw the john that picked her up. I don't want to know anythin' else. Help me. Why don't you help me? Come on, man, she was your girl.'

Curtis leaned against the wall and, to her astonishment, started to cry. Lorraine moved closer. 'She was picked up last time you saw her near Didi and Nula's patch, that right?' He nodded. She asked if he had seen anything, asked why Holly had been working the transsexual patch. He sniffed, wiping his face with the back of his hand. 'She'd had a fight further up the strip, that's all I know. She'd had this fight and we'd been talkin', she said she wanted to move further down the strip, I was sortin' it for her. I never got to tell her I really cared—'

'Now's your chance to make it up to her, Curtis. If you hear anything, know anybody that saw anything, will you contact me?'

'I don't work for cops.'

'I'm not a cop.'

She made him write her telephone number on the back of his hand. Then he walked off down the alley.

Lorraine sighed. She was about to walk back the way she came when it hit her.

'Freeze.'

The boy ran on, his Superman stripe lit up in the neon lights.

'Freeze.'

He didn't turn because he hadn't even heard her, because it wasn't a gun in his hand but a Sony Walkman.

Sweat broke out all over her body. Her mouth felt dry and rancid. All she could think of was getting a drink. She started to run, back up the alley, along the strip, banging into passers-by, her whole body aching, her brain screaming for a drink. '*No, no, I won't, don't do it, don't do it, just keep walking, keep walking.*' A lethal, whispering voice repeated over and over, 'You killed the poor kid, he wasn't involved, you emptied your gun into a little kid's back. How does that make you feel, you drunken bitch? You killed him.'

Lorraine walked until the panic attack subsided. She sat on a wall, gasping for breath, waiting for her heart to slow down. She knew what she had done, but refused to face it. She had never faced it.

'You okay?' Didi limped towards her. 'You ran right past me like you'd seen a ghost.'

'I did. I was just running from a drink.'

Didi laughed, understanding. 'Well, if you're okay I guess I'd better get a move on.'

'No, please, I need to ask you something, about the night Holly died. *Please* just wait.'

Didi hobbled closer. 'Listen, I don't know nothin', I didn't see nothin' and I don't know why I'm talkin' to you. We had cops asking questions, we can't get a shoot together, we're broke, all down to you.'

Lorraine faced her out. 'I'm not a cop. I was once but so long ago even I can't remember it. I've been hookin' for years and drunk for as many, you know that.'

Didi pursed her lips. 'Once one, always one.'

Lorraine caught hold of Didi's sleeve. She gripped her hand, feeling the heavy ring on Didi's finger. 'Please just tell me about the guy. The one Nula said you saw. He picked her up right on your patch.'

'I don't remember nothin', not even that night, they're all the same to me.'

'Come on, Didi, it was the night you got beat up. Did you see the john that picked her up, see his car?'

Didi shrugged. 'Maybe. Nula's been talkin' to you, has she?'

'Yeah, and Curtis. They both want to help me, so please, just tell me what happened that night.'

Didi told Lorraine almost the same story as Nula – how the car had cruised down the road, stopped, driven on, how Holly had run across the road and got into the passenger seat.

'You think he really wanted maybe you or Nula?'

'If he did we're lucky then, aren't we?'

'Close your eyes and think, Didi. Was he dark, blond, balding? Think about him.'

Didi tried but her mind was blank.

'Did he wear glasses, kind of rimless, pinkish-lensed glasses?' Lorraine prompted.

'Yeah, yeah, maybe he did.'

'Was his mouth wide, wet? Did he have a crew-cut? Short-haired, blondish hair?'

'Yeah, yeah, that's right.'

'He never cruised by you before?'

'I remember anyone that's near to a regular, darlin'. I'd never seen this guy.'

Lorraine cocked her head to one side. 'You're not holding anythin' out on me, are you? You're not just saying, yeah, yeah, because that's what I said?'

'Why would I do that? He kind of fitted the description you said but it was a while ago. Listen, I knew Holly, and like everybody else round here, we'd like that piece of shit put away, right?'

'If you think of anything, will you call me?'

Didi nodded and limped off to earn her night's cash.

Lorraine arrived home to find a note from Rosie saying Rooney had called and she had gone to a meeting. Rooney was not at the station so she called his home. When she got through he sounded hoarser than ever, she could hear his heavy rasping breathing. 'You can go see Fellows now, he's expecting you – and I'm expecting somethin' soon for my dough, understand?'

Lorraine fixed some food, stuffed vitamins down herself and, a little refreshed, left the apartment.

Rosie, meanwhile, had returned to Janklow's house on Beverly Glen. At night it was easier to park and remain semi-hidden. She pulled out the camera, double-checked the instruction manual and then took a few practice shots. She heard a car come up the hill behind her and stop in front of the barred gates. It was the Mercedes. Crouching, Rosie inched up over the front seat. 'Come on, you bastard, get out of the car, lemme get a good shot.'

The driver opened the gates by remote control, never looking in Rosie's direction. She could see the glint of his glasses but nothing more – the top of his head was hidden by the roof of the car. The gates closed behind him as he drove up to the house. Rosie got out and, still carrying the camera and keeping close to the hedges, made her way cautiously towards the gates, hoping to get a second shot as he got out of the car to go into the house. She fiddled and muttered, the zoom lens was loose, and by the time she had it tightened the man was inside.

Rosie returned to the car. She'd tried, she told herself. As she turned on the ignition, the engine coughed and died. She tried again, it coughed, spluttered and then died again with a low, whirring sound. 'Oh, fuck it!' She tried another three times to start it but the ominous whirring sound grew fainter and she was miles away from the main road. She got out and started to walk.

The road she was in was badly lit, so she kept to the centre as much as possible. Two cars passed her going down the Glen and, even though she stuck out her thumb, they didn't stop. Her feet were aching and she was working up quite a sweat. She wished she'd locked the camera in the trunk; it was heavy and the strap cut into her shoulder.

When Rosie reached the main road, she was past caring about Janklow or anything else. She was hungry and it was getting chilly. She heard a car behind her and looked up to the traffic light. The 'Walk' sign was blinking and she reckoned she'd never make it across the wide road before it blinked off, so she hovered at the kerb. The Mercedes paused at the red light just as Rosie realized it was the car. She fumbled with the camera and made out she was taking a shot of the sign 'Hollywood Stars' Homes Maps Here'. She had the bonnet of the car in focus just as the lights changed to green, and then the car moved off. It was not a man driving, but a blonde woman, wearing dark glasses, a silk scarf wrapped round her throat.

Rosie got two, possibly three, reasonably clear-angled

shots before the car disappeared out of sight. She caught a bus and got off at Sunset, called home, but when there was no reply decided she'd take the film round to the all-night Photomat Snap store, and get a set of prints made up while she waited. She also had to arrange with the rental company to collect the car. Suddenly being busy rather than in limbo, as she'd been for so long, made it all okay again. She handed over the roll of film and settled down outside the store with an ice-cream cone. She had half finished the big strawberry and chocolate ice cream when she saw the Janklow Mercedes passing. The blonde woman was alone, hunched over the driving wheel and wearing black gloves. She reminded Rosie of an old movie star, with her thick make-up, black sun-glasses, or maybe someone else, but she couldn't put her finger on it. Rosie sucked her hand, sticky with ice cream. She was good at remembering faces. She could match those puzzles, the jigsaw faces of stars, faster than a bat of the eye. Julie Andrews's lips, Goldie Hawn's eyes, Jane Fonda's nose. She concentrated and then remembered. She was sure she'd seen the blonde woman at the art gallery, the one Lorraine had worked at. Confident she was right, Rosie returned to the store and collected the photographs.

As she waited for the bus back to Pasadena, she ripped open the envelope and sifted through the pictures. On the whole they were disappointing, especially the ones she had taken up in Beverly Glen, but there was one clear set of the blonde woman. She couldn't wait to tell Lorraine but, to her disappointment, the apartment was still empty when she got home. It was way after ten and she began to worry. She fed the cat, and then sat by the phone but when Lorraine didn't call she started to lay out the photographs on the table. She turned the one of the woman round, held it up, studied it from every angle, and then it hit her. It was not a woman at all, but a man. When she squinted at the photograph of the driver who had first pulled through those gates in the Mercedes, even though it revealed only half his face, Rosie was sure that the blonde woman, and the man they presumed to be Steven Janklow, were one and the same.

CHAPTER 11

A T THE University of California, Lorraine paid off the cab and headed for the main entrance and reception. She went up to a janitor who was polishing the floor.

'Excuse me, I've come to see a Mr Fellows.'

He switched off the noisy machine. 'He's not here, was he expecting you?' Lorraine nodded. The janitor checked in the visitor's book. 'He's not in the laboratory but I think he's over on the squash courts.'

No one paid her any attention as she approached the entrance. A group of students wearing tennis whites passed her, laughing and talking loudly; young tanned limbs, healthy fresh-faced kids, gleaming teeth, shiny hair. They made her feel old, unclean and uneasy.

Professor Fellows was on court six with a partner called Brad Thorburn, according to the booking card on the gate. The sound of the squash ball was like cracking thunder and more thunder emanated from court six than any other. Lorraine slipped into a seat at the end of a row overlooking the court. As neither player looked up to acknowledge her, she was able to watch both men and wonder which was Fellows.

She leaned forward, her concentration on the man she thought must be him, red-faced and sweating profusely as he lunged and hurtled round the court. She was sure Red-face had to be Fellows, hoped it was, because his partner attracted her. She had not been attracted to any man for so long that it threw her slightly, but it was not until she had sized up Fellows that she slowly turned her attention to Thorburn. He didn't yell but gave small grunts of satisfaction, like a man fucking somebody well, those short hard grunts. He snapped out, 'Yes, yes, yes,' every time he did a good shot and gave a smile of recognition when he missed one. It was his smile, a half parting of his lips, that attracted her. He was much taller than Fellows, she reckoned about six two, maybe more. His body was perfectly proportioned with long, muscular legs, dark-tanned with not too much hair, though she knew he would have a thick thatch around his genitals – a man with black hair always had. Because he was sweating, his hair clung to his head, thick, short hair, and she knew he would have a chest to match – she could see it, just, through his high-sleeved, fashionable T-shirt. This man was very different from Fellows. He kept hitching up his shorts as he swung his racket back and forth, bending forward as Fellows lined up a shot, and dragging his wristband across his forehead. His hands were strong and big. Lorraine inched further forward to get a better view of his face. His dark eyebrows were fine and his eyes . . . He turned and looked up. They were dark greenish-blue.

Fellows looked up and waved. 'Are you Lorraine Page?' She nodded. 'Won't be long.'

The game continued for another ten minutes and then she presumed Fellows won as he yelled his head off and flung his arm around his partner, who picked up a pristine white towel and wiped his face, arms and neck before draping it round his shoulders. He didn't acknowledge Lorraine as he walked out of the court. Fellows, however, gave a wide grin and shouted that he would meet her in reception in five minutes.

She sat for a few moments. She pressed her crotch. It shocked her just how attractive she had found Brad Thorburn. She hadn't wanted a man since she could remember and this one had sneaked up like the hard black ball they had been thrashing around the court. It felt as if it had hit her in the groin: she ached, she was wet, and she was scared to walk out and face him. Not until she felt the old Lieutenant Page surface, the one that didn't give a shit what any man said or made her feel, did she leave her seat.

Lorraine waited in the main reception. An even pinker-faced Fellows finally emerged with his kitbag, now wearing slacks and a shirt with a sweater tied round his neck. 'Sorry to keep you waiting but Captain Rooney didn't give me an exact time.'

'That's okay.' She looked past him, half hoping his partner would come out, half hoping he wouldn't. He didn't. Fellows took her by the elbow and walked her out into the cool night. He continued to chatter in an open, friendly manner as they crossed the courtyard and returned to the main hall. He hoped she didn't mind having their discussion at his apartment as the main laboratories and his office were closed for the evening. He picked up his car keys from the janitor and, still with a light gentlemanly touch to her elbow, guided Lorraine to the staff parking lot where an English MG sports car, like Mike's wife's, Lorraine remembered, headed towards them. Fellows waved and Lorraine purposely didn't look as she knew it would be Brad Thorburn. Instead she kept her attention on Fellows, saying how kind it was of him to see her. When she was seated in the passenger seat of Fellows's odd little Japanese car, she clenched her buttocks, angry because she was still sexually aroused. She had wanted to see Thorburn, wanted to see a man that had made her feel like a woman again.

'It was a very interesting game,' she said rather lamely.

'Yes, first time I've beaten him this year. He's an old friend – we were at Harvard together.'

'Does he teach here too?'

'Good God, no. He's rich as Croesus. He's a writer, but he runs a big vintage car garage out in Santa Monica. He imports the cars, has them refurbished and then sells them at immense profit. It's just a pastime really, because he's got a garage full of his own. He started up to keep them in good condition and now it's a flourishing business. Anything that man touches flourishes. He's got the Midas touch but you'd never know it. He's a charming, unassuming man. I'm sorry I didn't have time to introduce you but you didn't come to meet my old college buddy, did you, Miss Page?'

Fellows chatted on about real estate and how his property had lost its value. Nothing he said was of any importance but he was trying to work out what had suddenly made her so tense and distracted. He wondered if she was uncomfortable being driven to a stranger's home but she didn't seem the type who couldn't take care of herself, especially after what Rooney had told him about her. As if she had read his mind, she suddenly asked what Rooney had said to him.

'That you used to be a lieutenant, and a good one.'

She laughed and he found it attractive, a low, soft gurgle more than a laugh.

'Was that all?'

He paused at traffic lights. 'Yes, well, he implied that you made a mess but he didn't embroider.'

'So what did he tell you?'

Fellows drove on, turning into Marmont Avenue. 'Something about a drinking problem.'

Before they could continue, he turned into a driveway. The house was as neat as Fellows, a swimming pool taking up most of the garden. Lorraine calculated the property would be worth around one and a quarter million dollars, perhaps more.

Fellows opened Lorraine's door for her and waited for her to get out. The front door opened and a pleasant, rather

223

plump woman waved from the porch. 'Dilly, this is Lorraine Page. She's working on the case I told you about.'

Lorraine felt an immediate warmth towards Dilly, short for Dylisandra. The interior of the house mirrored her generous personality – open plan, comfortable, not ostentatious. The sitting room was filled with deep, inviting sofas and thick Moroccan-style coffee tables, big lamps, spotlights focusing on large, bright canvases. The one that hung over a stone fireplace was of a man reclining, stark naked. The painting was impressive: no matter where you sat in the room you couldn't help but be drawn to the figure, or, more specifically, to his large penis and balls that were over-prominent.

Dilly worked in the kitchen, opening wine, talking nineteen to the dozen as she listed who had called and left messages. Fellows took himself off to his study and his answer machine, excusing himself.

The meal was simple – tossed salad, steak – but served beautifully. Lorraine was relaxing and enjoying their company, when Dilly brought the conversation round to Brad Thorburn. 'Now there's a man I could go for,' she said to Lorraine. 'That's his portrait over the fireplace, by the way. I know it doesn't look like him – that's because he refused to sit still long enough for me to get his head right, but I think I got everything else okay. Well, Andy says I've been a little optimistic about the genital area but I'm not. I just painted what I saw and, to be perfectly honest, at times it was very difficult to hold my brushes straight.' She laughed loudly, tossing her head back.

Fellows smiled adoringly at his wife, without a hint of jealousy. 'I've tried to introduce him to more girlfriends than you could imagine. They all fall for him but he's a real choosy guy.'

He suddenly stood up, ruffling his wife's hair. 'We've not come here to talk about Brad Thorburn. Can you bring coffee into the den?'

'Sure. How do you take it, Lorraine?'

'Black, honey if you've got it.'

Fellows said, 'I thought you'd take it that way. It fits with how clean-cut you are, direct.'

Dilly snorted. 'Don't pay attention to him, he's always saying things like that! It used to be his big pulling trick, now he just does it for effect!'

Fellows's study was lined with books and photographs, many of them featuring Thorburn. Lorraine walked round the room, with its leather armchairs and wide stacked desk. She looked at a photograph of Fellows and Thorburn together on a fishing trip. Fellows stood behind her.

'Where does he live?'

'Up in the Canyon. It's the family home, he's got them littered all over the world but that's his sort of base. He had quite a strange upbringing. His father left his mother when he was just a toddler and remarried God knows how many times.'

'Is he an only child, then?'

'No, I think there was an older brother but Brad was left the money.'

Dilly appeared with the coffee and bade them goodnight. Lorraine liked her and Fellows too. He was a man she felt she could talk to, a man she *wanted* to talk to, but not about the murder. She felt he would be dependable, honest, a man with no ulterior motive, a rare creature. Fellows briefly outlined his interest in the murder. She listened intently, knowing much of what he was saying because she had read the files, but she liked the reassuring sound of his voice.

'I hear there's been a development with Norman Hastings – cross-dresser. Well, I said Rooney would probably find something. Interesting, huh?'

He had thrown the ball neatly into her court.

'Yes, it is.'

'You asked to see me. For what reason?'

'To see if you knew more.'

'You think I do?'

'I don't know.'

'I think *you* do.'

She met his steady gaze. Lorraine was the one to break the look. 'Why do you think he kills?'

Fellows leaned back. 'Lorraine, nobody knows what makes a man kill, if not in the armed forces or under pressure or supreme emotional strain. I don't believe any man simply kills. There is always a reason.'

'What reason is behind our killer?'

'I don't know because there is no cohesive pattern. They are not all hard-faced prostitutes. One was a cross-dresser, one a seventeen-year-old.'

'What if the seventeen-year-old was a mistake?'

'What do you mean?'

Lorraine repeated what she had discussed with Nula and Didi, and Fellows leaned forward, frowning. 'So you're saying our killer was after one of your friends. Is she blonde?'

'Bleached. She said the driver stopped and Holly ran across the road to him, got into the car. I think Hastings knew the killer,' Lorraine continued, 'and that the killer is a cross-dresser or a transvestite.'

'Why?' Fellows asked.

'Because he seems to hate women, maybe women his own age. I think he hates the woman he becomes, the woman he attempts to be when he's dressed up.'

Fellows closed his eyes. 'Where does Hastings fit in?'

'Hastings may have known him and been suspicious. Perhaps he was about to expose him to the police . . .'

Fellows tugged at his ears. 'There is one person who must be found, the woman he attacked, the one in the parking lot. I don't think the police realize the importance of this witness. She saw him, his face, smelt him, he attacked her and, according to the witnesses, she was covered in blood. Both they and the cab driver have described her – tough, hard-faced, tooth missing, scrawny, lank-haired . . .'

Lorraine's heart was thudding.

'I don't think she was a whore, though, or at least not like the other women. I think this one was different. She was educated, knew enough to . . .' He looked directly at Lorraine. 'Did you read the transcripts of that phone call she made? Clear, concise description. I told Rooney it was almost like a professional description, as if she had been attached to the police in some capacity.'

Lorraine coughed. He was bloody good – did he know? 'I agree but I don't think they'll find her.'

He shrugged. 'Then they're not looking, are they? Because she's still in this area.'

'Why?'

'Because she wouldn't give her name. She wants to remain anonymous.'

'That doesn't mean she didn't pick up a trucker and is out of town. Just because she didn't give her name doesn't mean anything.'

'She wanted him caught! If she was moving on, why bother calling the police? I think she's still around.'

'Will he kill again?'

'Of course, when the mood takes him. He must be feeling good – he has to know that the police have nothing. Even the press has died down.' He paused, then went on, 'This is his sex life, his action, and it's connected to his own sexuality. He will get no pleasure from masturbation, he's probably impotent so his masculinity is warped. He is both male and female, and he is killing as a man. We know this because the anonymous caller gave a good description of what he was wearing. So we're not looking for a man who dresses as a woman and then kills. We're looking for a man who consistently wants to kill. Just as you said, I too think he wants to kill the woman inside him.'

Fellows sat on the arm of his chair, swinging one leg. 'You killed a boy, Rooney told me. He said you were drunk on duty.'

Lorraine felt as if she'd been punched. She didn't like the way he was looking at her.

'Do you remember what it felt like?'

He had to strain to hear what she said. 'I had to kill a number of people in the line of duty and you never forget one of them.'

'You did not answer the question. I asked if you recalled what it felt like to kill that boy.'

'Yes,' she said quietly, 'of course I remember.'

He stared at her intently, knew she was lying but he was astonished at the way she held his gaze and didn't flinch away.

'But you were intoxicated.'

'Yes.'

'But you remember.'

She broke his gaze and he knew she was in trouble. Lorraine stood up, pulling her skirt straight. 'It's not something I'm likely to forget.'

'Why?'

'Because it must be fucking obvious why. The boy was innocent and I was drunk.'

'Even though you were intoxicated, you remember. As you said, you never forget. What exactly don't you forget?'

Lorraine sighed and lit a cigarette. 'I don't see the point of this.' She inhaled deeply, let the smoke drift, was about to take another drag when she paused and, without any emotion, described the boy's jacket, the yellow Superman stripe, the way he fell, as if in slow motion, the way his body folded, the way his head rested against his outstretched arm, the way his soft hair fanned out, the way his body jerked a few times before he became still. Once she had begun she couldn't stop, remembering Rooney pushing past, ordering her into the patrol car, displaying in his filthy

228

handkerchief the boy's Walkman, the tape still in the deck. That there had been no gun, that she had fired six times. She fell silent. Fellows had expected her to break down and weep.

'What about afterwards?' he asked softly. She intrigued him.

Lorraine stubbed out her cigarette, becoming annoyed that he had swung their meeting over to her life rather than the killer's.

'I felt fucking angry, desperate, disgusted, and all I wanted was to forget it.'

'How did you do that?'

'With booze, of course.'

'And did it block it out?'

She shook her head. 'Yes. I suppose you want me to say no, that it was always there, that it always will be. Well, I'm sorry to disappoint you, I don't think about it.'

Fellows picked up a paperweight. 'But you were drinking before this boy. What made you dependent on alcohol?'

'I was just addicted to it, like my mother. It's supposed to be inherited, isn't it?'

'Why did you drink, Lorraine?'

'I guess I liked the way it made me feel, the confidence it gave me – not having to think or feel. Now, can we get back to the reason I asked to see you?'

'What main thing did you not feel?' He looked into her eyes, with an expression of concern, almost apologetic. 'I'm sorry, I don't mean to pry.'

She laughed. 'Can't help yourself, huh?'

He gently touched her cheek. 'You're a clever woman, a strong woman – possibly the strongest I've ever met. I'm sorry to delve into your private life but I'm trying to get you to think like him, understand him. Like you felt the compulsion to have another drink, he will feel this compulsion to kill. He will be in a kind of torment because maybe something happened to him that twisted him, hurt him, and the only way he is able to live in society and carry on in a state of apparent normality is like this. When this consuming pain takes hold of him like a rage, he will control it, contain it, and release it when he hammers a victim to death. Only then does the rage subside and calm or normality return.'

Fellows paced up and down his banks of books, all of which were serial killers' histories, and slapped each in turn. 'I have pinpointed the rage syndrome in so many of these cases. It manifests itself in an overpowering need to wound, to destroy, to hurt, to inflict pain. Time and again it is sexual: stalking, peeping, watching and knowing what they were about to commit will be exquisite, relished – and enjoyed. Many collect the newspaper cuttings to gloat over. The fact they are clever enough not to be detected adds to the overall feeling of enjoyment. And when it's over they integrate back into their homes, their work. Their secret is like a lover, precious, nurtured, controlled until the pain starts again. It's a horrific vicious circle that cannot be broken until the killer is caught.'

Lorraine put her cigarettes and lighter into her purse. 'I really must go. Would you call me a cab?'

Fellows reached for the phone, and started to punch the buttons. Seemingly intent on his task, he asked calmly why, if she wanted to assist in the inquiry, she hadn't admitted that she was the woman the killer picked up.

'Because, Professor Fellows, I am not.'

He ordered the cab and stuffed his hands into his trouser pockets. 'I know you were a prostitute, I know the address you've just given to me for the cab tonight was also close to the area where the witness was dropped off by a cab driver. Ex-cop, it was you who called the station, you who gave the description. I just don't understand why you're lying.'

'I'm not.' She stared at him.

'He said you were one of the best he'd ever worked with.'

Lorraine snapped that Rooney had a big mouth, but he knew nothing about her life since she'd left the force.

Fellows became equally tetchy, opening a file and pushing it across the desk. 'I'd say this is pretty informative.'

She pursed her lips as she saw the copy of her record. 'The bastard,' she said, and then she deflated, slumping into the big leather chair. 'Does he know? Rooney?'

'No, in fact I wasn't sure, until I met you, talked with you. You're in a very precarious position, my dear.'

'How did you work it out?'

'I just took one almighty guess.' He snickered. 'I threw in a wild card.'

She laughed, tilting her head back, a deep, warm laugh that made him smile.

'The description in the files fits – tall, blonde – except the missing tooth.'

'I had it capped.'

Fellows sat on the arm of her chair. 'I can't see any need to tell Rooney, unless you're holding anything else back?'

Lorraine took hold of his hand, gave it a squeeze, and then looked up into his face. 'I'm not holding anything back, Prof. Just wish I had something else to get me fifty bucks a day when Rooney's off the case. I doubt if anyone else would trust me.'

'They're fools. Does that mean the FBI will take over?'

'Yes, within the next forty-eight hours. What about dates? Is there anything in the dates the killings took place?'

Fellows frowned. 'I doubt it. He just kills when he feels the urge, no specific date code.' He sighed. 'I'm sorry I couldn't be more help but if I sift through the files again, find something, can I call you?'

She nodded.

'Good, and will you call me if you find anything? It's interesting to me or I wouldn't have spent so much time on it already, and, I might add, with no fifty bucks a day.'

The doorbell rang. He walked her to the cab. 'It's paid for, so don't worry. And if you need me, call me.'

She smiled her thanks and he remained watching her until the cab turned out of the drive.

Back in the den, he picked up the dirty ashtray piled high with cigarette stubs – fifteen. He tipped it into the waste basket, then straightened the leather cushions, and went upstairs to the bedroom.

Dilly was sleeping, her arms entwined round a pillow. She hardly stirred when he slipped into bed and turned off his bedside lamp. He rested his head on his arms and thought about Lorraine. There was an arrogance about her that attracted him and a directness he admired. There was also, he detected, a deep, hidden pain which, in his professional opinion, was about to erupt.

CHAPTER 12

LORRAINE ASKED the cab driver to take her to Beverly Glen. She would meet any extra costs. By the time they parked outside Janklow's house, she was already annoyed with herself for not asking Fellows if the name meant anything to him or had any connection to Brad Thorburn. She was also confused as to why she had told the cab driver to take her there.

She stood a short distance from the gates. The dog was still loose, sleeping about ten feet inside. He woke and growled, his tawny eyes daring her to lay so much as a hand on the gate. As the rental car had been towed away, nothing indicated that Rosie had been back. The house was in darkness, shutters closed on the lower-floor windows, and the drive was empty. It seemed ominously quiet and yet there was nothing creepy about the property, quite the opposite. Lorraine stepped closer and her body set off the automatic security lights. The gardens, the lower storey of the house, the gates, even the road she was standing in, were suddenly bathed in brilliant light.

She started back to the taxi when she heard someone calling. She paused and looked back.

'Bruno must have set the security lights off again. *Bruno!*'

Brad Thorburn, wearing shorts and flip-flops, appeared at the front door. The dog ran to him, standing on its hind legs to lick his face. Brad ruffled its fur and scanned the garden for an intruder, but his voice was mocking when he clapped his hands and said to the dog, 'See them off, go on, good boy.'

Lorraine whipped round as the cab driver tooted his horn. 'You want to stay here much longer? Only I got another fare to pick up.'

She had her hand on the door when the gates opened. Thorburn looked over the road and was about to close the gates, when he looked again. 'Hey! Were you at the college earlier?'

'Sorry,' Lorraine said innocently. 'Are you talking to me?'

He nodded. 'I was playing with Andrew Fellows.'

Lorraine smiled. 'What a coincidence.'

She turned back to the driver. 'Give me five minutes.'

'You got a problem?' Thorburn asked.

Lorraine walked over to join him. 'No, not really. I was supposed to drop in to collect something for a friend of mine. I thought it was number three eight hundred but I must have been mistaken.'

'Do you need to make a call? You can use my phone.'

'I won't be a second,' she called to the driver, who gave a surly nod. She grinned at Thorburn. 'My driver's fed up as we've been up and down the Glen. I didn't like to start ringing doorbells, with all the security around here.'

Thorburn pressed the gates closed and released the dog, which immediately launched itself at Lorraine, wagging its tail and slobbering. 'He's not quite got it together yet, he's only a puppy. This way . . .'

The hallway alone took her breath away. It was an antique mixture of Baroque furniture, massive chandeliers and gilt mirrors, but it was not oppressive because the pieces were not crowded together. The hallway was of such a grand scale, it could easily have accommodated a number of vehicles parked side by side.

'Phone's on the table just through that arch. I'm Brad Thorburn.'

234

'Lorraine Page.'

He walked off and Lorraine went towards the wide archway. The room was sunken, with deep white sofas and a single glass-topped coffee table with a basket of flowers the like of which Lorraine had only seen in magazines. The paintings were all huge and the white telephone was the smallest object in the room. She called Rosie.

'Hi, it's me.'

Without a pause for breath, Rosie gave her a tongue lashing – how worried she was, that she was just about to call Jake and get a search party out looking for her.

'I'm sorry, I got lost. I'll come straight home now.'

Rosie tried to tell her about the photo session but Lorraine could hear the sound of the flip-flops across the white marble hallway.

'I won't bother tonight, I've got a taxi waiting. Goodnight.'

She replaced the receiver before Rosie could utter another word.

'Can I get you a drink?' He had put on a loose white caftan over his shorts.

'Ah, no, I'd better go, but thanks for the offer and the use of your phone.' She could feel herself blushing, so she dipped her head.

'Did you go over to Andrew's?'

'Yes, we had a relaxed dinner, just Dilly and Andrew.'

He smiled. 'I've offered her money to take that painting down. I know you've seen it because you won't look at me.'

She hadn't even thought of the painting, it was him she couldn't look at. They walked towards the front door, which was still ajar. As they stepped onto the porch, her taxi drove off.

'Since your transport has departed, will you change your mind?'

'No, thanks all the same, but if you could call me another cab . . .'

'Don't you drive?'

'Yes, I do but I also used to drink. The two didn't go together. Now I don't drink or drive.'

He took her elbow. 'Come and sit down. Let me fix you a soft drink, or tea or coffee, if you'd prefer?'

Brad took her into the kitchen. It was like a movie set — more appliances and high-tech equipment than she'd seen in any restaurant. He poured her a glass of iced water, then crossed to a wall phone, asking her what she did for a living. She told him she worked part-time for an art gallery. He turned to look at her. 'Anyone I'd know of?'

'I doubt it, it's not very successful.' She knew she had to concentrate on using this situation and told herself to stop acting like a tongue-tied teenager. This was too good an opportunity to pass over. Maybe she did fancy him but she had to ignore it. It was unlikely he'd have any interest in her — Dilly had said that all his women were young, perfect beauties. But she was sure, unless she was kidding herself, that — wasn't he putting out signals? She gave him a hooded glance as he picked up the receiver but he turned and caught her looking at him. He didn't smile but met her eyes and then his attention was drawn to the phone.

'The cab will be here in about fifteen minutes.'

'Thanks.' She decided to start doing the job she was there for. 'You have a wonderful home, do you live here alone?'

'No, my brother's here as well. You want me to show you around?' Politely, he led her through one vast ornate room after another. He was obviously uninterested, so they viewed each quickly and Lorraine hardly said a word. It was not until they went upstairs that his closeness made her feel uncomfortable. He touched her elbow as he showed off the master bedroom, with floor-to-ceiling white silk curtains that Barbara Stanwyck might have draped herself in. It lacked the freshness of the other rooms.

'This room's different,' Lorraine said, and walked further inside, her feet sinking into thick-piled, soft rose-coloured carpets.

'My mother's room. She likes it kept this way.'

She saw photographs in heavy silver frames, at least fifteen, clustered on the dressing table. The main one was of an astonishingly beautiful woman, pale blonde hair, elegant, a classic beauty.

'My mother.'

'She's stunning, very beautiful.'

'Yes, she is – or was. She's now made herself into a plaster cast, hardly recognizable as the same person. I don't think she has a single feature she hasn't attempted to freeze in time. She refused to age gracefully. And that was my father. I think the only reason it's here is because she looks so wonderful in the same photograph. He died a long time ago.'

Lorraine picked up a smaller picture frame. 'That's my brother, well, a half-brother. I think I was four, he'd be about twelve, different fathers.'

They heard the sound of a car heading up the drive. He replaced the picture and, crossing to the window, drew back the drape.

'Is that my cab?'

'No, they'll call from outside. It's just the staff returning.' He walked briskly to the door, impatient for her to follow, yet he remained the gentleman, holding the door open until she passed him, about to head down the stairs.

'No, come into my office.' He gripped her elbow and they walked along the landing and through another archway. 'Go in and sit down, I'll be right with you.'

He crossed to the banisters and looked down as the front door slammed. 'Don't put the alarms on, I'm waiting for a cab.'

'Are you going out?'

Lorraine was just about to go into the office. She paused. Although she had heard a man's voice, she had also heard the *click-click* of high heels.

'I've got somebody here – they're just going so stay down there.'

The *click-click* faded and a door below closed. Brad beckoned her into his so-called office, which was mostly windows with a vast array of books lining the walls. A modern desk was covered with a word processor and stacks of manuscripts.

'What kind of books do you write?'

He closed the door. 'You mean attempt to write! I haven't done it yet.'

He frowned as footsteps could be heard on the polished wooden stairs but they carried on up to the floor above them. Then he seemed to relax, pointing to a photograph of a vintage car. 'I have a collection.'

'Do you keep them all here?' Lorraine asked.

'No, I have a garage. I bought it to house my own vehicles, then I hired a mechanic to keep them in condition, and every other day somebody with a comparable car would appear and ask if my mechanic could help them repair it or where they could get a part, so I opened up a garage, dealing only in vintage imported or American cars.'

He looked up as the footsteps passed over the ceiling from the room above. 'Excuse me.'

He walked out and closed the door. As soon as it shut, Lorraine was at his desk, opening drawers, checking. She found stacks of notepaper with the S and A logo, envelopes, drawers full of magazines and more manuscripts. She looked over the bookcase – novels, theology, medicine, dictionaries, biography, autobiography – then opened a door into another room and saw the professionally equipped gym. She suddenly looked up as she heard low voices arguing. It was frustrating because she couldn't hear a word they were saying. A door slammed and then there were running footsteps. Lorraine hurried to sit down as Brad returned.

'Maybe you should call me another cab.'

He walked to the bookcase and removed a book. The entire wall fell back to reveal a large bedroom.

Brad bowed. 'There's even a private staircase leading out and down to the garden. If the cab hasn't arrived by the time we get there, I'll run you home.'

Lorraine passed him to walk into the bedroom. The king-size bed had several mirrors above it yet it didn't feel overtly sexual. The room was too orderly, everything pale oatmeal, even the polished wooden floors. The walls were covered with photographs, mostly of blonde women.

'My harem, as Dilly calls them.' Lorraine moved closer and he stood directly behind her. 'She says they were interchangeable. What do you think?'

She could feel the heat of him but she calmly looked from one girl to the next. 'I think they're lovely.'

He touched her shoulder, a light feather touch, and then slowly traced down her arm. He reached for her hand and drew it back slightly to feel his erection.

'I want to fuck you.' His voice was hardly audible.

She did not withdraw her hand but allowed him to press it against his erect cock. Her whole body seemed to catch fire, and then she laughed. 'Dilly's painting doesn't exaggerate, does it?'

She moved her hand, without his assistance, slowly over his erection and he moaned. She closed her eyes, she didn't want it to happen. He pressed closer and his right hand began slowly to unbutton her blouse, pushed beneath her bra to feel her nipples. They were hard and he knew she was aroused. He bent his head to kiss her neck. His tongue licked as he pulled her blouse further open, while her legs began to spread as if out of her control.

'No,' she whispered. 'Please don't do this to me. I don't want this, I have to go.'

She wanted to scream, wanted him to go on. She could feel herself start to pant as he massaged her nipples. She knew that if he reached down, put his hand between her legs, she wouldn't be able to resist – but she had to make it stop, walk away from him. She pushed his hands off but he turned her roughly to face him and kissed her lips. It was a sweet, gentle kiss and she craved more and pressed against him. She felt her arms lifting to hold him.

'How did you get this?' He traced the scar on her cheek. 'It drives me crazy, you know that? It's so sexy, the way you tilt your head. You have beautiful eyes. I want to make love to you, Lorraine.'

She was embarrassed about her body, her scars, and hearing his husky voice, saying things she had never expected to hear from any man, let alone one as handsome as he was, made her want to weep.

'I have to go.'

'No, not yet.'

'Yes. Just get away from me.'

He stepped back as she buttoned her blouse, pulled down her skirt. She had to keep talking because if he laid so much as a finger on her again, she'd be unable to say no. 'I don't know what you think I am but you've got a fucking nerve. Now just stay the hell away from me – go fuck one of your classy blonde college kids but don't come on to me because I'd make you pay, sweetheart. You picked the wrong lady.'

He stepped away from her, his face like a boy's in his confusion. She ran her hands through her hair and looked up to the mirrors. 'They may get turned on by this crap with the mirrors but please don't play out your fantasies with somebody you don't know, and will never know. Now, did you really call me a cab or was that all part of your pussy-suckin' game?'

'How much do you charge?' His face was taut with anger.

'*I* choose my clients. Now how do I get out of here?'

He grabbed her wrist and she did a quick twist, released her hand and brought it up to slap his face. 'Stay off me, rich boy.'

'I said, how much?'

She could feel her stomach lurch, wanting him to hold her, wanting him to stop her foul mouth, wanting him to kiss her just like he had a moment ago.

'Name your price!'

She looked for the door to get out. Shocking him hadn't worked. He was humiliated, angry, and even more attractive.

'I said name your price.'

She glared at him. 'You don't have it.'

'Want to bet? Five hundred? You want more? Seven fifty? You don't look like a thousand-dollar whore to me but if that's your price . . .'

He crossed to a wardrobe, opened one of the drawers and took out a wad of notes. Just as he was about to proffer them, the telephone rang. He tossed the money at her as he picked up the receiver. He listened and then let it drop. 'It's your cab. Why don't you leave me your number? Maybe we'll make it another night.'

She laughed as he opened the hidden door leading to the staircase into the garden. She didn't wait for him to direct her but headed straight down. He didn't follow, but stood, watching her.

'I meant what I said, Lorraine.'

She paused and looked up at him. 'I'm not a whore, Brad. I don't want you or your money. Goodnight.'

He waited until the door below closed, then relocked it automatically, stood to see her stride down the pathway, and pause to give the dog a few words. Then he used the remote switch on the main gates, saw her hesitate as they swung open, but she didn't look back. Maybe she didn't know he could see her.

241

He lay down on his bed, looking up at himself in the mirror, confused and still smarting from her rejection. He was not used to it, nor was he used to meeting a woman who excited him so much. The phone rang. He sighed with irritation and snatched it up.

'What do you want?'

'Did you switch the security lock on the gates?'

'Yes.'

Steven Janklow replaced the phone and walked into his bathroom, closing the door silently. Locked inside the house he felt safe and secure. He let his silk dressing gown fall away from his body, gazing at himself admiringly as he stepped into the perfumed water. As he slid slowly beneath the soft warm bubbles, he sighed with satisfaction.

Lorraine travelled home in style. The car was a stretch Mercedes, the driver wearing uniform. He did not say a word the entire journey. She was glad, she didn't feel like talking. Rosie, however, was still up and ready to launch in as soon as Lorraine opened the front door.

'You cut me off before I could tell you.'

'Rosie, I'm real tired. Can't this wait until morning?'

'No. I got the photographs developed. I went back to the Janklow house.'

'You did *what*?' Lorraine snapped.

Lorraine chucked her purse down. 'Listen to me, Rosie. This is not a game. You *never* – do you understand me? – *never* do anything unless you run it by me first. This is work for me.'

Rosie stuck out her lower lip like a child. 'I was only trying to help and then the car broke down. I hadda walk miles and get it towed back. I walked from the Janklow house all the way down—'

Lorraine interrupted, 'Jesus Christ, you broke down outside the house? I don't believe it.'

'Good thing I did because I saw the Mercedes and I got a good picture of the driver.'

Lorraine was hooked. 'Janklow?'

'Yeah, well, I think so. You tell me.'

Lorraine stared at the photographs, lingering longest on the blonde woman driver.

'Is that a man or a woman? You tell me.' Rosie made an elaborate show of matching the two sets of photographs, the ones with Steven Janklow driving, and the ones with the blonde woman.

'It would be hard to tell if it wasn't for the mouth.'

It was a wide mouth, a mouth Lorraine was sure belonged to the man who had attacked her. But she was concerned about Rosie, that she was becoming too involved and might do something that would get her into trouble or, even worse, get her hurt. 'We'll see if we can get them enlarged. Now, if it's okay with you, I'm going to bed.'

Lorraine slipped into her bed on the couch and drew the covers close up around her chin. She gripped the sheet tight, twisting it round her knuckles. She had wanted to be loved tonight, she had wanted to be held, kissed, but she had been so afraid because, after all this time, after so much loss, she didn't think she had any feelings left. Lubrinski's death had been the worst moment of her life. He was the only person who had given her the love she craved from her husband, who had loved her for what she was and asked nothing in return.

It began with a single, dry sob, wrenching upwards from the pit of her stomach. Afraid Rosie would hear, she bit the sheet, held it between her teeth as the second sob shook her body. She told herself to get control. 'Fucking take control of yourself, Page. People depend on you to be a rock. You start howling and you'll make us a laughing stock. There's a mother out there needing to know if her little girl is alive or dead – you show any emotion and she won't be able to take it. You want to weep, do it in your home, never on duty. You hearing me, Page?'

'Mrs Bradley, I'm sorry but we've found Laura, and I'm sorry to tell you . . . Laura's dead, Mrs Bradley.'

Rosie sat up. Something had woken her and she was afraid for a moment. Then she heard the strangled, awful sounds. She threw back the blanket and went in to Lorraine. She was rigid, the sheet clenched between her teeth, her knuckles white from the strain of gripping her fingers so tightly. The sound was like a wounded animal, a low mewing sound, as she tried to suppress the desire to scream. Rosie reached over and picked her up in her arms, holding her and rocking her. 'Let it go, Lorraine, let it free. It's only me, it's only big fat Rosie. You have a cry, let's hear you cry . . .'

The dam broke and the mewing sound erupted into gasping sobs as the tears flowed. Lorraine held onto Rosie as if she was drowning, as if she was terrified to let her go. She sobbed for almost two hours. She wept for everything she had lost, for her children, her husband, her dead mother, her brother, her father. She cried for the boy she had shot, she cried for Lubrinski and called out that she was sorry, sorry, and at long last she wept for herself, for what she had done to herself, for what she had forced herself to become.

At last the crying stopped. She was drained, so exhausted she couldn't speak. Her body still shook, and she made soft, hiccuping sounds as Rosie gently dried her face and together they walked into the bedroom. Rosie helped her into the bed, rinsed a facecloth so she could pat her face cool, and then got in beside her. Lorraine rested her head against Rosie, whose big fat arms cradled her friend as she said softly over and over, 'It's all over now, everything's going to be better now, honey. It's gonna be easy now.'

*

The ring of the telephone by the bed made Rooney's heart thud so loudly he thought he was having a heart attack. It was Bean. They had just got a report in. The body of a white woman, aged somewhere between thirty and forty, had been discovered in the trunk of a stolen vehicle. Judging by the look of the corpse, the killer had struck the victim from behind with a hammer, and she also had horrific facial injuries. Rooney flopped back, cradling the phone against his chest. His wife peered up at him, her face masked with nightcream.

'Dear God, we've got another one. He's done another.'

CHAPTER 13

ROONEY AND his lieutenant waited in the anteroom of the City Morgue. They could do little until they had further information from the pathologist. The stolen vehicle, a Lincoln Continental, had been towed to the yard and was being checked over by forensic experts. The owner of the vehicle had been traced, having reported his car stolen the previous day from outside his bungalow in Ashcroft Avenue, LA. Rooney was morose, knowing that the press would be on to the killing and had, more than likely, given it front-page coverage as he had declined to say anything to the photographers and reporters waiting outside the mortuary.

The Lincoln had been left in the third storey of a garage where it could have remained for days, along with all the other cars on long-term contracts. The only reason it had been investigated was that the alarm had been triggered off when another car accidentally touched the rear fender. According to the attendant, the ringing had been driving him nuts for almost an hour so he had gone to take a look. No long-term parking ticket was displayed on the window or on the dashboard, and he was about to return to his booth when he saw something dripping from beneath the trunk. At first he presumed it was oil but on closer inspection, realized it was blood and called the police.

Rooney sighed. 'He give a description of the driver?'

Bean shook his head. 'He said he wasn't on duty until

246

late and the car was already parked. We've got a number for the daytime attendant but we've not spoken to him yet.'

Rooney checked his watch. 'Get on to that right now.'

'I'm on my way.'

Rooney waited another two hours before the doors opened and the masked and gowned attendant gestured for him to follow. Draped in green sheeting, the body dominated the white-tiled room, whose strip-lighting gave a surreal white brightness to all the rows of instruments and enamel sinks.

'Morning, Bill,' said Nick Arnold, the pathologist, as he washed his hands at a large sink. 'You're pretty impatient for this one, aren't you? I hear you've been hovering outside – you should have come in.'

Rooney hated being anywhere near an autopsy. He'd never gotten used to the way corpses were sliced open, never been able to stand hearing the hiss of stinking gases or looking at the blood pumping out; the open, sightless eyes of the victim as their body was systematically inspected.

Arnold knew Rooney of old and understood he wouldn't want to take a close look. He appeared distinctly greenish already. 'Come and have a coffee,' he said pleasantly. 'It'll be a while before we get the photographs and tests completed.' He yawned. 'Got called out of bed for this one.'

'So did I,' muttered Rooney as he slumped into a low chair, its cushioned seat puffing loudly as his bulk made contact. 'So what you got for me?'

'Death occurred late evening – can't be more specific. Until I get my reports back, I can't pinpoint the exact time but it was evening and the last meal was banana bread.'

'That's a big help,' Rooney slurped his coffee.

'Victim's age was late thirties, may even be forty, but fit – good muscle tone.'

'Was she blonde?' Rooney asked.

'Yep, but who said "she" was female?'

'What?'

247

Arnold grinned. 'He was almost a she and at first glance I'd have said definitely female, heavy breasts, but he was also well endowed in the nether regions. Transsexual, Bill, one who'd been on a lot of hormone replacement treatment, Adam's apple has also been removed at some time.' He stood up and pointed to drawings. 'Hammer blow here to the base of the skull, which would have almost certainly rendered her unconscious. Her face was beaten to a pulp, nose, cheekbones and frontal lobe shattered, very heavy blows, one eye forced back into this region and the other socket split open by the force of the hammer. Not a pretty sight now but I would say she or he had at one time been quite attractive. Hair is bleached blonde, well cut. We've also got nothing from under her fingernails so the first blow was unexpected. She put up no resistance.'

Rooney went into the forensic laboratories to see the victim's clothes. They were reasonably expensive, some with well-known labels, but only the shoes would be helpful. They were large-sized, high-heeled stilettos and made in a specialist shoe store that catered for transsexuals and transvestites. As Rooney jotted down the information, he was sure he could get an identification of the victim quickly.

Bean joined up with him back at base. He had talked to the parking attendant, who had no recollection of the driver of the vehicle. He was sure the car had been parked there for more than twenty-four hours. The car's owner had been away for a week and only knew the car was missing when he returned home. Neither of the attendants could be certain of when the Lincoln had been left.

Rooney instructed officers to check out the garage. Perhaps the killer had stolen the car, left it there, then returned in another vehicle with his victim. Forensic reports from inside the Lincoln yielded no bloodstains, no fingerprints in the interior or the glove compartment, and the driving wheel had been wiped clean. They did, however, find long strands of blonde hair which were sent to be

248

tested and matched to the victim's. All this took considerable time – time Rooney did not have. At nine thirty Chief Michael Berillo summoned him.

Rooney listened to him glumly. He was still to lead the officers in the inquiry but only until the FBI officers had familiarized themselves with the evidence. Then they would take over and, as Rooney's chief had said, 'You can start mowing the lawn, Bill.' He'd sounded gloating, even if unintentionally. Mowing the lawn was not something that Rooney pictured himself doing even if he'd retired of his own free will. Now this enforced 'release from duty' sat uneasily on his wide, sloping shoulders. 'You mustn't feel you've been ousted due to any unprofessional conduct or lack of ability. It's just that—'

Rooney leaned on the Chief's desk. 'You gotta have a scapegoat, someone to blame for not making an arrest. Sure, I understand. I just didn't expect to go out this way. I've given the best years of my life to the force but it don't matter. Somebody's got to pay for not finding this crazy bastard, so why not make me the sucker?'

'I'm sorry you feel that way, Bill.'

'At least I should have a chance to talk to this guy they brought in with them.'

The Chief coughed. 'They're with him now but I'm sure they'll let you talk to him later.'

Rooney knew they'd all been aware of the possibility he'd be replaced but his men seemed taken aback that it was happening so quickly. For all his bad-tempered ways, he was well liked. Bean, too, felt a trifle embarrassed. If Rooney was being moved, it meant that everyone on the case would be scrutinized. He repeated Rooney's request that until the FBI formally took over, they must all work double time.

No one attached to the case had yet had access to

Brendan Murphy or had seen him brought in. Bean patted Rooney's shoulder. 'Be just our luck if they walk in with a suspect and pin the whole string on him. They'll get all the glory and we'll be made to look fools.'

'We want to know who he or she is so that's our first priority.' Rooney jerked his head at the pictures of the last victim, already being pinned up, and plodded out of the incident room. He had decided to have one more crack at Mrs Hastings. The link between her husband, victim and cross-dresser, and the latest victim, was too much of a coincidence.

'Captain, should I take what we've got over to Andrew Fellows?' Bean called after Rooney. 'See if he can help us out at all?'

'Sure. I'll be interested to hear what Big Ears has to say.'

While Bean went off in search of Fellows, the rest of the team split up to make inquiries with known transsexuals, shoe and clothing stores that might recall the victim. Rooney assigned two men to run checks on the employees at the S and A vintage car garage in Santa Monica but told them to keep it low key.

Rooney stepped into the lift and went down to the basement. He proceeded along the brightly lit corridor towards the holding cells. He had to pass through innumerable security doors and left his weapon in the locker outside the last before he took the key. Then he joined the duty sergeant at his computerized board, which indicated every occupied cell and every corridor, a maze of small red and green lights.

'Where they got the suspect?'

The sergeant indicated cell fourteen.

'Any way I can hear what's going on?'

The sergeant gave him a sidelong look and flicked a switch. 'FBI been with him for hours.'

Rooney crossed to the bank of screens and gazed at the one showing the occupant of cell fourteen. Brendan

250

Murphy was sitting on the bunk bed, his hands held loosely in front of him. He was wearing a denim jacket and a stained T-shirt. His shoes had been removed. His beer gut, even larger than Rooney's, hung over his baggy old jeans. Rooney could not see who was in the cell with him but he heard the soft voice asking him to start from the beginning again and to take his time. Murphy seemed to stare directly into the camera and then ran his thick stubby hand over his square jaw.

'Jesus Christ, I'm gettin' confused, I'm hungry, I want some cigarettes. I dunno how many more times I can tell you I'd not seen my wife for almost ten months. I've not met the other woman more'n once or twice and that was fucking years ago. You got the wrong man.'

Rooney dragged on his cigarette. Murphy did not resemble the only description they had of the killer – nothing could be more different. He was thickset, overweight, at least six two and, by the look of him, had never worn a jacket in his life. Murphy listed plaintively where he had been on the night of the murder and then stood up, angrily swinging his fist. 'I wasn't even in Los Angeles, for chrissakes. I told you all this in Detroit. You're gonna make me lose my job.'

Rooney had seen enough. He did not believe for a minute that Murphy was their man so let the FBI question him. The longer they were out of his hair the better.

He drove to Mrs Hastings, pausing on the way to buy some bourbon and a packet of mints. He took three heavy slugs from the bottle as he drove on, then unwrapped a peppermint to disguise the smell.

Rosie was woken by Lorraine presenting her with a cup of tea. She was dressed for a workout. 'I'll be back for breakfast,' she said brightly.

She pushed herself at the gym and Hector monitored her

weights. She also did a full step aerobic class. Then she had an ice cold shower and felt fit and sharp. She even ran from the bus back to the apartment – long, slow, steady strides, not pushing herself or working up a sweat.

Rosie had laid out all her vitamins, the protein drink, cereal, fruit and yogurt. Lorraine ate hungrily. It was still not nine o'clock but even after all her exertion she didn't feel tired. She was feeling like the old Lorraine Page used to feel before she hit the bottle.

'I met this guy called Brad Thorburn last night,' she said to Rosie. 'He knew the lecturer I went to see at the college, Andrew Fellows. They were playing squash and . . .' Lorraine stared into space, seeing him again, his handsome face, his athletic body. 'He lives at that house in Beverly Glen. He owns it. And that vintage car garage.'

Rosie pulled out a chair and sat down as Lorraine sifted through her photographs. She looked closely at the Mercedes, then at the man they presumed was Steven Janklow. All they had in focus was his chin and a bit of his right nostril. She drew the clearer photograph of the blonde woman beside it. 'I think you're right – this is the same person.'

Lorraine flipped through the files, checking for Norman Hastings's section. 'I want to go and talk to Hastings's wife. While I'm doing that, I want you to hire another car and pick me up there in a couple of hours. But first see if you can get a section of this picture of the woman blown up so we get to see more of his or her face.' Lorraine counted out some cash. It was running low again.

'Any chance you can touch that friend of yours to pay us a bit more?'

'I'll try but I doubt it.' Lorraine handed out sixty dollars, plus Mrs Hastings's address.

'You going to tell him about those photos?' Rosie asked.

'Not yet. We need more, I don't want to foul this up.'

Rosie picked up the newspaper from the steps outside and tossed it to Lorraine. 'See you later.'

As the screen door slammed after Rosie, Lorraine opened the paper. She couldn't miss the blazing headlines: 'HAMMER KILLER STRIKES AGAIN'. She laid the paper out flat on the table: no name for the victim, just that she was white, aged between late thirties and forties and found in the trunk of a stolen vehicle. The murder had taken place early evening, the licence plate number was given and the location where it had been found, along with a request to the public for any information that would assist the police inquiry. A suspect was being held.

Lorraine called Rooney but was told that he was not at the station. She checked her watch. It was too late to change her plans.

Rooney had been waiting outside Mrs Hastings's house for fifteen minutes. She was not in but, according to a neighbour, was probably taking her daughters to school so would not be long. He took another few swigs of bourbon, screwed on the cap tightly, then unwrapped another peppermint. He settled back, reached for one of the newspapers he had bought and broke wind loudly as he glared at the front page.

Mrs Hastings finally returned. She parked her car in the drive and carried a bag of groceries inside. Rooney figured he'd wait a while longer before paying his visit. He looked into his driving mirror and saw Lorraine walking up the road. She paused as if checking she had the correct address. As she walked past his car, Rooney lowered the window. 'Morning,' he said loudly.

When she saw it was Rooney Lorraine said, 'Hi, I was going to talk to Mrs Hastings.'

'I'll come in with you.'

Rooney saw her hesitate and then, 'Fine, but maybe I can get more out of her without you.'

'You seen this morning's paper? It's not public yet but it wasn't a she, it was a he – or an it, according to the pathologist. That's why I came here – thought I'd have another go at Mrs Hastings.'

Lorraine didn't react to the information. This was the moment she should have discussed Janklow but she didn't.

'Says they got a suspect in custody.'

'Brendan Murphy, husband of one of the victims. The suits have arrived. They brought him in from Detroit. I've not even had access to him yet but . . .'

'But?'

'It's not him, I know it. Let's talk to Mrs Hastings.'

'Let me try before you, Bill. You been checking out that vintage car garage?'

'I got two guys on it this morning.'

She could smell liquor on his breath. 'You okay?'

He shook his head. 'Nah, they gave me the fucking kiss-off this morning. Well, until the FBI are ready to roll. They want me for a briefing later today.'

Lorraine straightened. 'You mind if I say something, Bill? It's just that I can smell the booze – that and peppermints. If I was you, I'd grab a cup of coffee. Mrs Hastings sounds like the type of woman who'd report you and you don't want to give the FBI a rope to swing you on . . .'

Rooney swore and cupped his hands round his mouth, blowing into them. His jowled face wobbled childishly. 'Okay, I'll be back in fifteen. I'll grab a bite to eat. If you're through wait for me on the roadside.'

He found a deli about four blocks along and parked the car. As he waited for his order he thought how incongruous it was for Lorraine to be telling him to sober up. He'd always been a heavy drinker but now he was drinking more during working hours than he ever had. He wondered if that was the way Lorraine had started. She'd had marital problems but, then, so did all the men. He dreaded the thought of being retired and at home with his wife. It gave him nightmares, as she wittered on about them getting a trailer and travelling round the country. He could think of nothing worse. He couldn't recall the last time he had taken his wife out to dinner, or, for that matter, when he had taken her anywhere. He became more and more despondent as he ploughed through his breakfast. Everything he did revolved around his station, his men, and now it was going to end. Pushing these morose thoughts out of his mind, he tried to concentrate on the case. He wondered why Lorraine had wanted him to check out the vintage car garage. Did she have something for him, something she'd held back? She hadn't made it sound important, but in the old days Lorraine always kept her cards close to her chest. He'd reprimanded her about it, reminding her that she was not a one-woman agent but part of a team. He remembered her snapping back at him, saying the day the men treated her as part of the team, she would work with them. She had put him down hard and fast because at that time she held a higher rank. It had always needled him, needled a lot of men, that she had gained her stripes before them.

'You got a problem with the men?' he could see himself leaning against his old wooden desk as she stood straight-backed in front of him. 'You want to make a complaint?'

'No complaints, but if one of them sends me out on any more fucking wild goose chases with that Merton, who wants to open fire on any kid he sees within ten yards of him, then I will. He's a lousy back-up, he's in need of treatment and everyone on this unit knows it.'

Rooney had promised to look into it but he never did. Even when the shoot-out happened and she was almost killed he had not given her anyone decent. Just suggested she take a refresher course at the shooting training gallery.

'I'm the crack shot, Bill. I wouldn't be here if I wasn't

and neither would my partner. It's him that needs a refresher course.'

Lorraine had taken two weeks off for further training and her ex-partner died in a shoot-out the next time he was called out. Maybe she'd been right but no one ever bothered to make an official inquiry. Officer Colin Merton was given a posthumous medal for bravery and Lorraine a new partner. Rooney had expected fireworks from John Lubrinski when he'd been told he was to partner a woman but he'd said nothing. He wondered if it was Lubrinski that had started Lorraine on her drinking sessions. The two of them were always in the bars together, Lubrinski a famous hard drinker, and it was rumoured that she was matching him. It was Lubrinski who nicknamed her Hollow Legs.

They were partners for three years. When he was injured in cross-fire, she'd made a tourniquet round his leg with her tights. He'd taken three bullets, one in his thigh, one in his shoulder and a third in his stomach. It was the last that had killed him. She had returned to duty the next week and had never spoken about Lubrinski until the internal investigation. He, too, received a posthumous award and she gained a commendation, which many of the men opposed, insinuating that, had the officer had one of them as back-up instead of a woman, they would still be alive. She had never complained or asked for an easier assignment or taken up the offer of a few weeks' compassionate leave. She had gone straight back to work and remained on the same beat for another year. Rooney wondered if perhaps she had begun drinking alone then. Then, at her own request, she was moved from Vice to the Drug Squad. Six months later she had shot the kid. No one ever knew what she had felt on that night or why she had been drinking.

Rooney pushed his half-eaten ham and eggs across the table. For the first time he felt guilty that he, like everyone else, had given Lorraine the cold shoulder. He decided that, even though it was too late, he would talk it through with her. Maybe because he himself felt as if he could finish his bottle of bourbon and not care that he was on duty. He was past caring and he wondered if she had felt that way all those years ago. Angry. In some ways they were similar because he had never complained; he was the man who had always drummed into his officers, get on with the job no matter how tough, never complain, complaints are for losers. It didn't matter if they were male or female, nobody deserved any favours. If they couldn't take it then they weren't tough enough to gain respect. Nobody respected him now, he reckoned, and nobody had respected Lorraine Page.

'My name is Lorraine Page,' she said to a nervous Mrs Hastings. 'I wonder if I could come in and talk to you for a few moments, to iron out a few things about the inquiry into your husband's murder. It won't take long.'

Sitting in the living room, Lorraine was relaxed and complimentary about the neat house, calming Mrs Hastings's nerves.

'I've told that detective Rooney everything. I just can't understand what more there is to discuss. This only makes it worse, these constant questions.'

Lorraine opened her file and smiled. 'Well, let's get this over with as fast as possible, shall we?'

She asked if Norman Hastings had ever owned a vintage car, or used a garage in Santa Monica, which specialized in imported vehicles. She went through the different makes of car to see if Mrs Hastings reacted, but the woman shook her head and said that her husband could never have afforded anything so expensive. Lorraine asked if he owned a car before they were married.

'Yes, of course, but I've no idea what kind it was.'

Lorraine said nothing, seemingly more interested in her file. 'I've got a photograph of it, I think,' Mrs Hastings added.

Lorraine looked up and smiled encouragingly. 'Can I see it?'

Mrs Hastings left the room and Lorraine took out the photographs she and Rosie had taken. She then made a quick drawing on a blank sheet of paper. Mrs Hastings returned with a photograph album and began to sift through the pages until she found what she was looking for. 'I think that's it. I've no idea what make it was and I'm sure it wasn't one of the cars you mentioned.'

Lorraine looked at the snapshot taken in 1979, the date neatly printed below the photograph. Norman Hastings, in shirt sleeves, stood beside the car. It was a low sports car, a British-made Morgan – and, by the look of it, quite an old model.

'Do you have any idea where he bought it?'

Mrs Hastings shook her head again. She had never seen it.

'Your husband was a few years older than you,' Lorraine observed, about to turn the album page, but Mrs Hastings took it back.

'Yes, fifteen, but we were happy.' She hesitated. 'I suppose you know about Norman's little problem. I told that man Rooney.'

'I don't think we need discuss it. You were brave to tell Captain Rooney about it – it must have been very distressing.'

Lorraine passed over her drawing. 'This isn't very good but I wondered if your husband owned a pair of cufflinks like these? They could be gold or silver but with that distinct S and A logo in the centre.'

Mrs Hastings looked at the picture. 'They're silver, but the chain's broken.'

'Do you still have them?'

She left the room again and Lorraine leaned back in the sofa. Next she wanted Mrs Hastings to look at the photographs. It was going well but the woman was tricky, nervous and jumpy. Lorraine wanted her nice and calm. The cufflinks were still in their little cardboard box and one was broken. Lorraine examined the links, then looked at the box. No date, just the same logo and the Santa Monica address.

'What do you want to see these for?' Mrs Hastings asked.

Lorraine replaced the cufflinks, shut the box. 'We may have a possible link to the killer. We think he was wearing something similar. Can I keep these?'

Mrs Hastings agreed. She was beginning to pluck at her dress in agitation. 'Will it all come out? About Norman?'

Lorraine put the box into her purse. 'I doubt it. I always think personal details that have no connection to the case should not be released to the press, especially if the family have requested them not to be.'

Mrs Hastings clasped Lorraine's wrist. 'Oh, thank you. I've been so worried – the children – then there's Norman's parents and his friends at work.'

'He was an engineer, wasn't he?'

'Yes, yes, he was, for ice-boxes and domestic appliances.'

'Did he work on his car engines?'

'He could repair anything from a toaster to a car. The neighbours were always asking him to fix things and he was such a kind man, he'd never say no.'

Lorraine used the opening and showed the photograph of Janklow. 'Did he ever help this man out?'

'I couldn't tell, there's not all his face there, but I don't think so.'

Lorraine showed the second picture, each one taken at the S and A garage. Mrs Hastings looked at one after the other and then tapped one. 'This one. He came here once to talk to Norman about his car.'

Then she showed the photo of the white Mercedes

259

driven by Janklow in blonde wig and make-up. Mrs Hastings glanced at it. 'I don't know her.'

'Have you ever seen the car?'

Mrs Hastings took the photograph and stared at it. 'I don't know, a lot of people came to see him. As I said, he was always helping people out.'

'It's a Mercedes sports car, drop head. It would also have a hard top. Maybe you saw it with that on?'

Mrs Hastings frowned. 'I don't know. There's something familiar about it, it's difficult to say. What colour is the hard-topped hood?'

Lorraine took a chance, reckoning if the body was white maybe the roof was too.

'Well, no, I remember a similar car out in the drive once but it had a black top, sort of dipped.'

Lorraine began to put away the photographs, still relaxed. 'Did you see who was driving it? Who it belonged to?'

'No, they were in the garage out in the yard. Norman used to keep odd spare parts out there so that was another reason why he had so many people coming round. He'd charge them – just expenses, it was his hobby but I hated it. It made his hands all dirty, and oil on everything.'

Lorraine stood up and smiled. 'Thank you very much. You've been very helpful, and I really appreciate it. Would you mind if I come back if I get a better photograph of the man in the Mercedes?'

'No, I don't mind. In fact, I haven't minded talking to you at all.'

Rooney was just drawing up when he saw Lorraine walk out. She waved to Mrs Hastings and he saw her glance towards his car. He opened the passenger door as Mrs Hastings shut her front door and Lorraine got in beside him. 'I'd stay clear of her – she's nervous, more worried about her husband's "little problem", as she calls it, getting out to the press than she is about the murder.'

Rooney sniffed. 'You got anything for me?'

'I might have a suspect but until I'm sure I'd prefer to do a bit more digging around – maybe in a few days.'

'I need anything you've got now. I don't have a few days.'

She pursed her lips. 'Give me until the end of the day. I also need anything you've got on the latest victim.'

'I told you all I've got. Until they've finished the tests, that's it. She was a man and her last meal was banana bread.' She had her hand on the door ready to leave when he said, 'You and Lubrinski, were you an item?'

'Why do you want to know?'

'I'm just trying to figure you out.'

'Bit late for that, isn't it?'

'Yeah, I know. I was just mulling things over, and I started to think about him, he was a great guy.'

She nodded but made no reply. He reached down for his bourbon and unscrewed the cap. He drank from the bottle and she turned to look at him. 'It's the bourbon that reminds you of him. Because he always had a bottle under his seat. Why are you drinking, anyway?'

He gritted his teeth as the bourbon hit his stomach. He took another swig. 'I need it. Did you drink with him?'

'You know I did.'

'On duty?'

'Sometimes, but mostly we saved the session until we were off.'

'Did he get you started on the booze?'

She laughed. 'I didn't need Lubrinski to start me drinking, Bill, I managed it all by myself.'

'Why?'

She suddenly became tetchy. 'How about I was just screwed up, tense and scared I'd foul up, and there's nobody else to blame but myself.'

261

'Your husband? The kids, was that it?'

'For chrissakes, back off me. Why do you want to start on this?'

He took another swig and screwed on the cap. 'Because I'd like to know, and maybe I feel guilty. Maybe this is a conversation I should have had with you years ago.'

She got out of the car and leaned in. 'You're too late, Bill, there's nothing you can do now. What happened happened. It's over.'

'I'm sorry.' He said it gruffly, not looking at her, and she straightened up, about to slam the car door, when she bent down to look at him again.

'About Lubrinski, Bill, he was the best friend I ever had. I trusted him with my life but he was a crazy fool, he took risks, got into a lot of things that I tried to stop, but he wouldn't listen to me, he never listened to anyone and, in answer to your question, we were not an item, we were just partners.'

Then she shut the door and walked off just as Rosie appeared on the opposite side of the road. Rooney drove away in a cloud of exhaust fumes.

'How'd it go?' Rosie said cheerfully.

Lorraine told her to drive to the S and A garage in Santa Monica. Then she closed her eyes and leaned back. She could see Lubrinski's face as clear as if it was yesterday. They had got drunk together on many evenings, they'd talked about everything under the sun, always carefully skirting round themselves. But eventually it had happened. She'd been boozing heavily and he'd insisted she sober up at his place before Mike saw her and threw a punch at him. He was always joking about Mike, snide one-liners about her house-proud husband, but she wouldn't let him run Mike down. He should try and clean up his own act, his wife was no angel. They had squabbled like teenagers and eventually called a truce, that neither of them would discuss their partners. They had shaken hands and Lubrinski had drawn her close.

'Does this make you a single woman now?'

She had tried to slap him but he ducked so she hit the window of the patrol car. Her knuckles hurt and she sucked her fist. He reached over and caught her hand, drawing it to his lips.

That night she had been totally smashed. Even though she had drunk as much as he had, he seemed never to show it. Not until she watched him attempting to brew the coffee did she know he was as drunk as she was. 'You're plastered, Lubrinski, talk about the blind leading the blind. Here, lemme do it.'

He lay back on his unmade bed in his one-room apartment with dirty clothes strewn all around. Lorraine offered to come by and clean it up for him. He said he liked it this way, he knew where everything was, but after they'd finished the coffee he couldn't find the patrol car keys. He started throwing things about, swearing. Then he threw up his hands and laughed his wonderful, deep bellow. 'I'm lying, they're in my pocket.' He pulled them out and dangled them. 'I just wanted to keep you here a while longer but now I'm stone cold sober I don't have the guts.'

'For what?' She was still laughing at him.

'To hold you. You ever think how much I want to hold you, Lorraine Page?'

She stopped laughing, got off the bed, went to him and gently slipped her arms round him. He held her close, he didn't kiss her, he didn't fondle her, he did exactly what he had said he wanted to do: he held her in his arms. She rested her head against his chest, could feel his heart beat, could feel him tremble. She had smiled up at him and then released herself. 'I got to get back to the kids.'

'You love him, don't you?' he asked.

She was confused. She didn't really know. The rows and

bitter arguments had been wearing her out. Mike hated Lubrinski, constantly implied that he was more than just a working partner. He also hated the way she had started drinking so much. He blamed that on Lubrinski as well. Mike blamed everything on anything and anyone but himself.

'Yes, I love Mike. Now I got to go home. We both got enough problems without starting up any new ones.'

She had never seen Lubrinski ill at ease but he was that night, pulling at his thick black curly hair. 'It is kind of different for me, Lorraine.' He shook his head, looking at her. 'You don't know, do you? You got no idea. Jesus Christ, Lorraine, I love you. Some days I don't know what to do with myself I love you so much and sometimes I get scared for you, and I know that's not a good thing but I can't stop it, can't stop loving you, wanting you. And sitting so close to you, day in day out, is driving me crazy. I'm gonna ask for a transfer. It's nothing to do with you being a good or bad partner, it's just that I want you and . . . well, now you know.'

Two nights later he was shot. When she tore off her tights to wrap around his thigh as he was bleeding to death, Lubrinski had joked that at long last he was getting her pants down – he knew he would in time. If he'd known she'd do it when he was shot, he'd have stood up months before . . .

She held him in the ambulance. His breathing became laboured, his eyes unfocused. She kept telling him to hold on, to keep talking. The last thing he said was that he loved her and the last thing he heard before he died was Lorraine saying that he was a stupid, dumb bastard because she loved him too, and if he didn't hold on and pull through she'd strangle him with her tights. She saw the light go from his eyes in disbelief. She'd seen so much death, been so close to it, but this was like losing her own soul, as if he was taking it with him.

Lorraine went back to her apartment, needing Mike more than ever, but he wasn't there. She drank herself into a stupor and collapsed on the bed. Mike came back about two hours later. As soon as he saw her he shouted that Lubrinski had got her drunk again and she had said quietly that this time Lubrinski had nothing to do with it.

'I don't believe you. I'm gonna see him, report him.'

'Try the City Morgue, Mike, but I doubt if he'll talk back to you, he's dead.'

Mike was stunned, had tried to hold her, but she couldn't stand him near her, couldn't bear anyone to touch her. All she wanted was to drink herself into oblivion. Poor Mike had tried to understand, to persuade her to take leave when it was offered, but she refused; she couldn't stand not to be busy, not to be working. She began to believe that Lubrinski had taken a part of her with him when he died. Nothing she did made any sense, neither did anything Mike said. She was irritable with the girls, she was bad-tempered and uncooperative at work, but somehow she carried on until she finally lost control and killed an innocent boy.

'We're almost there,' said Rosie.

Lorraine opened her eyes. She wanted a drink. That was all she could think about. She didn't care about anything else. 'I want a drink.'

Rosie drew up outside a grocery store and hurried inside. She returned with a pack of Coke. 'Here, you wanted a drink!' Lorraine opened a can and gulped it down. Rosie opened one for herself and then proffered a piece of home-made banana bread.

Lorraine sat bolt upright. What had Rooney said? The latest victim, all they had on her or him was that his last meal was banana bread. She felt her body break out in a cold sweat. Was it Didi or Nula that was always making banana bread? Could it possibly be one of them? Didi was blonde, the right age. He had said it was a transsexual – but it couldn't be, it was impossible.

'I got to make a call, Rosie.'

Rosie looked at her. 'Oh, yeah, like you just got to go in there and make a phone call. You think I'm dumb. I know what you'll be making, a bottle of vodka. No way.'

Lorraine had her hand on the car door. 'Shit, if you feel I can't be trusted then come in with me.'

Lorraine had Rosie right at her elbow as she placed the call to Nula and Didi's apartment. Nula answered, her voice drowsy. 'It's Lorraine, who am I speaking to?'

'It's Nula, sweetheart, how you doin'?'

'I'm great, Nula. Is Didi there? I need to speak to her.'

'Nope, she's not come in, been out all night, the dirty cow. She'll be back soonish because she's got a girl comin' to have her hair cut. You want me to get her to call you?'

'Do you know where she is?' Lorraine asked, trying to keep her voice laid back.

Just then the doorbell rang at Nula's end. It was probably Didi just coming home, she said; if Lorraine wanted to hang on and wait she'd bring Didi to the phone.

'No, I got to go, I'll call later.'

Rosie waited, head on one side. 'What was that all about?'

Lorraine shrugged. 'I thought maybe something had happened to Didi but she'd just gotten home.'

They left the grocery store and drove off to the S and A garage. This time Lorraine was going to go in. She needed to speak to the man Mrs Hastings had recognized. She also knew that Steven Janklow might be there and if he was, she was going to have to come up with a good reason for her presence.

Nula fetched her coat. The two officers didn't say why they wanted her to accompany them to the station, but she knew it was something to do with Didi because they had asked for photographs of her. If she had just been arrested for prostitution, Nula knew they wouldn't want photographs. It was something else, something bad. All they had asked was if she knew David Burrows. Nobody ever called Didi David, only the cops. Half an hour later Nula identified Didi's body. She was in such a state of shock she was unable to speak coherently. All she could do was whisper Didi's name over and over. The face didn't resemble that of her beloved friend. Only the red nails and the big topaz ring made Nula sure it was Didi. Two uniformed officers returned her home by patrol car. They helped her inside the apartment, before they asked when she had last seen Didi.

The FBI checked into the complex list of dates and pick-ups that Brendan Murphy could remember. They contacted the trucking agencies he worked for and released him. He had not lied: Brendan Murphy was not in Los Angeles when his wife Helen had been killed and neither had he been near any of the other locations where victims had been found. Deprived of a suspect, they began to study the case history. Having been brought in to trace Murphy, they were now assigned to the murder investigation.

CHAPTER 14

LORRAINE SAT with Rosie in the parking lot adjacent to S and A Vintage Cars. 'Right, here I go. You wait here and if I'm not out—'

'I'll shoot myself.' Rosie laughed.

Lorraine got out of the car, gave her jacket a quick tug to straighten the back and walked briskly towards the main reception area. No one was around and the vast stretch of the polished mahogany counter held leaflets sprayed out like fans. Dull soft music, songs from the twenties, was in the air. A number of Oscar-like statues, racing cups and awards stood in glass cabinets and everywhere there were pictures of vintage cars.

Five gleaming automobiles were lined up in front of the showroom windows: a Silver Cloud Rolls-Royce, a Rolls Corniche, a 1950s Bentley, a Bristol and a two-door Mercedes sports. The leather interiors were as immaculate as the gleaming chrome, wooden dashboards, large steering wheels, by today's standards almost fragile-looking. Lorraine could see her distorted image reflected in the hub caps. She looked squat.

'Hi, how can I help you?'

She turned to the equally polished salesman. His hair gleamed, as did his teeth, his deep tan, his eyes. He had the S and A logo on the pocket of his navy blazer and on his maroon tie. He smiled expectantly, one hand shifting his immaculate starched cuff closer to his wrist, he was all logo-ed out. She wondered why he hadn't had S and A stamped on his forehead.

'Do you have an office? I'd like to discuss something with you.'

The teeth gleamed as his lips drew slightly apart in another fake smile. 'Would you like to tell me what it's about?'

'Sure, if you have an office. I am Mrs Page, and you are?'

He stepped behind the counter. 'Alan Hunter. I am the chief sales assistant. How can I help you, Mrs Page?'

He gave her a cool, studied appraisal. Even though his eyes didn't seem to leave hers, she felt as if he was scrutinizing her from her worn shoes to her second-hand suit. 'May I ask what you're selling?'

She would have liked to hit him in the face. She used to love times like this, times when, confronted by a real smart-ass prick, you drew out your ID and said in a low voice, 'You want to check my ID, sonny?'

'I'm not selling and I'm not buying. I need to talk to you in private. What did you say your name was?'

Something in her voice unnerved him so he hesitated and repeated his name.

'Right, Mr Hunter. I don't want to waste any more time and I don't want to discuss anything in this swimming pool of a lobby.'

He touched the knot of his tie and gestured towards a glass-windowed door.

Lorraine walked across the reception area and paused when she saw a picture of Brad Thorburn. He was sitting on the wing of a racing car wearing a white racing-driver's suit. One arm clasped a helmet, the other lifted a glass of champagne. To right and left were more pictures of him posing at racetracks.

Hunter opened his office door, motioning her to enter ahead of him. 'Are you with the police?'

She placed her purse on his empty polished mahogany desk and took out her cigarettes. 'Do you mind if I smoke?'

Hunter did not demur and Lorraine surveyed the room. 'You don't appear to be very busy.'

'We are, I assure you. Most of our customers wait for us to deliver, few come to the building. We have hangars and workshops out at the rear of the showroom. Can I ask what you wanted to talk to me about? Is it traffic violations?'

Lorraine sat in the perfectly positioned chair, not too far away from the desk. 'No. It's not about traffic violations.'

'Is it connected with . . .' Hunter opened his desk drawer and withdrew a card. 'A Lieutenant Josh Bean?'

'No, it isn't.'

'He was here earlier, some kind of check on stolen vehicles.'

'That's not my department. I'm investigating an insurance claim.' She took out Rosie's pictures. 'Do you recognize any of these men?'

Hunter leaned forward, sifting methodically through the photographs. He put seven aside. She watched as he glanced at the one of Steven Janklow. He frowned, hesitated a moment, and then looked up. 'These seven men work here in various capacities.'

She tapped Steven Janklow's picture. 'How about him?'

Hunter picked up the photograph. 'This could be Mr Janklow. He's one of the partners but it's not a very good picture. I recognize the car more than the face. It's one of ours – it's actually owned by Brad Thorburn. Is it something to do with Mr Thorburn?'

Lorraine nodded, looking around for an ashtray. As Hunter passed her a silver one with the S and A logo stamped into the centre, she noticed his gold cufflinks which also carried the insignia. She tapped the ash from her cigarette and eased out the picture of the woman driving the Mercedes. 'Do you know her?'

He stuck out his bottom lip, shaking his head. 'No. It could be Mrs Thorburn, Mr Thorburn's mother, but I really wouldn't know as I've never met her. But the car is the same. It belongs, as I said, to Mr Thorburn. Has it been in an accident?'

'No.' Lorraine packed away the pictures. 'Do you have a schedule of who was on or off duty over a period of time?'

He nodded, tapping his foot. She then pulled out Norman Hastings's picture. 'Do you recognize this man?'

Hunter sighed irritably. 'His name was Norman Hastings. Is it his insurance? He was murdered, is that what this is about?'

Lorraine assented.

'Well, I'm sorry, but I never dealt with him. All I know is he was a pain in the butt. He bought a car from us, long time ago before I joined the company.' He leaned back, splaying out his hands affectedly. 'If you buy one of our vehicles at the prices we ask, we have first-class mechanics and maintenance engineers at your service. We attempt to make sure no vehicle ever leaves here without its engine having been rechecked, rebuilt if necessary. Many purchasers have the cars customized to their own specifications. Every modification is made to ensure a trouble-free vehicle, but, that said, we're not dealing in new cars. Some of these are twenty, even thirty years old, and sometimes there will be problems. But we give a six-month guarantee to every vehicle, and for the first six months we will collect and redeliver should any mechanical fault occur.'

He laughed like an actor, his speech, even his own humour rehearsed. 'We had someone here not long ago, I think he had a Bentley, and he called us out simply because he was unsure where he should put the gas!'

'Norman Hastings?' Lorraine said quietly.

'His car was a Morgan. He was on the phone almost every day wanting it collected and tested. And then we

271

discovered that the faults were self-inflicted because he was constantly taking the engine apart and rebuilding it – or that's what Mr Janklow said.'

'Is Mr Janklow here today?'

'Yes.'

Lorraine asked if it were possible to find out who was on or off work at the time of Hastings's murder and that included Mr Janklow.

Hunter plucked at his lip. 'Why would you want that for an insurance claim? Anyway, Mr Janklow doesn't work on any schedule system. He comes and goes when he likes.'

Lorraine asked if Janklow was around on the evening when Holly was murdered but Hunter shrugged his shoulders. He stared at a wall calendar. 'I simply couldn't tell you. All I know is he arrives and leaves when he feels like it.'

'Is there a place for parking workers' cars?'

'Out back. It's like an old aircraft hangar – there's always cars there – our own, some waiting for work to be done, others that have just been shipped in.'

Lorraine opened her notebook and reeled off the car each body had been found in but to little effect. Hunter could not recall any of them. He was becoming puzzled by the dates and lists of cars. She played a wild card. 'Not even, say, Norman Hastings's blue Sedan?'

'Ah, yes, he left that here on a number of occasions.'

Lorraine felt her heart jump, like a kick of pleasure at her own cleverness. 'Would you just check the last time you saw it here.'

Hunter looked at his watch. He picked up the phone. 'Sheena, can you please check the last time Norman Hastings came in and left his vehicle? Thank you.' He hung up. 'The police asked this, and they've already been over the hangars.'

Lorraine lit another cigarette and tossed the match into the ashtray. 'Hastings sold his car, didn't he? Quite a few years ago. Do you know if he purchased any other vintage car? Did he sell it via S and A?'

'Not to my knowledge but I didn't have anything to do with him.'

'Did Mr Thorburn also know Hastings?'

'I believe so.'

The phone rang and Hunter answered it. He drew a notepad towards him, said 'yes' a few times, thanked the caller and ripped off the page. 'Hastings apparently had some arrangement to leave his car here – my secretary isn't sure who he made it with or the last time he came.'

'So he parked his own car here and yet he hadn't owned one of your vehicles recently?'

'Seems so.'

'Do you think the arrangement would have been with Mr Janklow?'

'I've no idea. My direct boss is Mr Thorburn, not Mr Janklow.'

'What do you think of him?' she asked nonchalantly.

'Brad? He's great to work for. He's firm, you know where you are with him, but he's also fun, loves a good laugh.'

'I meant Steven Janklow.'

Hunter pursed his lips in distaste. 'I have little to do with him so I can't say what he's like.'

'You could try.'

'I don't see eye to eye with him, that's all. He's volatile. One day he's friendly, the next he'll cut you dead. He's witty but it's that put-down humour, that's all.'

'Is he married?'

'No.'

'Is he homosexual?'

Hunter was shocked. 'I don't know.'

'Do you think he could be? Or could he be something else?'

'Like normal?'

Lorraine stood up. 'Fine, so you think he's a nice, normal guy. I'm sorry, but my firm insists on me completing these amazing questionnaires.'

'But I told you, he's not that nice.'

Hunter gave her a hooded look and she smiled broadly. 'How about not that normal either?' she said. She was beginning to like the Ivy League car salesman. She reckoned he was being honest with her and was green enough to have taken her at face value as an insurance claim officer. She looked through the white blind to the front yard.

'Is he suspected of something?' Hunter asked. 'The police asked a lot of questions to some of the other staff but they weren't very interested in me. I wasn't here the week of the Hastings murder.' He sounded disappointed.

Lorraine got out the photographs again. 'What about taking another look at that photo of the blonde woman? Can you tell me if it could be Janklow?'

Hunter picked up the photograph. He studied it and his voice went quiet. 'I honestly don't know, Mrs Page, and I would hate to embarrass Mr Thorburn. He's a good friend.'

'Norman Hastings's family cannot sell his car or claim any monies on his insurance until I have completed my questionnaire.'

'Is Mr Janklow under suspicion?'

Lorraine ran her fingers through her hair. It was difficult to ask what she wanted to know without getting into trouble.

'There are rumours,' he said suddenly. She waited as Hunter determined whether or not to continue. 'I don't know if I should repeat them as they are just rumours.' He came to a decision. 'He has some odd mannerisms and he can be affected. Nobody here knows much about his private life, just that a few years ago there was an inquiry. He was interviewed by the Vice Squad, arrested. Nothing came of it.'

There was a light tap on the door and a pretty girl peered

in. 'I'm sorry to interrupt, Mr Hunter, but you have a customer waiting.'

Hunter introduced his secretary, Sheena. Lorraine asked if she and Sheena could have a quick chat and look at the hangar where the cars were kept. He said he had better ask his superior.

'I'll wait here with Sheena then,' Lorraine said.

Sheena looked at Lorraine. 'You wanna know about Norman Hastings? He used to come here quite a lot. He used to park his car out back – loved to look over the new arrivals. I had to check back this morning for the police. As far as I can remember these were the dates when his car was left here. I gave the officers a copy too.' She passed over a neatly typed list. 'I was so shocked when I read about his murder. He was such a quiet, unassuming man, like my dad.'

Lorraine looked over the dates and then smiled warmly at her. 'If I were to give you a list of other cars, could you see if they were parked out in the hangar at any time?'

Sheena bit her lip. 'I've already got one list from the police but I told them it's not a garage, we just let the workers park there and a few friends. Sometimes there's no free space.'

'Could we take a look at the hangar?'

Lorraine followed Sheena across a wide yard. There were a number of outbuildings and she could see cars on ramps and mechanics working. The business seemed to be thriving and she calculated that there were a lot more employees than Rosie had said.

The hangar was boiling hot and there were rows of cars, fender to fender. Some had tarpaulins over them and seemed to have been left for a considerable time. Dust covered others waiting to be reconditioned and then came a large section of what looked like the workers' cars.

'Mr Thorburn likes the employees' vehicles out of sight, says it's not a good advertisement. We park here and

275

this is where Mr Hastings's car usually was, just for a few hours at a time, but he always left the keys. We have to leave the keys in case they need to be moved if a delivery arrives.'

They reached the back of the hangar and looked over three racing cars, all draped in protective silver covers. 'These are Mr Thorburn's specials. He used to race a lot, but not so much nowadays. One of his wives created a stink about it . . .' Sheena opened a door at the back of the hangar into a corridor. It was air-conditioned, freezing cold compared with the hangar. They passed large offices with white blinds on the windows. One was Brad Thorburn's, his name on a wood plaque cut into the door. They arrived at Sheena's where she took out a large log book to check the list of cars Lorraine had given her. 'It's the same list the police gave me. I told them there was just the one. Mr Hastings's.'

The phone rang. She answered it, listened and then said, 'I'd better go. I've got to take the sales invoices to Mr Hunter. Every week the top salesman gets a bonus.'

'Can I wait?'

'Sure. I'll tell Mr Hunter you're in here.'

Sheena gathered up a file and walked out. She left the door ajar. As soon as she was half-way down the corridor, Lorraine closed the door, picked up the log book and began to search through it. She was getting close, she knew it. She felt herself growing excited. She was sure Steven Janklow was connected to the case.

Rosie got out of the car, her dress sticking to her in the heat. A number of people had already taken a good look at her, noticing that she was parked in their yard. She walked round the car, fanning herself with her hand. She was thirsty and Lorraine had been gone over an hour. Just as she thought she would go into S and A, a mechanic walked out of the building and headed towards her. 'This is a private road, you want something?'

'No. My friend's inside.' She pointed to the S and A building.

'Why don't you wait over there? We're expecting a delivery any minute. Go on, move.'

Rosie returned to the car and started up the engine. She backed out and parked for a while in the street. Then she circled the block. She was heading past S and A when a white Mercedes passed her and drove onto the forecourt. Rosie watched Steven Janklow head round to the rear of the building and disappear before she could get her camera out. She dabbed her sweating face with a tissue. 'Come on, for God's sake, Lorraine, what are you doing in there?' she muttered. From where she was parked, opposite the garage, she could see a smart salesman talking to two Japanese men. All three disappeared inside. Still no Lorraine.

The door opened and Sheena came back in. 'Sorry, but I got held up. I haven't been able to speak to Mr Hunter yet – he's still with a couple of clients and I think they want a test drive.' A voice from one of the other offices called, 'Good morning, Mr Janklow.'

Sheena pulled a face. 'He's here. Look, I'd better go and tell Mr Hunter that you're still waiting.'

Lorraine picked up her purse. 'No, it's okay. I'll find him myself. Thank you for the coffee.'

'I hope I was of some help. It was just so terrible, poor Mr Hastings.'

'Did you see him when he was here the last time?'

'No, but when he came to see Mr Janklow, he'd pop in and leave me his car keys. I think he banked up the street, but his office isn't far away. He was always anxious about parking fines. Funny, really, worrying about something as small as that and then . . . he gets killed.'

'But Mr Janklow was here *then*?'

'Yes. Do you want to speak to him?'

'Maybe later. I'll just go see Mr Hunter. Thanks for everything.'

Lorraine walked out, into the blast of cold air in the corridor. Her heart jumped as she passed Janklow's office but he was not inside; through the blinds, she could see a secretary placing papers on the desk. She continued along the corridor, came into the hangar and walked quickly out into the sunshine. She stood for a moment to get her bearings and then took off towards the path winding around the building, intending to go back to Rosie. Then she saw the Mercedes parked by a car-wash area. She hugged the wall when she saw a man talking to one of the attendants. He was gesturing to the car's wheels. Then he leaned into it and pointed to the interior. She saw the attendant nod, then heard him tell two black kids to wash and vacuum Mr Janklow's car, and polish up the chrome on the hub caps and fenders.

Lorraine waited, half wanting Janklow to turn round so that she could see his face but not wanting him to catch sight of her. He was wearing a pale blue linen jacket, white slacks and sandals. Slim, immaculate, his hair cut short and tight to his head – blondish-brown hair – just as she remembered. Steven Janklow was the man who had attacked her, she was sure of it. If only she could get a good look at his face.

Hunter appeared at the showroom doors. 'We've a customer who wants a trial drive, Mr Janklow. It's the Silver Cloud but we've already got someone that asked if we'd contact them if it looked like we'd got a sale.'

Janklow walked slowly towards him and Lorraine pressed closer to the wall. They were about to enter the building, Hunter stepping aside to allow Janklow to go in ahead, when Hunter saw her and waved. 'I won't be a moment, Mrs Page, I'm sorry to keep you waiting.' As soon

278

as they disappeared, Lorraine hurried along the wide lane, past the Mercedes, to the road, hoping that Janklow's attention would be on the customers.

As Janklow was walking towards the Japanese customers, Hunter mentioned that the police had been to speak to him that morning about Norman Hastings. He added, 'There's another insurance broker, or something to do with Hastings's car, here. She was in my office but I just saw her outside. She wanted to know about Hastings parking his car in the hangar.'

Hunter was used to Janklow's mood changes but he was stunned when the man pushed past him and walked back out the way they had come in.

'What about the Silver Cloud, Mr Janklow?'

Janklow's fists were clenched as he strode along the corridor to Sheena's office and opened the door. She gave a nervous smile at the sight of him. 'Where is this woman from the insurance company?' he demanded.

'She just left me, Mr Janklow.'

'What did she want?'

Sheena swallowed. 'Same as the other two officers. She was making inquiries about vehicles we allowed to be parked in the hangar.'

Janklow picked up the log book. 'Did you get her name?'

'I presumed Mr Hunter must have. She was interviewing him this morning.'

'What do you mean, interviewing?'

'Well, just talking to him. I don't know what he said or anything. I was only doing what I was told, Mr Janklow.'

He walked out and into his own office, banging down the heavy book in a fury. He then rang through to the showroom.

Hunter was turning the engine over, the Japanese looking on with interest, when the phone went. Hunter excused himself and went to answer it. Janklow seemed hysterical, screaming for him to get into his office immediately. He didn't care if they had customers, he wanted to speak to Hunter this second. If he valued his job he would get himself over there. Before Hunter could reply the phone was banged down.

Lorraine ran towards Rosie and climbed in beside her.

'Thanks a lot, I've been roasting alive out here. Have you any idea how long I've been waiting? I've been round the block four times and I'm dying of thirst.'

Lorraine told Rosie to get out of sight of S and A. She hit the dashboard with her fist. 'I've got him, Rosie, I know he did it. Maybe he did them all but I'm damned sure for one that Janklow killed Norman Hastings. We got an A-1 suspect for Rooney.'

Rooney was sweating in spite of the chill of his air-conditioned office. He expected the FBI any minute to talk to him and the rest of the day would be spent discussing the murders, and his lack of progress. He'd finished the bottle of bourbon, his nose was redder than ever and his eyes were bloodshot. Bean put a large mug of black coffee and a packet of peppermints in front of him. Rooney had seemed less than interested in the new victim; he'd merely glanced at the reports and photographs. 'What was she? Man, woman or what?' Rooney muttered.

'A transsexual prostitute. It's in the report, happened last night around ten thirty.'

The only thing different about this one was that she had been hammered to the side of the head first, and had no rear scalp wound but multiple facial injuries. It had not yet been ascertained if the weapon was the same as that used in the previous murders.

'Any witnesses?' Rooney asked.

'Nope. She or he was seen on the streets, then said she was going to have a break because she'd got something wrong with her right foot.'

'That it?'

Bean nodded.

'Well, let these smart-alecks sort it. Any sign of them yet?'

'Due any time. They went out for lunch. Oh, you wanted a low-key inquiry run off at the S and A garage about the workers. Well, it's all here. Hastings's car was parked there in a hangar but he removed it the day before he was killed. He used it as a free parking lot – he knew the management. Place belongs to the Thorburns.' Bean tweaked two fingers up when he said the name. 'You want to take it further?'

'If his fuckin' car wasn't parked there on the day he died then it's not much use to us, is it?'

The phone rang and Rooney motioned for Bean to leave. Out of the corner of his eye, Bean saw Rooney swivel round to face the wall behind him, the report of the morning's interviews at S and A left untouched on his desk. He hoped Rooney would get his act together before the FBI grilled him. He looked shot and stank of liquor.

Lorraine was using a public call box.

'You got something for me?' Rooney snapped.

'Yeah, but I don't want to discuss it over the phone.'

'Dunno if I can get away. There's been another one.' He gave Didi's real name and that she was a transsexual prostitute. 'She was in the car like the others, similar head wounds. Car was reported stolen a few hours after we found it.'

'When did it happen?' she asked bluntly.

'Last night, around ten. Nicknamed Didi. You ever heard the name?'

They agreed to meet in an hour and a half's time at Rooney's favourite Indian restaurant. Just as he picked up the reports, the phone rang again. He was required in the Chief's office. The FBI were waiting.

Lorraine joined Rosie in the car. 'Where to now, partner?' Rosie asked.

'Didi's dead – one of the transsexuals you met at the gallery.'

Rosie switched on the engine and Lorraine told her to put her foot down: she was meeting Rooney but wanted to talk to Nula first.

'You going to tell him everything?' Rosie yelled over the noise of the car engine. 'Only you could maybe get some more dough out of him if you got a suspect.'

Rooney slipped the knot of his tie closer to his sweat-stained collar. The Chief cracked his knuckles, waiting impatiently for an answer. 'I don't need this, Bill. Who the fuck did you send there?'

Rooney shifted his weight. 'Lieutenant Bean and another officer.'

'The complaint was about a woman.'

'She used to be a cop and she's been doing some work for me on the streets.'

'This isn't on the street, Bill, this is somebody impersonating a police officer.' Rooney pulled at his tie again. He had no idea what Lorraine had been doing at the S and A, or why his chief was getting so hot under the collar. 'It's not in any report, Bill. What was she fucking doing there? That family have big connections and they're screaming about this. I want you to go there personally, iron it out. We've got enough bad press as it is and I don't intend losing my job over this.'

Rooney gave a half smile. 'Yes, sir. They that powerful? This garage a big deal, huh?'

The Chief glared. 'It's the Thorburn family, old money, big money. Fucking back off them. Go on, get out.'

'What about the suits? I thought I was having a briefing with them.'

'Sort this out first.'

Rooney knew who the Thorburns were, not that you heard much about them nowadays but their donations to police charities were legendary. Lorraine Page had better have something for him.

Nula was distraught. Her face, devoid of make-up, looked haggard, her eyes without their false eyelashes were puffy and red from weeping. As soon as she saw Lorraine she broke down again. She wore a silk kimono and bedroom slippers. In the raw light of day the apartment was claustrophobic with its drapes and stuffed animals. Rosie hovered, finding it difficult not to stare at the overtly sexual pictures that hung on all available wall space. Lorraine fetched a glass of water and sat by Nula, holding her hand.

'Tell me what happened.'

Nula wiped her face with a sodden tissue. 'She used to have a number of regulars, she often stayed out all night. When she didn't come back I thought she'd scored. It wasn't her at the door when you phoned – it was the cops to tell me.'

'Do you have a list of her regulars?' Lorraine asked.

'No, of course I don't. Nothing was ever arranged, they'd just turn up on the streets and sometimes she used that motel Roselee, but the rooms there were getting expensive. Sometimes she brought them back here, I dunno their names. I've got my own clients and she's got . . . Oh, God—I don't know what I'm going to do without her.'

'Can you describe any of her johns? Did you see any that night?'

'*No!* She was with me one minute and then she just walked off.'

Lorraine opened the envelope. 'Will you look at these photographs and tell me if there's anyone you recognize?' Nula looked at each one, sniffing and blowing her nose. Lorraine saved the blonde in the Mercedes until last. 'What about this woman?'

Nula took the photograph. It was the only one she showed any interest in, but she shook her head.

'Are you sure? Keep looking at it, Nula, look at the car – it's an old Mercedes sports car. Look at the woman . . . is it a woman?'

Nula turned away. 'I don't know, I don't *know*. I want to be left alone, please, *please* just leave me alone.'

Rosie leaned forward. 'That car was driving along Sunset last night. Did you see Didi speak to the driver – maybe get into the car?'

Lorraine gave Rosie a discreet wink. Rosie remained silent, eyes swinging from Lorraine to Nula; she was impressed with her friend, she was hot shit.

Nula scrutinized the picture of the blonde. 'Does this woman have something to do with Didi?' Nula asked. 'Do you think she had something to do with her murder?'

'She might, but do you recognize her?'

'No, I just said so, didn't I?' Nula passed the picture back.

Lorraine stood up and packed away the photographs. Nula began to sob again, burying her face in her hands.

'We'll let ourselves out, Nula, and I'm so sorry, really sorry.'

Nula hugged her kimono tighter around herself, the tissue in shreds now as she plucked at it with her long, painted fingernails. 'She was the nicest person I've ever known. I'm all on my own now, I've nobody, she was my best friend. I don't know what I'll do. I can't afford this place – I've got no money.'

'What about Art? Do you know where you can contact him?'

'He's left town. We haven't heard from him since the gallery closed. I'm not sure where he is.'

Nula waited until she heard their car driving away before she went into the bedroom and opened a drawer in the bedside table. She took out a black diary and thumbed through the pages. Just seeing Didi's childish scrawled writing made her want to weep again but she gulped back her tears, flicking over the pages until she found what she was looking for. She went back to the hallway and picked up the phone. She pressed each digit and waited.

'Hi, this is Art. I'm not in, but please leave me your name and number, and I'll get back to you, okay? And wait for the tone before you leave your message.'

'Art, it's Nula. Will you call me? It's very urgent. We have to talk.'

She replaced the receiver and went into the bathroom. She'd have a long perfumed soak, that would make her feel better, and she was going to feel better. But before she turned on the taps, she went into the bedroom and knelt down by the bedside table. Lifting the curtain, she opened the bottom drawer and withdrew a large, square manilla envelope. She pulled out a number of photographs, then sat back on her heels. The one she wanted was black and white, of a woman sitting on a bed, wearing a long fifties evening gown with padded shoulders, a bit like Barbara Stanwyck, of that era. She was elegant, exceptionally beautiful. He had wanted to look like her, had brought the photograph for Didi to match, and she had worked for hours on him. The wig had been on a stand for days as she had teased and set it, ready for him. He had paid a lot of money for the session and Art had taken the photographs, draping the room to his specifications, down to the flower arrangements. The blonde woman was the same as the one in the picture Lorraine had shown her. Nula didn't panic. She slowly got to her feet and began to search through all the stacks of photographic files.

Rosie dropped Lorraine outside the Indian and drove off.

Rooney was already sitting at a table with a glass of beer. 'This had better be good and you'd better have a fucking good reason for barging into that S and A place. What the fuck were you doing there?'

Lorraine picked up the menu, asked if he'd ordered, but he said he wasn't hungry.

'You run a check on the S and A employees like I asked?' she said.

Rooney swigged his beer, banging the glass onto the table.

'There was a vice charge against Steven Janklow. You got a record of it? Be a few years back. Picked up for pavement crawlin', I think. He part owns the garage. His brother is Brad Thorburn.'

'What's your interest in him?'

Lorraine laid her hands flat on the table. 'I think he's your killer.'

Rooney pulled at his nose. 'What evidence have you got?'

She rubbed her cheek. 'I don't, but I do know that Hastings's car was left in their hangar.'

'You any idea who Janklow's family is?'

She shrugged. 'I guess they must be important if they've got you running. Can you check if there was a vice charge? If there was, you can get him for questioning, see if he can account for himself over Hastings. It's him, Bill, I'm sure.'

'Why?'

Lorraine took her time to outline the reasons before she told him that she was sure Janklow was the man who had attacked her. It didn't sink in for a while. Then he looked up.

'You wanna say that again?'

'I said, I think he was the man who attacked me, the man that I bit a chunk out of his neck.'

He leaned back, partly in disbelief, then got out his cigarettes and stuck one in his mouth. He stared fixedly around the restaurant, feeling as if the floor was opening up, and inhaled deeply. 'You stupid bitch.'

'I'm sorry, I was scared to come forward. I picked him up—'

'Sweet Jesus.' Rooney shook his head.

'He attacked me with a claw hammer. I'm sure it was Steven Janklow.'

'You seen him face to face? Or, more to the point, has he seen you?'

'No, I've held off facing him, I don't want to tip him off.'

Lorraine's order was placed in front of her. Rooney waited until the waiter had moved off before he leaned towards her. 'Say it *is* him — say he's the guy that attacked you. You can identify him . . .'

She had picked up her fork but put it down again. 'I identify him, he denies it, he walks. It's just the word of an ex-hooker, ex-drunkard against a fine, upstanding citizen, right? All he's got to say is he wasn't anywhere near the street I was picked up in and I got to admit I was picking him up for a few bucks. It wasn't his car, it was Hastings's car and Hastings's body was in the trunk. Now who's gonna believe who?'

Rooney drained his beer and beckoned the waiter to bring another.

Lorraine messed around with the food on her plate, then pushed it away. 'I think he's a transvestite.'

Rooney ran his hands through his hair. '*What?*'

'I think Janklow's a transvestite.'

287

'*Think?* I need more than you fucking thinking, I need evidence, I need *facts*. Jesus Christ, Lorraine, you know how crazy this all sounds?' He put his head in his hands. The more she told him, the worse it all sounded. 'You think the guy that hit on you was Steven Janklow, right? You also think Steven Janklow is a transvestite. Is there anything else you might have just glossed over – that maybe he has two heads?'

'Back off me. All the dead women have a similar look, similar age.'

'What about Holly?'

'I think she's the mistake. Because of the last one, Didi.'

Lorraine explained that she thought the killer was trying to pick up Nula or Didi on the night Holly was murdered. She told him how they had both seen a car, had both seen Holly run across the road to a punter. Her pimp Curtis saw her – but maybe the john was trying to pick up Didi or Nula. Once he'd got Holly he had to get rid of her. Maybe he panicked.

Rooney argued that it didn't make sense. Why didn't he just kick her out, if he'd got the wrong one? His head throbbed and he still couldn't believe how she'd held out on him like this.

Lorraine banged the table. 'Wait a minute! The wrong one. What if they were all the wrong ones? What if he was looking specifically for Didi all along? They're all the same age, all dyed or bleached blondes, but he can't find the one he's looking for, the main one.'

'Are you trying to tell me that this guy clubs seven women to death because he's looking for one, and we forget Norman Hastings? Did he think he was one as well? This is dumb, Lorraine. You lost your touch, sweetheart. We're looking at someone who's bumped off these women over five years, and he's doing it because of mistaken identity? Nuts!'

Lorraine twiddled her fork. 'Okay, let's try something

else. Let's go through every victim, including Hastings. He was a drag artist, right? He used to park his car at S and A years after he was doing any business with them but he knew Janklow. Maybe he found out something?'

Rooney delved in his pocket for his wallet. 'Maybe I'm wasting my time. I got to go take a leak.'

'But listen to me, there's every type of tool and hammer at the S and A. Can't someone check there? Match them? What if the hammers came from there?'

Rooney jabbed the air with his finger. 'Stay away from that place, is that understood? From now on you don't go anywhere near it. I'll have the place looked over again – in fact, I'll do it personally – but you stay well away.' He squinted at the bill and looked up at her. 'I'll check out what I think fit.'

'The Vice Squad, can you check that for me? See what Janklow was picked up for?'

'For *you*? Who in chrissakes do you think is runnin' this show? I'll take it from here. If you wanna press charges for assault—'

She leaned back. 'You know I won't do that but if you get more evidence, then I can be used as a lever. We let him confront me, let him know I'm alive and can identify him, and then see what he does. Use me to catch him. I'm willing.'

Rooney hauled his bulk out of the booth. 'Lemme think on it.'

She followed him as he headed for the restroom. 'Bill, he used a hammer on me. It's him.'

He whipped round. 'I could have you for withholding evidence. I only paid you to get out on the streets to talk to the hookers, so back off. I'll contact you when I need you.'

'I need a few dollars, I'm flat broke.'

'Not my problem,' he said as he pushed open the restroom door, and let it swing closed.

When he came out of the restaurant she was waiting by

his patrol car. She gave that strange, lopsided smile and he relaxed slightly. Although he was loath to admit it, she had pushed the investigation further – had even supplied him with a suspect.

'Lemme see what I come up with – but you do nothing until you hear from me, okay? Here's a few bucks, go home, wait for me to call. If it's Janklow, leave him to me.'

She took the money and watched him drive off. She checked the time – just after two thirty. As she walked to the bus stop she was thinking over everything she had said to Rooney. She had been clutching at straws, but what if she was right? What if there was a connection between Didi and Janklow? She hailed a taxi and, instead of returning home, told the driver to take her to Nula's place.

CHAPTER 15

NULA DIDN'T answer the door. Lorraine waited for almost an hour and then went home. There she hung about in case Rooney called but when it got to after six, she decided he'd got cold feet. 'I guess he mulled it all over and decided against it.'

Rosie wondered what they should do next. Without Rooney she was worried it could be dangerous to try to see Janklow again. Lorraine grabbed her purse.

'Where are you going?' Rosie asked nervously.

'You stay put so I can call Rooney back if he makes contact.'

'Don't you need me with you?'

'I'd prefer it if you stayed put in case he calls. I've got to keep him sweet, 'cos if I don't the old bastard is quite likely to get me arrested.'

Rosie sat moodily in front of the TV. She didn't even say goodbye as Lorraine let herself out. So much for partnership – all she'd been doing was sitting waiting for Lorraine in the apartment. When she heard the rental car starting up Rosie shot to the window as fast as her bulk allowed her. She pushed up the window and was about to yell after Lorraine but it was too late, she was already at the corner.

*

It had been so long since Lorraine had driven that her knees were shaking but she talked herself down, hoping she wouldn't get pulled over.

The lights were on in Nula's apartment. Lorraine sighed with relief, locked the car and headed into the apartment block. She rang the bell and waited. Nula's voice asked who it was but Lorraine rang again, afraid if she said her name that Nula wouldn't let her in. She kept her hand on the bell, and eventually Nula peered out, the chain still on.

'Fuck off.'

'Let me in, Nula, I'll stay here all night if needs be.'

Nula eventually opened up the door. Lorraine looked around. Suitcases had been dragged down from the wardrobes. Nula was on the move.

'What happened?'

'I'm going away.'

'Why do you have to go?'

Nula hurled a cushion at her. 'Stop asking me questions, just leave me alone.'

Lorraine took out the picture of Steven Janklow in drag. 'Will you have another look at this, Nula?'

Nula picked up the cushion and hugged it to her chest. Lorraine dangled the photograph between finger and thumb. 'It won't hurt you to have a look at it. Is it Steven Janklow?'

'If you fucking know who it is, why are you asking me?'

'Because I need to be sure.'

'I don't know, do I?'

Lorraine was deflated. She didn't know what her next move should be. She flopped back on the sofa.

'You gonna leave now?'

Lorraine slipped the photograph back into the envelope and stood up, facing the big four-sectioned screen behind which the models changed for a session. It was plastered with photographs of males and females, males and males, part females. Nula looked at her, then to the screen.

Lorraine started to move out then stopped and glanced back to Nula, who hid her face in the cushion. She stared at the screen. At first she wasn't sure that she was right so she moved closer, then she bent down and peered. She straightened up and waved the file. 'You don't know him? Then why is his photograph up on the screen?'

'Because it fitted the hole.'

'Who took the photograph?'

'Why?'

'Because if you don't know who it is, then whoever took the photograph might. Who took the picture, Nula?'

'Art.'

Lorraine could feel the adrenalin pumping; it was all as crazy as Rooney had said. 'What's Art's scene apart from the porno?'

'Use your head, clever bitch. Where do you think he gets all his dough from?'

'Why don't you tell me?'

Nula stood up and leaned against the doorframe to the bedroom. 'Blackmail. Some fucking detective you are. Art blackmails everybody, he's a bleeder – you should know, you copped a few grand from one of his little leech jobs. I don't know that blonde in that photo on the screen and I don't know whoever it is in your precious folder. That's not my screen, it's Art's. Now would you get out and leave me alone?'

'Where's Art?'

'I don't know.'

Lorraine followed Nula into the bedroom. 'Was he blackmailing Steven Janklow?'

Nula kicked out at the wardrobe and screamed, '*I don't know, leave me alone.*' She began to pull clothes out of her wardrobe.

'He was blackmailing him, wasn't he?'

Nula was hurling dresses onto the bed.

'The night Didi died—'

'*Yes, what about the night Didi died?*'

Lorraine kept her distance. Nula was becoming increasingly hysterical, dragging things off their hangers, dropping them, kicking them. She suddenly turned to Lorraine in a fury. 'He used us. If we had a john, he was sniffing around. He never let us have any peace, but then we couldn't have any because he'd give a few dollars here, a few dollars there, he let us have this apartment, okay? He said we never had to pay rent, okay? Well, if you believe that you're dumb. Art used me, used Didi, he made us both pay. Now if you don't get out and leave me alone I swear before God I'll scream this place down and have you arrested.'

Lorraine didn't budge. 'Was Art blackmailing Norman Hastings?'

Lorraine looked over the screen at the laminated photographs. She was frantically glancing from one blonde to another in a vague hope that one or other of the dead women as well as Hastings would have been photographed. 'When did Art make this screen?'

'Years ago. He brought it here with him when he left Santa Monica – he had a place there on the beach.' Nula stood, hands on hips, smirking. She had decided to try another tactic to get rid of Lorraine.

'Did he ever own a vintage car?'

Nula rolled her eyes. 'What do you mean?'

'A custom-made car or an old sports car.'

'Nah, he had a Bentley once for about six months, then he went broke again and sold it.'

'The blonde in the photograph, the one I showed you on the screen, did you meet him?'

Nula sighed. 'No.'

'What about Didi?'

Nula was holding a long chiffon dress. 'This was her favourite. It never fitted her but she wouldn't throw it out.'

'Nula, please, did Didi know the blonde?'

'She may have, she used to do wigs, she was always good

294

with hair. Art used her sometimes for photo sessions, so she may have, I don't know who she knew.'

'Did Didi know Art before you?'

'Yes, I met him through her.'

Lorraine's mind was racing, trying to put two and two together but she wasn't sure what she was trying to come up with. There was no point in staying any longer. Her priority now was to contact the photographer who had taken pictures of Norman Hastings. She asked Nula if she could use her phone.

Rosie was still watching TV when Lorraine called. No, there had been no contact from Rooney. Lorraine asked her to check in the files for the name and address of Hastings's photographer. She hung on, waiting impatiently, until eventually Rosie found his name: Craig Lyall. She gave the address and phone number. Lorraine said she would call in again. If Rooney made contact, Rosie was to tell him that she would be back in about an hour: it was imperative she speak with him.

'Have you ever heard of Craig Lyall, a photographer?' she asked Nula.

Nula clicked the suitcase shut. 'Professional, is he?'

'Yeah, takes family shots, portraits.'

Nula shrugged. 'Name isn't familiar but then I'm never good with names.'

'What about Didi? Do you have her address book? Maybe she has his number.'

Nula took a small key and locked the case. 'No, she never kept one, and now, if you'll excuse me, I am going to take a bath. Unless you want to watch me soaping my tits I suggest you leave.'

'You need a lift? I've got a car.'

'I'll get a cab.'

'Can I ask where you're going?'

'You can, but I don't see why I should tell you.'

'Just in case I need to get in touch with you.'

Nula carried her cases to the door, dumped them and went back to pick up two more bags.

'Curtis knows how to contact me.'

Lorraine reached out to shake Nula's hand but she turned away. 'Goodbye, and thanks.'

Nula stood in the centre of the room, arms folded. As soon as she heard the front door slam behind Lorraine, she clutched the sides of her head and started to scream, ripping off her wig and hurling it across the room. She screamed and screamed.

Lorraine drove to Craig Lyall's studio. She looked around for a phone kiosk to check with Rosie if Rooney had called. He hadn't but two uniformed police officers had been there. Rosie hadn't been unduly worried when they arrived, partly because she was expecting Rooney. She even asked if they were there because of him. They did not answer her questions but moved from room to room, even swishing back the shower curtain. When they asked if there were any other ways into the apartment, Rosie started to get uneasy. She was edgy after they left because they remained outside in their patrol car and didn't look as if they had any intention of driving off.

Lorraine wondered what Rooney was playing at. She told Rosie she would call him right away and see her in a while.

'Where are you?'

'Ventura Highway. I'm gonna talk to this Craig Lyall. See you later.' She hung up and called Rooney's office.

'Where are you?' he barked.

'Oh, just having a quick coffee, then I'm on my way home.'

'Do me a favour and bring yourself to the station.'

'You got a development?'

'Maybe. I want you here where I can see you.'

'I got something I want you to check out. Photographer, guy called Art Mathews. I think he's involved, blackmailer, porno stuff. He knows Janklow . . . hello?' The beep-beep-beep of her money running out cut off the call.

Rooney let the receiver drop back on the cradle. He waited, half hoping she would call again, wandering round his office, hitching up his pants. Through his venetian blind he could see the suits working with the computer officers, sifting through the investigations. He let the blind fall back into place. He was, in some way, hiding out – he'd skirted around them all afternoon and evening.

Bean breezed in and Rooney jumped. 'Fuckin' knock, for chrissakes, you give me a heart attack. You ever heard of a porno photographer, Art Mathews?'

'Nope.'

'Run a trace on him, will you? And then bring him in. I want to have a talk to him.'

'Okay, will do. You wanted to know if Vice had anything on a Steven Janklow? There's no record, nothing . . . but the Thorburn family funded an entire section of the LAPD forensic lab and—'

'Thank you,' grunted Rooney.

'You're welcome,' said Bean as he walked out.

Lorraine moved up the wood-slatted staircase to the small photographic studio belonging to Craig Lyall. She pressed the intercom and waited. Asked to identify herself, she said she was a friend of Art Mathews. Lyall unbolted the door. Small and dapper, he was shorter than Lorraine.

'What do you want? You a cop?'

'No, just a friend of Art's.'

Lorraine followed Lyall up the narrow staircase towards his studio apartment. The TV was on loudly and he switched it off. 'I was working in the dark room. Let me sort out these negs then I'll be right with you. Make yourself at home.'

Lorraine put down her purse and remained standing, looking at all the framed photographs. She then crossed to two heavyweight albums, filled with portraits of kids and families. She turned over the heavy pages, awful smiling brats in over-colourful dresses, all much the same, similar to the pictures she had seen in Mrs Hastings's home.

Lyall returned and offered her a drink. He seemed jumpy.

'Art's told me a lot about you.'

'Really?'

'Yeah. He's in trouble, you know that?'

'He's always been in trouble, ever since I've known him.'

'Yeah, well, this time he's involved in murder.'

Lyall pursed his lips. 'Jesus Christ, it's not this fucking Hastings thing again. I've had them here, you know, asking me all kinds of questions. All I did was take some photographs – poor bastard liked to drag up, right? What's wrong in that?'

Lorraine perched on the edge of a hard-back chair. 'Can I see them? Just out of interest. I'm trying to help Art. I wasn't all that honest with you – I'm a private investigator and I need to get as much –'

Lyall jumped almost a foot in the air. 'I've got nothing to do with him! I know him, that's all, I just know him, and a few times I've taken the odd photo for him, or if he's sent somebody to me. I'm discreet, okay? That's all there is to it.'

Lyall was even more nervous now, walking up and down.

'Did you ever use a transsexual called Didi?'

'How do you mean?'

'Did you ever take photographs of her? Pornographic ones.'

'No way. I wasn't into that kind of thing. I just do straight portraits.'

'But sometimes you photographed transsexuals, or transvestites?'

'Yeah, they just wanted a photo of themselves, nothing wrong in that, is there?' He fidgeted, repeating that it wasn't against the law and that he'd answered all the questions about Hastings; the police had been to question him, he'd given them his photos.

'Did you know Didi well?'

'Yes and no. She was useful sometimes. She did their make-up and hair, that's all.'

'Did she do Norman Hastings's wigs?'

'Yeah, I think so.' Lorraine watched as he bent down to a chest and took out some envelopes. 'She was good, knew her stuff, could make even Hastings look reasonable.' He showed her two or three photographs of Hastings. Lorraine complimented each photo, and Lyall preened himself, started to take out more. She asked nonchalantly if he'd ever photographed a man called Steven Janklow.

Lyall was still looking through his work admiringly and didn't hear so she repeated the name and he straightened. 'Look, I don't always ask who my clients are. This is a private thing between me and them. I have to make them feel at ease – they get quite excited, and then when Didi has finished with them, they're almost orgasmic. It's a big turn-on for them and after the session they take away their photos and that's it.'

Lorraine nodded. She didn't immediately mention Janklow's name again but took her time, letting Lyall relax.

'Did Art help out on any sessions?'

'Not for years. He did once – I didn't have a dark room of my own and he had a big place over in Santa Monica, so I used to use his facilities. If I'm honest, he taught me a lot. Many of them have a bit of a problem – you know, the skin. Art taught me how to airbrush all that out, lines. I can make them look beautiful.'

She tried again. 'Did you photograph this Janklow?' Lyall paused. 'I really don't know. Some of them use assumed names, or call themselves by their female name. Is it important?'

'He's Art's alibi.'

'Why don't you ask Janklow?'

'I can't trace him and Art thinks he wouldn't want to come forward – doesn't want his family to know about his private life.'

Lyall repacked his photographs in their envelopes.

'Do you know the S and A vintage car garage?'

'Yes, it's in Santa Monica. I'm going back years now, but Art used to wheel around in an outrageous Bentley. He bought it from them but he's useless mechanically. It was always going wrong. Art just about knew where to put the gas in.'

Lorraine took out the photo of the blonde woman and gave it to Lyall. 'Have you ever taken that person's photograph?' she asked.

'I can't say. You've seen how many I've done and they're just the recent ones.'

Lorraine took it back, and asked if the clients took away their negatives. That was part of the deal, Lyall said, suddenly becoming evasive again. 'Look, I know what you're inferring. My clients always have the negatives. Some even wait until I've done them. I've never been in trouble with the police and I would never – Look, we all know about Art and I've always said that's his business. No way do I get involved.'

'You mean his pornography?'

'No. Blackmail.'

Lorraine nodded. 'Yes, I've warned him about it and I think that's why this witness won't come forward. I reckon Art was blackmailing him.'

Lyall groaned. 'Art's been in prison and that didn't stop him. He's always after making the quick buck but it disgusts me. These poor bastards, they come here and they're like kids, you know, shaking with excitement, and they're so harmless. I mean, who does it hurt if a man likes to pretty himself up? It's no crime but society makes them hide.'

Lorraine agreed. 'I feel sorry for the guys Art's been tapping. Poor Norman Hastings, a decent married man, scared it would come out—'

Lyall looked anxious. 'I never told that to the police – I couldn't, it would incriminate me. Then I'd have to tell them about Art.'

Lorraine asked if she could smoke. 'I get asthma but go ahead.' He fetched an ashtray and turned up the air-conditioning. She lit a cigarette and blew the smoke away from him.

'How did Art get hold of Hastings's pictures if, as you said, they always take the negatives away?'

Lyall flushed. 'I don't know.'

'You didn't give them to him, did you?'

'No, of course not, but . . . maybe his friend did. I photographed Hastings's family – I knew them and I wouldn't want to hurt them. They're not even wealthy, but that was Art, he'd even settle for fifty dollars a month – awful, I hated it.'

'By his friend, do you mean Didi?'

'Yes, I suspected it was her. She was here, she made Norman up – made a very good job of it.'

'She's dead.'

Lyall gaped. 'But you were just talking about her. When? Why didn't Nula call me? Or Art? I don't believe it.'

'Last night.'

Lyall seemed genuinely shocked, so she said, 'Will you take another look at the photo I brought, in case you might remember. I think it's a cross-dresser, don't you?'

Lyall took the photograph again and held it to the lamp.

He viewed the picture through an eyeglass for at least thirty seconds before he nodded. 'Yes, but it's a very good wig and make-up . . . It's the jaw-line, I can always tell.'

'You don't recognize him then?'

'No, I don't think so, but I do so many . . .'

'He never came here with Hastings?'

'Norman was always alone, unless he was with his family.'

A buzzer sounded from the dark room and Lyall checked his watch. 'I've got to get these ready for tomorrow. It's a twenty-first portrait.'

Lorraine was heading for the door, when Lyall exclaimed, 'Of course! Let me see that picture again.'

Lorraine watched him, almost willing him to say that he *had* taken pictures of Janklow. Instead he shook his head. 'There was a famous society hostess, very wealthy – now, what was her name? She came for a sitting, very crippled, arthritic, in a wheelchair. She had two sessions, I think, but turned the pictures down. Well, honestly, if I'd airbrushed any more of her she'd not have had any face left, not a line left, and they paid just the sitting fee. That's why I remember it, because I was out of pocket, and I'm going back a few years.' He traced his thin lips with his tongue as he tried to remember, and then he beamed. 'Thorburn, that was the name, Della Thorburn, and it must have been at least eight, maybe nine years ago. She could even be dead by now. Isn't it strange? Really weird.' Lorraine waited for him to continue. 'It's odd that I can remember her so well and from that photograph, it's just that . . . Let me have another look at it.' He used his eyeglass again. 'It isn't her – she couldn't drive, she was very crippled. But the way the scarf is draped reminds me of her. She always wore these chiffon scarves to hide her neck, and the blonde hair, that old-fashioned style, a Grace Kelly roll at the back or just flicked at the sides.'

'Did Didi do her make-up and hair?'

'Good God, no. She was Society. She wouldn't want somebody like Didi around. I'm talking old money.'

Lorraine wasn't sure where this new development was leading. She asked if Mrs Thorburn had been accompanied by anyone. 'Yes, of course, she was in a chair. Her son, if I can recollect, he brought her.'

'Did you hear his name?'

'Well, I presumed it was Thorburn.'

'Can you describe him?'

Lyall screwed up his eyes. 'God, I'm going back years, and I'm sorry I can't. But Art maybe could, he has a mind-blowing memory – he can even remember phone numbers.'

'Art was here?'

'Oh, no, it was in Santa Monica, I told you, we worked together, had our own clients. But then I left and came here.'

'Was Art doing similar photo sessions, with transvestites or transsexuals?'

'Oh, yes – in fact he started me off, sent me clients. I told you before.'

His dark-room buzzer rang loudly again. 'I've really got to go, I can't leave them soaking any longer.'

Lorraine returned to the car. She sat a while as she went over everything Lyall had told her. She now had a link between Hastings and Janklow. She even had a tentative link between Didi and both men, and Art was linked to them all. Art was blackmailing Norman Hastings, she concluded, and Hastings might have discussed this with Janklow. But what if Art was blackmailing Janklow as well?

She drove home deep in thought. What if she was wrong about Janklow and Art was the killer? But she knew that couldn't be right. Her attacker hadn't been Art Mathews. What was the link between each of the dead women who, apart from Holly, all resembled each other in age? But then she thought again about Holly's murder; according to Didi, the killer had gestured to her, had wanted her. She had even said to Lorraine that she was lucky because if Holly hadn't been picked up then it could have been her. What if it *was* Didi the killer had wanted? Just as she had said to Rooney the women were or could possibly have all been mistaken for Didi. She, Lorraine, was tall, about the same height as Didi, and blonde. Was the killer looking for one woman in particular, a woman he knew worked the streets, a woman he knew was a transsexual?

Lorraine had to pull over, her head throbbing with all the jagged sections of information. Her attempts at trying to make them all fit exhausted her. She closed her eyes. She had left Art Mathews in the gallery the night Holly had died. What had he done after she left and where did he go? Were he, Didi, Nula even, all connected to the murders? She was too tired to get it together, tired and hungry. She started the car again and headed back onto the freeway towards Pasadena.

Art Mathews had been brought in for questioning. He had attempted to run from the police, who had been about to tell him that he was not being charged with anything but was required to assist their inquiries. As they entered his new studio, though, he had dived past them, which aroused their suspicions and they gave chase. He gave himself up after an abortive run between oncoming cars, zig-zagging across the road, nearly getting himself killed. A routine search of his studio yielded a vast selection of pornography stills.

Rooney had begun to question Mathews as soon as he was brought in. He was expansive and over-talkative, as if high on drugs. He had not as yet asked for a lawyer. He admitted to mild pornography but it was not until one of the officers entered the room with a black and white photograph of Holly that the interview took an upward spiral. Art admitted knowing her; he had even taken

304

photographs of her. Agitated and sweating, the little man tried to recall where he was on the night of her murder.

At almost every turn he incriminated himself. When he admitted that he also knew the most recent murdered transsexual, Didi, Rooney could feel the hair lift on the back of his neck. He knew they had to get legal representation for Art and fast, and suggested as much to him. If he so wished, they would be prepared to wait. Rooney had also asked for a doctor to examine him: if he was drugged up they needed to know as they would have to wait until he came down from whatever he was on.

Suddenly Art jumped up, spittle forming at the sides of his mouth. 'This is crazy! You think I killed Holly? Why would I do a thing like that? This is all a misunderstanding.'

At no time had Rooney suggested there was any suspicion that Art was involved in the murder. He had him on selling pornographic material by his own admission. Now it seemed he was about to talk himself into being accused of murder.

As the interview swung up a notch, the tension in the room grew tighter. Rooney began to ask him about each of the victims.

'What? Why?' Art began to screech, his voice getting higher and higher in his agitation. 'Why are you asking me about these women? This is insanity. You think I had anything to do with those murders? This is crazy. I've admitted I knew Holly, okay, I knew Didi—'

Rooney probed into Art's business, his background, his previous criminal record. Only then did he detect the fear. Art now demanded legal representation: he would not answer any more questions. Rooney knew that most of what he had admitted might not hold up in court, especially as he had still not been checked out for drugs. He was so wired up when they brought him in, he could have confessed to any number of crimes. But Rooney was pushing, he was excited, he felt that old rush of adrenalin. Art

Mathews was like a scared rabbit almost caught in a trap and Rooney was eager to snap the door shut on him. So much was riding on his gaining results, on grabbing them right under the FBI's noses.

When Art eventually quietened, Rooney took it as a sign of guilt. It was obvious to all in the interrogation room that he had only become uncooperative when the murders were mentioned. While they waited for the lawyer to arrive, Art continued to declare his innocence. He kept rubbing his shining bald head, looking from one man to the next. 'Just because I knew Didi and Holly doesn't mean I'd kill them. This is some kind of frame-up. Did somebody tip you off about me? Is that what this is all about? Did some piece of shit put me in it?'

He demanded to know what time Didi had been killed, as he had been with friends the entire evening, but when told and asked where he was between nine and ten thirty he suddenly refused to say where he was or who he was with until he had a lawyer present. A doctor examined him and gave him the all-clear but suggested they give him plenty to drink as he was sweating so much from nerves.

His lawyer arrived and he was allowed a private discussion. Once that had been completed, he was faced yet again with all the questions that had been asked earlier. One of the reasons he had refused to state where he was on the night Didi died was also that he had been filming a session. Having already served time for selling pornographic videos and working with under-age kids, he was scared that he'd be charged with a similar offence. He was also becoming increasingly alarmed that details of his blackmail activities might leak out. The more he was questioned the more nervous he became. When the lists of the dead women started unfolding he became hysterical, screaming that they were setting him up, and some of the murders had happened so long ago he couldn't remember where he had

306

been living. He might even have been serving a sentence. Meanwhile, his new studio was being ransacked, and more pornography discovered.

He was taken down to the cells. It was almost three in the morning and both Rooney and Bean were still working. Rooney's head ached but he was back on form, though he was sure now that Art was not their killer. He had found out that when two of the earlier murders had been committed, Art had been in jail.

When he returned to his office, Bean was waiting. 'They still haven't brought your informant in, this Lorraine Page.'

'I think we've been wasting our time, Bean. That little bastard should be locked up but not for murder. He's just into his porno and probably the blackmail rackets again.'

Bean threw up his hands in despair. 'Does that mean Lorraine Page is into all that as well?'

Rooney sighed. 'I don't know. Maybe you should get this information ready for the suits. Lay it out on the Chief's desk, let him see we've worked our butts off tonight.'

Bean took Mathews's prison record to the FBI agents' office and Rooney glanced at his watch. In all fairness it was too late to call Lorraine but he reckoned he wouldn't get any sleep. He'd give it a couple more hours and call her after he'd shaved and washed.

He was running his small battery-operated shaver over his fat chin when Bean peered into the washroom. Rooney gave him a worn-out smile and clicked off the shaver. 'I don't suppose we just got lucky and Art Mathews admitted killing eight women and Norman Hastings?' he asked sarcastically.

Bean ran the cold water into the basin. 'No. Prime suspect is sobbing his heart out down there in the cells. Meanwhile his lawyer doesn't want us to press criminal charges if he admits to what he was doing on the night of the last murder. He has already remembered where he was when Holly was murdered and this you're not gonna believe.'

'Try me,' Rooney said heavily.

'Art Mathews was working in that gallery right next to your Indian curry place. He worked there until late, all night, and Lorraine Page is one of his alibis.'

Rooney stared at his reflection. Bean dried his hands on the roller towel. 'Any money the FBI'll release him on bail, he'll get locked up for a few years for his porno trade. Been a long night for nothing. Pity we don't have something – there's press outside. Somebody tipped them off we got a suspect.'

Rooney hitched up his pants. 'Yeah, maybe the same person who tipped us off about Art Mathews. I'm going to call that two-faced bitch now.'

Bean followed Rooney down the corridor. 'You know they got Andrew Fellows coming in to talk to the FBI later this morning? Maybe you should hang around – canteen'll be open soon.'

Rooney had been about to call Lorraine even though it was only five thirty. He changed his mind. He didn't give a shit if he woke her up or not. He was gonna go one better and do it personally. As he drove out of the station yard, he watched two new patrol cars pulling in with the FBI men all bright-eyed and bushy-tailed even if they had been hauled out of their beds at this ungodly hour. He drove away, his anger mounting. Art Mathews had been another of Lorraine's theories. She had been partly right: he *had* known Holly and Didi, but he had no connection with Steven Janklow. There was no record on him in Vice. Rooney might even force her to give him back his dough. Maybe he'd have her hauled in, spill it about her being the witness they'd been searching for. He'd like to grab her by her scrawny throat and strangle her. He was through, period. The more he drove, the angrier he became. As he headed towards Lorraine's apartment, he was ready to explode. He really needed to sound off at somebody so it might as well be her! The two-faced, lying whore.

Rosie shot out of bed when the doorbell rang. She grabbed a robe and scuttled to the door. Lorraine was sitting up on the sofa yawning. 'What time is it?'

'Six o'clock in the morning! Who the hell is ringing the bell at this time?'

Rosie opened the door and stepped back. Rooney was leaning against the doorframe. He looked past Rosie to Lorraine. 'I'm gonna arrest you.'

Lorraine drew a cardigan around her nightdress. 'Arrest me? Why, for chrissakes?'

He sauntered in. 'Art Mathews, sweetheart. You were with him the night the . . .' He couldn't remember Holly's name. 'You were with him the night she was murdered, you're his fucking alibi. *You!*'

Lorraine filled a tumbler with water and drank it straight down. 'Is that why you sent cops here? Did you do that to me?'

Rooney tossed his hat aside. 'Be the FBI wanting you next, sweetheart, time's up.'

She faced him in a fury. 'Did you tell them about me? Bill, did you tell them I was attacked?'

'You know I didn't but I sure as hell intend to because you are full of bullshit and you've lied to me right along the way. When I tried to help you out, all you did was lie.'

Lorraine glared at him. 'They still holding Mathews?'

'Far as I know. Maybe you were mistaken about this Janklow and maybe it was Mathews attacked you in the gallery when you were working together, hanging up pictures, the night Holly died.'

She sighed. 'That's stupid. He's right-handed.'

'What?'

'Art Mathews is right-handed. The guy who attacked me was left-handed, according to all the forensic and pathology reports and even the reports from Andrew Fellows. The killer is left-handed, opens the glove compartment with his right, holds their heads down with his left . . .'

Rooney looked at her, then turned away. 'Get dressed. We're out of here.'

'No. You sit right where you are.'

He pouted and then tugged a bottle of bourbon out of his pocket. He slowly unscrewed the cap and took a heavy pull. He dangled the bottle towards Lorraine.

Rosie eyed it and then eyed Lorraine. She was walking towards it.

Rooney watched Lorraine. 'Want a drink?'

Lorraine snatched the bottle and marched to the sink, about to pour it down the drain, when the smell suddenly hit her. She wanted a drink, everything started to crystallize, all she could think of was reaching for a glass and drinking. She didn't care about Art Mathews or Steven Janklow, she wanted a drink. She slowly lifted the bottle to her lips, closing her eyes in anticipation.

'Don't do it, Lorraine.' It was Rooney. 'Chuck it out, don't do it. I'm sorry. Here, Lorraine, give it to me.'

Rooney had to prise her hands away from the bottle. It shocked him, made him feel wretched. He leaned on the sink pouring the booze away, as Lorraine tried to wrest the bottle from him. He turned on the taps so the water splashed into the sink and over him. 'Shit. I'm soaking wet.'

'Aren't we all?' snapped Lorraine. 'Old washed-up soaks,' she said as she took down coffee cups. 'I suppose it's black coffee all round?'

There was a sudden hard tap at the front door. Rosie went to open it but Rooney stopped her. He peered out of the window and told Lorraine to get into the bedroom. She obeyed immediately, closing the door behind her as the front door was tapped hard again.

'Don't say anything,' Rooney said quietly to Rosie. 'Just leave this to me.'

The two officers framed in the doorway asked for Lorraine Page. Rosie held the door wider to reveal Rooney standing in the centre of the room with a cup of coffee in his hand. They seemed fazed by his presence and made no move to enter the room.

'Captain Rooney.'

'You come to pick her up?'

They nodded, and one passed him a warrant for Lorraine's arrest.

'I'll hang on to this. I'm staying put until she shows. Go back to base. Soon as I got her I'll call in.'

Rooney pocketed the warrant, carried his coffee towards the sofa, and sat down. 'Unless you want to hang around here.'

'We'll leave it to you, Captain.'

A few moments later Lorraine came out of the bedroom. She leaned against the doorframe, looking at the squat Rooney. 'Why did you do that, Bill?'

'Christ only knows, I must be nuts.'

She cradled her coffee cup in her hands and sat in the easy chair opposite him while Rosie hovered, uncomfortable and ill-at-ease with them.

'I'm sorry for bringing the booze in,' Rooney said.

'That's okay,' and Rosie wandered to her bedroom, feeling in the way.

'She seems a nice woman,' Rooney said.

'Rosie's great.' Lorraine got up for a refill. She leaned over the back of the sofa towards Rooney. 'You wanna hear my developments? What I've come up with this evening?'

He wanted to say no but he didn't. Instead he let her talk without interruption, listening intently as she pieced together her talk with Nula, then her meeting with Craig Lyall.

Lorraine's face was expressionless as she explained

clearly, emotionlessly, what had happened when she had been attacked. She described walking up to the car, how he had driven her to the parking space, how she had fought him, bitten hard into his neck, hung on for her life as he tried to push her away from him. He was strong, she said. The grip on her hair had been like a vice, and it had taken all her strength to lever up her body to turn and bite. She was sure if they hadn't been disturbed by the Summerses, she would have been dead. She then told Rooney that she had also taken Norman Hastings's wallet.

Rooney closed his eyes and kept them closed. He was scared that if he opened them he'd charge at her like a mad bull with fury.

'There's something else. At first I didn't think it was important. It was his cufflinks. They had a logo. I didn't think it was important until I saw the same logo on a letterhead. At my husband's place – Mike, you remember Mike? He has nothing to do with this, I know that, but it gave me the first clue to the killer.'

Rooney was fighting to control his temper. She looked directly at him and continued. She described how she and Rosie had gone to S and A's garage, how she had narrowed the list of cufflink owners down and taken photographs of suspects. None resembled the man who had attacked her. She took the photographs out and passed them to Rooney and leant close to him as he examined the one of the blonde woman.

'I think this is Steven Janklow. I think he's a transvestite, and that he had a photographic session with either Mathews or Lyall. It could have been as far back as nine to ten years ago, maybe when he was just daring to come out. I think Mathews subsequently discovered who he was and started blackmailing him, realizing he'd found the golden goose. I think Art and Didi may have worked as a team. She was used or hired to do wigs and make-up. She made up Norman Hastings, fixed his hair for the photo session.

Maybe she even tipped off Art, as Lyall said most of his clients always took the negatives. You interviewed Lyall, too, didn't you?'

Rooney nodded. They'd come up with nothing as concrete as Lorraine. He couldn't help but give a tight smile: she was good, always had been good. Now she began pacing up and down. There was something about the way she moved, tensing, relaxing her hands, and she rubbed her body, sexually, her face becoming more and more alive. She was exciting to watch, as she became increasingly animated.

'I've got Hastings linked to Janklow – maybe they discussed the blackmail. Who knows what they discussed? Possible theory is, when Hastings went to the bank that morning, was he going to pay off Mathews? Pay off somebody? The strange thing is all his bank statements have been checked and the major transactions are accounted for.' She suddenly stopped and clicked her fingers. 'Unless Hastings was also tapping Janklow for money. It seems strange that he was allowed to park his car in the hangar. Nobody seems to know why he should have been when he no longer owned one of their cars. Did you know that at one time he owned a vintage car? Maybe that was where he could have found out that he and Janklow were the same kind of men. Whatever, we know they're linked, and linked to Mathews through Didi. She's very important. She may not have collected from Mathews's blackmailing activities, but I'm beginning to think she may have been the go-between or, and this is a wild guess, maybe she was the person Janklow believed was blackmailing him. So that brings me to the last bit of guesswork.'

Lorraine took out the victims' photographs and laid them along the sofa for Rooney to look at. 'They have one thing in common apart from prostitution. Look at the make-up, the type of clothes they wore. Now, look at the morgue shots of Didi . . . Put her beside each one. You didn't believe me earlier but what if Janklow was only after

313

her – was only interested in tracking *her* down and killing her? He's a Thorburn, right? His mother was a big society hostess, his brother is holding all the purse strings. What if Janklow has been paying out blackmail money because he's scared his family will find out and it might be made public? Just as Hastings hid his private life from everyone who knew him.'

Lorraine tapped Rooney's shoulder. He edged away, annoyed by her but more angry with himself. She had run rings around him and his department, and it infuriated him. But the only thing against her that he could think of was that she had withheld vital evidence.

'You got to break Art Mathews – get him to admit this blackmail. If you do, then you got a clean motive and you've got Janklow – or at least enough to arrest him and take him in for questioning.'

Rooney's head was spinning, and as he tried to assimilate everything she had told him he felt dizzy. She added, 'And the guy has got to have some mark from where I bit him. Maybe the skin's healed, even the bruising, but I held on for grim death.'

Rooney was unnerved by her toughness. 'You faced him yet?'

'I told you I hadn't, I'm not stupid.'

'You are one hell of a witness, you know that, don't you?'

'Yeah.' She stepped back, suddenly wary of him. He was a big man and when he stood up straight instead of his usual slouch it was surprising how much it added to his size.

'You'll have to come in with me. I'm sorry, Lorraine, there's no way out of it now.'

'Come on, Bill, don't make me have to go to court, not now, not when I'm getting myself back together. I go to court, they can start throwing old charges at me, make me admit to what I was and they'll dish the dirt on me, even bring up the shooting. Don't do it to me, Bill.'

'You were fucking attacked! That's what you'd be in court for, nothing else.'

'I know what he did but I won't go to court. Don't make them call me out, Bill.'

'You've withheld evidence, and you even had Norman Hastings's goddamned wallet! You never even told me about the cufflinks, so what do you expect me to do? You are the only witness. You gave me weeks of fucking waste of time. If you'd been upfront with me I'd have cracked this, I'd have been—'

She yelled, 'Patted on the back and given a commendation before you retired, that's what you're pissed off about right now! Instead of moving on what I've just been spewing out for the past hour, you're gettin' the needle to me. You want me to face out Steven Janklow, then I'll do it right now, I'll go over to his place in Beverly Glen with you, with anyone you want, but I won't go to court. Bill, I'm not standing up as ex-cop, ex-alcoholic, ex-hooker so you can get a slap on the back. I won't do it, I'll pack up and walk out right now and you won't see me for dust.'

He waved the warrant. 'I can take you in, Lorraine.'

'Try it, *just try it*.' Hands on hips she glowered at him. 'Go get Art Mathews to talk, Bill, that's what you should be doing. You know it, so stop bullshitting and get on with it. I won't be taken in and I warn you, if they drag me into court, then I won't pour the next bottle down the drain.'

He pointed at her with his index finger. 'You don't leave this apartment, you hear me? If you want I can make sure. I can have a squad car out front in two minutes. I can have you watched day and night, right round the clock, have guys on your doorstep.'

She sat down. 'I won't leave, Bill, I give you my word. Maybe just to the corner for groceries but I'll stay put.'

His upright position relaxed and he resumed his habitual slouch. 'I'll call you, see what I can do, lie about you, I suppose. But don't let me down, Lorraine, I couldn't take it.'

She hugged him tightly. He smelt of cigarettes and booze and food and he grunted at her to get away from him. He walked out of the door without a word and slammed it behind him.

Lorraine slumped onto the sofa. She was hot, angry, frustrated and a little scared. She should have kept her mouth shut about Hastings's wallet. There was no need for her to have mentioned it – that had been a big mistake. She wondered if Rooney would have the balls to keep her identity secret and not make her go to court. To have all her past made public, to have her daughters and Mike read about her made her anger turn to humiliation. For the first time she faced her shame. She was disgusted with herself. Tears slid down her cheeks, but she made no sound. Had she really been stupid enough to think that she could start a new career? Who would want to hire her if her past life was splashed across every tabloid? She knew they'd love it, that she'd be hounded, and she knew they'd rake up why she'd been forced to quit the police. She saw him again, the yellow zig-zag stripe down his jacket, his face as he fell, his hair flopping.

Rosie opened the bedroom door and Lorraine heard the heavy, plodding feet crossing the room. She waited, praying for Rosie to leave her in peace. She bit harder into her hand as she felt her friend's weight subsiding on the edge of the sofa. Rosie stroked her hair. 'I listened at the door just in case you needed me.'

Lorraine sighed. She never had any privacy. She almost forgot that this was Rosie's place.

'You serious about going into the investigation business? For real?' Rosie asked quietly.

'No, I'd never get a licence, I was just kidding myself.'

'You shouldn't. I was real proud of the way you just

316

talked to Rooney, the way you were piecing it together. You're good, you know, clever.'

Lorraine gazed up at the big plump face. 'Did you hear it all?'

'Yep, and that's another thing you're good at. He was right, you sure as hell can lie better than anyone I know.'

Lorraine laughed softly. 'Yeah, I guess you just get used to it, part of a cop's life that, you know. "No cause for alarm", when a whole building's about to collapse.'

Rosie rubbed Lorraine's back, like a mother would her child's. 'Maybe if you had to go to court it wouldn't be such a bad thing. Maybe your kids *should* know, maybe they'll be proud that you're fighting back, proving yourself – proving your worth.'

Lorraine grinned. 'Rosie, you're such an optimist.'

'Yeah, but I'm looking out for me too. I think I could get used to this kind of work – being a private investigator's more interesting than sticking down envelopes – computers, even!'

Lorraine moved away from the soothing warmth of Rosie's reassuring hand. 'You don't know it all, Rosie. It's not just the drinking, the whoring, it's not just that . . .' and she told her about the fourteen-year-old boy. Rosie didn't say anything but she felt even more warmth towards Lorraine, and especially when after the telling of the story, she tilted her face slightly and gave her a sweet, sad smile. 'I'm gonna take a shower now.'

The telephone rang and Rosie answered it. It was Rooney and she knew something was wrong straight away.

'She's just taking a shower, Captain Rooney, you want me to fetch her?'

Rooney coughed. 'Rosie, I've got some bad news. Art Mathews committed suicide.'

Rosie gasped. 'My God, but how – how did he do—'

Rooney interrupted, 'I'm sorry, but you'd better warn

Lorraine. There's not a hope in hell of me keeping her out of this now, you understand?'

'How long does she have before they get here?'

'They're already on their way.'

Rosie looked at the closed bedroom door. 'She'll be ready.'

Rooney wanted to say more but there was too much going on so he hung up. Rosie opened the bedroom door: she could hear Lorraine singing in the shower. 'Run, rabbit, run, rabbit, run, run, run . . .'

CHAPTER 16

J AKE LISTENED without interrupting. When Rosie had called him before he'd even had his breakfast, his first thought was it was she who needed him 'urgently'. He was relieved to find her waiting at her front door stone cold sober. As she drew him into the apartment, she put her finger to her lips, indicating the bedroom. She didn't want Lorraine to hear what she was saying but she knew she had to make it fast. 'They arrest her, Jake, and everything she's accomplished so far will be over. She'll go back on the booze – she as good as said it.'

It was hard for him to take in everything Rosie said. Just the pertinent facts were enough to make him break out in a sweat. Lorraine had been attacked by the so-called hammer killer; she was the witness the police were searching for; she was also investigating or assisting the police in their inquiries. It was hard to believe, and even more so when Rosie slipped in that Lorraine's 'partner' was also helping the investigation.

They couldn't carry on the conversation as Lorraine walked in. She was surprised to see Jake.

'You come for breakfast?'

'Nope. I was wondering if you wanted to come to a meeting.'

'What? Are you nuts? It's not even nine o'clock. Besides, I can't. I got to stay in the apartment.'

'I'm gonna get dressed,' Rosie said, eyeing Jake and

jerking her head towards Lorraine, who watched her go out and then started to wash the cups.

She ran water into the sink. 'So, what has she told you?'

Jake fiddled with his collar.

'Is it about me admitting I wanted a drink?'

Jake shrugged. 'You may not know it, Lorraine, but you just broke through, and you'll make it even if it doesn't look or feel like it right now. But I want you to come to a meeting with me this morning. According to Rosie you might need a morale boost.'

Lorraine put her head on one side. 'She tell you I might be arrested?'

'Is it true?'

She put down the dishcloth. 'It's true, and I think I'm gonna need a lot more than just a morale boost.'

'Then you'll come to the early-morning meeting?'

Bean strode into Rooney's office, hands in his pockets. 'Ambulance just taken his body away.'

Rooney pulled at his nose. 'How the hell did he do it?'

'Broke his glasses and slit his wrists.'

'FBI must be shitting themselves.' Rooney snorted with a half-derisive laugh and sneer.

'Yep, all in there blaming each other and patting each other on the back at the same time.'

Rooney gaped. 'What you mean?'

'Well, it's obvious, isn't it? I mean, why kill yourself if you're innocent? They reckon he must be the one.'

Rooney snorted again. 'That's bullshit. We know he couldn't have done two of them because he was inside. They got the report of his criminal record, didn't they?'

Bean said that they might have found some discrepancies over the dates. Whatever, they were not digging too deep as the Chief was putting out a press release that the suspect in custody had admitted his guilt.

'Had he?' Rooney asked, astonished, because when he'd last seen Mathews he hadn't – far from it.

'They reckon so, but they still want to question his accomplice.'

'His what?'

'Lorraine Page. I was told you were bringing her in. They've been waiting for you.'

Rooney could feel the warrant in his pocket. He took it out and passed it to Bean, his heart pounding. He felt sick, needed time to plan what he was going to do with the information Lorraine had passed him. He had already decided not to mention the theft of Norman Hastings's wallet, and would maybe tell her to leave out the cufflinks. He was even toying with trying to keep the attack on her out of his statements; now it looked as if it was out of his hands. He asked himself why he'd go out on a limb for her like this, but all he came up with was that he liked her, but if it got out that he'd used her, paid her, and had been privy to the information, he'd not only be out in the cold but his hoped-for bonus was shrinking by the minute.

The squad car drew up outside Rosie's apartment just moments after they'd left for the AA meeting. All vehicles were instructed to be on the look-out for the prostitute Lorraine Page, described as five feet nine, short blonde hair, last seen wearing a cream suit and silk shirt. She was to be arrested on sight.

Lorraine was still uncertain as to why she had let Jake and Rosie talk her into coming to the meeting. Maybe, if the truth was to be admitted, it was because she was at a loss and she was also scared.

The woman was neatly dressed in printed cotton, her hair well cut, parted in the centre and constantly falling forwards to hide her face. She spoke quietly, nervously. 'My name is Carol. Nine months ago I was sleeping rough, I felt there was no hope for me. I felt no shame, I felt nothing. I had lost my husband, my children, my home and my job. I had turned to prostitution to feed my drinking. I was a prostitute, a thief. I owned only what I stood up in, I had nothing, and no respect for anyone, least of all myself.' Carol continued to talk and Lorraine held tightly to Rosie's hand, understanding for the first time what she felt, what she had been through and that she was not alone. Everyone at the meeting, she now began to realize, had felt shame and rejection, knew loss and humiliation.

When they stood and warmly applauded Carol, when they embraced her and congratulated her, Lorraine was one of the first to leave her seat. She was shy, at first proffering her hand, but then she put her arms around her. 'I've been there too. I know how you feel,' she said simply.

Carol hugged Lorraine back. 'We've all been there, that's why we're here.'

'What was the hardest thing for you?' Lorraine asked.

'Facing myself, not being angry or ashamed. It wasn't me but the drink. I hid behind it, I know that now, and I'm determined to stay sober. I got a job today. I was scared but I told them I'm an alcoholic and now that I know that's what I am, I feel free. For the first time in years I'm not hiding.'

'You said you hid behind drink. What did you mean?'

'I was afraid of failing. I'm a nurse and I had a patient, a child, who died. I gave the wrong medication and I was never able to face the guilt or come to terms with it. I have now. It will always be with me but I can deal with it, I'm taking responsibility for myself and I want to stay sober. I *have* to stay sober or I'll go down again.'

Jake was watching Lorraine. He winked at Rosie. 'It was good we came. You were right, Rosie, it was important for her.'

'And for me too. If Lorraine had started drinking I'd have probably joined her,' Rosie replied, and Jake smiled.

Lorraine joined them. 'Thanks for bringing me. Now we should get back in case Rooney needs me.'

Rooney watched the FBI agents talking to his chief. He sat in a hard-backed chair at the rear of the room; when anyone looked to him for an opinion he made no comment. The press had been given statements and the suits felt that, by the arrest of Art Mathews, they had been able at least to gain time. Even if they couldn't provide evidence that Mathews had murdered all the victims, they were satisfied that by his own admittance and subsequent suicide he had been guilty of at least three.

Andrew Fellows had come in and they had been in deep discussion with him for two hours. He did not disagree with their conclusions but raised doubts that Mathews was the killer. Not until they seemed to have grown tired of their own voices did Rooney ease his bulk from the chair. 'You mind if I put my two cents in?'

They had forgotten he was even in the room. The Chief looked pointedly at his watch. 'Is it about the Lorraine Page woman?'

Andrew Fellows frowned. 'Lorraine Page?'

'We're still looking for her but it shouldn't be long.'

Rooney squeezed between a row of chairs.

'Lorraine Page?' Fellows asked again, but no one answered him and she was forgotten as Rooney prodded the photograph of Didi, the last victim.

'What if our killer – and I'm excluding Mathews just for a moment – was looking for this particular woman or man – the transsexual? Looking for her because she and Mathews were blackmailing him.' There was a low murmur and Rooney held up his hand. 'Let me finish. Take a look at them. Tough, hard-faced women, all bleached blondes, all prostitutes, as was this victim.' Again he tapped Didi's picture. 'It's a possible motive because I think Hastings was also being blackmailed and possibly by Mathews . . .'

The men listened, giving each other sidelong looks. The Chief loosened his tie. Mathews had admitted at no time to blackmailing anyone. Rooney continued to repeat almost verbatim what Lorraine had said to him. He did not mention her part in piecing it together, or that she was the witness who had been attacked by the killer. Just before he gave the name of her suspect, he felt a hot flush spread through his body. The Thorburn family were powerful and all Rooney had was Lorraine's theory. They did not have enough evidence: her own admission that Janklow had been her attacker would, as she rightly surmised, be tough to prove. As she had said, it would be her word against his. And as yet no incriminating evidence linked him to the murders. Until he had more on Janklow, Rooney decided he would keep his identity to himself.

The room was silent. The Chief stared at Rooney – they all did – and Andrew Fellows's face wore a half smile. It was hard to determine whether it was through disbelief or because he was impressed.

Rooney decided he might as well go for the big prize. He nodded to Hastings's picture. 'He used a garage to park his car, the S and A company. I've not gone into this in any depth but a number of the company's employees were checked out against the description we had from the anonymous witness. The S and A garage is owned by a Brad Thorburn.' Fellows gasped at this but no one paid him any attention. Rooney continued, 'I'm not suggesting anything without further evidence. Obviously considering the family's connections, I have not, until tonight, even voiced my suspicions.'

'Just what are you implying?' Fellows asked, his face pink with agitation. Rooney looked at him then, and at the Chief who became aware that Fellows should not have been

324

privy to this statement and suggested that he might wish to leave.

Fellows had not disclosed that he knew Brad Thorburn. He was unsure as to why not but, then, he hadn't been asked. He intended to drive straight home but changed his mind and headed for Thorburn's house.

Jake saw the patrol car even before he turned into the road. Lorraine was in the back seat.

'You want me to drive past the cops?' Jake asked.

'Yeah, but not for the reason you think. I'll go in but in my own time. There's somebody I want to talk to first. I misjudged Rooney. He must have told them about me.'

She ducked out of sight as Jake passed the police car, turning left at the top of the road before he stopped.

'Where we going?' Rosie asked.

'I need to talk to Andrew Fellows. I won't do anything crazy, believe me. I just want to run a few things past him.'

'I'll drive you,' said Rosie.

Lorraine hesitated before she agreed. Jake got out and Rosie moved into the driving seat. He watched them drawing away from the pavement but not until they were almost out of sight did he walk off.

The car backfired. Jake whipped round. It had sounded like a gun blast. It made him uneasy and he wished he'd stayed with the two women. He also wished he'd asked a lot more questions, but as he walked on he also realized that he had been part of Lorraine's cover-up story about the attack. He shook his head. He had known as soon as he saw the injury that it hadn't been caused by a fall, as she'd said. With all her lies, Lorraine had not only used Rosie but himself. The more he thought about it, the more angry he became, and now he started to wonder where Lorraine got all that money from. He remembered the way she clutched it when he'd stitched up her wound. She was one hell of a liar, he told himself. Maybe there was more to the cops hanging around than either he or Rosie knew.

Rooney had now told the agents about Craig Lyall, again using Lorraine's evidence. When the Chief got back, Rooney was in the hot seat. Berillo wanted to know why he had been withholding so much evidence, and neither discussed it with him nor provided the agents with the information on Mathews's blackmailing activities.

'I only pieced it together tonight. Like I said, it's just supposition. I've been up all night on this. I hadn't finished interviewing Mathews when the FBI took over. You tell *me* how such an important suspect with all this high-tech surveillance on his cell was able to slit his wrists. Don't lay that on me, I wasn't even in the station. It's down to the FBI.'

The agents took his gibes and accusations without expression. One of them, a blond, square-jawed man, was making copious notes as Rooney spoke.

'You're seriously saying that Brad Thorburn is a suspect?' demanded his chief. The atmosphere in the room was uneasy. Bean remained silent throughout: he was wondering why Rooney had never mentioned any of his findings to him.

'I never said Thorburn *was* a suspect. I believe it's his brother, Steven Janklow.'

The blond agent, tight-lipped with anger, asked if Janklow fitted the description of the killer given to Rooney's department after Hastings's body had been found. Rooney shifted uneasily. As he had never seen Janklow or interviewed him, he was hesitant.

'I've not interviewed him. All I know is he knew Hastings and—'

'And?' snapped the Chief. Rooney felt as if they were all against him, closing in on him. He pulled at his bulbous

326

nose, half wishing he'd kept his big mouth shut. He took a flyer, lying through his teeth. 'I held back giving you this information until I'd checked in the files for a possible vice charge against Janklow in the past. So far I've not been able to trace it and it was just told to me by one of the workers at the garage. I didn't want to act on hearsay – well, not until I'd run it past you. I could be wrong on all counts.'

The Chief glanced at his watch and then said, 'You go through those vice records, Bill, immediately – but until you have more evidence we make no contact with the Thorburn family for two reasons. If our man is Janklow, we need hard facts to arrest him, and the Thorburn family is high society and powerful.' The Chief said the last sentence directly to the blond FBI man: 'In other words, back off the Thorburns until I say so.'

The agents departed, with a show of obvious irritation towards Rooney, and the Chief called him into his office. He turned on him in a fury, demanding to know what the fuck he'd been playing at.

'Just trying to do my job.'

'Come on, Bill, who are you kiddin'? You're just pissed off because the FBI have been brought in. If you'd even had half of what you blurted out tonight we could have held them off. What else are you holding back? You'd better come clean with me, Bill.' He stared hard at Rooney and then asked about Lorraine Page.

Rooney covered like an old trooper. 'She's my informant but I didn't know until tonight that she knew Mathews or that she was with him the night Holly was murdered.'

'I want her brought in because I want to talk to her. I want to know just what the hell Mathews was up to.'

'It's in his file. He's been in for blackmail and extortion, along with his porno rap.'

'Is that it?'

'That's it. Like I said, let me dig into Janklow's past a bit more and then I'll get straight back to you.'

The Chief agreed but told Rooney to call him, no matter what the time was, if he discovered anything else.

Rooney returned to his office where Bean was waiting. He couldn't stop smiling; he felt he'd shown the bastards. He kicked the door closed. 'You and me got work to do.'

Bean took off his jacket and hung it over the back of a chair. Rooney was rummaging through his desk drawers. 'What about Lorraine Page?' Bean asked. 'According to officers Hully and Maynard you were at her place. They said you were bringing her in.'

'I left when she didn't show – that all right with you?'

Bean's face was quizzical. 'You just done a hell of a lot of legwork since you left here last night, but you've not mentioned any of this to me – Janklow, the Thorburn family. If you'd seen those agents' faces, talk about jaws dropping open. I was impressed. They were really pissed. They were patting each other on the back ten minutes earlier about Art Mathews. They really upped the pressure on him, you know, he was crying his eyes out. She tip you off about him?'

Rooney raised his eyebrow in mock surprise. 'God no, that was supreme detective work on my part, Lieutenant.' Then he scowled. 'If Mathews said he killed them, I reckon he'd have said he'd shot his mother just to get those suits off him. He was scared – I reckon he was scared shitless about being done for blackmail again. He'd have done eighteen years this time and the little prick knew it. They just wanted to make an arrest, period. I reckon they were lucky he did kill himself because if I'd got my hands on him, I might have got a different result, like negative.'

Bean sighed. 'So why did he kill himself, then?'

'Because maybe he knew he was in very deep and we'd have dug up something. Christ almighty, I gave them his fucking file, he was serving time when two of the victims were done. I don't care what any of that FBI crowd want to say about copy-cat killings, those victims were all done by the same man.'

Bean sucked in his breath. 'Or woman. That's what Fellows threw in tonight.'

'Bullshit.'

'No. He said that all the crap that's written about male or female strength is hyped up out of all proportion. If a woman wanted to kill, she could have done it. He even said that was why the victims took a blow to the back of the head first – incapacitated them.'

'Well, Fellows is looking up his own tight-assed backside. We got that witness, the one that gave us the description, right?' He almost disclosed who she was but stopped himself. Instead he leaned over the desk. 'She described her attacker as a man, right?'

Bean jangled the change in his pocket. 'Lorraine Page. Where does she figure in it all, then? What if they were doing it together? She was with Mathews the night Holly was murdered, he said so.'

'I know, I know . . .' He felt his stomach turn over. What if Bean was right? Could she be that much involved?

Bean sank into a chair. 'Well, you put the cat among the pigeons. It sounded like hot shit to me.' Rooney looked puzzled. 'It was nice to watch you in action, Captain.'

Rooney smiled. 'I was always one of the best. Now, why don't you go get some sandwiches and coffee?'

Bean picked up his jacket again. 'Gonna be a long night, is it?'

As the door closed behind him Rooney slumped in his chair. He wasn't one of the best – he doubted if he ever had been – but she was. It was *she* who was hot shit and she'd proved it. He just hoped to God she was right, that she hadn't done a runner. Did he want to crack this so badly he was going to let her risk her neck? He knew he still had the trump card that she was the witness. If he was forced into a corner he'd bring it out. He wondered how long it would be before they brought her in, then suddenly felt cold. What if Bean was right? What if she had been ducking and diving all along? What if she'd never been a witness but a killer, and the description was just to put them all off the scent? He picked up the phone and punched out her number. No answer. Where the hell was she? If she wasn't brought in within the hour, he'd go out looking for her personally. She wasn't the killer – that was dumb, that was *crazy* – but he felt a horrible nag at his gut. She was connected to Didi and Mathews; he'd told the FBI that she had been with Mathews the night Holly was murdered. He should have brought her in with him, he shouldn't have trusted her. She might even now be in some bar drinking herself into a stupor – she'd threatened as much . . .

Bean came in. He'd called for a takeout to be brought in rather than schlepp out for it himself.

'What else did Fellows say about it maybe being a woman?'

'None of the victims had been sexually abused, there'd been no trace of semen, not even on Holly. Victims all struck from behind, just their faces mangled.'

Rooney swallowed and tapped the edge of his desk. 'Is Lorraine Page being brought in?'

'Changing your theory, are you?'

Rooney sniffed and waved to Bean to get out, but he hovered at the door. 'She was an ex-cop, right? She's capable of taking care of herself, she's tough, I've heard you say it, and she's been out hooking. She's got a record. Maybe, just maybe, she's also got a lot of venom in her, a hatred of women that look like her.'

Rooney hit the desk hard. 'No. No way.'

He watched Bean walk away down the corridor. He couldn't have lost his touch to that extent. He shut his eyes and recalled Lorraine's face, the way her pale eyes bored into him, the scar making her face switch between vulnerable and street tough. He read through her file again: the arrests, the charges, the no-shows at court, the attacks on arresting officers, even that she had been held in a strait-jacket. Drunk and disorderly was recorded time and again. Drunk in charge of a vehicle, drunk when arrested for breaking into a liquor store – she had fought the arresting officer, bitten him, kicked him and punched him in the face. It had taken four of them to get her into the wagon. She'd been held in the cells for three days, charged with assault and spent two months in the women's jail. If he hadn't known her, he would have described her without hesitation as dangerous. Could she be capable of murder? His feet ached as he walked up and down, swearing alternately at Fellows – for throwing this 'woman killer' angle into the investigation – at Lorraine, and lastly at himself.

When Bean returned with the food, Rooney seemed distracted and had taken a bottle from one of the drawers. He took the top off his coffee, gulped a few mouthfuls and topped it up with bourbon. 'Check that vice charge, the Janklow thing, get on that first.' Bean didn't say he was already working on it, he just left Rooney alone. He'd seen these dark moods often and didn't want to be at the receiving end of one today.

Rooney closed Lorraine's file. She had sunk lower than he could ever have imagined and he felt a certain remorse. The question uppermost in his mind was, had she sunk so low then forced herself back up just to take revenge? Should he warn all officers that she might be dangerous? He knew if he gave that out, and she resisted arrest, she might be shot.

Rooney opened the lowest drawer in his desk, took out his gun and searched for his holster. He rarely, if ever, wore it, even though he knew he should. Now he strapped it on, checked the weapon, and slipped it into place. He shrugged back into his jacket and was just about to walk out when

Bean returned. 'We got no record in any Vice section regarding Steven Janklow. This is the second time I've checked, so now I've requested they go back in Records to the time of the first murder. There's nothing on him or the Thorburns. Nothing. Even if there had been a possible charge, we'd at least have a record or it would have been on file – that includes if charges were dropped for any reason, like string-pulling.'

Rooney passed Bean, reeking of bourbon. 'You got your peppermints handy?' he asked him, as if he knew what he was thinking.

'You going home?' Bean asked.

'Nope, I'll call in. I need some fresh air.'

'What about the extra cars out looking for Lorraine Page? They still haven't picked her up.'

'I'll bring her. Just hang out here until I find her.'

'Don't you want me to drive?'

Rooney turned on him. 'No, I fucking don't. Just stay put – I'll call in soon as I find her!'

He slammed the door so hard the blinds rattled.

Lorraine asked Rosie to wait and she walked up the drive to Andrew Fellows's home. She rang a couple of times before Dilly answered. She was wearing a nightgown with a shawl wrapped round her shoulders.

'I'm sorry, did I get you out of bed?'

'No, didn't feel like getting up today, I was just watching TV. Sit down, I'll get us some tea. He shouldn't be too long – he called in to say he was on his way home hours ago.'

Lorraine sat down within sight of Brad's portrait. Dilly came to sit on the sofa, curling her feet up beneath her. 'He went to meet the FBI agents at the station. He gets talking and then he forgets the time.'

'Dilly, tell me about Brad.'

She giggled. 'Oh, another conquest, is it? Well, just let me warn you, he's some hunk but don't get too interested. He's got a terrible reputation – screws them, sometimes marries them, but then he gets icy, ditches them. He's ditched more than I can count.'

The kettle boiled and she went to make the tea. Lorraine looked at the portrait again.

'He had it all, you see, given on a plate. Loaded and handsome, always a fatal combination.' Dilly's head appeared above the kitchen counter. 'He's so glamorous, motor racing – God, he looks so sexy in those white jumpsuits. Now he's writing thrillers, or whatever he calls them, but he'll never finish a book, I know him . . . Do you take sugar?'

'What about his family?' Lorraine asked.

'Oh, you *are* hooked – or are you seeing cash registers?'

'Just interested.'

'I bet. His family are mega-rich. I'll tell you something weird. His brother – he's got an older brother, did I tell you?'

'Go on . . .'

Dilly snuggled down and sipped her tea. She loved to gossip. 'Well I only met him once. They're like chalk and cheese. He's quite small whereas Brad is tall and well-built, dark. Steven's fairish, short-sighted, sort of prissy. I only saw him for a few minutes when I was up at their house. They have Christ knows how many homes – well, Brad does, he was left everything. They have different fathers – obvious, I suppose, they got different names, right? Janklow was her first husband, wealthy, I think, but it was Thorburn who had the big bucks. She was a great socialite, beautiful, pampered and I think she was in movies at one time, very early on. She's ancient.'

'And she's still alive?'

'Oh, yeah, in some expensive home. I've never met her but I think Andrew has. But he's useless, I ask him all these questions about his patients and he won't gossip but I love it.'

'She was a patient?'

'Oh no – well, I don't think so. I just knew he met her once and she sometimes stays with Brad. She has this bedroom, very Greta-Garbo-style, different from Brad's taste. His is all macho wood and the bare essentials.'

Lorraine was getting impatient.

'How long will Andrew be, do you think?'

Dilly shrugged. 'You asking me? All I know is he phoned to say he was on his way. Do you want another cup of tea?'

Brad offered Fellows a glass of wine, which he refused. They walked into the living room.

'What did you want to talk to me about?'

Fellows sat down, unsure how to begin. 'Is Steven home?'

Brad looked perplexed. 'He may be. He keeps to his part of the house. Why do you ask?'

Fellows fiddled with the fringe on the sofa. 'Just something I overheard tonight. I was at the cop shop – FBI agents, they've been brought in to oversee these murders. Have you read about them?'

Brad sipped his wine. 'Be hard not to. Are you working on them?'

Fellows tugged frantically at his ear. 'They brought up this guy Norman Hastings, one of the victims. Did we talk about him?'

Brad leaned back. 'I don't remember.'

'Well, I suggested they dig deep – may be they'd missed something. As it turned out, I was right.' He smiled. 'He was a cross-dresser, you know, a transvestite.'

'And?' Brad said softly. His voice was deep, attractive, and he sank down lower on the sofa.

Fellows looked away. 'I don't think I was supposed to

hear it, about this Hastings guy. Did you know he parked his car at your garage?'

Brad frowned. 'Somebody mentioned it to me but I have no idea who parks there half the time. It's supposed to be just for the employees.'

'Have you been questioned?'

'No, but the police have been talking to all the employees – in fact I was meaning to talk to you about it . . . because I think I might write something, and I know you sometimes assist the homicide squad. I just thought maybe you could help me.'

Fellows stood up. 'Maybe I'll have a glass of wine, after all.'

'Sure,' Brad said easily. He uncoiled his perfect body, picked up his glass and walked out towards the kitchen. Fellows followed. As he passed the stairs he looked upwards, instinctively, as if he knew someone was looking down at him, but there was no one in sight. 'Is Steven home?' Fellows asked again. Brad poured two glasses of Chablis and offered one to him. 'Just I thought I saw someone on the landing.'

'You asked that already, Andrew! You tired or something? You never did say why you came. Are you cancelling our squash game?'

'Oh, no, that's fine, it was—'

Brad walked ahead of him. 'Remember the last time we played? That woman was waiting to see you – Lorraine Page? Maybe I should have told you, she came here.' Brad was sprawled on the sofa again. 'She was looking for someone up the road.'

Fellows sipped his wine, wondering if he should tell his friend what he had come to say. He couldn't make up his mind.

Brad balanced his glass on the sofa arm, twisting the stem. 'Actually, she's rather attractive, has an odd way of looking at you, sort of sly but not—'

Fellows drained his glass and stood up. 'Stay away from her, she's bad news. She's not what she seems.'

'What's that supposed to mean? I thought she was a friend of yours. She was at your place for dinner, wasn't she?'

Fellows decided he'd tell Brad, whether it was ethical or not. 'She's a hooker and a police informer. She's also wanted in connection with these murders. But there's something else . . . The cops were discussing your garage and the fact that Hastings parked his car there.'

'They don't suspect anyone at the garage, do they?'

'They were discussing your brother. Apparently he knew Hastings. He was found dead in his own car so maybe someone at your place had access to it. Look, I'm just repeating what I overheard. Maybe you can tip Steven off, have a chat to him.'

Brad walked Fellows to the front door. 'He's not mentioned any of this to me but we're not exactly best of friends. But thanks, I'll have a word with him.'

Fellows stood on the porch. 'This is advice, Brad. I'd stay clear of Lorraine Page if she should make contact. The lady could be desirable but her past life isn't.'

Brad watched Fellows drive away. He would have liked his friend to explain himself, but then he saw Steven standing on the first-floor balcony. Brad banged the gate with his fist and walked back into the house. He ran up the stairs two and three at a time until he reached his brother's quarters. He tried the door, but it was locked. 'Steven, open the door – I know you're in there so open the fucking door. I want to talk to you.' He waited, hit the door again, but there was silence. 'Steven, open the door or I'll get the master keys. *Steven?*'

He pressed his ear to the door. He could hear water running. He fetched the spare keys. He returned to his brother's bedroom and slipped in the key. He walked inside, bare-foot, leaving the door wide open behind him.

Brad looked round the immaculate room. He could still hear the sound of the bathwater running as he crept across the room. He'd wait, Steven would have to come out at some time. The room was different from his own, but similar to his mother's – floral drapes at the window, a canopied bed with swathes of silk caught in a coronet and tied with large satin bows. The carpet was oyster pink, as were the silk-covered walls. The stereo equipment was built into banks of mirrors; the television section was mirror-fronted to match the rows of wardrobes. Steven's tapes and videos were neatly stacked and listed in alphabetical order, hundreds of CDs, old records and tapes. Brad caught his own reflection over and over again. There was no corner of the room in which you couldn't see yourself. It was all elegant, expensive, even tasteful, if you liked that kind of décor. Brad hated it.

He looked over the dressing table – more fitting for a woman than a man, with jars of creams and perfumes in neat symmetrical rows, silver-backed mirrors and hair-brushes, and rows of silver-framed photographs. Brad had only ever entered this room two or three times and now he looked around slowly, taking everything in. He opened one wardrobe door after another to reveal rows of linen jackets and a vast array of shirts, each one covered in plastic. The shoes were packed in boxes with colour coordinations marked. There were racks of ties, silk handkerchiefs, even straw hats, a few he recognized as having belonged to his father.

He could hear the bathwater draining away. He knocked, waited a moment, then knocked again. The softly playing classical music was turned off.

'Come on, Steven, I have to talk to you. It's important.' He punched the bathroom door. 'Okay, fucking stay in there. You can come to me, I'm not waiting any longer. But you'd better come and see me, you hear? That was Andrew Fellows, my friend from the college, the professor.

He's working with the police. He had something to tell me about you, about that Norman Hastings friend of yours. If you want to know what he told me, then . . . screw you, Steven!'

Brad waited another few moments, then spotted the briefcase, placed neatly at the side of the dressing table. He picked it up and tried to open it, but it was locked. He looked over the dressing table and found a thin paper-knife. He prised open the lock, removed a file of papers, and then replaced the briefcase. His brother had still not made a sound so he left.

Two minutes later the bathroom door opened and Janklow walked out, draped in a silk dressing gown, naked beneath it. He bolted the bedroom door, to ensure his privacy, then walked casually towards the dressing table and sat on the small frilled stool. He opened a bottle of lotion and began carefully to cream his hands. Every move was studied, each finger massaged, each perfectly manicured nail scrutinized. He used pointed cotton-wool sticks to wipe around the cuticles and then looked along his row of clear varnishes, choosing one and carefully painting each nail. His hands were steady; he was calm. He slipped off the robe and stood naked, surveying himself in the mirrors. His slim body was still pinkish from the bath, a pale, white-skinned body, but muscular. He never went in the sun, unlike Brad – he never did any of the things Brad did, not as a child or as a man.

He began to do his yoga exercises, studying every posture in his mirrors. His testicles were small, like marbles, and his penis flaccid. He knelt forwards, squeezing his thighs together, pushing his penis out of sight until he knelt upwards, seemingly devoid of any sex organ. His nipples were erect, pink, and he slowly massaged his breasts, breathing deeply. The only blemish on his hairless skin was the mark at the side of his neck. He had used oil of arnica, even make-up to disguise the toothmarks of the bitch who had bitten him. He had been desperate to find her again. She could hurt him much more than the bite had. He breathed deeply, not wanting to become agitated.

It was almost over, he was almost free. It had been a terrible long nightmare. He had even thought of suffocating his mother just so that she would never find out; he had done it all for her because he loved her with an all-consuming passion. But they were not like mother and son, they were one. That was why he couldn't kill her. He couldn't bear the thought of losing her, just as he could not tolerate her knowing about him.

Brad stood in his mother's room. He wasn't sure why he had come here, possibly because it reminded him of Steven's. He stood at her dressing table looking at the photographs and then slipped his finger into the small drawer in the centre. Everything here had a place and not one perfume bottle was out of line. He sniffed a cut-glass stopper and recognized the same smell from his brother's room. As he was about to replace the stopper, he accidentally knocked over the bottle, which tipped into the open drawer, perfume splashing over the leather jewel boxes. He swore, snatched a tissue from the white-embroidered box and dabbed at the leather, then took out the large, fan-styled box to make sure it was not stained. He clicked it open. The velvet-lined case that had once contained four fabulous ropes of perfectly matched pearls was empty. He closed it and then opened the other boxes. All were empty.

He whistled softly as he shut the drawers. He checked that the perfume bottle was once more in line with the others and walked out.

Just as Brad left his mother's room, he heard the front door close. 'Steven? *Steven?*'

He ran down the stairs just in time to see his brother drive out in the Mercedes.

Lorraine hadn't seen it coming. She was totally taken aback when Dilly Fellows, midway through talking about Brad Thorburn, burst into tears. She sobbed loudly, hands over her face. 'This is so stupid, but just talking about him hurts me so much because I love him. I don't know what to do about it sometimes. I can usually control it but sometimes it just bursts out of me.'

Lorraine stood up. 'Look, I'd better go. My friend's waiting outside.'

Dilly sniffed. 'You should have brought her in. I don't know what's happened to Andrew and I'm so sorry about this, I don't know what you must think of me. Andrew doesn't know. Oh, God, you won't tell him, will you?' Lorraine shook her head. 'He's got no idea. He knows I had a passion for Brad – well, it was obvious to begin with – but he doesn't know just how much I care. I think about him all the time, I make up excuses to call him. I'm like a teenager – but I like it. I like this feeling. It's like a pain, it's almost sexual it gets so intense, and then when he comes here with Andrew, I have an orgasm just looking at him. I do, I honestly do, and it's an incredible feeling. I put it back into my work when he's been around, I can paint for hours. Did he touch you?'

Lorraine felt more and more uneasy. Dilly was over-bright, over-excited and her voice was verging on hysterical. 'Why did you ask me all those questions about him? Did you fuck him?'

Lorraine picked up her purse. 'No, I didn't, and I have to go. Thank you for the tea.' She couldn't wait to get into the car.

*

'Jesus, you took your time, I was just about to come in and get you. A few minutes, you said,' Rosie growled. She was hungry and it was way past lunchtime.

Lorraine apologized. 'That woman is freaky. I really liked her at first – she seemed so warm and friendly, so bloody normal.'

They drove off. 'Where to next, home or what?' Rosie asked.

Lorraine hesitated. 'Look, we drive home, then I've got to go some place else. I'll take the car on alone because I don't want to keep you hanging around any longer.'

'Great, some fucking partner I am, I'm not in on anything. I don't know what you're talking about half the time.'

Lorraine jerked her thumb back at the house. 'That was the wife of the guy the cops brought in to help solve the case. He's a professor of psychology, working for Rooney. If you ask me, he should do some work on his wife. She just blurted out she was infatuated with Brad Thorburn, I couldn't believe it.'

Lorraine knew she would go and see him, as soon as she got rid of Rosie, and it was strange, she had a dull, low ache in the pit of her stomach. She wanted to see him but it wasn't just about the case. She wouldn't admit that to herself, or that she was feeling sexually aroused. She refused even to contemplate that.

Rosie was still pissed off about being dumped back home when Lorraine dropped her off a little way from the apartment. Just as she turned the corner past the grocery store, Rooney screeched to a halt alongside her.

'Where's Lorraine? This is important, Rosie, there's a warrant out for her arrest. If you know where she is you'll be doing her a favour because they got every available officer out looking for her and if she resists arrest, she could get hurt.' Rosie said nothing and Rooney got out of the car. 'Come on, sweetheart, where is she? If you care anything about her you'll tell me.'

Rosie looked down the road. 'She's gone off in the car.'

Rooney asked her for the registration number. Rosie was in a quandary but then she blurted it out. She'd said enough now and started off down the road.

'Where you going?'

'I got to go home, feed my cat.'

Rooney told her to stay in the apartment. If Lorraine came back she was to call him immediately. 'You sure you don't know where she is or where she was heading? When did you last see her?'

Rosie shouted that she'd told him all she knew and she hadn't seen Lorraine since early morning. She hurried to her apartment and went up the stairs. She looked down at Rooney as he parked opposite the house watching her. 'I don't know where she is!' she yelled as she let herself in and slammed the screen door behind her. She looked out of the window. Rooney was still there. She was about to call Jake when she heard Rooney's car move off. She decided to wait for half an hour or so. If Lorraine hadn't returned, if she hadn't heard anything, she'd call Jake and ask him what she should do.

Andrew Fellows let himself in and called his wife. She gave no answer. In the kitchen, he noticed the two cups and saucers left on the draining board. He found her in the bedroom, huddled beneath the duvet, the TV on. 'You had a visitor?' She looked at him, eyes red-rimmed. 'You okay?'

'I'm fine. It's a sad movie.'

'Who was here?'

Dilly sat up. 'Your friend Lorraine Page. She wanted to speak to you – waited ages.' She swallowed and her eyes filled with tears. 'She asked me questions about Brad and then she left. She had a friend waiting, she said.'

Fellows sat on the edge of the bed. 'Just tell me exactly what she said, what questions she asked.'

Dilly switched off the TV by remote control. She repeated everything Lorraine had said but deleted any reference to her own outburst. Fellows went into his den. He called the police station.

Bean listened as Fellows reported that Lorraine Page had been at his home and had talked to his wife. He was very agitated and angry. Bean said he would send someone over straight away.

'She's not here now, she's left.'

Bean called Rooney to let him know that Lorraine had been with Fellows's wife. Rooney took the address; he was on his way. He'd just left Lorraine's place, and had already put out the registration number of her vehicle. It would only be a matter of time before they brought her in.

Brad sifted through the file he had taken from Steven's room, bank statements and other private papers. He knew it had been going on for some considerable time – it was obvious from the receipts. Steven, meticulous as ever, had carefully recorded each sale of every item he had removed from his mother's jewel drawer. The four strands of pearls had been sold for five thousand dollars, although they were insured for three times that amount. The diamond rings, necklaces, the ruby and sapphire bracelets, the topaz ring, all had been listed but with a dash at the side of each item. Brad calculated that his brother had accrued over a hundred and fifty thousand dollars, yet he had not paid it into his own bank accounts – unless he had another one somewhere.

Brad was aware that on his mother's death she would leave the jewels to Steven. But that was no reason for him to have been selling them off without her permission – unless she knew of it. It was just after three. He decided against calling the nursing home: better to face Steven first when he came home.

He replaced the papers in the briefcase, then went back

into his mother's room. One of the wardrobe doors was slightly ajar and he opened it to close it properly. He looked at the rows of her wigs. He found them distasteful, as he found everything about her obsessive drive to retain her youth. The wardrobe was crammed with flimsy gowns and négligés, not fitting for a woman in her seventies, of an era when she had been in her prime. Brad was sweating from the overheated room and the cloying smell of her perfume. He felt slightly nauseous, also guilty. She had always hated anyone touching her things. She herself had never liked to be touched. How often as a child he had run to embrace her, but she had always held up her perfectly manicured hands as if she was scared to be held by her own child. It had been different with Steven. If anything, she had encouraged him because he was so much older than Brad. She pointedly preferred his company. Brad remembered his father in one of his rages shouting up the stairs, as she stood quivering in pale lime chiffon, that if she didn't want him, he would find other women who did. 'Other women?' She had leered down at his father, her perfect red lips drawn back in a snarling smile. 'No decent woman would come within a mile of you. Whores! You can only get a whore and that's because you pay her!'

'You'd know all about that, wouldn't you? Janklow picked you out of the chorus line. You were a ten-cent stripper – you think I don't know? Movie star? The closest you ever got to a real movie was paying at the ticket window.'

She would throw things, she would rant and rage at him whenever he referred to her first husband, or her chorus line days, and he would roar with laughter, enjoying her fury, her humiliation, encouraging Brad to listen, warning him never to marry someone else's used goods. She would become so hysterical that she would smash mirrors and crockery, and lock herself into her room for days on end. The only person who was ever able to calm her was Steven.

Back in his own room, Brad lay down, looking up at his mirrored ceiling. The mirror remained, a legacy from Tom Thorburn. Brad wondered if the other legacy was his predilection for young blondes. He had certainly married enough of them. But of late, like his father, he chose to go with whores rather than get involved in yet another relationship. It was rare for women to say no to him: on the polo field, at the racetrack, they were always available, like clutches of twittering starlings.

He was a man to whom few women said no. That was why he had liked Lorraine Page. She had said no but she had almost said yes. Just thinking about her gave him an erection. He was no longer pondering on his brother or what Andrew Fellows had hinted at. He was even able to put aside the Norman Hastings query, simply because he felt sure that the reason Steven had been so secretive was because of his systematic siphoning off of his mother's jewellery. He wished he had just come out and asked Andrew for Lorraine's phone number.

But even his relationship with Andrew was a mess because his wife was always wanting Brad to screw her, and she wasn't the first – a lot of his friends' wives wanted him. Some he had obliged but it always ended badly.

His erection dispersed as he looked over his life. He had wasted it, he knew that. Even his attempt at writing a novel was futile. He had millions at his disposal, his vast charitable donations taken care of by trustees, but there never seemed any point. He hated what he had become: a dilettante, worse, a clone of his father.

Lorraine headed up Beverly Glen. She passed Brad Thorburn's home, parking the car a few houses up, half hidden from the road. She then walked back, wishing Rosie was with her. The house looked peacefully silent, the faint sound of a lawn mower buzzing from somewhere in the grounds, and she pressed the intercom at the side of the gates. She rang again as the dog appeared. He barked and then stood looking at her through the gates. Brad answered. 'Who is it?'

'Lorraine Page.' She was fazed when he laughed. He didn't say anything else but the gates clicked open. He stepped out onto the porch and leaned against the door frame, a glass of wine in his hand. He was smiling, watching her as she walked slowly towards him. She was so tall and the sun made her hair seem more white than blonde. She wore high-heeled slingback shoes, a straight skirt with a slit to one side, revealing a fraction of her thigh. The jacket was ill-fitting, a little too large, and she had a white shirt beneath, open at the neck. She wore no jewellery and it didn't look as if she had on any make-up. She carried only a clutch purse, in her right hand. As she reached the first white stone step on the porch, she tilted her head; even from this distance, he could see the scar on her cheek.

'I was just thinking about you,' he said quietly. She wasn't expecting him to be so gentle, just as she didn't expect him to hold out his hand to her. It felt strong, gripping hers tightly. 'Do you know the police are looking for you?' he said, not taking his eyes from hers, trying to see what she wanted from him, but her fine hair hid her face.

'Yes, but I have to talk to you.'

He guided her towards the hallway, his hand now at her elbow, with a firm but not threatening hold. They walked into the drawing room. He remained at the door, finishing his wine, watching her.

'Is your brother home?'

'No.'

'Are there any servants here?'

'Just the housekeeper, she'll be leaving at four.' He ran his hand over his neck to the back of his hairline. The T-shirt moved aside and she could see part of his shoulder.

She was silent. She stared hard at him and his eyes slid away, as if embarrassed by her clear, direct gaze. She opened her purse and took out her cigarettes, flicked open the packet and placed one between her lips. 'Do you have a light?'

He came in and put down his empty glass. She thought he was going to pick up a table lighter but instead he came close, took the cigarette out of her mouth and tossed it aside. He then slipped his hand to the small of her back and pressed her to him. In her high heels she was almost as tall as he was. He kissed her and let his hand fall to her buttocks, pulling her even closer to him. He kissed her again and she responded, her tongue traced his mouth and she moved back just a fraction, taking his free hand to place on her heart. She was trembling. He scooped her up into his arms – she was so incredibly light – and carried her with ease out of the drawing room and up the stairs. One of her shoes fell off, then the other, as she rested against him. She was crying, her head buried in his shoulder. He had never known such sweetness, and by the time he laid her down on his bed, she was sobbing. He just held her, rocking her, soothing her, kissing her hair, kissing the tears that poured down her cheeks. He looked up and saw himself cradling her as if she was a child. He was scared of his own tenderness towards this woman, who both excited him sexually and aroused emotions he had not thought himself still capable of having. His arms tightened around her, until the weeping subsided and she lifted her lips to him. This time his kiss was not gentle but passionate, hard and crushing, and she responded.

Steven Janklow walked into the house. He looked into the spotless empty kitchen. The housekeeper had already left. He picked up his brother's empty wine-glass, took it into the kitchen, and put it carefully in the dishwasher. He lifted the lids of two covered dishes left out for dinner. He was hungry but he didn't know what he felt like eating; nothing tempted him.

He started up the stairs and stopped. He saw Lorraine's shoes, first one then the other. He held them in disgust, cheap shoes, and carried them up the stairs, turning towards his brother's quarters. He was just about to put them outside his door – he'd done it before, not just with shoes, but brassières, skirts and, more often than not, panties – when, as he drew closer, he could hear a high-pitched moan, like a mewing. It made him cringe. They all sounded alike, all his brother's whores – even his wives. Janklow had intended simply to leave the shoes but the door was ajar. He put out his hand to close it, averting his eyes in case he got so much as a glimpse of their writhing naked bodies. The woman moaned again, and even though he didn't want to look, he couldn't help himself.

Her face was tilted towards him, eyes closed, mouth half open. She was astride his brother, her body like a young boy's rather than a woman's – that, perhaps, was what had made him stare. As she moved, thrusting forwards, Janklow gasped, quickly covering his mouth with his hand. He didn't shut the door; he didn't dare make a sound as he backed away silently. Not until he was safely along the corridor did he turn and run. He clung to the toilet rim as he vomited, retching with terror, his whole body breaking out in an icy sweat. He couldn't be mistaken, it wasn't possible. There couldn't be two women with that face, that scar. It was *her* – the woman he had picked up, the woman who had bitten his neck until he bled like a pig.

He ran cold water over his face to try to calm himself, but his hands trembled violently. His mind screamed out questions. Why was she here? How could she have got to him here, traced him here? He tried to control his breathing, stop himself panting. Brad often dragged back whores and cheap bitches but he'd never have believed he would have sunk this low, not with *that* woman – she was disgusting. He flopped on his bed, saying to himself it was just a coincidence, it was that and nothing more, just a terrible coincidence. He rolled over, clenching his fists, trying not to break down and weep with fear. It was then that he saw his briefcase, knew at a glance that it had been moved, and worse, that it had been opened.

A thought struck him. He got up and went to his mother's room where he checked her jewellery drawer. He knew that the boxes had been taken out – they were all in the wrong order. Someone had been in here and into his own room, checking him out. Was it Brad? Or was it that woman? He returned to his bedroom and bolted the door. He had to get rid of her. If she was a call-girl, if Brad had done his usual, brought her back to the house, he would just have to wait. They never stayed all night. When he saw her leave, he would follow. It was simple. He would kill her as he had almost done before, only this time he would make sure. He looked at his bedside clock, it was almost five. If she was like the others, she would probably be leaving after an hour or so to start work at night. Walking the streets as she had been doing when she had picked him up. He remembered how she had rested her hand on the car door, asked if he needed her help. There hadn't been a car in the drive, had she come by taxi? Or parked out in the street?

Janklow crept around the house. He found Lorraine's purse, opened it and searched through. She had little money, no cards or check books. All she had in her purse was a packet of cigarettes, a used lipstick, a comb, and, he smiled to himself, car keys.

He left the house and went down the driveway. He saw Bruno look up and wag his tail, and hoped he wouldn't start barking. He stood, frozen to the spot, until the dog lowered his head. The gardener was on the other side of the tennis courts, using some kind of spray, intent on his work. Janklow opened the gates and walked along the road, sure that no one had seen him. There was no one on the road and not even a car passed him.

He found Lorraine's car and checked the keys against the registration number. He was feeling better now, more in control, already working out in his mind how he would kill her, because she was going to die.

Rooney rang Andrew Fellows's doorbell, keeping his finger on the button. Fellows opened up and sighed when he saw who it was. 'I said everything on the phone to Lieutenant Bean. I didn't think it was necessary for anyone to come out, especially not now. She was here before lunch.'

Rooney smiled. 'Sorry about this. I just wanted to go over a few things, and I'd like to speak to Mrs Fellows.'

They went into the kitchen where Dilly was sitting. She looked upset, tear-stained. She repeated everything to Rooney, again without any mention of her disclosure to Lorraine about Brad Thorburn.

'Can I speak to you alone, Professor?' Rooney asked.

'Of course. Dilly, this won't take long.'

Fellows took Rooney into his den. He looked a little sheepish.

'You know the Thorburns?'

'Yes.'

'You didn't mention it this morning.'

'No one asked me if I did or didn't know them.'

'When you left the station, did you come straight back home?'

Fellows flushed a deep red. 'No, I did not. I – I went to the Thorburn house.'

Rooney stared hard, in disbelief as Fellows told him what he had said to Brad. He was obviously ashamed and knew he had behaved unethically. Rooney asked for Thorburn's address and phone number. He left shortly after, not reprimanding Fellows, not saying much at all.

Fellows found his wife in the bedroom. She was crying again. He stared at her for a moment and then walked out. In a fit of rage he dragged Brad's portrait off the wall, smashed it against the open fireplace until the canvas ripped apart and the frame snapped. He stamped on it, then lit the log fire and watched it blaze. He had never felt so angry in his life – angry and bitter, but above all foolish. He hated that most of all. He had just jeopardized his work with the police and doubted if he would ever be called upon again.

As the flames slowly destroyed the painting, his anger subsided. Now he felt nothing but humiliation. Brad Thorburn's nakedness had dominated his home and he had allowed it, joked about it, encouraged Brad to visit Dilly. What made it worse was that Brad had known of her instability, which made his affair with her even more of a betrayal. Fellows vowed never to speak to or see him again. He couldn't even stay in this room, even though the painting was no longer hanging on the wall. The vast space where the life-size portrait had hung added insult to injury. He picked up a cup of cold coffee and headed into the den. As he shut the door, he could hear his wife still crying but he had no intention of discussing Brad with her again. Fellows didn't care if he had screwed her once or twice, it was immaterial. The fact that he had fucked her at all was what mattered.

Fellows found little solace in his den. There were photographs of him and Brad together all over the walls, the two of them fishing, playing baseball, water-skiing in Miami, at squash tournaments, on tennis courts. Brad Thorburn and Andrew Fellows had known each other for many years, had always been competitive with each other as sportsmen. In the women stakes, Fellows had never moved in Brad's social sphere, had never wanted to, could never have been any competition there. No man could, not with Brad's looks and wealth.

Fellows sat at his desk. He drew the file on the murder

investigation closer and began to go over every detail once again. He had been so sure that Brad Thorburn could have no connection with the killings but what if he had been wrong? What if he had missed something? If he had, he was determined to find it. It made him feel better. He wanted to hurt Brad Thorburn – better still, destroy him.

Rooney reached his car and picked up the radio to tell Bean he was now on his way to the Thorburns'.

'You going to interview Janklow?' Bean asked.

'Nope, I think Lorraine Page is trying to though so get a squad car out there. It's Beverly Glen, you got the address? Okay, I'll see you.'

CHAPTER 17

THEY LAY naked side by side, the sheet loosely covering their bodies. She was face downwards, her eyes closed. Brad drew the sheet back and brushed his hand gently over her body. 'How did you get these marks?' He leaned up on his elbow, to trace the scar on her face. 'And this?'

She pulled away from him, and suddenly swished the entire sheet from the bed and wrapped it around herself. 'I'd better get dressed.'

He remained lying naked on the bed as she crossed the room. Trailing the sheet, she started to pick up her clothes. Skirt in one hand, she looked around. 'Where are my shoes?'

Brad got up and opened a wardrobe. He took out a white kaftan and dragged it on over his head. 'They must be downstairs. I'll get them.' He stood behind her and wrapped his arms round her, kissing the nape of her neck. Then he frowned and brushed the short hair at the nape of her neck upwards. 'Jesus Christ, how did you get this one?'

The scar, still pink and raised, zig-zagged across her hair line. She tried to move away but he gripped her tightly. 'Why don't you answer me? Who did this to you?'

She tried to release herself but he held her tighter. 'I need to get dressed.'

He let go of her shoulders. 'I'll be downstairs.'

'Don't go, not yet, we have to talk, the reason I came here.'

Brad sighed. 'You want to talk but if I ask you a question you refuse to answer. So you go ahead, you talk.' His face was tight with anger because he had thought she had come to see him, be with him. She continued to gather her clothes as he sat waiting.

'Look, if it makes it any easier I know you're a whore, you told me that yourself. Is it money you want?'

She moved so fast and it was so unexpected that he did nothing to defend himself. The slap was hard and it hurt. He rubbed his cheek and laughed.

'I didn't come here for what we just did.' She stepped back and her fists were clenched. He reached out his hand to her but she wouldn't take it. She began to pace up and down, the sheet trailing on the floor. She looked astonishingly beautiful. There was a mannish quality to her as she tightened the sheet round her body. 'The scars I got from times when I was on the streets. I used to get drunk, I don't know what I did, who I went with. I'm not proud of the hideous things or the cigarette burns, but I never felt them. I didn't care enough about myself to care.'

'And now?' he asked.

'Now I just want you to listen – don't interrupt me, just listen.'

'Fine.' He leaned back against the pillows. He was not disgusted by anything she had said – in some ways he didn't really believe it.

'The scar on my cheek was a bar-room fight over a bottle of vodka, that's about as much as I can remember, nothing dramatic, nothing romantic. I got it, I live with it, and I was, so I was told, lucky not to lose the sight of my eye. I was a hooker but who I was with and when I don't know. I don't have AIDS, or any venereal disease, just in case you're freaking out. I had myself checked. There's a lot of my life I don't remember. But I do know about this scar, this one at the back of my head, because this is one of the reasons I'm here.'

She was very still, standing like a statue in front of him. She seemed to be watching him for a reaction, some kind of revulsion that would help her continue, but he gave none. Instead he patted the bed, indicating for her to lie beside him, but she shook her head.

'I used to be a police officer. I was a lieutenant with the LAPD Homicide Unit.'

He half smiled and she glared at him. He lifted his hands in an apologetic gesture. She continued: she was now acting as a paid street informer for Captain Rooney. He had hired her because she knew the girls on the streets and he needed information about the hammer killer. She looked directly at him as he sat up, no longer smiling, but staring at her. Without any emotion she told him about the night she had been attacked, half turning to reveal the scar again. She then told him how she had made an anonymous call to the police describing the man who had attacked her. As she gave Brad the description, she didn't take her eyes off him. If she had described his brother, he showed not the slightest sign of recognition. She explained how she had taken Hastings's wallet. She watched him all the time as she told him about Art Mathews, Didi and Nula. He listened in silence. He only became tense when she described the cufflinks, the S and A logo, the cufflinks worn by the man who had attacked her. Brad got off the bed and crossed to a pine dresser. He opened the drawer and took out a small leather case. He threw it onto the bed. 'Like those?'

Lorraine opened the box and took out the cufflinks. She looked at them and nodded. He stood with his hands on his hips and after a moment he asked her to go on. She told him how she had gone to his garage, checked out the workers, checked out the cars in the hangar and had discovered that Norman Hastings had parked his car there the day before he was murdered. That no one could recall what time he had removed it or if he took it away himself. Perhaps it had been taken by someone working at the company.

Brad returned to the bed. Seeing a muscle working at the side of his neck, she knew he was on edge. His eyes also betrayed him, but he never mentioned his brother, just indicated for her to continue. The more she talked, the more he realized that, just as she had said, Lorraine Page had not come to his home for any sexual or romantic reason, but for information. He had misjudged her, misjudged his own prowess, he didn't know this woman at all; he was becoming more and more wary of her.

Lorraine detected his anxiety but continued, keeping her eyes on him constantly. She noticed that it was almost five thirty on the bedside clock, and she started to hurry, telling Brad how she and her friend had photographed each of the workers and had eliminated them one by one. The reason she was outside his house was to continue the elimination process. 'You mean me?' he asked.

'Yes, we even took some photographs of your brother, but none were of much use, so I returned to the Hastings murder, to his wife, and to the man who had taken photographs of Hastings. His name is Craig Lyall.' She waited a beat but he didn't react so she continued.

'Norman Hastings was a transvestite.'

Brad's eyebrows lifted slightly. It was an open reaction without guilt.

'I think the killer was being blackmailed,' Lorraine went on, 'and probably for some considerable time. I think Hastings was too, but he was only able to pay small sums that wouldn't alert his wife and family. He was very protective towards them, terrified his private life would be disclosed. I believe the blackmailers were Art Mathews and Didi, one of the victims, transsexual. She made up the men for photographs taken by Lyall. She was then able to tip off Mathews and he, I think, instigated the blackmail.'

She had seen it, just a flicker in his eyes, on the word blackmail but he covered it well, nodding as if he wanted her to continue. She was combing her hair, watching him in the mirror. 'I wouldn't mind a cup of coffee,' she said, and smiled, then remembered the housekeeper would have left.

He stood up immediately. 'I'll make it.'

'And I still can't find my shoes.'

Brad opened the bedroom door. The shoes were neatly placed outside. He picked them up, held them by the straps and tossed them to her. Lorraine slipped her feet into them before she remembered they had fallen off as he carried her up the stairs. Who had placed them outside the door? The housekeeper? Or someone else? Down in the kitchen, Brad sweated. Had Steven come home? He couldn't recollect the alarm being triggered, and the security system worked on a timer device so would have automatically switched on. By now the gardener would also have left. He looked out of the window and couldn't see the Mercedes. He was sure he hadn't heard Steven return. Maybe he was still out. But if he was, who had put Lorraine's shoes outside the bedroom door?

Brad jumped when he heard her footsteps on the marble hall. She went into the drawing room and collected her purse and then he heard her walking towards the kitchen.

'Did you say the housekeeper left at four?' she asked nonchalantly, as he ground the coffee beans. She was trying to remember what time they had gone up to the bedroom. 'I wondered who left my shoes outside your door.'

'Probably Maria, she's obsessively tidy. Am I one of your suspects?' he asked, smiling.

'No, of course not.'

He sat on the stool next to her. 'Do you need me to call you a cab?'

She touched his face. 'No, I have a car. Now, can we

stop playing games?' She withdrew her hand. 'Tell me about Steven.'

'What about him? Oh, you wanted to see him. Well, he's out but if you leave me your number I can get him to call you tomorrow.'

'Don't protect him, Brad. You'd better be honest with me. That's what I meant about stopping playing games. I want to talk about him, I want to see him to eliminate him. It was your brother I came to see – see him face to face.'

Brad pointed at her. 'Why don't *you* stop? You eliminate him? *You?* There's a warrant out for your arrest, as we both know.' Brad smiled as he poured the coffee. 'You know, I've been fascinated by this monologue you've just delivered. The rogue cop, is that how you see yourself? Maybe the booze did something to your head, Lorraine. I know why you're here.'

She was off the stool, heading towards him. 'Who told *you* about the warrant out for me? – was it Rooney? Did he speak to your brother?' Brad put his cup down. She'd changed suddenly. He thought she was just scared but she said, steadily, 'You'd better tell me, Brad. This man has killed nine times. He knows I'm alive and he's looking for me. I'll be the next. Who was here and what did he tell you? Was it Captain Rooney?'

'No, it wasn't him, whoever he is.'

She pushed at him. 'Who was it? Did he speak to Steven? *For God's sake, stop playing around and tell me who was here.*'

Brad gripped her wrist. 'It doesn't matter. What matters to me is you have to stop this right now – whatever you've dug up on Steven, whatever filth you want to make up about him, about this family.'

She jerked free. 'What are you talking about?'

'How much do you fucking want? You're very clever at what you do, Lorraine. I've had it before, I just didn't think I could be so wrong about someone. So how much and what have you got on Steven? Is that why you took such

358

pains to explain the blackmail by those two whatever-their-names-were?'

'You think I want to blackmail you?'

'Isn't that what you came here for? This family has always been an easy mark, so name your price.'

She snatched up her purse. 'Nothing you could pay, Brad Thorburn. You just think what you want, I didn't come here for any other reason than to—'

'What?' he interrupted. He was angry but controlled.

'I think your brother is a killer. You won't be able to protect him or buy him out of this. You know why? Because I'll prove it.'

Brad sneered, 'You expect me to believe a word you've told me? I've had threats from a lot better than you, sweetheart.'

'What about your brother? Has he had threats?'

'My brother is no concern of yours. Now get the hell out of my house! Now! Get out!' Lorraine turned on her heel. He could hear her walking across the marble hallway, the front door slamming behind her. He waited a moment before he called his lawyer, asking him to come to the house immediately.

She was almost at the gates when she saw a reflected blue light and knew a patrol car was near or heading close by. She pushed the gate closed and ran to the shrubbery. She only just made it out of sight as Rooney appeared.

The front doorbell rang and rang. Brad stared out of the window and could see a figure standing outside the gates. For a moment he thought Lorraine had returned. He went out onto the porch, and Rooney announced himself. Brad stood at the door as Rooney walked up the path and stopped on the bottom step. 'Is Steven Janklow home?'

Brad shook his head and introduced himself. Rooney showed his ID, badge and repeated his name as they entered the house, Brad ushering him ahead. As he closed the door, he saw a police patrol car draw up outside the gates.

Lorraine watched the interaction from the shrubbery. She felt safer now that Rooney was here. She wanted to get back inside the house and remembered the door at the rear opening onto the small corridor leading up to Brad's bedroom. She crossed her fingers that it would be open and that the alarms had not been switched on.

Rooney looked around the impressive drawing room. Brad offered a drink but he refused. 'Do you know where your brother is, Mr Thorburn?'

'No, I'm sorry, I don't. What is this about?'

'I think you know. Andrew Fellows called by earlier, didn't he? So let's cut the bullshit. Is Lorraine Page here?'

'She was but she left.'

'Do you know where she went?'

'No, I don't. I'm surprised you didn't see her, she was here about ten minutes ago.'

'Mr Thorburn, I won't keep you, I'd just like a recent picture of your brother, Steven Janklow.'

Rooney wandered over to a grand piano and looked at the silver-framed photographs. He picked one up and held it out. 'This him?'

Brad said no, it was his father. He suggested that the following morning, when he had had time to speak to his brother, he would ask him to let Rooney have a photograph.

'I'd like to take a look at one now,' Rooney said stubbornly.

'Is it really necessary?'

'Yes, sir. This is a murder investigation.'

Brad disappeared and Rooney stood with his feet planted apart. He was on dangerous ground, he knew, standing in the Thorburn household demanding a photograph without any warrant or back-up evidence except Lorraine's theory.

He waited, then crossed to the telephone and punched out Lorraine's number. Rosie answered.

'It's Rooney. Is she back yet?'

'No.'

'Call me as soon as she gets in.'

He put in another call to Bean. Still no sign of Lorraine. Suddenly, Rooney heard a car driving up the gravel path. He wondered if it was Janklow. His heart sank as he heard voices, Brad saying something about a police officer, a long, whispered conversation. Then Brad walked into the drawing room, with a small balding man wearing rimless glasses and carrying a briefcase.

'This is Alfred Kophch, Captain Rooney.'

Rooney shook the pallid little man's damp hand and remained standing. He didn't need to be told that the balding man was one of the most high-powered criminal lawyers in LA. Kophch sat down and opened his case. 'You want a photograph of my client Steven Janklow, is that correct? Do you have a warrant to be on the premises?'

Rooney huffed and said that at this stage of his inquiries he did not require a warrant. It was an informal visit and Brad Thorburn had invited him in.

'Why do you want a photograph of my client?'

Rooney went a deep red. 'Elimination purposes.'

'I would like to know why no one has contacted Mr Janklow before, and why you have made an informal house call at six thirty p.m.'

Rooney sat on the edge of the plush sofa. He was beginning to sweat, not with nerves but with contained agitation. This grilling made him feel as if he was the guilty party. He reached into his pocket and took out a dog-eared envelope with scrawled dates on the back.

'I would also like to ask – informally – Steven Janklow to tell me where he was on these dates. As he is not here, you can bring him with you in the morning, with a photograph.'

'Why do you need this photograph if Mr Janklow is prepared to come in to see you in person?'

'An attack took place in a multi-level garage. We believe the man that attacked the woman, our witness, is involved in the murders.'

Kophch sighed. 'So now you're saying that Mr Janklow is also a suspect for this attack?'

'Possibly.'

'And the name of the witness?'

Brad leaned forward. 'It's a prostitute called Lorraine Page. There's a warrant out for her arrest and she's involved in a blackmail case.'

'Is this correct?' snapped Kophch.

Rooney shuffled uneasily. 'I am not prepared to disclose the identity of the witness.'

Kophch gave Rooney a warning look. 'Blackmail? This is all getting out of hand, isn't it? I suggest that when you have charges you wish to relate to my client, you contact my office. Until then you should leave these premises immediately and I will forward a complaint to your superiors.'

Rooney stood up slowly. 'Fine. All I'm trying to do is track down a killer.'

Kophch faced Rooney. 'And I am protecting my client. As you must be aware, the Thorburns are an influential family and have in the past been subjected to various blackmail threats and—'

Rooney interrupted, taking a flyer, 'Then there was the vice charge against Mr Janklow that was dismissed. I am aware of certain activities in the past concerning this family, which is why I chose to make this an informal visit.' Suddenly, he was on a roll. He could see the hooded looks passing between the lawyer and Brad, and pushed it further. 'However, this is not just a homosexual cruising or pick-up, but a murder and one that has been the focus of huge media attention.'

Kophch was good. He didn't back off as Rooney had expected but came straight back at him. 'And in the late edition of the papers today there was an announcement that a man arrested for these murders had subsequently committed suicide. Are you now saying this man was not the perpetrator of these crimes?'

Rooney sniffed and pulled at his nose. 'Possibly not.'

His face tight with contained anger, Brad snapped, 'It appears that everything and everyone concerned in this investigation is only "possibly" attached. I suggest that my lawyer should contact your superior and discuss it with him. Now I'd like you to leave my house.'

Rooney was shown the door. The gates opened and he stepped out, hearing them clang shut behind him. As he crossed to his car, he looked down the road, walked a few yards and then squinted in the semi-darkness at the registration number of the parked vehicle. It was Lorraine's. Two uniformed officers were already peering inside. Rooney called his office again to check if Lorraine had been traced. When he heard that she had not, his heart sank. He walked back to the Thorburn house as the alarm floodlights went out. The house seemed ominously dark and quiet apart from the ground floor, where he suspected Thorburn and Kophch were still talking. The officers asked what he wanted done about Lorraine's car. 'Open it up and search it,' he snarled. In truth, he wasn't sure about his next move. He felt a dull panic. Where the hell was she?

Lorraine had found the hidden door open and, in darkness, had made her way back up the narrow staircase into Brad's bedroom. The sheet she had used was on the floor where it had dropped, the pillows on the bed where she and Brad had made love were still dented from his body.

Lorraine crept along the landing. She had seen Rooney enter, and the lawyer, though she didn't know who he was, but was glad of the diversion as she went silently towards the bedrooms, trying to determine which was Janklow's. Below she could hear Brad talking and the low tones of another male voice she wrongly presumed was Rooney's.

She tried two or three rooms before she entered what she thought must be Janklow's and quietly closed the door. She looked around, checked the bathroom and wardrobes, half hoping to find female clothes or wigs but there was nothing. She was disappointed. All she wanted was a photograph, something she could take with her, but while there were many of his mother, and of him and Brad as boys, there were none of Janklow as a man. She was about to leave the room when she saw the briefcase.

She picked it up and froze when the locks clicked open loudly but all she could hear was the low murmur from downstairs. She sifted through the papers as Brad had done, searching for a diary, anything that would give her an insight into Janklow. She found the receipts, all the recorded sales of jewellery, but replaced them and then studied Janklow's bank statements. Again, like Brad, she noted that none of the sums paid to him for the jewels had been put into his accounts. And there was the neat methodical list of jewellery items – maybe these were to be sold? She gave up and went out of the room.

Then she found the mother's bedroom. She went over to the dressing table and glanced at one silver-framed picture after another. Still none of Janklow as an adult. Lorraine picked up a photo of the glamorous Mrs Thorburn – so like the woman driving the Mercedes as photographed by Rosie. It looked posed, well lit and touched up. She turned the frame over, about to replace it, when she decided to see if the photographer was identified on the back of the picture.

As she opened the frame she almost dropped the glass but caught it in time. A second photograph had been placed

364

inside. At first glance it looked like another photograph of Mrs Thorburn, but on closer inspection it obviously wasn't. The blonde wig was identical, even the diamond necklace, the way the gloved hand rested beneath the sitter's chin. But this sitter was not Mrs Thorburn. It was someone attempting to look like her, but no amount of airbrushing and touching up could disguise the fact that the sitter was a man.

Lorraine took the photograph and replaced the frame. She checked three more before she found another hidden photograph of the same man. She could not be sure it was Janklow, or even the man who had attacked her, only that it was some man impersonating Mrs Thorburn. She then heard an ominous creaking sound from above: footsteps pacing up and down.

Quickly, she peered at the back of the photograph and made out a pale imprint of the photographer's name and contact number. It was so blurred that she needed more light, but she suspected it would be either Art Mathews or Craig Lyall. As she eased open the door, she jumped back as she heard voices, louder now. She hurried to the landing to look down to the hall. Should she confront Brad and Rooney together? Or get out, drive herself to the station, and show them the photographs? She crept further along the landing; they were still talking. Then she heard the same pacing coming from above. Was it Janklow? She dithered a moment and then moved silently down one stair at a time. She was within yards of the drawing room and she could hear clearly now.

'How serious is this?' she heard Brad ask.

'I have no idea but I will tomorrow, I'll go there personally. It's best not to worry about it. Just leave it with me.'

Lorraine was at the foot of the stairs, her heart pounding. She could easily have walked in, admitted being there – but why couldn't she hear Rooney's voice? She turned suddenly, certain someone was watching her. She pressed against the wall, trying to look up the stairs.

'You don't think there's any possibility of there being any truth in all this, do you?' Brad sounded tired. The clipped tone of the other man replied that he doubted there was anything to be worried about, he was fully aware of Steven's sexual preference and he would make sure it was never disclosed. But he would like to talk to him at the first opportunity. Where was he? Brad had no idea, but knew that he had been home earlier.

Why couldn't she hear Rooney's voice? Was he there? She looked to the open kitchen doorway, then back to the drawing room, and stepped out of her shoes. She made it to the kitchen and then stopped. She looked again to the first landing, again sure she had seen someone.

'I'll show you out.' It was Brad, and they were walking towards the hall. She dodged into the kitchen, seconds before the two men emerged from the drawing room. Lorraine could see them through a narrow chink between the door and its frame but she still couldn't see Rooney. He must have already left.

'One thing's bothering me, Alfred. Do you know if Mother instructed Steven to sell off her jewellery?'

'I don't deal with Mrs Thorburn's private accounts, it's an entirely different department, but I'll get it checked out.'

'I'm sure there'll be a reasonable explanation. I know the jewellery will be left to Steven on Mother's death – it's just that I find it strange that neither Mother nor Steven has mentioned it to me.'

Lorraine was terrified to move: they were so close. She was hoping and praying that if the front door was going to open, she could get out through the back door as the security system would be off. She was about to head for what she presumed was the back door when something Brad said made her freeze.

'This last business, I thought there was no possible way it could get out. You told me there would never be any repercussions and yet that Rooney brought it up as if it was still on the police files.'

Kophch again said that he would look into it. Although he had made certain there was no documented evidence left on any police file, he could not guarantee the silence of any officer who had been involved.

'Then pay them off, if necessary, whatever the cost.'

Lorraine flattened her body against the wall inching towards the back door.

'You know, Brad, there's only so much I can do. I cannot in any way jeopardize myself. Do you have any reason to believe that Steven could be involved in this? Because if you do, you must be honest with me. For example, this witness, do you know any more about her?'

Lorraine heard Brad discussing her visit, that he was sure she had only been trying to get money out of him. He sounded angry, his voice rising. 'Well, I can have her taken care of if she contacts me again.'

He was interrupted. 'No, you listen to me. If this woman shows up, you do nothing. Nothing. As I said, I was able to take care of things last time but this is bigger – this is murder, and if the press get wind that either you or your brother have any involvement, you'll be hounded. Now do you understand? You do not do anything without first discussing it with me!'

Brad walked out onto the porch with his lawyer. They shook hands and Brad watched Kophch take out his car keys. Then he walked back to the house, his hand on the buzzer to open the gates.

Lorraine edged to the back door. She tried the handle: it was open. She said a silent prayer, only to find she was in the garage rather than the garden as she had expected. The kitchen door closed behind her, just as Brad closed the front door and switched on the alarm circuit.

She looked round the vast dark garage, which had room for at least six cars. At the side of the sliding doors was a row of numbered buttons to open them and above the buttons was an ominous unblinking red dot. She tried to go back the way she had come, but the door was now locked. She was trapped inside the garage.

Rooney was sitting in his car as the lawyer drove past. Kophch stared at him but did not stop. Lorraine's car remained parked along the road; the two officers had found nothing inside. Rooney sat, hoping to see her and becoming more and more worried as the minutes ticked by. He wondered if she was in the house. He even wondered if he should go back in and demand to search the place, but he had no warrant.

The two officers hovered, waiting for instruction. Rooney rubbed his chin; his stubble itched. He was dog tired. 'I think she's maybe up at the house. I want one of you to call, ask if you can look around the grounds. I doubt if he'll let you in but it's worth a try. If we get no luck, take her car back to the station.'

Lorraine looked about her. A Rolls-Royce Silver Shadow, plus Brad's sports car, two Harley Davidson motorcycles, a Porsche and, hidden from her sight at first, the Mercedes. She was sure it would be alarmed, like everything else in the house. She looked at the garage doors, could see wires threaded everywhere. It was like a fortress. No way would she be able to get out that way; she'd have to return to the house. Then she heard the ringing of a distant doorbell. The garage doors began to slide open. She ducked behind a car as they began to whir and grind, pulling back. She peered up and could see Brad standing right outside the garage with a uniformed police officer.

'Take a look around in here and then wherever else you like but not in the house.'

She could see Brad's bare feet beneath the cars, and the dark trouser legs of the police officer, his black rubber-soled shoes.

'I'll show you round the back way,' Brad said. He hadn't expected to see Steven's car there and it had freaked him. He was sure his brother wasn't in but he covered his initial reaction by quickly offering to show the officer the gardens.

Lorraine waited until they were out of sight before she dashed out of the garage towards the grass verge and ran flat out until she reached the open gates.

Rooney and the officer were standing by her car, Rooney leaning forward for his cigarette to be lit. She headed to his car. It was open and she threw herself inside, onto the back seat. Rooney inhaled and let the smoke drift out of his nostrils. He checked the time again; it was almost seven o'clock. His stomach grumbling for food, he plodded back to the gates as the second officer appeared, a young, fresh-faced boy, who worked out. His muscles rippled beneath his pristine cop shirt and badge and he edged his night stick aside from his leg.

'There's no one in the grounds, Captain, and Mr Thorburn wants to lock up for the night. What do you want me to do? This place is alarmed all over, he's standing with his hand on the buzzer, says we can't go into the house.'

Rooney waddled towards him. 'You didn't see anything?'

'Been round the back, summer-house, tennis courts, swimming pool, checked all over. She's not in the grounds.'

Rooney went back to his car but he couldn't just walk away. As the two officers stood in the road waiting to know what he wanted them to do, he reached in for his radio.

'Don't let them take me in, Bill,' Lorraine said quietly from the back seat. 'Please don't.'

Rooney turned back to the officers but they hadn't seen

her. 'One of you take her car into the holding bays, the other follow. I'll see you back at base.'

Rooney got into his car and watched the two men split up, one going for Lorraine's car, the other getting a set of pliers out of the patrol car. He started his engine and drew away, leaving them as they decided who should drive Lorraine's car. The young muscular cop laughed as they reached down to fix the wires to start the engine. He said it had been a long time since he'd been caught doin' this.

'You go first, Rambo, I'll follow.'

Rooney didn't even head up Mulholland but pulled over about a mile away. She'd have felt better if he'd slammed on the brakes and yelled at her, but instead he engaged the handbrake gently and switched off the engine, then slowly swivelled around to face her.

'What the fuck do you think you're doing?' He hit the seat with the flat of his hand.

She unfolded the photographs. 'These were behind pictures of Mrs Thorburn. Look at the back. Can you see who took them?'

Rooney snatched the pictures and reached into his glove compartment for a torch. He shone it onto the creased photograph.

'Can you make it out?'

'Can you?' He passed the torch across to her and she shone it on the faded photographer's stamp. 'Professional Photo Studio,' she said slowly, disappointed it had not said Art Mathews – yet it could have been his studio, or even Craig Lyall's.

'So you got photographs of a woman,' Rooney said flatly.

'They're not of a woman, Bill, it's a man dressed up. And it's not just any woman he's dressed up to look like, but Mrs Thorburn. I think it's Janklow.'

'Jesus Christ, now what you tellin' me? That he's a homo

or a transvestite, or what? Is he or isn't he the man who fucking attacked you, Lorraine?'

'I don't know.'

'You don't know. Well, that is fucking great.'

'I didn't see him, Bill – that's why I went there.'

'I told you to stay in the apartment. You promised me. You done nothing but jerk me off, Lorraine.'

She sighed, watching her car being driven past followed by the patrol car. They tooted and waved at Rooney. As Lorraine's car drove away, the patrol car slowed.

'Everything okay, Captain?' The officer stared at Lorraine in the back seat.

Rooney jerked his thumb at Lorraine. 'Yeah, it's all fine. I found her. Go on, I'll see you back there.'

They watched the patrol car move off and Rooney turned back to her. 'I got to take you in. You got no option, I got no option.'

'I went to an AA meeting, I was going to go straight back and wait for you but . . .'

He fished in his pocket for his cigarettes, lighting one from the butt and tossing it out of his window. 'But you didn't. I've been running all over Pasadena, all over LA looking for you. They got half the cops on duty out looking for you. What the hell have you been doing?'

'Getting laid,' she said flippantly.

'Very funny, Lorraine, you always liked a joke. Well, this time the laugh is on me. Why didn't you tell me you were with Art Mathews the night of Holly's murder, with him all night? You were his friggin' alibi.'

She sighed, leaning forward to rest her arms along the seat. 'I wasn't with him all night. I left quite late . . . Rosie'll remember, maybe after twelve.'

He passed her a cigarette without her asking for one. 'I'm out of matches.'

She delved into her purse. 'What time was Holly

murdered, or near as damn it?' He took the matches, struck one, then held the flame out to her. 'Thanks.' She exhaled, waiting for him to answer her question.

Rooney plucked at his eyebrows. There had been so many murders, he couldn't remember offhand what time they had verified that Holly had died.

Lorraine tapped his arm. 'About eleven, wasn't it? She was just starting work so it'd be around ten thirty or eleven. I was with him so he couldn't have done it.'

Rooney lowered his window. 'Doesn't matter to him, he's dead, but it matters to *you* because the FBI got your name from him. I can't not take you in.'

He started the engine.

'Where are we going?' she asked.

'Back to the fucking station, where do you think? I just told you. I'm handing you over, I want you out of my hair, out of my life. You and your theory will land me in a strait-jacket, never mind retiring me. You've been feeding me a line of bullshit from day one.'

'Bill, I swear to you I haven't.'

He looked at her in the driving mirror, his eyes watering from tiredness and smoke. 'Holly was murdered after twelve. Lorraine, I was just testing you.'

She punched his shoulder. He stopped the car. Suddenly he was really angry, his jowled face set rigid. 'What the fuck were you doing at Thorburn's house? And from what I gathered, you weren't there for any interview with his brother. Trying to make a few bucks for yourself – is that what you were up to? I wouldn't put anything past you. Well, now I'm through with you.'

'Was he in there?' she asked.

'You tell me. We won't get a foot in there without more evidence than that load of shit you got. I'm gonna get it in the neck about this.'

He crashed the gears as the car shot forward. They headed up Mulholland, the road becoming steeper. His car coughed, protesting, but they picked up speed as they moved downhill. Suddenly Rooney stamped on his brakes as they came to the traffic lights at a dangerous multiple crossing. The patrol car was there plus two more cars, and rammed between them, the entire driver's side smashed to smithereens, was Lorraine's car. The officer was still inside, his blood spattering the broken windshield and soaking his muscular dead body.

Rooney barked at Lorraine to stay out of sight. As he got out and crossed to the wreckage, she peered out of the window. An ambulance and medic truck arrived and they began to release the driver.

When Rooney came back, he didn't turn to speak to her but stared straight ahead. 'He's dead. He was just a kid.'

'Was it an accident?' she asked.

'What would you say? There's one, two, three other vehicles involved. He jumped the lights, this junction's known to be a death trap. He drove straight into it.' He faced her. 'This is *your* fault. It's due to you, you hear me?'

'Why?' she snapped back. 'I wasn't driving the god-damned car, was I?'

Rooney walked back to the scene of the crash. A few people were gathering around to gawp, more police, and now they had the dead man free. Lorraine saw Rooney and another officer prise open the car's buckled hood. As they peered inside with a torch, another man crawled beneath it. Rooney was there for almost fifteen minutes. When he got back he sat half in and half out of his car, his feet still on the roadside. 'Brake cable's smothered in grease, sliced almost in two, and the handbrake cable's cut. Did anyone have access to the car keys?'

'They were in my purse.'

'They still there?'

Lorraine fumbled and took them out.

'Did you leave it unattended while you were there?'

'Yeah. For quite a while when I was talking to Brad

Thorburn. We were in the bedroom. I left my purse downstairs.' She flushed.

He looked at her and shook his head. 'Christ, I thought you were joking before. Did you screw him?'

'I wanted information, Bill.'

'I bet you did.'

'Why don't we go back up there, Bill, just you and me? If Janklow's there, it's him you should be taking in, never mind me! If I'd been in my car, it would have been me who was dead.'

Rooney slammed the car door and started the engine. 'No way. Not until I've discussed this with the Chief. I'm sorry, but that's the way it's got to be.'

Lorraine had been hoping against all hope that this would never happen but now there was no alternative. She would become a witness for the prosecution and all it entailed. Any idea she had had of starting up as a private investigator would be ruined: when the press got to hear about her part in the murder investigation she and her past would make the headlines. She stared out of the window as they drove towards the precinct. She wanted a drink, could feel it sweeping over her. She wanted a drink rather than face it all.

She hardly said a word as Rooney led her into the station. The duty sergeant noted down all her particulars, she was photographed, and her prints taken. Then she was led away to Rooney's office.

Rooney had called the Chief and was waiting for him. He had shaved and changed his shirt for what looked like an even more crumpled one from his locker. He was drinking coffee and talking to Bean when Lorraine was brought into the room. Rooney introduced Bean who shook her hand and drew out a chair. 'When we're ready, we'll take your statement. We'll also tape it and film you, okay?'

Lorraine asked if someone was preparing the movie

374

rights but no one laughed. Bean fetched her some water and cigarettes and, as he seemed so helpful, she asked him if she could call her friend Rosie to let her know she was okay.

Lorraine waited in Rooney's office for some time. She was told they'd be held up until the FBI agents arrived; neither Rooney nor the Chief could deny them access to her. When she was eventually taken into the large room where everyone was gathered, it was eleven thirty. She remained closeted there for a further four hours. In that time she gave a clear statement of everything that had happened since the day she had first been attacked in the car park. When asked why she had not come forward, she said it was because she had removed Norman Hastings's wallet. She didn't lie, she could see no point. She answered all their questions directly and truthfully. No one appeared impressed by her subsequent investigation or her attempts at piecing together the evidence she had accumulated.

'Why are you so keen on continuing this investigation, even placing yourself at risk?' one of the agents asked. She didn't like the look of this one: his square jaw, which worked overtime, his clean-cut face, his blond crew-cut and neat suit, like a comic-strip man.

She looked over at Rooney who nodded quickly. 'I needed the money, I was being paid to do it by Captain Rooney.'

Although they knew about her record since leaving the police force, they seemed loath to believe that that was the only reason she had taken such risks. Surely she had another motive?

'I suppose I did. I hoped that if I succeeded in assisting the department, then it would stand me in good stead for the future if I ever wanted to start up as a private investigator. But if I have to be a prosecution witness, then it'll destroy that chance. I know this case'll get a load of publicity and like me, well, they'll go for the jugular – that's a joke. The ex-cop ex-hooker'll make good copy, might

375

even get a headline "Madame Dracula". I doubt I'll be able to live it down. I might be able to move away, but I've got contacts here and you need contacts in the investigation business, right?'

They made no answer but glanced at each other before they all left the room, leaving her with a stone-faced policewoman. They returned an hour later. It was almost dawn. But Lorraine detected another undercurrent.

The Chief gave a grimace – she supposed it was some kind of smile but because he was so tense his lips just curled over his top teeth. 'Mrs Page, would you be willing to continue assisting this inquiry?' Rooney wouldn't meet her eyes and the Chief continued, 'There could be certain risks involved.'

Lorraine looked at the Chief, then Rooney. 'You want to make a deal with me, don't you? Well, I guess it would depend—'

'On what?' the Chief asked.

'On what exactly you want me to do. If I work with you, you'll have a tough time bringing me into court as a prosecution witness, won't you? I'd put any money on it that anything connected to the Thorburns you'll have to tread on lightly. What is it you want me to do? Is Janklow going in a line-up?'

'The situation is this. If you pick Steven Janklow out of a line-up, it will be his word against yours. You are a chronic alcoholic, ex-prostitute, drug user—'

She snapped, 'I am also an ex-cop.'

The FBI agent retorted, 'We know that, and we'd be out of our minds to put that out. With your record, it would make you sound an even worse witness than a hooker.'

The comic-strip man leaned on the desk. 'I think we got Janklow to agree to come into the station. He'll be accompanied by his lawyer. What we don't want is a line-up at this stage. But you came face to face with him, you were attacked, so what I want from you is just a good look. We'll set him up in an interview room with a one-way viewing section so you can watch him at your leisure. Because you have to be one hundred per cent sure that the man you say attacked you was Steven Janklow.'

Rooney took over. 'You're the only witness we have but, that said, we'll need a lot more. If he did attack you, then he will be charged with assault. If you're sure it's him, we can even press charges, but you and I both know, because of who you are and his powerful back-up, he'll walk.'

'What about the couple that saw me in the garage?'

'At no time were they able to describe the man in the car with you, so they can't be brought on as witnesses – well, not yet.'

So far Lorraine couldn't see any risk, but then she intercepted the looks between the men. As Rooney moved closer, Here it comes, she thought.

'You know Brad Thorburn, you've had sexual intercourse with him. He inferred that you may have been attempting to blackmail him. We don't know yet if he has played any part in the murders but he *is* Janklow's brother, and you've told us he even has a pair of cufflinks, so—'

'You want me to blackmail Brad Thorburn?' she asked smiling.

'No, we want you – and only if you're sure that Steven Janklow is the man who attacked you—'

The comic-strip man was gradually taking over and Lorraine began to try to assess him and to fathom what they wanted her to do. He was steely, assured. She determined that he was trying to make her offer to assist them without them saying it for themselves; whatever it was must be either illegal or, as they had implied, risky. They were all watching her, waiting for her to take the bait . . .

'I think I get what you're after. If I do recognize him and I'm a hundred per cent sure that the man who attacked me was Steven Janklow, then you've still only got him on assault. You want to use me to do – what? Put pressure on him and see what it throws up, and at the same time find out if Brad Thorburn is also involved?'

They all straightened and she knew she had not only bitten their bait but was offering to reel herself in. She looked over at Rooney and smiled. 'I'll do it but there are certain conditions. If I can get Janklow to admit his part in the murders, maybe by confronting him at his home, if I can get him to admit it and I'm wired up, you won't need to call me as a prosecution witness. So there will be a guilty plea? That what you're after?'

They didn't say a word.

'I'll have a try, but I want your word you won't release my part in any of this to the press.'

'We can't guarantee that,' snapped the Chief.

'Then bring him in and charge him. Just do what you have to do.'

There was a low murmur and she looked to the only other woman present and asked if she could go to the bathroom. She took her time: she was tired out and her clothes were crumpled. She sat on the toilet, thinking about everything they had discussed. When she was led back into the room, only Rooney and his chief remained. Everyone else had gone.

The Chief motioned her to a chair. 'We cannot agree to any deal, Lorraine, you know that, but what we will do is not press charges against you for withholding evidence, and we will endeavour to keep your name out of the proceedings. Your identity will be kept secret, but only if you're able to ascertain that Janklow is the killer.'

She looked at Rooney and gave a half smile. 'Okay, I'll do it. Though it's a very one-sided deal to your advantage. Now, I'll need some new clothes and I need to get some rest. I also need a car so I'll want a clean licence – just so I don't get picked up.'

Rooney winked at her as a warning not to press too hard for anything more.

'When is Janklow coming in?' she asked the Chief.

'Not sure, but we don't want to make it seem too urgent, so you'll have time to change and rest up.'

'Can Bill be my back-up?' she asked, and smiled at Rooney who looked at the ceiling. 'He was always a good back-up man, one of the best.'

'No, I'm afraid not. Bill's been seen in your company and by the look of him if he doesn't get some sleep, he'll fall down. You'll have his lieutenant, Josh Bean. He's a good man, and he's waiting to drive you home right now.'

Lorraine was confident, almost arrogant, as she said, 'He gonna take me shopping? I want to look good.'

The Chief replied that they might not need the new clothes. First she had to view Janklow, then they'd see about the other things she'd asked for – just as they'd also have to set her up with a wire. She walked out of the room before the Chief had finished talking, saying over her shoulder, 'I guess you'll call me when you need me.'

'Can we trust her?' the Chief asked Rooney.

'Much as any woman and she hasn't had a drink for nine months. She wants to go straight.'

'It never was your theory, was it?' the Chief said quietly and Rooney grunted. He knew that by bringing her in it'd come out in the open.

'No. She ran rings around most officers and, so help me God, I'll never know why she blew it those years ago.'

'Just hope she doesn't blow it with us. If she puts a foot out of line, Bill, I'll haul her in so fast, I'll have her charged and put away for a long time. You should make sure she's aware of just how serious this is. We've got to get this case wrapped up. And if she fucks up, it's not just us, it'll be the FBI who'll make sure she never works again, not here or in any other state. Let her know that. Make sure she knows we can't have any mistakes – there's been too many as it is.'

CHAPTER 18

ROONEY HAD shaved, and was wearing a clean-looking shirt and a new suit. He'd had a good lunch before he drove into the station. He knew that Janklow was being brought in by his lawyer at four thirty because his chief, who seemed to be in a growing state of panic, had called him three times.

Bean was sweating as he hit a traffic jam. Lorraine sat beside him. If she was nervous she didn't show it but Josh grew increasingly agitated. He kept on tapping the dashboard clock, then checking his wrist-watch. It was almost four. His hair was damp at the nape of his neck and he leaned out of the window to look at the lines of traffic up ahead. He knew if she wasn't at the station by four fifteen he'd be hauled over the carpet. He wiped his face.

Lorraine tapped his shoulder. 'Get your light on or we'll never make it. Shut it off before we get to the precinct.'

Subtle it wasn't but in the end Bean switched on his siren and his blinking roof-light and began to edge his way down the centre of the road. Even less subtly, he yelled out of the window for other drivers to move over.

On arrival at the station, they were met by Rooney.

'Is he here yet?' she asked breathlessly.

Rooney shook his head as he and Bean hurried her along towards the viewing room. It was just an anteroom, with a table and two hard-backed chairs facing a square-curtained window that adjoined the main interview room. There were microphones at ceiling level, the controls at the side of the room. Lorraine was ushered in. She noticed that, like Bean, Rooney was sweating. She knew a lot was riding for Rooney on her identification of Janklow.

'You just make notes and watch, look and listen. You'll be able to hear every word they say.'

'Come on, Bill, I know the set-up. Who's taking the interview?'

'Ed Bickerstaff, one of the suits. He's the blond crew-cut guy.'

It was four twenty-five, five minutes to go. Rooney left the room. Lorraine lit up and her hands were shaking. She picked up her pen and began to doodle on the notepad, then said to Bean, 'What if there's something I think Janklow should be asked?'

Bean hesitated. 'Give it to me and I'll see if I can go into the interview room but only if it's—'

'Important?' she said smiling.

'Yeah.'

'He's gonna know he's being viewed – any two-bit criminal knows by the window – so why all the secrecy?'

'Protection.'

'His?'

'Yours. You're a valuable witness, Mrs Page.'

Janklow and Kophch's arrival in a chauffeur-driven Cadillac sent whispers through almost every department. Even though secrecy had surrounded the request to bring in Janklow, rumour spread fast; any suspect being brought in for questioning about the hammer murders would have attracted interest, but a high-society man like one of the Thorburn family. . .

Rooney stood in the corridor as they filed past him. He was surprised at how confident Janklow appeared, not paying anyone any attention but staring ahead, his face partly hidden by dark glasses. As they passed, Rooney sniffed. He could smell expensive cologne like delicate flowers. He noticed the way Kophch stayed close to Janklow, his steely eyes taking in everyone and everything.

Bean replaced the intercom phone and looked at Lorraine. 'They're coming in now.' He drew back the curtain to expose the dark square window-pane and returned to his seat.

The microphones picked up the sounds of the room beyond. Bickerstaff was sitting to one side, hardly visible. The table was stacked with files and photographs. As the door opened, he rose to his feet. Lorraine leaned forward: she couldn't see Janklow as the men were introduced. Kophch turned and stared at the one-way glass, aware of what it was, but said nothing and drew out a chair for Janklow.

Lorraine watched closely as Janklow sat down facing her directly, his chair positioned towards the viewing window opposite Bickerstaff. Kophch sat on his left, and clicked open his briefcase. Janklow was wearing a fawn cashmere jacket and a white shirt with a tie, but Lorraine couldn't see his trousers. He had mouse-blond hair combed back from his face which was angular, more handsome than she had expected. His nose was thinnish, again not as she had remembered and she doubted immediately that this was the man by whom she had been attacked. She didn't recognize him. She sat back, her heart beating rapidly. She'd been wrong. She twisted her pen. 'Can they get him to take off his glasses?'

'They will, just relax.' Bean could see that she was tense: she was frowning, cocking her head first on one side then the other.

No one spoke in the adjoining room. It was eerie: the silence, the waiting.

'Would you please remove your glasses, Mr Janklow?' It was the quiet voice of Bickerstaff.

'If you require my client to look at any evidence, he will need to use his glasses. They are not decorative but prescription. I'm sorry but your request is denied.'

Bickerstaff opened his file. 'Take off your glasses, please, Mr Janklow. When it is required you may replace them.'

Janklow slowly removed them. Lorraine felt chilled for the first time. His eyes were pale blue, washed out, and he stared ahead as if straight at her. She caught her breath as he moistened his lips. His mouth had been tightly closed until this moment but when he licked round both lips his face took on a different quality, as if his lips had come to life, wide lips, wide, wet lips. She scribbled on her notepad. This was the man who had attacked her, she knew it. His lips had given him away.

'It's him,' she said softly, barely audible. Bean stared at her and then back to the window as the interview began in earnest.

Bickerstaff, quiet and authoritative, first explained that he would require from Mr Janklow his whereabouts on certain dates. He was aware that some were several years ago but he should answer to the best of his knowledge. When the date of the first murder was given, Janklow frowned. 'I have no idea.'

His lawyer jotted something in his leatherbound notebook. The second date and Janklow was unable to answer, the third and still nothing – he was even apologetic at his memory failure. Bickerstaff persisted. As the more recent dates came up, Janklow gave alibi times and places. He mentioned his brother and his mother. Both, his lawyer said, would verify his client's whereabouts.

Bickerstaff then laid out the victims' photographs in front of Janklow. He studied each one intently, in silence, before shaking his head. 'No, I don't know any of these people.'

Lorraine watched every gesture he made, his hands, long delicate fingers, and she made a note of the ring on his right-hand pinky finger. She was sure that this was the man who had attacked her, even though she didn't recognize his voice, or remember the ring. It was his face and hands that convinced her: he was left-handed.

Bickerstaff was unhurried, taking his time over each question, each photograph. He was saving Norman Hastings and Didi – or David Burrows – until last. When he presented Janklow with the picture of Hastings, Janklow said he knew him quite well. He described how Hastings had used his garage to park his car but denied any social interaction between them. When asked if he was aware of Hastings's transvestite tendencies he looked shocked, and when Bickerstaff asked if he knew Art Mathews he looked nonplussed. To his knowledge, he said, he had never heard the name. He was then asked if he knew Craig Lyall. This time he paused and touched his mouth, he started to shake his head and then changed his mind. 'Craig Lyall? Er, yes, I think I've been to his studio. He's a photographer. I took my mother there to be photographed, but he was not as professional as I'd hoped and the session was terminated. My mother is very particular, and this refers back to her days in the movies. She was a film star when she was in her twenties.'

Bickerstaff let him talk, quietly turning pages, before he interrupted. 'Were you being blackmailed, Mr Janklow?'

Janklow sat back in his chair. 'Blackmailed? Do you mean by Lyall?'

'By anyone,' Bickerstaff replied.

'Absolutely not.'

He now presented Janklow with the photograph of Didi. Again, Janklow spent a considerable time looking at it, shifting his glasses on and off. 'No, I've never met this woman.'

'It's a man.' Bickerstaff waited. 'She or he never made you up for a photograph?'

Lorraine saw Janklow's mouth snap shut. Then he licked

his lips again and gave a humourless laugh. 'No, I was never made up – I presume you mean in female attire – for any photograph.'

Bickerstaff didn't flicker but continued, head down, still nonchalant, as he asked if Janklow was homosexual.

'No, I am not,' Janklow snapped.

'Are you a transvestite?'

'No, I am not.'

'Have you ever in the past been charged with any homosexual crime?'

'No.'

Kophch reached out and touched Janklow's arm. He was becoming agitated and he constantly licked his lips. Lorraine chewed her pen, willing Bickerstaff to push for more, but he remained composed, even apologetic, looking at Kophch and saying that he was sorry if some of the questions were distasteful to his client but he must understand they had to be asked.

Kophch leaned towards Bickerstaff, his voice low. 'Mr Bickerstaff, please feel free to ask my client any question – that is what we are here for, to confirm my client's innocence – but please let me remind you, he is here of his own free will.'

'I am aware of that, Mr Kophch. The sooner we have completed all the questions, then the sooner your presence will no longer be necessary.'

Lorraine sighed. If anything, Bickerstaff seemed to be on Janklow's side. She had never witnessed anyone taking so long, pussy-footing around. His methodical approach was driving her crazy. She asked Bean when Bickerstaff was going to up the ante. He made no reply but stared at the glass partition.

Bickerstaff presented Holly's picture next and Janklow denied any knowledge of her. Then Bickerstaff gave him Didi's photograph again.

'I have already said I do not know this person.'

Bickerstaff pushed the photograph closer. 'This person sometimes calls herself Didi.'

'I don't know her – whoever it is. I don't know them.'

'You have also denied knowing or meeting Art Mathews.'

'I don't know him. You're repeating the same questions.'

Bickerstaff was beginning to step up the pressure, just a little. 'Now, Mr Janklow, can we return to the dates and the alibis you have given. It seems convenient that both your brother and your mother are always your only alibi. You have no other witness to—'

Janklow's voice rose as he interrupted. 'It happens to be the truth.'

'Mr Bickerstaff,' Kophch intervened, 'it is obvious that you are beginning to repeat yourself. If you have no further questions to ask my client, then perhaps we can close this interview.'

'I'm afraid not, Mr Kophch, because your client has so far been unable to present to me any alibi for a number of these cases.'

'But they took place some years ago. If we are given time we will attempt to present you with the whereabouts of my client on those specific dates.'

Kophch stood up but was ordered by Bickerstaff to remain seated. Lorraine clasped her hands tightly together. This was more like it.

'Mr Janklow, you've stated that you are not homosexual.'

'Yes.'

'You are not a transvestite.'

'No, I am not.'

'Is your brother?'

'No, that's ridiculous.'

'And you have never at any time in the past eight years been arrested on a homosexual-related incident.'

'No, I have not.'

'You have stated that on the night of Norman Hastings's death you were not in Santa Monica, you were not—'

'I was with my mother.'

'Is this your mother, Mr Janklow?'

Bickerstaff placed one of the photographs Lorraine had removed from the Thorburn house before him. Janklow looked at his lawyer, then looked back at the photographs. He was visibly shocked. 'Is this your mother, Mr Janklow?'

Kophch frowned and looked at the pictures. He seemed confused as Janklow sat tight-lipped with fury.

'Is this a photograph of your mother, Mr Janklow?'

'Yes.'

'Are you sure?'

'*Yes.*'

Bickerstaff removed a picture of Mrs Thorburn and placed it on the table. 'Do you notice any difference, Mr Janklow, between this photograph of Mrs Thorburn and the one I am now placing in front of you?'

The two photographs lay side by side, one of Mrs Thorburn, the other, everyone was certain, of Janklow himself.

He picked up the photographs and stared at them. 'Where did you get these?'

'Would your client please answer the question?'

Janklow was becoming agitated. Lorraine stood up. Bickerstaff should go for him now. *What was he waiting for? Why didn't he push Janklow now?* Kophch requested a few moments alone with his client. As they were led out, Lorraine slapped the table. 'I don't believe this – *I don't believe it!*'

The door opened; Bickerstaff walked in and asked quietly if she had anything to tell him.

'You bet I have! It's him and I would stand up in any court. In fact, if you want me to I'll walk in there and confront him.'

'No, you won't,' Bickerstaff said firmly, and left.

They waited over half an hour before Janklow and Kophch returned. Janklow was calm again. Kophch opened the interview this time.

'My client and I would like to know how you came by these photographs.'

Bickerstaff kept his head down as if studying his papers. 'I am afraid, Mr Kophch, I am unable to give that information to you. We feel we require to place your client under oath and that anything he subsequently says—'

'If you have any charges related to my client, I want to hear them. If any relate to these murders, then we will not, at this interview, discuss or refer—'

Bickerstaff snapped, 'You will not, Mr Kophch, tell me what I can or cannot do. I am more than aware of the law and I am now ready to charge your client with assault.'

'*What?*' Mr Kophch's studied calm cracked. He had been unprepared for an assault charge.

Bickerstaff continued, 'I wish formally to charge your client that he did, on the night of the seventeenth of April, assault a woman, whose identity I have every right at this stage of my inquiry not to disclose.'

'You never at any time told me my client was suspected of an assault,' Kophch interjected. 'You have brought my client and myself here on false pretences.'

Bickerstaff and Kophch argued for more than ten minutes. Lorraine was becoming impressed with Bickerstaff, who had remained in control. Kophch was one of the most high-powered lawyers and knew every legal loophole but Bickerstaff was one jump ahead. He had wanted, from the outset, to force Janklow to talk on oath but without Lorraine's verification of his identity he had not had sufficient evidence. Now he had, and at seven o'clock that evening Janklow was sworn in and read the charges of assault against him. As yet there was still not enough evidence to charge him with any of the murders. All were

388

more than aware that when Kophch received Lorraine's statements and was allowed access to the evidence against Janklow, they would be in trouble. But they had enough to hold him for another twenty-four hours.

At nine o'clock that evening, with only an hour's break for a light supper, Janklow was brought back into the interview room. He and Kophch had spent the time alone in a cell.

Lorraine had sat in the incident room with Bickerstaff over sandwiches and coffee.

'I think you should put more pressure on his homosexual activities.'

'The blackmail's a strong murder motive and if he and Hastings ever discussed the blackmail—'

Lorraine leaned close, excited. 'Of *course* he was being blackmailed. What about all the missing jewellery belonging to Mrs Thorburn? We don't know if it was sold with her permision but it's a good area to get Janklow to talk about – even more so as Mrs Thorburn is his only alibi for the night I was attacked.' Bickerstaff wiped a crumb from his lips with his paper napkin. 'Is anyone talking to her?' Lorraine asked.

Bickerstaff was getting irritated, but he listened – he felt obliged to. 'Don't tell me what I should and shouldn't do, Lorraine, I'm quite capable of interrogating a suspect.' He finally asked her if she felt that Janklow was the killer.

'Yes, I do,' she stated. 'He has the motive, heavy blackmail and possibly over a long period of time.'

'But you don't have any proof of that, it's just supposition and we don't have a motive for each of these women.'

Lorraine looked at Bickerstaff, her head on one side. 'What about Kophch? He's not as tough as I expected – he seems to be taking a back seat. Couple of times he could have got Janklow off the hook but he let it ride. Why?'

Bickerstaff grinned. 'We got him. Here, read that. This retired cop has spilled the beans, and that softly spoken

389

lawyer's in it up to his neck.' He pushed forward a neatly typed statement. 'Steven Janklow had been arrested for soliciting in a red-light district. He was given a warning, but three nights later was arrested again in the same area. This time they took him down to the station to book him. His lawyer subsequently bought off the vice charges against Janklow and paid the cop to pull his arrest sheet. Kophch would be struck off if it was known that the client he bought out subsequently went on to kill eight women. But don't let him fool you, he's a vicious little shark. His prowess is in court – you'd be surprised what he's like and what he can do. A lot of this is knocking him sideways – but don't think he's a pussy because he's got razor-sharp claws.'

The time was up. Janklow was being led back into the interview room. The session began again. Bickerstaff repeated almost every question he had asked earlier. Janklow answered virtually word for word. He denied any knowledge of the victims and confidently repeated the same alibis. It was only when he was asked about his sexuality that he became hesitant. He was quiet, subdued, when he admitted that he was homosexual but was now celibate; he had not had a relationship with any man for ten years. He was near tears when he admitted that he did, on occasion, use women's clothes, but only his mother's. He had never been outside his home dressed as a woman. The photographs Lorraine had found were taken a long time ago.

'Who took these photographs, Mr Janklow?'

Janklow became distressed. He sniffed, then took out a clean laundered handkerchief and blew his nose. 'Art Mathews, or one of his assistants.'

'Where, Mr Janklow?'

Again he sniffed, wiping his nose. 'Santa Monica.'

'Are you or were you being blackmailed by Mathews, Mr Janklow?'

'No, and I haven't seen that wretched man since that session.'

'Who did the hair and make-up for it?' Bickerstaff pressed, repeating the question.

Janklow wriggled in his seat. 'It might have been David.'

'David?'

'Oh, stop this! You know who I mean. That David Burrows – Didi.'

'So was David "Didi" Burrows blackmailing you, Mr Janklow?'

'*No.* Why do you keep asking me this? I've told you I'm not being blackmailed. Not by that Art, or Burrows or anybody. I haven't seen them since that session years ago.'

Bickerstaff doodled with his pencil. 'And you have not dressed as a woman for, as you said, many years?'

'*That is correct*,' he snapped loudly.

Janklow was now confronted by Rosie's photograph. He stared at it, pursed his lips. He seemed disgusted by it. '*That* isn't me.'

'Please look more closely, Mr Janklow. Is that person in the photograph you?'

'No, it is not. It's my mother.'

'Your mother?'

Janklow blew his nose again. His eyes watering, he wriggled and then whispered, 'It's me.' He had already lied – and under oath. Bickerstaff went after him again, demanding to know just how deeply entrenched he was in the world of transvestites and transsexuals, swinging his questioning round to prostitutes – whether Janklow had ever picked up transsexual prostitutes. 'No, I have not.'

'You sure about that, Steven? You never picked up other men like yourself, dressed like this . . .' He pushed the photo of Janklow forward again.

'I do not pick up any of the filth from the streets.'

'Tell me about David Burrows.'

'I don't know him.'

'Didi. Come on, Steven, you've admitted he made you up, fixed your hair for the photographs and now you're saying you didn't know him. You're lying.'

Janklow looked helplessly to Kophch who examined his nails, refusing to meet Janklow's eye.

Bickerstaff leaned back. 'Okay, Steven, you didn't know Didi, you didn't know Art Mathews. So tell me about the jewellery you've been selling off. It's a lot of money and it belongs to your mother.'

'You leave her out of this.' He was back on the defensive.

'But, Steven, if you've been selling it without her permission then we'll have to discuss it with her.'

'Leave her alone. She's not well.'

'I can't do that, Steven, because she's also your alibi for the night of the assault and the night of Norman Hastings's murder. We're going to have to bring her in, you must know that.'

Janklow slapped the table near to Kophch. 'Tell them they can't do that.'

'They can, Steven.'

Janklow put his head in his hands. When Bickerstaff asked him again about the jewellery, he began to sob. This was not what Bickerstaff wanted: if he became too distressed, by law Kophch could take a break. Bickerstaff switched the subject away from Mrs Thorburn.

Lorraine was furious. 'What the hell is he doing? He's got him sobbing his heart out. Why doesn't he push for more about the jewellery? I don't believe it.'

Rooney walked in and saw her angry face. 'Mrs Thorburn has just told us that she gave her son permission to sell all her jewellery and that he was, on the night he was supposed to have attacked you, with her . . . I got to tell Bickerstaff.'

'Shit.' Lorraine looked at him. 'But somebody must have got to her – like Brad.'

'According to the nursing staff she's had no visitors, just one phone call. Late last night. From Kophch. But as her legal advisor he has every right to call her, and I'm telling you, she's a tough old broad and she's got all her marbles – told me to get the hell out.'

Bickerstaff was back on the subject of Janklow's relationship with Norman Hastings.

'He was a fool, a stupid idiot.' Janklow was no longer tearful, and both Lorraine and Rooney listened intently. It was eerie watching him, his face twisted, his lips wetter and shinier. 'Stupid, boring, fat, bloated fool.' Kophch gave a warning touch to Janklow's arm. 'Get off me, don't *you* touch me, you're a useless waste of money. This is *your* fault, all your fault – you should never have brought me in here. I'd be better off on my own. I don't want you here any more.'

Bickerstaff ploughed on, asking Janklow why he didn't like Hastings, a man he had said he hardly knew. Janklow whipped round and pointed at Bickerstaff. Kophch attempted to calm him but he swiped him aside. 'You have nothing to keep me here! You've been fishing around for hours and I know you have not one shred of evidence against me.'

'What about a witness, Steven?'

'Lies. There was never any witness.' Janklow was pulling at his jacket and smirking now, rocking backwards and forwards in his chair.

'We have a witness, Steven, someone you attacked on the same day Norman Hastings was killed.'

Janklow laughed. 'Oh, yes? You think I don't know who she is? She'd never stand a chance coming up against me. She's an ex-cop, ex-drunkard with a string of vice charges against her. She killed a kid when she was on duty. I know who you're protecting! I know – and it's a joke.'

Kophch was white, his face so tight with anger because his client was blowing it. He should never have admitted

393

what he knew about Lorraine. Kophch rose to his feet. 'I insist we take a break now.'

'Sit down,' Janklow leered. 'I'm beginning to enjoy myself. This is fascinating. Go on, ask me anything you want.'

Bickerstaff said evenly, 'Listen to me, I don't care if we scooped a witness off the streets. All that matters to me is that she's a witness, you tried to kill her, you used a claw hammer. You know the type because there must be a hundred of them at your garage. I am quite prepared to let you go, Mr Janklow, but I will need a blood test. You see, you made a big mistake with the assault. She attacked you as well, didn't she? She made you bleed, didn't she? And, Mr Janklow, we have a sample of blood taken from the vehicle, the same vehicle into which you stuffed Norman Hastings's body. We have what I think is your blood. And now would you open your shirt.'

Janklow had become still, his face drawn, his hands clenched in front of him.

'Open your shirt and remove your tie.'

Lorraine clutched Rooney as Janklow slowly loosened his tie, slipping it away from his neck, and undid his shirt, one button after the next. It was horribly sexual – he was flicking glances to each of the men in the room and then he pulled away his shirt, revealing his white neck.

Bickerstaff got up, hiding Janklow from Lorraine and Rooney as he peered at the man's neck. He stepped back. 'You've got a mark the right side of your neck. Where did you get it?'

Janklow shrugged his shoulders. 'I have a German shepherd dog. He bit me a few weeks ago, maybe a couple of months. You can ask my brother, he was there, he saw it.'

Bickerstaff returned to his seat. He asked the other officer to contact Brad Thorburn. Janklow did up his shirt.

'Did you ever use Norman Hastings's car, Mr Janklow?'

'Oh, I might have – yes, I did . . . well, not drive it. I sat in it once, and – oh, I remember it very well. I was sitting talking to Norman, and I had a dreadful nosebleed because I have a weak septum.'

'What date would that be?'

'I borrowed his handkerchief to stem the bloodflow. Brad saw it, because I looked dreadful, very white and shaking. So I have a witness to that as well.'

Janklow buttoned up his shirt and unbelted his trousers as he tucked in the shirt tails, giving hideous flirtatious glances round the room. 'I did not kill anyone, I did not attack anyone, I am an innocent man, and now I would like to go home as I'm tired.'

Bickerstaff would not let up. He asked again where exactly Janklow had had the nosebleed, and on what date. Janklow yawned and said in the front seat of Hastings's car – he'd been parking it for him in the garage.

'What date would that have been?'

'I have no idea, around the sixteenth, I suppose. That was why I didn't come into work the following day, the seventeenth, because I felt poorly. I spent the day with my mother instead.'

Bickerstaff began to collect his files. 'I think, Mr Janklow, you can leave. We will, of course, have to check all this information, make inquiries to verify your alibis, both with Mr Brad Thorburn and Mrs Thorburn. I would also like you to pass to us further details of your whereabouts on the other dates you were unable to recall where you were.'

'Yes, of course. I'll check back in my diaries, give the relevant information to Mr Kophch and, as they say in the movies, I'll get back to you.'

Lorraine looked at Rooney in disbelief. 'He's going to walk! They're going to let him walk out of here.'

'Looks like it,' Rooney said bluntly.

'But it's obviously him! You know it, they must know it.'

'We're not through with him yet.'

Lorraine kicked at her chair. 'What about me? Don't I count? I've said it was him, I *know* it was him – he did *this* to me!' She showed Rooney the scar at the back of her head and then slumped in her chair. 'Jesus Christ, I even feel like some of the women I used to take statements from, the whores beaten within an inch of their lives. They always used to say to me, "Nothing will happen, nobody cares about us, nobody cares if they beat us to a pulp, because we don't matter." Are all those dead women of no consequence? Because you know, Rooney, if he walks now he'll never be brought back in.'

As if to confirm what she was saying, the chairs were scraping back in the interview room, Kophch assisting Janklow to stand up. He was joking about his crumpled shirt.

Lorraine pushed past Rooney and made for the door. He grabbed her. 'No, don't do it, Lorraine, you don't go out there.'

She wrenched her arm free. 'He's *walking out*, Bill! I swear before God I'll make a citizen's arrest! I'm not going to let him get away with this—'

'He just did. Now sit down.'

When Janklow and Kophch had departed, the atmosphere in the incident room was of exhaustion and depression. Bickerstaff looked at Lorraine and lifted his hands in a gesture of defeat. Lorraine's hands were on her hips. 'Get me a wire – get me set up. I'll get him to incriminate himself. I swear before God I'll bring that piece of shit in.'

Bickerstaff was worn out, but he grinned at her. 'That's what I hoped you'd say. Go home and get some rest. We'll talk in the morning.'

Bean drove her home and, as he had been instructed, remained with her, sleeping outside in the patrol car. Bickerstaff had taken him aside and warned him to keep her under watch day and night. Janklow knew who she was, maybe even knew her address. The following morning he was to get her some decent clothes before he brought her back into the precinct. Now she was all they had and everything depended on her. He was not to let her out of his sight for a moment.

Lorraine, accompanied by Bean and Rosie, set off early for Rodeo Drive. She chose an elegant suit, with a tight, pencil-slim skirt with a thigh-length slit, and loose jacket with a soft creamy silk blouse beneath. She chose high-heeled shoes with matching clutch bag. Conscious that she was to be wired, she also bought a fitted, slightly padded, brassière and matching panties. A suspender belt and fine pale stockings completed the outfit. She had her hair streaked, cut and blown dry, a manicure and a facial. Rosie and Bean trailed from one place to the next, sitting in the salon as she was made up by an expert. The whole process took three hours so she did not arrive at the station until after twelve.

Rooney gaped at the bill and even more when he saw her. He flushed with embarrassment. She always had been one hell of a looker, but now she was stunning. He blew it, however, when he said, intending a compliment, 'Holy shit, they sure done a hell of a job on you.'

Rooney was not the only one taken aback by Lorraine's appearance. Bickerstaff's jaw dropped and the Chief, who had screamed bloody murder when he had seen the cost, also complimented her. Lorraine found it almost amusing the way they suddenly drew out chairs for her, jumped to light her cigarette. She loved the feel of the soft kid leather handbag, containing new lipstick, powder compact, silk handkerchief, calf-leather wallet, silver lighter and cigarette case.

She was to wear a small pick-up mike disguised as a decorative pin attached to a gold chain round her neck. It was in the shape of a heart and could record from a five-mile radius. She was impressed by its sophistication: she had half expected the old box in a belt strapped to her waist as she had been used to in the past. Even if she was stripped naked, Rooney said half in jest, it would be hard to find. She had flicked him a look, wondering if they were all aware she had been to bed with Brad Thorburn. It seemed likely as she was warned that the only time she would lose contact with the radio surveillance truck would be if she took a shower.

Lorraine was then closeted with Bickerstaff and his team, Rooney standing glumly to one side as they discussed her approach to Janklow. They knew he was at home and they also knew that Brad Thorburn was with him but a telephone tap had revealed that Thorburn was intending to leave for France and had been arranging his flight. Janklow had returned to the house directly after leaving the precinct but had made no phone calls. Mrs Thorburn had been interviewed again and repeated the statement she had made. Brad Thorburn had also verified everything his brother had said. Two calls had been recorded from the tap on the Thorburn home, both from Alfred Kophch, requesting that Janklow visit him in his office at his earliest convenience. Kophch had also said that on no account should Janklow make outgoing calls, but speak to him only personally at his office.

As Bickerstaff and Lorraine discussed the new developments, a report came in that Mrs Thorburn had just called Brad and asked him to visit her. She had refused to speak to Steven.

'That's good,' Lorraine said. 'The only time I saw Janklow really upset was whenever you made any reference to her and if she's not talking to her nasty little pervert son, he might be even more on edge.'

'You're very confident, Lorraine. How can you be sure you'll get into the Thorburn house?'

'I'm sure.'

Bickerstaff was growing to like her. He patted her shoulder. 'Well, you take care – and I mean it. Use your back-up and scream the fuckin' place down when you feel any kind of threat.'

Bickerstaff looked up as Rooney returned, tapping his wrist-watch. It was really time for Lorraine to leave. She tried to make light of it – they were all so concerned – and asked if Andrew Fellows was still working for them. Rooney dismissed him out of hand: the last thing he had suggested was that the killer might be a woman. They had all joked that she had even been under suspicion, and Lorraine laughed out loud.

She was presented with a clean driving licence and a Mustang, also wired up to the main base, was ready in the yard. The only thing she did not have was a weapon.

Rooney walked her to the car. He opened the driving door, winking to warn her not to say anything because she was wired. Then he took his gun from his shoulder holster and stashed it in the glove compartment. 'We're all with you and we'll be on hand. You know what to do?'

Lorraine nodded. They had given her the code word 'Rosie'. If she mentioned it the back-up cops were to stand by; it meant she was heading into deeper trouble than she could handle. If 'Rosie' was coupled with 'Partner' they were to come in no matter what else she said. This was an old scam she and Lubrinski had worked, just the name of someone they could start to talk about, which would give no warning to the suspect that it was, in fact, a warning.

Lorraine shut the glove compartment. 'Thanks, Bill.'

Rooney pulled at his nose. 'Fuck off, and get a move on.' He'd always said that and it touched her but she slammed the door and started the engine. She didn't look back but headed for Beverly Glen. It would take an easy hour and a quarter. She knew Brad and Janklow were in, and that no further outgoing or incoming calls had been made. The housekeeper and gardener were there but Lorraine knew they left about four. From then on, it would just be the brothers.

Moving way behind Lorraine was a dry-cleaning truck with two overalled police officers up front. In the back were Bickerstaff, Rooney and another FBI agent. Lorraine's car bleeped on the grid up ahead of them but they made no effort to sit on her tail. They didn't need to – they knew where she was heading and even if they were miles back they could still monitor the car, and her personal microphone.

Lorraine parked right outside the gates, clearly visible from the house, and rang the doorbell by the intercom. The dry cleaning truck parked a good distance down the tree-lined street.

'Who is it?'

Lorraine recognized Brad's voice. 'Let me come in – it's Lorraine.'

'Are you alone?'

'No, I got surveillance trucks and a couple of uniformed cops. What the hell do you think, Brad? Let me in.'

The gates opened and Brad came out onto the porch. He watched her as she walked up the gravel path, then frowned. 'What have you done to yourself?'

She did a slow turn, hands out, one holding her purse. 'I've spent all day at the beauty parlour. How do I look?'

'What do you want?' he asked abruptly.

'To talk.' He stared at her and she laughed. 'What are you so suspicious of? Here, you want to check my bag?' She tossed it to him and remained standing on the pathway.

He caught it in one hand but didn't open it. 'I don't think I've got anything to say to you.'

She moved closer. 'You let me in, though. How about a coffee?'

He looked back to the hallway and then down at her as she remained on the lower step. 'I'm going away – this isn't a good idea.'

'Why don't you just hear me out – hear why I've come? I have a reason.'

'I gathered,' he said, as he turned and walked into the house. She followed him, eyes flicking upwards to the bedroom above. Was he there? Was he watching her? She saw nothing; no curtain moved aside; it was very still.

In the kitchen, Brad took her things out of her bag, laid them all out.

'Satisfied?'

He went to the fridge and took out a bottle of chilled wine, held it up and then slammed the fridge door. He poured himself a glass as she perched on a stool and began to put everything back into her purse. He switched on the coffee percolator and leaned against the sink.

'Don't you ever wear shoes?' she asked, smiling.

'What's this, a rerun of last night?'

'I know they took your brother in for questioning.'

'They also released him.'

'So I gather.'

He sipped his wine, leaning against the sink.

'Where are you going?'

'France.'

'For how long?'

'I don't know. What do you want?'

She opened the cigarette case, held it up as if for his permission, and he fetched a cup for her coffee. She still found attractive every move he made, even just pouring coffee. He had such a great body, but his ease was what made him so sexy. When he moved close to give her the coffee he smelt of soap. 'You just showered?'

'Yeah, I had a game of tennis. I was going to play squash with Andrew but he refused to speak to me.'

'Why?'

He smiled. 'Maybe his wife has told him about her fantasy, that she and I were a hot number, but it's all in her head.'

'Is it made up, or did you fuck her?'

He passed her an ashtray. 'You like to talk dirty? What does it mean to you if I screwed her or not?'

'It was just a question. I like her – he's okay too.'

Brad picked up his glass, tilted it towards her, and drank the contents. 'What do you want?'

'Money.'

He ran his glass under the sink. 'So what's your hourly rate, then?'

She chortled. 'Oh, this isn't *hourly*! This is going to cost you and Steven a lot, lot more.'

'*Steven?*'

Lorraine blew on the hot black coffee, looking at him over the rim of the cup. 'Let's not waste any more time playing games. I want money, Brad. Your brother may have walked but you take a good look at me. Now put me in court in front of a jury. You think they're gonna say, "Oh, she's just a hooker, oh, she's just a fucked-up piece of shit, an ex-cop who killed a kid." You take a good look at me, Brad, because I reckon I look good. I look good enough to sway a jury, make them doubt all that shit about me, make them look at me, see the scar on the back of my head. They'll listen real good when I say it with tears, and I can conjure up tears, Brad, I'll have them running down my cheeks when I tell them what he did to me.'

He couldn't deal with her at all. It was as if she'd become two, even three people. This hard, sophisticated woman was not the same woman who had wept in his arms.

He looked so confused that she felt suddenly guilty, wanting to comfort him. It was stupid. She lit a cigarette, blowing the smoke out high above her head. 'I'll have your brother charged with assault and then they'll think again about the murders, same blow as the one to the back of my head. He wanted to kill me – he *tried* to kill me – and you may say in court that he was bitten by your dog, big Mr Brad Thorburn, but wait till I tell them, weeping, holding

402

my head in my hands, that when he struck me with the hammer I fought for my life. I bit him in the neck and I hung on until my teeth broke his skin, until he screamed like a stuck pig. . . It was Steven who attacked me, Brad. Why don't we stop all the bullshit and get down to just how much you'll pay me to keep my mouth shut?'

He looked at her with open hostility. She revolted him.

'Okay, I'll give you more. I had a tooth missing. They get a match on those marks on his neck, they'll be able to verify it was my teeth – not your dog's, but mine.'

He wouldn't look at her.

'You don't like hearing me talk this way? Well, why don't you get Steven down here? Why don't the three of us discuss just how much it'll take to buy me off, maybe to send *me* to France and forget I was ever attacked.'

'You'd do that?'

'Sure. You wanted to know why I was here, well, now you do.' Brad was so obviously out of his depth she felt almost sorry for him, sorry to have to be so hard, but she had no option. In some ways she wanted him to throw her out, wanted him to be straight and honest because she liked him so much.

'How much?' he said gruffly, not even looking at her.

She inhaled and let the smoke drift out slowly, then rested her chin on her hand. 'A million. You can afford it. But I want it in cash, used notes.'

He made a sound that was half laugh, half sob. 'A million.'

'And I guarantee that I'll disappear, any charges will be dropped. Suddenly he didn't look like your brother, suddenly I guess I was just mistaken. He'd never even have to go to court.'

'I doubt if he will, anyway,' Brad snapped.

'You want a bet? Because if they don't press charges, then I will take out a private prosecution. I'll have every feminist group backing me up. You wouldn't believe the stink I could create. You and your precious brother and your beloved mother would be hounded by the press. You won't buy out of that but you can buy me out now. Go talk to Steven. Is he in?'

Brad made it to the doorway, his fists clenched. He wanted to grab her by her hair and throw her out bodily. He had never felt such loathing for another human being – let alone a woman.

'Oh, I can see I got you real angry. Well, it's up to you, I think I'm being fair and square. What's a million to you, rich boy?' He moved so fast, one moment in the doorway the next at her side. He slapped her face hard. She held her cheek. 'That make you feel better, rich boy? It's just gone up another ten grand. Touch me again and, so help me God, I'll walk out of here and start screaming my fucking head off. Now go talk to your sick pervert of a brother – better still bring his ass down here. Let's hear what he has to say.'

He walked out. She was shaking all over – he had really hurt her. She rubbed her aching jaw and checked her face in her compact mirror. Her cheek was inflamed but otherwise she looked better than she had in years. She snapped the compact shut, moved to the hall and looked up. Brad was nowhere in sight. She went into the empty drawing room.

'He's gone upstairs, I'm now in the drawing room.' She said it softly, tilting her head down to the tiny gold heart.

Lorraine heard footsteps and leaned against the piano, as if she was looking over the framed photographs.

'He's agreed, a million, but he can't get it for at least a couple of months.'

Lorraine propped both elbows on the piano. 'No deal, I can't wait that long. I want it today. Why don't you pay me? You got the dough, haven't you?'

'This has nothing to do with me. I wouldn't pay you a cent.'

'No, but you'd stand up in court and tell a jury that your dog bit him on the neck, your mother would say on oath that her son was with her all day and all night on the night he nearly killed me. You're sick, you know that? Well, fuck you and fuck your brother. I'm getting out of here, I can make enough selling my story to the press.'

Brad stood across the door. 'He doesn't have that amount of cash and nor do I. Everything's tied up in property, trust funds. I can't get that amount of money released in a day, it would be impossible.'

'I don't believe you and I wanna talk to your brother. You're a pain in the butt. *Steven!*'

She heard footsteps; he was coming down the stairs.

Steven Janklow walked into view and stood in the hallway.

'Hi, you remember me, don't you, Steve? You said you needed to be sucked off in a public place, twenty dollars. We drove to the garage in the shopping mall. Sure you remember. Look at him, Brad, he remembers me. Maybe it's my scar.'

Janklow's face twisted in rage. 'I don't know you. Throw her out of here, Brad.'

Lorraine remained where she was. She felt safe with Brad between her and Janklow. 'Fine, Brad, you throw me out, but first fill him in, tell him what the deal is. If you don't have the cash, then I'll take a couple of items belonging to your mother. Art Mathews said he was getting good prices for the stuff in Europe.'

Janklow looked as if he would attack her but Brad gripped him. 'Just calm down, Steven. Have you ever seen her before?'

They moved out of sight further into the hall. Lorraine had to hold on to the piano top, her legs were shaking so much. She could hear Janklow insisting that he did not know her, that she was lying. She hurtled out and confronted both men. 'I'm lying, am I? Right, you'll see, and I'll see you in court.'

She strode into the kitchen and picked up her bag. She was about to walk past them to the front door, when she heard Brad's low voice, 'Give that to me! Give it.'

She turned round just in time to see Janklow with the gun but he hadn't even got it to waist level before Brad had taken it from him. Then he sank onto the bottom stair. Brad slipped the weapon into his pocket. He spoke to Lorraine.

'You'll get your money as soon as I can arrange it.'

'Well, what about the jewellery? Don't you have any left? Art seemed to think you had more'n the Queen of England.'

Janklow's head was in his hands, but he said, 'He was a thieving piece of shit.'

Lorraine sniggered. 'Yeah, he was that all right but you got no worries about him talking.' She was on firmer ground, testing how much she could say. 'They had him arrested for the murders, didn't you know? Apparently he even admitted to a couple, then he got scared and killed himself – cut his wrists on his glasses.'

Janklow looked at her with his pale, expressionless eyes. Lorraine held his gaze. 'You shouldn't have hurt Didi, though. She was a friend of mine. I know she was into the blackmail with Art, but he forced her to do it.'

Janklow looked up at his brother. 'There's nothing left, Brad. I've got no money – I can't pay her.'

'What about your mother? She's sitting on a load, isn't she? How would you think she'd feel if I paid her a visit? It's all the same to me. Look, I don't want to walk away empty-handed. If Art and Didi cleaned you out, then why not—'

'You don't go anywhere near my mother.' Janklow's temper surfaced.

'Then I'll just walk out of here. But I warned your

brother – you ask him – I'm not gonna let you off. I'll sell my story to the papers and then she'll wish she could get up and run because they won't leave her alone. They'll dig up every inch of dirt on her, on this family—'

Janklow shoved Brad away and dived at Lorraine, but again Brad caught him before he laid a finger on her. He pushed him up against the wall. 'Tell me the truth, Steven. Was it you who attacked her?'

He screamed and tried to wriggle out of Brad's grasp, but Brad thumped him in the stomach so hard he buckled over. Then he yanked his brother up against the wall by his hair. 'You'd better tell me, Steven, because if what she says is true, then we've got to pay her off.'

She pressed her back against the wall. 'He attacked me and he murdered the others. He did it, Brad! Ask him. *Go on, ask him!*'

'*Yes! Yes! Yes!*' screamed Janklow.

Brad released his hold but was still too close for his brother, who was gasping for breath, to try anything on her. Brad looked at Lorraine, then at Janklow. 'Okay, we'll pay. I'll pay you whatever you want.'

Janklow pulled at Brad's arm. 'You fool, you pay her and she'll be back like that other bitch. They'll never leave you alone. You let her walk out of here and she'll be on your back like a leech. She's a leech, a blood-sucker.'

'What you gonna do, Steven? Kill me like the others?'

Lorraine spat it out and Janklow tried again to reach her. Again Brad dragged him back, shoving him against the wall. He was frothing at the mouth with impotent fury, but Brad was too strong for him to escape. 'They deserved it! And even if he's stupid enough to pay you off, I'll find you, wherever you are, no matter how long it takes.'

She pointed at Janklow and then back at Brad. 'You did hear that, didn't you? You're gettin' off real light. He's killed eight women and all I'm doing is asking for a million dollars. I could push for a lot more.'

Brad looked first at her then Janklow as the implication sank in. His face was drained. He hauled his brother slowly to his feet, and stared into his twisted face. Janklow was near to weeping. 'Is this true, Steven?' Brad shook him so hard his head cracked against the wall. '*Is it true?*' He gripped his brother's face in his hands. '*Is it true?*'

Deflated, Janklow lifted his hands up like a child to his mother. He was half pleading with Brad to hold him. He started crying, his wet lips hung open as he blubbered and began slowly to slide down the wall. 'I'm taking him upstairs to his room. You stay down here.'

Lorraine watched as Brad half carried his brother upstairs. There was no fight or anger left in him: he was crying more loudly – she could hear him – he sounded like a little boy. 'Brad,' she said flatly. Half-way up the stairs, he stopped. 'You'd better stay with him. Will you put the gun down that you took from him?'

They both looked towards her, as different as Dilly Fellows had said, like chalk and cheese. Brad took the gun out of his pocket and for a split second she thought he was going to fire it straight into her head, but she said calmly, matter-of-fact, 'I'm wired up, Brad. Every word we've said has been recorded. Just put down the gun.'

He let it drop and half carried, half lifted Janklow into his room. As the door closed she went to the intercom in the hallway and said they should come in and that he was in the top right-hand front bedroom. She pressed open the gates and went to wait on the porch. The truck was now pulling up outside. Rooney was first out and gave her the thumbs-up. Next out was Bickerstaff. Lorraine had turned away to look over the beautiful gardens, the flowers, the swimming pool, the tennis courts. It was so perfect, so incongruously peaceful. The sound of squad cars arriving cut through the silence. Lorraine joined Rooney. She removed the wire from her neck and asked if she could go home. She was told by Bickerstaff that she must return to the station.

Brad Thorburn was led out between two uniformed police officers followed by Steven Janklow handcuffed between another two. Janklow began to sob out a wretched, sickening confession inside the vehicle, and two hours after he was arrested, admitted to six murders, but seemed vague about Holly and Didi, and one of the as yet unidentified victims. The other two remained unidentified because Janklow didn't know their names but agreed when shown the photographs that he had killed them. He said one was called Ellen and the other something like Susanna but he hadn't known their surnames.

Lorraine did not get home until late that night. Rosie was waiting expectantly to hear all that had happened. She gave her friend a bear hug and was disappointed when Lorraine didn't want to go out for a celebration dinner.

'But it's all over, isn't it?'

Lorraine sighed, exhausted. 'Yes, I guess it is, but I don't feel like celebrating.'

The next few days were long and drawn out. She was asked to be on call should they require her at the station. Something nagged at her but she couldn't pin it down. In the end she put it down to the possibility that she still might be used as a prosecution witness.

The good news came at the beginning of the following week. Janklow would plead guilty – which meant Lorraine would not have to take the stand – to five counts of murder.

A month after his brother's arrest, Brad Thorburn left Los Angeles to escape media attention, but remained in touch with his brother via their lawyer. Lorraine followed the progress of the case through Rooney, or by dropping into the station. Money was tight, and Rosie kept up her daily check of want ads, but their financial situation put paid to the prospect of starting up their own agency.

Rooney was the one to tell Lorraine that her theory had been wrong although so had everyone else's. Further interviews with Steven Janklow elicited that he had been blackmailed by Art Mathews for much longer than they had thought – almost nine years – but he had only met Art once. Didi had made the calls and collected the money and the jewellery. Janklow had always liked Didi, he said, because she fixed his wigs and make-up. The other women had been murdered because they were like his father's whores, dirty hookers he had brought home to flaunt in front of Janklow's beloved mother. There was no blackmail link to the dead women, only Didi. Norman Hastings had been killed because, as he was being blackmailed himself, he felt that he and Janklow could help each other out – even go to the police to press charges. Janklow had not wanted anyone to know about his private life; he was disgusted that a fat middle-aged man like Norman Hastings could ever think that they were alike, so he killed him. When pressed for further details on the murder of Angela 'Holly' Hollow and David 'Didi' Burrows he said that he couldn't remember and he supposed he must have killed them.

Janklow also admitted attacking Lorraine, again saying that she was just like his father's whores and he had been right to attack her as she was now his brother's whore. His obsessive love for his mother had so twisted him that half the time he believed that he was her, and when he eventually admitted everything he had done, did not hold it against her that she had not come to see him.

To his surprise Rooney was called in to see his chief and given a big bonus; a whip-round from all the officers had paid for a gold travel clock and leather case. He hated the thought of retirement but his part in tracking down Janklow had made good press coverage, and he grudgingly thanked Lorraine but then said that if the truth be known she should thank him.

Lorraine's part in Janklow's arrest was not leaked to the press. The only thing she got out of it was the few bucks from Rooney, the clean driving licence and the new clothes. She had to hand back Rooney's gun because he had to return it with his badge. She and Rosie were flat broke.

'The bastards! Don't you get a reward?'

Lorraine laughed. 'No! But I got my self respect, Rosie.'

'Well, it ain't gonna pay the rent, sweet face, so now what do you do?'

She was looking good, she knew it; she'd been back on form and she knew that too. Working again had filled in her days, her nights, and yet somehow she wanted or expected more. She studied her reflection in the bathroom mirror: so much for respect. If they really thought she was something, how come they didn't offer her a job? How come, at the end, she was still broke, and worse, back to square one? She gripped the washbasin and bowed her head.

'Tea's ready,' Rosie yelled out.

Lorraine looked up at herself; it wasn't over, she hadn' beaten it. 'Jesus Christ, I want a drink.'

Rosie cut a thick slice of banana bread and poured tea for each of them. 'Home-made that – got it at the deli near the corner.' Lorraine choked suddenly. 'What's the matter? Don't you like it?'

Rosie watched as she grabbed the file from the Janklow case and began to thumb through it. Half an hour later she looked up. 'I got to go out. If you want something to do can you find out who we contact to rent that place Art Mathews had as a gallery, and how much? I'm gonna see if I can raise some dough, then we'll open up Page Investigation Services. I'll be back or I'll call in, okay?'

Rosie followed her onto the steps outside the apartment. 'Where are you going?'

Lorraine ran down the stairs, turning at the bottom. She waved and called back something about the banana bread, then she formed her right hand into the shape of a gun, and pretended to fire it. Rosie went back inside and glanced at the papers wondering what Lorraine had been so excited about. The file was open at Didi's autopsy report. Rosie grimaced in distaste and went back to her bread. It didn't taste so good. The pathologist's findings stated that David Burrows's last meal had been banana bread.

CHAPTER 19

E D BICKERSTAFF had been in a heavy meeting all morning discussing Janklow's mental deterioration. His family, via their lawyers, were insisting he be declared insane and therefore incapable of standing trial.

Bickerstaff had spent many hours with Janklow since his arrest, during which he talked compulsively, almost with pride, about what he had done. He showed no guilt or remorse, but the reverse; he gloated in detailing how the women had died. He was still sketchy when it came to Didi and Holly, but was adamant that he had killed them. He was constantly smiling, always polite and cheerful, and continued to talk freely when he was alone in his cell.

The last meeting Bickerstaff had with Janklow had been two days ago. His head was bruised and swollen and he was wearing a white gown with ties at the back as he had just been for a brain scan. He sat on the bed dangling his feet, and midway through the interview he started to sing some long-forgotten song. He could only remember the chorus, and repeated the same words over and over. 'If you say you love me, do you care? If you say you love me, do you care?'

When Bickerstaff was told that Lorraine Page was asking for him, he agreed to see her. He hadn't liked the way she'd been hanging around the station so he intended making this meeting short and sweet. She was ushered into his office – Rooney's old patch. He got up as she entered and shook hands.

'Is he insane, then?' she asked without any preamble.

'Well, they're certainly trying to prove it.'

'What do you think?' she asked.

'Well, he may be putting up one hell of a performance – who's to tell? I don't know.'

Bickerstaff rested his chin in his hands. 'That was one hell of a performance you gave at his place. Class act – but then old Rooney said you were good. What he never said was just how good. You mind if I ask you something personal?'

'Go ahead.'

'That shooting incident – one with the kid – how come you fired six times when you could have brought him down with one shot?'

She hadn't expected him to bring up the shooting and it caught her off guard. 'I'd had a few drinks. I didn't see the boy, just his jacket. It had this yellow stripe down the back . . . I had a partner I was fond of. He was in a shoot-out. The man that killed him had a black sweater with a yellow stripe and I didn't see the boy – it wasn't him I was firing at but somebody else.'

He stood up and, just like Rooney used to do, flicked at the blind. 'You could be useful to me, maybe, sometime in the future. You got any plans?'

Lorraine reminded him about the investigation agency. She caught him looking at his watch and knew he wanted her to leave, but she hadn't come for praise or even a tentative offer of future work. Not that she believed him about that. 'I need money. I'm broke.'

He frowned. She lit a cigarette and kept it between her lips as she spoke. 'I don't think Janklow murdered David Burrows or Holly.'

Bickerstaff leaned on the back of his chair. 'He's admitted both.'

'Way it sounds, he's admitting to any stiff we had in or around LA since nineteen sixty-five.' He laughed and she took the cigarette out of her mouth. 'How much if I get you proof that it was Art Mathews? You wouldn't look so dumb about his suicide. As it stands now, Janklow said he killed them which makes Art Mathews look as if he was put under so much pressure he killed himself—'

'You want me to hire you?'

'You can call it what you like. I just need cash to get cards printed, a word processor, pay a bit of rent.'

'You withholding further evidence, Mrs Page?'

'No, and maybe I'm wrong but I think Art Mathews killed both Holly and Didi. And if he didn't, I'd like to find out who did. And, if you don't have Janklow on the stand, maybe you'll have somebody else, because I'm sure Art didn't do the murders alone.'

'You gonna give me a name?'

'I don't have one yet, but I'm workin' on it. Come on, I know there's a kitty for informers – you can call me that if you like. It's not as if the FBI are broke, and it might be useful to you, Mr Bickerstaff.'

He smarted at her audacity. 'How much?'

She stubbed out her cigarette. 'Ten grand, in cash, in an envelope.'

He sucked in his breath and stuffed his hands in his pockets. 'Make it five and you've got a deal – if you get the proof that Art Mathews did the murders.'

She tossed the hair out of her eyes. 'You just got a deal, Mr Bickerstaff. I'll be in touch.'

Lorraine headed off in search of Curtis. She found him in a bar with a blonde Holly-lookalike on his arm. When he saw her he whistled and she pivoted for him like a model.

'I want to talk to you, Curtis, some place private.' She swore she was on the level and they headed into a back room. They were only there for about ten minutes before they returned to the bar.

'You want a drink, Lorraine?'

'I'm not drinking today, but thanks for the offer.' She banged out of the bar into the brilliant afternoon sunshine. She hadn't thought he'd bite but he *had* cared for Holly and what was a couple of grand? His girls were making that in a night for him.

She hailed a taxi and went home, where Rosie was waiting. Half an hour later they left together with an overnight bag. They hired not a wreck but a decent car. They had a long drive ahead of them, maybe six or seven hours: they were heading for San Francisco.

Rosie did most of the driving while Lorraine map-read. They only stopped for gasoline but it was after midnight when they arrived in San Francisco and booked into a cheap motel on the outskirts. Rosie was hungry so went out for a takeout hamburger and french fries, bringing one back for Lorraine, who was deeply asleep so Rosie ate it herself. She couldn't sleep, and tossed and turned, her bed creaking ominously, but Lorraine slept on. Rosie propped herself up on her elbow and looked over to her friend. In the blue light from the forecourt that broke through the motel's thin curtains, she studied Lorraine's sleeping face. The transformation from when they had first met was astonishing. She was a different woman in every way – less aggressive, more content within herself, more confident, more womanly.

Lorraine woke early. Rosie was dead to the world so she slipped into the bathroom and took a shower. As she soaped herself she thought about Brad Thorburn. She heard the way she had spoken to him, saw him so hurt, so bewildered. They would probably never meet again and he would never know just how much he had meant to her, what he had done for her. He had made her feel loved, wanted, had made some dead part of her revive. Brad Thorburn had woken her as a woman.

After breakfast, Lorraine took a street map of San Francisco, marked their destination with a cross and passed it over to Rosie. 'You're the driver. That's where we got to get to.'

'Who we seeing?'

Lorraine hesitated. In all fairness Rosie should know why they had come here. 'I *think* that Janklow didn't kill Holly or Didi. Nula lied to me. She said that she and Didi were working together the night Holly was killed but Holly's pimp said Nula was on her own. I think it's got something to do with Art. Also, I think Nula lied about where Didi was the night she was murdered. It's Nula we're going to see. Curtis gave me the address but I don't want to scare her off. I just want her to tell me a few things.'

'Are you gonna get paid for this?'

'Five thousand dollars from Ed Bickerstaff, and Curtis said he'd give me two grand if I got Holly's killer, so we'll have enough to open the agency.'

Lorraine called Nula's number. A sleepy voice answered and she hung up. She recognized Nula's voice.

She and Rosie left the motel, bought a morning paper and Rosie headed into the city. They were hemmed in by traffic and the streets were a confusing mass of one-way systems but they finally turned into Delaware Road.

'Slow right down, real slow,' Lorraine said. 'Let's check the numbers, it's apartment building 182. There it is!'

Rosie pulled up outside a dilapidated four-storey building.

Lorraine gazed up at it, checked the fire escape and then opened the car door. 'I'll be about half an hour. Sit tight.' Rosie picked up the newspaper and prepared herself for the

417

wait. Lorraine checked the names on the apartments and then made her way up an old stone staircase littered with garbage to the third floor. She rapped hard on the door of apartment 23 and waited.

'Who is it?'

'Surprise, Nula, open up, it's me.'

The eye-hole slid back, and bolts and chain locks were removed. Nula opened the door. 'Jesus Christ, how did you find me?'

'Curtis said you were here. As I was passing, I thought I'd call in.' Nula opened the door wider and Lorraine stepped inside. Nula was wearing a tatty kimono and she was barefoot. 'It's only nine o'clock, for chrissakes.'

Lorraine apologized and followed her into the bed-sitting room. It was a mess, crammed with dresses and bags, cases half unpacked and old food cartons. 'I just moved in, bit of a come-down but then I'm not gonna be here permanently. It used to belong to a friend and they're on tour in a big show so I've got it for a few months. Sit down.' Nula folded her arms and looked over Lorraine. She pursed her lips. 'Looking very chic, dear, come into money? That's a very expensive suit.' She sat at her dressing table, fiddled with her hair and checked her face. 'I look like a piece of shit but I was working nearly all night. Girl's got to do what she has to do to earn a living but Christ, this is a shit-hole. The pay isn't half as good as in LA.'

Lorraine told Nula about Janklow, how he had admitted all the murders, including Didi and Holly. Nula closed her eyes. 'Thank God. I've been praying they get the bastard and I know about Art. I cried my heart out but he took his life so I guess that's what he wanted. Those bastards pushed him, the shits, and he was innocent. But why are you here?'

'Work. I'm with an investigation agency.'

Nula shrieked with laughter, then pointed at Lorraine. 'You were a cop, weren't you? Well, I hope you've not

418

come to arrest me.' She brushed her hair, looking at Lorraine in the mirror. She was getting uneasy, Lorraine could sense it.

'What *do* you want?' Nula asked.

'Well, I'm trying to piece a few things together. You said on the night Holly died Didi was with you, that you both saw her cross the road but Curtis said Didi wasn't there, you were alone.' She paused.

Nula motioned for her to continue.

'Nula, I think Art killed Holly *and* Didi but I got to have evidence to prove it. Whatever you tell me won't be used against you – I'll keep your name out of it and it won't hurt Art because he's dead. It'll really help me. It's Mrs Thorburn's jewellery I'm interested in or what pieces you've got left.'

Nula blinked rapidly and swivelled round. 'I don't know what you're talking about.'

Lorraine got up and walked towards Nula. 'The last meal Didi ate was home-made banana bread. She was at home, wasn't she? Not, as you said, out working. Curtis said she didn't show that night because her foot was still hurting. You said she'd been out all day with a regular, but that wasn't true, was it? Now, did Art come round?'

Nula began to paint her nails. 'Bullshit, dear. She went out, and then I was told she'd been murdered. You even called the apartment.'

'The ring on Didi's finger, the one you said she couldn't take off, was Mrs Thorburn's, wasn't it? Well, I'd never seen her wearing it before so she must have been able to get it off. So I think it's something to do with that ring. Is that why Art killed her? Because of the ring?'

Nula painted the last nail of her right hand and began on the left with studied concentration. Lorraine moved closer. 'Didi and Art were blackmailing Steven Janklow. Art was cleaning up, wasn't he? He used Didi to make contact and to pick up the jewels. Where did she pick them up

419

from? Janklow's garage? Was that where they did the exchange?'

Nula continued to paint her nails. 'Listen, dear, why don't you go and do your Perry Mason someplace else? Didi was my closest friend, we adored each other and we both loved little Holly – neither of us would hurt her. Whatever she was doing with Art – she never let on about it to me.'

'Maybe not, but Art might have got angry with her. Maybe it was Art that picked Holly up?'

Nula wafted her nails about to dry them. 'To be honest, dear, I don't know what you're getting at. You've had a wasted journey.'

'Come on, Nula, I know you have to be in on it. Janklow listed a lot of Mrs Thorburn's jewellery but he didn't sell it. Did he give it to Art?'

'I don't know,' Nula snapped.

Lorraine shrugged. 'Fine, I'll go, but I won't keep quiet. You must know something because you had to be in on it.' She tried a different tactic. 'Look, I don't like to do this but I'm broke. Maybe I'll keep quiet if you give me a cut. I want money to keep my mouth shut, Nula. I lied about the agency crap – who's ever gonna employ me?

Nula began to shake a bottle of foundation cream furiously and started to make up her face. 'Obviously I have so much money that I get some perverse kick out of living in this shit-hole and getting twenty dollars a blow-job if I'm lucky. I don't have any dough, all right?'

Lorraine walked slowly to the door. 'Well, if you won't help me, Nula, I'll go to the cops – see if they'll dole me out a few dollars for the information.'

Nula smirked and then said loudly, 'Craig, why don't you come in and say hello to Perry Mason, dear?'

Lorraine pressed her back against the door as Craig Lyall walked in from the bathroom. Nula started to collect her clothes, relaxed and seemingly no longer interested in

420

Lorraine. She held up a dress, checking herself in the mirror, while Lyall moved closer to Lorraine.

Nula giggled. 'Sit down, sweetheart. We're going to have a little party, just the three of us. Well, *you* are. Open the bottle, Craig dear, she won't be able to resist.' She minced out into the bathroom.

Lorraine's heart thudded. How long had she been in the apartment? Ten, fifteen minutes? Would Rosie do anything? Did she even know which was Nula's apartment?

Lyall produced a bottle of vodka.

'Don't do this, Craig. I just wanted a cut of the jewellery, nothing more, and Janklow's already admitted the murders. I won't go to the cops, I promise, it was just a threat. I didn't mean it – all I wanted was some dough.'

Nula shrieked from the bathroom, 'What do you think we are? What are you so scared about? All we're going to do is have a little party.'

She reappeared, wearing a black silk underskirt and stockings. She held out a pair of shoes. 'If you think your shoes are nice, look at these, three hundred dollars, hand-made.' She slipped on first one then the other.

Lyall opened a bottle of vodka and poured a tumblerful. 'Have a drink, Lorraine dear. *Go on, drink it!*'

She swiped Lyall's hand away. The glass smashed against the wall.

'Hold her down and pour it down her throat.' Nula had opened a suitcase full of new clothes. She selected a smart navy dress with a white collar. Lyall gripped Lorraine's wrist and dragged her towards the bed. She struggled and Nula smacked her hard across the face. 'Listen, you'd better do what we want or we'll mark your other cheek. Is that what you want, Miss Goody-Two-Shoes? I knew you were a cunt the moment you ripped us off at the gallery. You blackmailed Art. Now *drink*.'

Lorraine was trying to locate the fire escape. Did the apartment face the street? How long had she told Rosie she would be? She'd fouled up so badly. Had she really felt so sure she'd be able to face out Nula, get the information she needed and return to Bickerstaff? She'd been so off the wall, she'd lost her touch – she almost needed a drink she was so angry with herself.

'Drink,' Lyall said, but she still hadn't taken the glass.

Nula moved to his side. 'Pour it down her throat! What are you waiting for? Few glasses and she'll be begging for more. Go on, do it.'

Lorraine looked up into his scared face. 'Don't do this to me, Craig. I promise I won't tell anybody you've got the jewellery—'

He gripped her cheeks and forced the glass to her lips. Nula grabbed her hair and held her head back, screaming at Lyall to get on with it.

Rosie had read the entire newspaper. She tossed it aside and checked her watch. She looked at the front entrance, drumming her fingers on the steering wheel. Then she got out of the car, trying to remember the name of the person Lorraine was seeing. She looked down the row of names by the intercom but most were scratched out or blank. She pushed open the main door, walked into the corridor, which stank of urine, and climbed the stairs to the first floor. Half-way up she stopped when a door opened and two kids ran out. She had to flatten herself against the stairwell as they charged past her. A woman came to the door and Rosie hurried towards her. 'Have you seen a tall blonde woman?' The door slammed in her face.

She continued up to the second floor, where a male voice demanded to know what she wanted. She turned to face an elderly black man wearing overalls and carrying a broom. 'You live here? What you doin' here?' Rosie explained she was looking for someone. 'What apartment?' he demanded.

'I dunno. She came in about half an hour ago to visit a friend – Nula. You know anyone called Nula?'

He shook his head and shoved the brush at her feet. 'Get out, go on, get out. This is private property.'

She got to the car in time to see the kids who had pushed past her breaking one of its rear-view mirrors and the window on the driver's side had been smashed. Rosie kicked at the glass in fury as the kids ran off shrieking. She carefully removed the glass from the seat. Where the hell was Lorraine? As she straightened up she saw a man walking out of the building with two suitcases. He was in one hell of a hurry and she was about to shout to him when he turned into a yard. Rosie followed, reaching the entrance as the man was throwing suitcases into the trunk of a car. Just as she was about to cross towards him, a woman shouted and he looked up to the fire escape.

Nula was leaning over the railings. 'Get another bottle, and hurry up.'

Lyall got into his car and started the engine. Rosie stared hard at Nula, sure it was the right woman. She wasn't sure what to do. If Lorraine was with her, maybe they were just talking and she'd go nuts if Rosie suddenly barged in. On the other hand, if Lorraine was in trouble and Rosie did nothing she'd be just as mad. 'Think like a detective, Rosie, come on,' she muttered. 'What would Mrs Super Sleuth Lorraine Page do?'

Standing on an old crate, she managed to drag the pull-ladder of the fire escape loose and started to climb upwards. One or two rungs snapped off as she put her weight on them so she almost fell back to the ground. Half-way up she wondered what the hell she was doing but by then she was almost at the first landing.

She grabbed the railings and ducked under the barrier to stand on the first escape. She was scared that if someone saw her they might push her off, so she picked up a garbage bag and tried to look like a resident dumping it. She passed one window after another, peering in, looking for Lorraine. The apartments were run down and squalid, and she saw no one until the fourth window revealed a couple eating. She dodged back the way she had come and headed up towards the second floor. Suddenly, the bag split and refuse clattered down the fire escape. She froze. The landing window opened below. 'What the fuck's goin' on up there?' The window banged shut again and Rosie held on grimly, heart pounding. She nearly fell off again when another of the rusted steps gave way and felt her arm wrench almost out of its socket as she hung on. It was only her anger with Lorraine that kept her climbing.

It took Lyall just a few minutes to get to the corner store, buy two more bottles of vodka and return to the apartment block. He parked right behind Rosie's car, ran up the stairs two at a time to the third floor, and banged on the door for Nula to let him in.

Lorraine was on the bed, her feet tied together with a pair of Nula's tights and her hands bound in front of her. The empty bottle was on the bed beside her. Nula was dressed and everything was packed ready to leave. Lyall locked the door and chucked the bottles onto the bed beside Lorraine. He was sweating with nerves. 'There's a car smashed up outside, a rental from LA – that hers?'

'Why don't you ask her yourself?' Nula snapped.

Lyall picked up the cases. 'I'm not hanging around, Nula, I'm getting out now with or without you. If that bitch could find us so can the cops. She's probably workin' for them.'

Nula was unscrewing the cap of a fresh bottle, glaring at him. 'You'll do just what I tell you and so will she.' Nula pushed the bottle between Lorraine's lips, tilting it. The vodka dribbled down her chin covering her chest. 'Drink it, Lorraine! *Swallow it!*'

The vodka hit the back of Lorraine's throat. She had to swallow but she turned her head away. Nula slapped her face hard and pinched her nose so that when she forced the bottle between Lorraine's lips she had to swallow. The liquor made her body feel as if it was on fire and the room began to blur. 'That's a good girl, come on, let's see you finish the bottle.'

Lyall was frightened. 'Christ, you'll kill her.'

Nula laughed. 'What the fuck do you think I'm trying to do? Get those bags down to the car.' He opened the door and suddenly Nula sprang off the bed and ran towards him. '*No!* I don't want you pissing your pants and driving off. We'll go together. Open the other bottle.'

'I'm not doing it!'

Nula punched him and pushed him up against the wall. 'We got to do this, we've no choice. She knows enough to get them sniffing round us and if they pick me up I swear before God you'll go down with me.'

Nula sat astride Lorraine pouring the vodka down her throat. Lorraine heaved as if to vomit and Nula withdrew the bottle and again slapped her hard across the face. Her eyes closed and her body went limp, and Nula poured the rest into her slack mouth. The liquid dribbled down her face, into her hair, saturating her.

Nula got off the bed, Lorraine was motionless. 'Let's go,' Lyall pressed. 'We'll miss the plane, Nula! *Come on!*'

Rosie, meanwhile, was on the third floor, edging along the fire escape, peering into one window after another, as Nula and Lyall got into their car and drove off. Her legs were shaking, her hands cut from the rusted rails as she inched towards the landing window. She'd break the glass if need be – she was not going to go any higher or climb down. Now she didn't even care if she was arrested for breaking and entering. She got to her knees and began to crawl the last few yards. It was then she saw Lorraine.

She banged on the window. Lorraine half turned her head but then went back to untying her legs. She kept flopping over and she was giggling. Rosie banged on the window again but Lorraine seemed oblivious. Rosie attempted to open the window but it held firm. She pressed her face closer as Lorraine tried to stand, lurching into the wall, then into the dressing table. She rolled around laughing and then she saw the bottle of vodka that had fallen off the bed.

Rosie kicked at the window. The glass cracked but only after she had used both feet was there a hole big enough for her to undo the lock.

Lorraine paid her no attention. She was trying unsuccessfully to drink from the bottle. Rosie heaved her bulk through the window. The glass cut her leg and she was gasping for breath from the effort. She reached Lorraine as she lifted up the bottle to drink and grabbed it. Lorraine screamed and tried to hold onto it but Rosie wouldn't give way. She tore the bottle from her, ran with it into the bathroom and poured the contents down the sink.

She became aware of an ominous silence from the other room and dropped the bottle. Lorraine had passed out. She looked green, her breathing rasping, rattling. Rosie was terrified that she was choking and dragged her to the bathroom, hung her over the bath, then ran water over her, pushing at her lungs. Lorraine heaved and coughed, then vomited. Rosie forced her under the cold water tap. She was like a pitiful rag doll, unable to fend Rosie off, unable to do anything as she retched.

Rosie got her to her feet and forced her to walk up and down. Her head lolled on her chest; she couldn't speak; her eyes were unfocused and she didn't seem to know who Rosie was. She mumbled incoherently and then slithered to the floor. 'Lemme sleep.'

Rosie dragged her up again, walking her up and down.

She was crying – she was so afraid. She didn't know if she should call an ambulance and she kept asking Lorraine her name but she couldn't reply, just kept saying that she wanted to sleep. It wasn't until she had been violently sick again that Rosie helped her to the bed. She stripped off Lorraine's clothes and drew back the sheets, rolling her naked body further onto the bed.

'Lorraine? It's Rosie.'

Lorraine's eyes drooped and she gave a weak smile. Rosie went into the filthy kitchen, where she brewed some coffee. She went back to the bed and shook Lorraine, who moaned and flapped at Rosie to leave her alone. But Rosie persisted, made her sit up and tried to get her to drink the coffee. After half an hour, Rosie could tell she was coming round. She asked where she was and Rosie said they were in San Francisco but it didn't seem to sink in. She closed her eyes again but Rosie still wouldn't let her sleep: she pressed ice cubes wrapped in a pillow slip to Lorraine's head. 'Rosie, I have to sleep. Leave me alone.'

Finally, Rosie lost patience. '*Right*. I'm going to leave you. You disgust me – just as you got everything going for you. Why did you do it?'

Lorraine threw aside the sheet. 'I got to have a drink, Rosie, I'm going crazy, my head aches. Just get me a drink.' She held her head in her hands. 'I got to make a call – got to call Bickerstaff. Is there a phone here?'

'The state you're in you can't call anyone.'

Lorraine squinted up at her. 'They forced it down me.' She tried to stand but the room spun and she had to sit down again. 'Nula, you got to get her arrested, she's with that photographer Craig Lyall. I got to call Bickerstaff.'

Rosie didn't know whether to believe her or not. She stood with her feet planted like a solid oak. 'Well, you can't do nothin' about that now. They've gone.'

'Shit.' Lorraine picked up the ice pack and rested it against her head. 'You saw them leave?'

'Yeah.'

Rosie poured more coffee and a glass of water. 'Start drinking this and as much water as you can take – go on, take it.'

Lorraine did as she was told but when she attempted to move off the bed she felt faint. 'Rosie, start looking in the garbage. See if they left anything that might tell us where they're heading.'

Rosie found nothing in the kitchen but in the bedroom she spotted a small trash can by the dressing table filled with cotton-wool balls and tissues smeared with make-up. She tipped them out onto an old newspaper and poked around. She found nothing and wrapped up the mess in the newspaper – then opened it again. There were marks around the air-flight ads. 'There's this. What do you think?'

Lorraine forced herself to look at the paper: two airlines had been underlined and there were crosses against them. 'Call these airlines, see if any flights are leaving this afternoon with a Mr Lyall on board.'

'They won't tell me. They never tell you what passengers are boarding – that's a law, isn't it?'

Lorraine craved a drink – her whole body screamed for one – but she gulped the water. 'Say it's an emergency, something to do with kids ... Anything, just find out which airline they're with.' Lorraine hung on to the bed-head as she stood up. She inched her way into the bathroom where she saw the vodka bottle and reached out for it. A single drop remained in the bottom and she drank it before she retched again, clinging to the wash-basin. She saw herself in the mirror: her face was pale green, her eyes red-rimmed and her lips swollen.

Rosie barged in. 'Two seats booked by Mr Lyall for the four-fifteen flight to Las Vegas. Now what?'

Lorraine's eyes were closed. 'Did they go off in a cab?'

'No, a car. So, now what do I do?'

She told Rosie to call Ed Bickerstaff. 'This is what you say to him. Tell him you're my partner – Jesus, just tell him anything – that it's to do with the murders of David Burrows and Holly, you got that?'

Rosie reached for the phone as Lorraine crashed to the floor.

Ed Bickerstaff hung up. He wondered if he could trust the information. He would have been happier if it had been Lorraine herself who had called – she have never made any mention of a partner. He decided there was nothing to lose so he put in the call to send agents to Las Vegas to arrest Craig Lyall and his companion. He then arranged for a search warrant to look over Lyall's studio. As he was leaving his office, he received the phone call he had been half expecting: Steven Janklow's plea would stand as guilty on seven counts of murder, but his mental state had been scrutinized and eight doctors and four psychiatrists had declared him criminally insane and medically unfit to stand trial. He would be held in a secure mental institution for life, with no hope of release. Mrs Thorburn had still not made any contact with him. Brad Thorburn continued to monitor his brother's welfare via the family lawyers but no more than that.

The subsequent arrest of Lyall and Nula would be welcome as a show of the FBI's thoroughness but Bickerstaff was wondering if he had made a mistake. He called Rooney to double-check on Lorraine but he was away, and although he'd already ordered that Nula and Lyall be brought in he still had to run it by the Chief. Bickerstaff embroidered the facts a little, pointing out that Lyall's arrest might further clarify Janklow's guilt. It might also confirm that Art Mathews had instigated the murders of Angela Hollow and David Burrows. It sounded so good to him that he felt more confident.

'Who's the informant, Ed? And how come you haven't discussed this with anyone else from my department?'

Bickerstaff flushed. 'It's Lorraine Page.'

The Chief gave a fish-eyed stare.

'Lorraine Page? You'd better hope to Christ that it pans out as well as the Janklow tapes she did.' He hesitated. 'Has she got something else on Janklow?'

'I'll get back to you as soon as I hear anything.'

The Chief glared. 'So you'll be staying on?'

Bickerstaff seemed fazed. 'Of course. This is tied in with the original investigation.'

'You sure it's not tied in with you trying to whitewash your fuck-up with Art Mathews?'

Bickerstaff stood square-jawed in front of the desk. He'd have liked to punch a hole right through it but he retained his composure. 'I'm just trying to do my job. Nothing has been whitewashed and I'm not making any excuses for the Art Mathews fuck-up but I would like to check any new evidence that may come to light.'

'How much did Page hit you for?'

Bickerstaff smiled but it was without humour. 'She doesn't get a cent.' He closed the door behind him silently. He had not added that Lorraine's payout depended on her providing Bickerstaff with evidence that proved Mathews's part in the hammer murders. If she could, it would help cover the FBI's public humiliation at having erroneously named Mathews as the sole killer. If she did bring in the goods, five thousand dollars was not much to pay for the FBI coming out smelling like roses.

As Bickerstaff was about to enter his office, he was handed a fax informing him that Lyall and Nula had been arrested in Las Vegas. Lyall insisted they were there to get married and they had said they had nothing to do with Steven Janklow. Bickerstaff requested they be brought in for questioning in connection with a 'homicide investigation' and a possible 'accessory to murder' charge.

He grew impatient as he received no reply to his calls to Lorraine's apartment. Nula and Lyall were on their way to Pasadena from Las Vegas and he hadn't the slightest idea what he was going to question them about. What had they overlooked in previous interviews? Or was it possible that Lorraine Page had, yet again, withheld vital evidence? If she had she was now in dangerous waters and Bickerstaff would make sure she drowned.

Rosie and Lorraine hardly spoke throughout the long drive home. It took all Lorraine's will-power not to beg Rosie to buy a bottle. The need to drink was stronger than her headache and sickness. She felt despairing and, worse, inadequate. It was the end of the agency, the partnership – she was back at square one again and it hurt. But nothing was stronger than the urge to drink. She had not beaten it. She felt it had beaten her.

The phone was ringing as they opened the front door. It was Bickerstaff. Rosie asked him to call back, and hung up before he could remonstrate. She then called Jake who said he'd be right over. When he arrived Rosie had cooked some spaghetti and laid the table. Jake put his arm round her shoulder. 'How you doing?'

'Fucked! I had a future and a job yesterday but today, well, I dunno. You got to talk to her – this guy Bickerstaff keeps calling.'

Jake nodded and went into the bedroom. Lorraine was awake, sitting on the edge of the bed. She had on a bathrobe and looked pale, sickly. She gave that look of hers, tilting her head, that slight squint. 'It's no good, Jake, I'm not going to make it. I blew it so badly. I got over-confident, arrogant. You know, I thought I was so damned clever, and if it wasn't for Rosie I'd probably be dead.'

He squeezed her hand. 'It'll always be a part of your life. You can never have one drink. Even if you think you're

431

strong enough to deal with it you won't be because it's an illness, Lorraine.'

Lorraine was crying. 'All I want is a drink, Jake.'

He stood up. 'Lemme tell you something. I want one, Rosie wants one, we all want one, you're no different. We all feel like you do so get your ass off that bed and come in and eat.'

He walked out and she got up slowly. When she joined them at the table, he drew out a chair.

'Thanks for helping me out this afternoon, Rosie.'

'Think nothing of it, partner, but next time you tell me to wait outside, I want to know how many minutes, who you're going to see and why.'

Lorraine doubted if there would be another time. The phone rang. Rosie answered and handed it to Lorraine. 'You better talk to him, it's Bickerstaff.'

'Hi, Ed. We just got back. It was a long drive . . . Yeah, yeah, no problem. I'll be there . . . sure, thanks.' She hung up. 'They want me at the station. They're sending a squad car. I can't think straight – I can't even see straight. They're going to take one look at me and they're gonna know. I'm still plastered.'

Jake took off his jacket and rolled up his sleeves.

'Let's get that shower running.'

Lorraine looked at them dead-eyed. 'Oh, God, not again . . .'

CHAPTER 20

NULA HAD been separated from Lyall on the way to Pasadena but the flight to Las Vegas had been long enough for them to get their story straight. Lorraine had not arrived at the station when their lawyer angrily confronted Bickerstaff, insinuating that he was wrongfully holding them on the word of a known drunkard, a woman who had arrived at his clients' apartment in San Francisco attempting to blackmail them. He doubted if Bickerstaff would be able to make any sense of what Mrs Page had levelled against his clients as she had been so drunk when they had last seen her that they had left her in the apartment. Time was against Bickerstaff because without strong evidence implicating them he could not hold Lyall and Nula longer than twenty-four hours. He was in a hot-seat of his own making and could ask for no help from the local police. This had been an FBI arrest and Bickerstaff was on his own.

Jake and Rosie were still plying Lorraine with water and coffee. She had no hangover now but her confidence had gone. She was afraid to confront Bickerstaff, and Rosie knew it.

The doorbell rang, and Lorraine jumped. Bickerstaff stood on the step, his shirt sticking to him, his tie loosened.

'I was just on my way,' Lorraine said lamely.

'Let's move it. We've got them for twenty-four hours and time's running out. You'd better have a fucking good reason for setting this scene up. I got my boss and their lawyer at me and I got the entire department wondering what the hell is goin' on and they aren't the only ones.'

Lorraine followed him down the stairs. She stepped into the back of the patrol car, he slammed the door, and got into the front.

'They both said you were drunk.'

'They poured a bottle of vodka down my throat, so I guess I was.'

'You okay now?'

'Just a bit shaky.'

'You should have told me who you were going after, and more important why. You wanna fill me in before we get there?'

Lorraine took a deep breath. 'I wasn't sure, I knew Nula was possibly involved. What I didn't know was that Lyall was too.'

Ed started the engine. 'I've given them both a tough grilling and they stuck to their story. They were in Vegas to get married, or were gonna try for some kind of ceremony – they got preachers there that'd marry them. They also maintain they don't know nothin' about Holly's or David Burrows's murder and they know that Janklow's admitted to killing them. They also said you were drunk when you visited them and that they told you if you needed them they'd fly back after they got hitched.'

There was silence for a moment. Then Bickerstaff asked bluntly, 'How do you want to work this?'

Lorraine was desperate for a drink. She didn't dare take out a cigarette as her hands were shaking so much. 'Maybe talk to Lyall first, break him. I don't think he killed anybody. He's dominated by Nula, maybe even scared of her, so go for him first.'

Bickerstaff was uneasy. His brain ticked like the small hand on his watch as he tried to assimilate what she had just said.

434

'It's something to do with Mrs Thorburn's jewellery,' she added. 'I need to look at the lists Janklow made out and I want to see the morgue shot of Didi – David Burrows.'

Lorraine followed Bickerstaff through the corridors, stopping off at his office. He asked for Lyall to be brought up from the cells and taken to a small interview room with a one-way glass. Lyall was nervous and asked repeatedly for his lawyer. He sat with his hands splayed out on the small bare table, his face set, his mouth a rigid line. Watched by Lorraine and Bickerstaff, he stared around the small windowless room and then looked directly at the one-way glass.

'You want to go in?' Bickerstaff asked.

Lorraine could feel the tension disappearing. 'Just let him sweat a few more minutes. I'll need a glass of water, some kind of official-looking file, good photographs of the dead women, lot of documents, pens, notepad – and keep his lawyer out for as long as you can.'

Bickerstaff glanced at his watch, constantly monitoring the time as it ticked away. Lorraine was calmly checking down Janklow's list of jewellery. She felt positive. She looked through the glass partition at Lyall, watching his every move, the way he clenched and unclenched his hands, ran a finger round the inside of his collar and cleared his throat. They could hear him crossing and uncrossing his legs, his shoes scuffing the floor.

Ten minutes later Bickerstaff handed Lorraine the articles she had requested. She patted her pockets to make sure she had the cigarettes and lighter; she was no longer shaking but was feeling a buzz inside her. She was almost ready.

'Get someone to take water and glasses in, but not to say a word, even if he asks a question.'

She watched an officer enter the room. They heard Lyall asking how long he was to be kept waiting but the officer

435

didn't even look at him. Lorraine nodded to Bickerstaff. 'I'm ready.'

As she left the room, he murmured, 'Good luck,' but she didn't turn back.

When Lorraine walked in, Lyall covered his surprise fast, turning away as she sat in the chair opposite. She paid him no attention but opened the dummy file and her notebook, carefully laid out her pens, cigarettes and lighter. Then she reached over to the jug and poured herself a glass of water.

Lyall cleared his throat again and tapped his foot. Bickerstaff waited.

Lorraine slowly got out the photographs of Holly and placed them in front of Lyall. 'Please look at the photographs, Craig.'

He turned away.

'She was only seventeen and she was beautiful, wasn't she? Take a look at her pretty face.'

He glanced at the ten-by-six photograph. Then Lorraine pointed to the morgue shots, which showed the injuries that virtually obliterated her face, broken nose, eye-sockets filled with blood and the gaping mouth with the front teeth smashed.

'Someone hammered her face, broke her skull, her nose, even her teeth. What kind of person do you think would do this? What kind of *madness* did this?'

Lyall wouldn't look at the photographs but kept his eyes on the wall.

'I keep on telling them that you couldn't have done it but they won't believe me, you know why? Because—'

'I didn't do that. I'm innocent.' His voice was high-pitched, bordering on hysterical.

'I know you are – of course you are – all you were involved in was blackmail. I know that but—'

'Janklow did it, he admitted it – so why don't you piss off and leave me alone? I want my lawyer here.' He sounded less hesitant now, his voice lower.

'Your lawyer will be here, Craig, but he's just finalizing Nula's release. She's going, so I hope you've made arrangements for your share of any money you had, because she . . .'

Bickerstaff covered his face. She was really pushing it.

'I don't believe you,' Lyall said sullenly.

'Believe what? That she's being released?' Lorraine flicked through the dummy documents. 'This is her statement. You can read it, if you like, but you won't be released, Craig, because Nula has stated that you were involved in murdering this girl and David Burrows.'

Lyall sneered, 'I know you're lying.'

Lorraine pushed forward Didi's photographs, the before and after shots. 'Am I? That's naïve of you, Craig. You know Nula killed Didi, even though she insists that you did it – that you drove her to the apartment, sat and drank tea, even offered her the banana bread. Didi lived on that banana bread of hers, didn't she? Anyway, according to Nula, the three of you started to argue because Didi had kept a ring, one of Mrs Thorburn's pieces. You'd all agreed to get rid of everything because the items could be traced, but Didi kept a ring. This one. Look at this picture, Craig – that is the ring, isn't it? On the third finger of her right hand.'

Bickerstaff had no idea what Lorraine was talking about. What ring? Was it in the files? He turned to his back-up. 'Get me the files down here, will you? And fast.' He turned his attention back to the interview room.

Lyall's fists were clenched so tight the knuckles stood out white. Lorraine placed in front of him the full-length mortuary shot of Didi in which she was wearing the ring.

'Just nod if it is the ring, Craig. You don't have to say anything. I'm only trying to help you, you must know that. I'm not even pressing charges about your part in trying to kill me.'

'What are you?' he snapped.

437

'I'm a private investigator, not even attached to the station or the FBI, but because I was there in San Francisco they're allowing me to talk to you. You both tried to kill me and you almost succeeded but what you didn't know was that I was wired, so everything you said in that apartment has been recorded. That's why you were both arrested in Las Vegas.'

He still didn't believe a word.

'Nula knew that she had to frame somebody to get herself released and that was you, Craig, because as soon as she saw me with the FBI agents she knew the game was up. She's been talking since they brought her in. Look at these statements. Don't you think it's strange your lawyer isn't here?'

Bickerstaff could feel sweat running down his back. He was relieved no one else was privy to what Lorraine was saying as all hell would have broken loose.

'I never killed anybody,' Lyall snapped, but his hands were shaking now.

Lorraine sipped her water. 'I know that, Craig, but let me read you a section of Nula's statement . . .'

Lyall was sweating even more than Bickerstaff, who couldn't believe Lorraine's audacity – the way she was lying.

She sifted through the dummy documents, and continued to talk quietly and calmly. She drew a page forward and started to read.

'"It started as an argument between the three of us. Didi wouldn't give the ring back, she said she couldn't get it off her finger so then Craig said he would cut it off and she started to get hysterical."'

'That's not true,' he interjected. Lorraine held up her hand as if to tell him to be patient, then carried on reading in the same steady voice.

'"Craig became more and more angry because Didi could get us all into trouble. We'd been selling Mrs Thorburn's jewellery for years, bits and pieces. Art would find the buyer

438

and we would just collect, but because of the killings it was dangerous for Didi to walk around showing off this big ring. It was a topaz with a row of diamonds around it and it was worth a lot of money."'

Lorraine was making it up as she went along. All she had pieced together was that according to Janklow's lists and description the ring belonged to Mrs Thorburn and it was possibly the ring Didi was wearing. She looked at Lyall. 'I presume when she says Art she is referring to Art Mathews, is that correct?'

'Why are you asking me these questions?'

'I used to be a cop, now I'm freelance, insurance claims, that kind of thing. Before they charge you I want to get my facts straight and until your lawyer is available they can't talk to you. There's nothing illegal about it – there's nobody else here.'

He was really sweating now. 'You mean it's true? They're releasing Nula?'

She nodded, tapped the dummy file. 'She's given her statement and all I want to do is get onto her for my clients and before she skips the country. I don't care who did what to whom just so long as I hold onto my job.'

Lyall tried to fathom how she was sitting in front of him. He knew she'd been dead drunk. How in hell had she got herself together?

Bickerstaff shook his head. Lorraine was giving to him, piece by piece, a section of the jigsaw puzzle, the stolen jewellery, the blackmail scam, but Lyall had not as yet implicated himself in any way.

Lorraine asked, 'You took the photographs of Janklow, didn't you?'

Lyall sighed. 'Art did. Well, some of them, years ago when he had a studio in Santa Monica. Janklow had this thing about looking like his mother, you know, all dragged up. At first Art didn't know who he was – he'd used some false name, they all do – and then he saw him at some society dinner with his mother, years ago, and started milking him. That's all I know. I swear before God, I honestly had nothing to do with it. I didn't even know it was going on . . .' He trailed off. 'I don't know what to do,' he said suddenly, helplessly.

'Maybe tell me the truth. Then I'll tell you what I think, as a friend, you should do, and in return, you tell me about the whereabouts of the stolen jewellery. I'm not interested in the murders. If you did them with Nula that's your business.'

'I didn't,' he said flatly. 'I'm so confused, I don't know who I can trust and I don't believe a word you're telling me.'

Lorraine snapped the file closed. 'If that's the way you feel I'll walk. All I wanted to do was get my insurance claims sorted out. There's more than three million dollars' worth of gems missing. Mrs Thorburn's son Brad asked me to look into it. They've let me talk to you because they aren't quite ready to charge you.' Bickerstaff's mouth was bone dry. She was fishing in dangerous waters again: actually *naming* people – that could get him into real trouble.

'They can't charge me with anything,' Lyall said shrilly.

Lorraine slapped her hand hard on the table and Lyall jumped. 'Don't be so fucking stupid. Nula's named you as Holly and Didi's killer. You're crazy if you think they're not going to lock you up for a very long time. Art Mathews is dead so she's only got you to blame. Now, if you're saying you didn't have any part in those murders then you'd better have a good alibi because she's given them evidence to prove you killed them both. Because you were in Didi's apartment, weren't you? If you didn't kill her then Nula did, right?'

He sniffed. 'I didn't touch her.'

'So who did?'

'She did, of course. Nula.'

Lorraine felt as if she had been punched. She'd expected him to say Mathews, not Nula.

'You saw her?'

Lyall put his head in his hands. 'Yes, she said she pushed Didi and she fell and hit her head against the coffee table. We couldn't find any pulse and she began to panic. Well, she had reason to.'

'Because of Mrs Thorburn's jewellery?'

'*Yes*. And then I panicked, it was just all confused and terrible. We couldn't get it off her finger, the ring . . . we couldn't get it off.'

He broke down and started to sob.

'So who decided to make it look as if it was one of the hammer murders?'

'She did. She said no one would believe it if they just found her, especially not after Holly.'

He sobbed, muttered to himself that it wasn't him, he hadn't done anything.

Lorraine touched his hand. 'Craig, what do you mean "after Holly"? What about Holly?'

Lyall flapped his hands wildly. 'Oh, Christ, this is terrible, it isn't right, I know it.'

'Come on, Craig, get it off your chest, tell me.'

He steadied himself. 'Holly had somehow found out about the blackmail – God knows how but she had. She'd been picked up by some john, taken back to his place and—'

'Do you know who it was?'

Lyall chewed his lip. 'I think it was – you said his name before – Brad Thorburn.'

Lorraine couldn't believe what she was hearing. '*Brad Thorburn*? You mean he's involved in all this?'

'Yes, in as much as he picked up Holly and took her back to his house. I dunno what happened but she somehow knew what we were all doing – maybe she saw Janklow there – but she started pushing Nula and Didi for money.

They got on to Art – they were really worried – and next thing I read she was murdered. I don't know which one of them did it but they got away with it because they made it look like this serial killer had done it. I think Art was involved. I swear before God I don't know. I was caught up in it all because I'd taken photographs of that Norman Hastings and he was a friend of Janklow's but I didn't know that. It was just, well, I knew *they* were doing it and it seemed so easy.'

Lorraine was trying to take on board what he was saying and then it clicked. 'Were you blackmailing Norman Hastings?'

'Yes, but then he went to Janklow and asked him what he should do about it. I suppose the two of them discussed it together. I've told you all I know. I had nothing to do with any of the murders. All I did was a bit of blackmail.'

Bickerstaff checked his watch, told one of his aides to bring in Brad Thorburn. He said he didn't give a shit if he was still in France. He was feeling elated and couldn't wait to get his own hands on Lyall. And he couldn't wait to lay it all before the Chief for the sheer pleasure of seeing his face.

Lorraine continued to question Lyall as he sobbed out his part in the blackmail racket. She made only a few notes, knowing that Bickerstaff would go over everything. She didn't even feel self-congratulatory. She couldn't stop Brad Thorburn's face drifting into her mind and she only half listened as Lyall talked, freely now as if relieved it was all out in the open.

Lyall had used Didi to make up the men who came to him for secret photographic sessions. They had met through Mathews when they worked together in Santa Monica. When they met again in Los Angeles they continued their old tricks and Mathews let Didi and Nula use his apartment for photo sessions. He moved out, leaving them there. Didi continued to pass on potential blackmail victims. Janklow was paying first Art, then all three to keep silent. None had any indication that he was also a killer. He had always paid up without argument, regaining one negative after another, until he began to get edgy, saying he had no more money, no more jewellery.

Lyall asked for water, sipped it and then traced the rim of the glass with his finger. 'Hastings didn't have much cash but he paid up, fifty bucks here and there. But when Art found out he went crazy.' The rim of the glass squeaked as he ran his finger round and round.

'Did you kill Norman Hastings, Craig?'

'No, I didn't, and I had nothing to do with any of those others.'

Lorraine leaned forward. 'What about Didi?'

Lyall closed his eyes and sighed. 'I saw her – she was already dead, she was at their apartment. Nula called me. She was lying on the floor. I never touched her. I think they had something to do with that girl Holly, but I don't know what – they knew something, I'm sure of it.'

'What about Mathews? Was he involved in Holly's murder? That's what you're suggesting, isn't it? That Nula and Didi had something to do with Holly's death?'

His voice was quiet, almost a whisper. 'Yes, but I don't know if Art was involved.' He started to cry, biting his bottom lip to stop the tears. 'I swear all I'm guilty of is helping Nula to—' He broke down, and Lorraine waited until he had composed himself. 'I helped move her body, carry it to the stolen car.'

'When you carried Didi, did she have these injuries?'

Lorraine brought out the photograph of Didi's hideously beaten face again and he straightened up.

'No. When I last saw her her head was covered in a black plastic bag, I never saw her face, and after she was put in the car, I went home.'

When he had finished Lyall seemed more relaxed. He had stopped crying and seemed resigned. As Lorraine gathered her notes and files together, he gave her a weak smile. 'I loved her, you know, really loved Nula. We were going to be married in Vegas – that's why I helped her. It wasn't anything but that, I didn't do anything.'

Lorraine walked across to the door. 'They'll want a statement from you, Craig, and I think you'd be wise to tell them everything you know, just as you've told me. Don't let her get away with it.'

Bickerstaff didn't congratulate Lorraine. He almost grabbed her notes from her while directing his men to begin the detailed requestioning of Craig Lyall. Lorraine sat in his office, drained, as the atmosphere around grew charged with excitement. She felt ill, her head thudded, but all she could think of was Brad Thorburn. Had she been wrong? Could he be implicated in the murders? Had he always known more than he had indicated?

'What about Thorburn?' she asked Bickerstaff quietly.

'We're having him brought back from France.' He hesitated and leaned over her. 'How involved do you reckon the smooth bastard is?'

'I don't know.'

'You mean there's something you *don't* know about this business?'

'I didn't think he was involved.'

Bickerstaff tapped her shoulder. 'We'll find out soon enough.'

Now it was Nula's turn. Bickerstaff was moving like a man on speed, talking non-stop, firing instructions right, left and centre. Lorraine remained sitting in his office until they were ready for her, thinking about Brad Thorburn.

Nula was brought up from the cells. She screamed for her lawyer and wanted to see Lyall. She was aggressive and abusive, and had to be half dragged into an interview room, kicking and spitting. Only when she saw Lorraine did she quieten down. As the door closed behind her, Lorraine entered the adjoining room, looking through the one-way glass as Nula knocked over the jug of water.

She refused to say one word without her lawyer present. He was, in fact, sitting beside Lyall, now under oath to tell the truth. He made a formal statement detailing his part in the blackmail of Norman Hastings and describing how Nula had killed Didi. He could give no details about Holly's murder as he had not been involved.

Bickerstaff waited until Lyall's statement was ready before interviewing Nula. By law she had to be allowed time to talk to the lawyer and he would be present throughout. Bickerstaff formally requested that Lorraine not only be present but a party to the interrogation. The entire station was buzzing with the new developments. There was no animosity, just strong professional back-up: anything Bickerstaff wanted he got.

They were ready to interrogate Nula, the last piece in the jigsaw. She now knew how serious the charges were, and that there was no hope of her being released from custody. She had become calmer, having been kept waiting for hours. She was sitting at the table, and had redone her make-up and hair. She looked almost perfect, every hair in place, her lips a deep dark vermilion with a sheen of gloss but small flecks of the lipstick stained her front teeth.

Bickerstaff, two uniformed officers and a stenographer entered the room, followed by Lorraine. Nula turned slowly to face her and then laughed. 'I underestimated you,' she said, completely relaxed, and apparently unconcerned by the formidable line-up. If anything, she seemed almost to be enjoying the attention. Her lawyer waited until everyone had been seated and the tape recorder switched on; the stenographer's hands were poised.

Nula was facing two separate charges: blackmail and extortion, and first degree murder. She stated that her birth name was Nigel Simmons. Her lawyer now turned to

Bickerstaff. 'My client categorically denies any part in the charges levelled at her and she has the right to remain silent. She has been made aware of certain statements by Craig Lyall, implicating her in these said crimes, and again denies playing any part in the said crimes but will, if required, be prepared to stand trial for the prosecution and to implicate Craig Lyall as being solely responsible for the crimes.'

There was a short pause before Bickerstaff began by asking Nula directly if she had been involved in the blackmail of Steven Janklow.

No comment.

Had she struck David Burrows (Didi) during an argument and then with the assistance of Craig Lyall, carried his body to a stolen car and deposited it?

No comment.

Bickerstaff asked detailed questions for almost half an hour. Each one was answered with, 'No comment.'

Throughout, Nula sat checking her nails, fixing her skirt, straightening her frilled blouse. She sometimes looked at Lorraine, raising an eyebrow, and then, as if bored by the proceedings, yawned, crossing and recrossing her legs. When the photographs of Didi were displayed, she averted her face and stared at the wall. When she was asked again to look at the photographs, she sighed and glanced down, then looked at her lawyer.

Holly's pictures were laid in front of her. This time her lawyer asked her to look at the photographs as requested. She picked one up, glared around the room, and then let it drop back on the table, drumming her nails on it.

'No comment.'

'Are you saying you do not recognize her? Or that you do not know her?' Bickerstaff asked impatiently.

'My client refuses to answer that question in case it may implicate her request to act as a prosecution witness.'

Bickerstaff turned towards Lorraine. He gave a brief nod

and they requested a break in the interview to enable them to confer. Both left the room.

Bickerstaff shoved his hands into his pockets. 'This could go on for days. You want to have a try, see if we can hurry it up in there?'

'Okay. Is it legal for the same lawyer to represent both parties?'

'Lyall has already given his statement. It'll be up to him to hire someone else. I would, if I was him, but that's not my main concern right now.'

They went back into the interview room and the tape was turned on again. Lorraine pulled her chair up close. Nula giggled and leaned across the table. 'Your turn now, is it?'

Lorraine ignored her remark. 'She was just seventeen, Nula. Why did you have to kill her? What harm had she ever done you?'

Nula conferred with her lawyer and then sat back.

'My client wants to know why Mrs Page is present at this interview. She is aware that she is not attached to the FBI or the police homicide division. She is also aware that Mrs Page is a chronic alcoholic. I would also like to lodge my own formal complaint as to such a woman being present.'

Bickerstaff leaned back in his chair. 'No comment.'

'Is she some kind of witness?' the lawyer asked tersely.

Nula smirked. 'They couldn't get her on a stand in any court of law, she'd be laughed off. She's a drunkard, she's a whore and she's even been paid for working with Art Mathews. She more than likely instigated the blackmail – she was certainly paid enough to keep quiet. Ask her! Has anyone asked her how much Art Mathews paid her? I never touched Holly, nor did I hurt my best friend. She's making it all up, probably with that pervert Lyall. I can even smell the booze on her – it's coming out of her pores. Look at the way her hands are shaking.'

Lorraine refused to be goaded. She turned to Bickerstaff and got a steely glint stare. She leaned back and imitated Nula's smiling face. 'I'm as sober as she is and she's lying. I was never paid a cent by Art Mathews.'

'You lying cunt,' Nula spat out.

'Takes one to know one,' Lorraine snapped back. 'But then you don't have one. Is that your problem? Is that why you had to kill little Holly? Because she was young, beautiful, everything you wanted to be but—'

Nula stood up, pushing away the restraining hand of her lawyer. 'She was about as innocent as my ass!'

'Taking your clients away, was she?' Lorraine shot out and Nula swiped at her across the table.

Lorraine was on her feet. 'That's it, Nula, come on, show what you're really like. Show just what a mean bitch you are – and you *are* mean. The way you hammered poor Didi's face after all she'd done for you.'

No one in the room acknowledged what was going on. They sat stony-faced as Nula and Lorraine shouted at each other. At one point, an officer half rose but Bickerstaff glared. He wanted this row to continue.

Nula snarled, 'It was *me* that did everything for *her*. Don't you know anything?' She pointed a red-tipped talon at Lorraine. 'She doesn't know what she's talking about.'

'Without Didi you were nothing. She had to tout you around—you couldn't even pick up a john without her.'

'Fuck you, that's bullshit.' Nula's hands were on her hips. Her lawyer tried to make her sit down but she stepped away.

'She told me, said you were a useless piece of garbage.'

Nula swiped at her again.

'And then when you found out she'd kept a ring, you just snapped, didn't you?'

Nula looked at them all smugly. 'I know what you're trying to do. Well, I'm not saying another word.'

She sat down and smoothed her skirt as Lorraine walked

to the side of the room and propped herself against the wall. 'Nobody's asking you to, Nula, because we know. We know that you tried to get the ring off her finger – even threatened to cut it off – but she wouldn't part with it. She told you to piss off so you punched her, like the man you really are. All this paint and wig, all the glam clothes, you're just a heavy-handed man underneath it all, aren't you, Mr Simmons? But Didi, she was really beautiful, wasn't she?'

Nula elbowed her lawyer. 'Tell her to shut the fuck up. This isn't legal. I want to leave.'

Bickerstaff calmly looked at the lawyer. 'Tell her she won't be leaving here for a long time.'

Nula stood up again and lunged forward. 'You're all jerks, all of you, you've got nothing on me, nothin' but what that wimp Lyall has told you and he's full of shit.'

'Then why don't you tell us what really happened?' Bickerstaff asked.

'No fucking way, you asshole, I'm not sayin' another word. I know my rights, I don't have to tell you anything because I know all you've got is his word against mine. That's *all* you've got and until we make a deal and make me a prosecution witness, I'm not talking.'

Lorraine was still standing by the wall, arms folded. 'Tell us about Holly. Why did you kill Holly?'

Nula shouted, 'I never touched her, I never touched Didi, I never did anything and I know you got nothing on me, nothing. Janklow killed them, just like he killed all the others – it's in the papers. It's Janklow – I've got nothin' to do with anything.'

'But he didn't kill Holly and he didn't kill Didi.'

'*Yes, he did.*' Nula was red in the face with fury. 'He was a sicko, everybody knows it, he's nuts, can't even stand trial. Don't you follow what's going on with your so-called investigations? I know what you did. You put poor Art in prison and you killed him. You gave a big press conference, "We got the killer" and you were wrong. How come nobody is standing trial for that? He was innocent. I'm innocent.'

Getting no reaction from anyone she turned back to Lorraine, pointing at her. 'I'll scream it all out to the papers about you, Mrs Page, about what's going on in this room. Janklow has admitted to killing Holly and Didi, Janklow is a sicko, a pervert and—'

'So are you,' Lorraine said softly.

'Get her out of this room or I'll—'

'You'll what, Nula? Kill me like Holly?'

'This isn't right, she shouldn't be allowed to do this to me, she's saying things to get me going. Well, I'm not gonna say another word. If you got the evidence then arrest me, charge me. Go on, let's hear you do it.'

Bickerstaff checked his watch. It was almost nine thirty. He suggested they take a break and continue the interview the following morning.

'Does that mean I can go?' Nula asked.

'You will be held in custody pending further inquiries.'

'But you haven't charged me,' she said. 'Can they do this?' she asked the lawyer.

'Yes.'

'Bastards,' she muttered.

'You'll meet plenty of them, Nigel,' Lorraine said quietly. 'How many will be in her cell with her? Three or four?' she asked Bickerstaff. He made no answer.

'I want to be put in the women's section,' Nula demanded.

'That won't be possible,' Bickerstaff said flatly and turned to the lawyer. 'Please explain to your client that as she is listed as male on her birth certificate she cannot be placed in a female wing.'

For the first time, Nula seemed frightened. She clung to her lawyer. 'But I'm a woman. They can't do this to me.' He whispered to her and she looked at Bickerstaff, then Lorraine, lunging at her, knocking over the table. 'You bitch! *You did this to me!* You know what'll happen to me in with those animals.'

Lorraine ducked and sidestepped Nula as an officer grabbed her. 'Then talk, Nula. At least they can segregate you. Tell us the truth about Holly.'

'Shut up, you schmuck.'

'Tell the truth, Nula. It was an accident, wasn't it? You never meant to kill Didi, did you? She was your best friend – I know that, I've seen you two together.' Lorraine saw the change sweep over Nula in her body language; she lost all the fight.

'Yes, she was,' Nula said softly, and then averted her face. Her eyes filled with tears. 'Best friend I ever had.'

The room fell silent as if everyone knew it was coming. Nula looked up at the ceiling, her eyes brimming with tears, and Lorraine moved silently back to her own seat. Nula blew her nose on a tissue and then began plucking at it. 'Oh, all right, there's no point, is there? You'll find out, I suppose. She fell and hit her head on the side of the glass coffee table. Craig started to panic because we couldn't find her pulse. We thought she was dead and what with—'

'The blackmail? You were worried about that, were you?' Lorraine asked softly.

'It was all getting out of hand, right? We suspected Janklow was doing these killings because he was a real crazy fucker. He always paid up like it was a joke, like he got off on it. He never argued or nothing but paid up once a month regular as clockwork. But Art began to get greedy, kept on pushing him for more and what was so sick, we were blackmailing him because of all his drag pictures but he still wanted more of them. We all kinda knew he was going to crack someday. That was maybe why Art kept asking him for more money, more jewellery, like he knew he was gonna break.'

'But why did you think it was him murdering these women?'

451

Nula was tired; she supported herself on her elbow. 'Art put it all together, don't ask me how. He always was an intuitive shit but instead of backing off, he asked for more. We were against it but he wouldn't listen to us. I mean, we were doing okay, we had dough and then he opened that gallery. There was no need to be so greedy, we even had the other business, the photo sessions. We'd all never had it so good—'

'How did you collect the money?'

'We'd just go to his garage, one or other of us, pretend we were looking for cars. Art used to drive an old Bentley. He'd bought it from S and A, so he was able to go in and out of Janklow's place. We'd not go in dragged up, anything like that. We were pretty cool, changed into straight gear.'

'How did Hastings fit into it?' Lorraine asked.

'Well, Art and Didi saw him at the garage. Didi recognized Hastings, because she'd been doing his wigs and make-up at Craig's studio. Well, this panicked Art for a while, then he discovered that Craig's at it, like he's picked up our tricks and he's only doing Norman Hastings himself. Craig's such an oaf, he couldn't even pick a guy with dough. Art was furious – it could've all come out – and what got him worried was that Janklow and Hastings knew each other, and could put two and two together, cause trouble.'

'But Janklow must have known who you were?' Lorraine said.

Nula shrugged. 'Maybe, but if he did he never contacted the cops. Like I said, he seemed to get off on it, like it was punishment. Anyway, we thought we should just back off – besides Art had plenty more, not with as much dough as Janklow, but he did all right . . .'

'So did Hastings talk to Janklow about the blackmail?'

Nula sighed. 'I dunno, but when he was found dead, we freaked. Then fucking Janklow appeared and said he needed Art to cover for him, like say he was someplace when he wasn't. He'd done something.'

Lorraine asked if Nula remembered the date. She thought for a moment and then said it was the fifteenth, she wasn't too sure. But it was the same date Lorraine had been attacked. Nula cried for a few moments and then sniffed, wiping her cheek with her hand. 'He said he'd pay well for Art to cover for him. He couldn't get cash so he handed over a box of jewellery, said it was all he had left.'

'Did you sell it?'

Nula blew her nose. 'In the past when we'd got a few things we'd used Curtis to fence it for us. We didn't say where we got it and he wasn't going to ask.' Nula sighed. Everyone hung on her every word. 'Curtis gave one of the pieces we were selling off – a ring – to Holly and she used to wear it, showed it to everyone. He'd said it was like an engagement ring. It was the big topaz, with diamonds round it. Anyway, she gets picked up by a john who takes her back to his place and he says where did she get the ring as his mother had one like it but—'

'Who was it?'

'Janklow's brother. Anyway, Holly puts two and two together and comes up with sixteen. She asks us about the stuff we fenced to Curtis and then tells us about this john, Brad Thorburn. We tell Art and he's going fucking ape-shit because he knows it's bloody Janklow's brother, and that Curtis, if he smells a good racket, would want in on it, and Curtis would cause trouble.'

Lorraine lit two cigarettes and passed one to Nula. She puffed for a while and then bowed her head. 'We had to do something about the ring – we could have all been implicated, know what I mean? She showed it off to everyone – not that Curtis would have ever married her. He's got a wife and kids anyway.' She sucked at the cigarette. 'We knew we had to get rid of Holly. We figured she hadn't said anything to Curtis – he never came on to us. Art was working the night we decided to do it at the gallery. After we left, we went back to the apartment and Didi got into men's gear. We nabbed a car and parked it not far away from the apartment. Didi left, then I left. I went on my patch, waited for Holly to arrive.'

She sobbed and was given a clean tissue. She took the cigarette from the ashtray and smoked. 'Holly, well, she was always jumping into johns' cars. We knew if she saw a decent car she'd duck and dive to it. Didi drew up across the road and sort of waved towards Holly and, sure enough, she shot across the road so fast I had a tough time following her. Course, soon as she got into the car she knew something was up but by that time I'd gone over, got the back door open and got in; then Didi drove off. We wanted just to get the bloody ring off her, warn her, but she was like a wildcat. We didn't even drive far – we couldn't, she was screaming and shouting so much. I think Didi hit her first, then me, but we never meant . . . We didn't mean to hurt her. She was suddenly just like a rag doll, it was awful, so we stuffed her into the trunk. Didi was supposed to dump it, leave her in it and get back to work, meet up with me. I went back on the streets, to sort of give us an alibi, you know, saying Didi had got a john and I was to talk to Curtis.'

'So where did Art come into all this?'

Nula stubbed out the cigarette. 'That stupid bitch Didi, she didn't turn up. We'd agreed to meet in the Bar Q but she never showed because she went back to the gallery. She was hysterical because as she was driving around, Holly must have come round. She started banging on the trunk, screaming again.' Nula rested her head in her hands. 'Art was mad as hell that she'd gone to the gallery with Holly in the car and Didi's face was scratched and bruised. Holly was a tough kid – she'd put up a fight. If she hadn't we'd never have hurt her.'

'So what happened at the gallery?'

Nula licked her lips. 'I'm not sure but Art said he'd check on Holly, and he went out. Then he came back in and got a hammer. Didi knew what he was gonna do and tried to stop him and it fell on her foot. Anyway, Art did it and came back and told Didi to dump the car. He gave her the ring – he'd taken it off Holly.'

'So Didi got back in the car, knowing Holly was dead in the trunk. Then what?'

'All the stupid cow had to do was dump it and piss off, but she gets into a terrible state. Her foot all swelled up, and she drove home in it because she said she couldn't have walked and she was scared of anyone seeing her. *I* had to dump it. I gave it a good clean in case there were any prints. It wasn't so bad because there was no blood or anything. In fact it wasn't until I got out and was walking past it that I saw this bit of cloth sticking out and then freaked. I just ran like hell back home.'

Lorraine sounded friendly and understanding. 'It must have been realy hard for you.'

'It was, but then it was un-fucking-believable. Didi started wearing the ring. And she wouldn't part with it, it was like some kind of obsession, as if she wanted to be caught. She was always crying and she couldn't sleep. Nothin' I said made any difference. She wouldn't listen to me and that's why we had this row. I was trying to get it off her but she went hysterical, saying it was hers.'

'So you had to get the ring away from Didi, is that right?'

'Course I did but she wouldn't give it up and so we had this argument. She pushed me, then I pushed her and she fell. I thought she was dead, but when . . . It was like Holly happening all over again.'

Nula started to cry, her shoulders shaking, and Lorraine reached across the table for her hand. 'It's okay, everything's going to be okay. After she'd fallen what happened?'

Nula's lipstick smeared, her mascara running down her face. 'I called Art and he came over. He said we should make it look like this serial killer had murdered her, like we'd done with Holly. But he said as he'd fixed it with Holly, I should do Didi, that he was having nothing to do with it and then he left—'

'And?' Lorraine asked.

'I hit her with the hammer and it must have been just like Holly because she moaned. She was still alive, just like Holly. I could hear her voice, telling me about Holly, and I just kept on hitting and hitting her until she was quiet.' Nula accepted another cigarette, inhaled deeply and then sipped some water. 'After I'd done it, I didn't know what to do next. I couldn't lift her by myself so I called Craig. All he did was help me get her to the car.' She fell silent. No one spoke. She smoked the cigarette down to the cork, then looked at it.

Lorraine took the stub from her and tossed it into the ashtray. She stood up.

'Where are you going?' Nula asked.

'They can charge you now.'

Nula watched fearfully as Lorraine walked to the door. She didn't even look back; she just walked out.

It was after midnight. Ed Bickerstaff was jubilant. Lyall's and Nula's statements were signed and they had been taken to their cells. He passed a small white envelope to Lorraine. 'Five thousand dollars in used notes. You did good. I didn't think she'd crack.'

'I won't be needed at the trial, will I?'

'Not unless she changes her plea but I don't think she will.'

'What about Brad Thorburn?'

'I reckon the only thing he was guilty of was screwing a prostitute but we'll need him for questioning. He's on his way back from France.'

Bickerstaff guided her to the door, then paused. 'If I ever need you again . . .'

Lorraine smiled. 'I'll send you my card. I can set up an office now.'

'Just one more thing, if you don't mind me asking. You seemed pretty friendly in there with Nula.'

'Just doing my job. She's scum – she almost killed me.'

'You don't want to press charges, though, do you?'

She gave him a wry look. 'No.'

Rosie was sitting on the sofa watching TV when Lorraine got home. Lorraine looked at her and grinned. 'You're a good friend, Rosie.'

'Bed's all made up. I'll kip on the sofa.'

Lorraine winked. 'Thanks.'

Just as she walked into the bedroom, the phone rang. 'If that's for me, I'm not back yet.' She switched on the shower and couldn't hear properly what Rosie was calling through the door. She had to switch it off.

'That was Brad Thorburn. He said he'd ring again tomorrow morning.'

Lorraine stripped off and stepped beneath the cool water, tilting her face up to the jet spray. She was unnerved by his call and she hadn't expected to hear from him again.

'Is he back in LA?' she shouted.

Rosie appeared in the doorway again. 'On his way, be here in the morning. He said he was at the airport in Paris. Did you want to speak to him?'

Lorraine wrapped the towel around herself and frowned. Brad had picked up Holly, taken her back to that house, had probably screwed her in the same bed as he'd fucked her in, little seventeen-year-old Holly. Brad Thorburn would probably always pick up the wrong kind. As much as she wanted to see him, she thought he was probably calling her to find out if she knew why the police wanted to talk to him.

'If he calls again, I'm out. He's no good – well, not for me.'

'Okay, whatever you say. You want a cup of tea?'

'Sounds good.'

Lorraine lay down on the bed. Tomorrow she would open up the agency, get cards made, get a word processor. By the time Rosie came in with the tea she was deeply asleep. Rosie didn't wake her but gently wrapped the bedcover over her. Lorraine didn't stir.

The last item on her list had been blurred, only half considered, but it was the first thing she thought of in the morning.

Rosie looked up sleepily from the couch when Lorraine walked in. 'What did you say?'

'Let's go to a meeting this morning.'

Brad Thorburn stared around the empty house with all its furnishings draped in dust sheets. He walked out, slamming the front door. He drove to the police station and was introduced to Ed Bickerstaff. The interview was formal and he gave a detailed statement of the night he had picked up a young blonde hooker. He couldn't recall her name; she was just one of so many. Bickerstaff questioned him as to what time of night, how long she had stayed and then asked if on the night in question he had noticed anything unusual about her. Brad shrugged, he couldn't remember clearly.

'How about an item of jewellery?'

Brad thought, and then it dawned on him. 'She was wearing a large ring. I only remember because it was similar to one my mother used to wear, but she took it off and slipped it into her purse and I never gave it much thought.'

'Was this it?' Bickerstaff held out the ring taken from Didi's finger.

Brad stared at it. 'Yes, well, it was similar.'

'Could this be your mother's ring?'

'Possibly. It *is* similar but whether it's hers or not I couldn't say. She had a large collection of jewels – she was a collector. Some of them were worth thousands, others cheap replicas. She was always terrified of being mugged. I'm sorry not to be of more help.'

Bickerstaff didn't bother to explain how important the ring had been in so many people's lives – or deaths.

Brad left and returned to his car. He drove to the real-estate agents, signed over the documents for the contents of the house to be sold along with the property, and then went to Beverly Glen. The sale notices already hung outside. Brad collected the items he wanted to take with him and put little red stickers on the rest so the storage men would be able to ascertain which articles were to be removed. He walked from room to room in the shrouded house. There was little he needed or wanted, it was mostly his personal belongings from his own quarters. He did, however, stick red dots on all the silver-framed family photographs. He found it difficult to look at the faces of his brother and mother but went about his work as fast as possible. Steven's room was more difficult than he had anticipated, with his precious collections of shells and snuff-boxes, the banks of photographs of their mother. He closed the door, refusing to allow himself to think about Steven. Not until he was in his own room did he relax as he checked his books and record collections, his sports equipment. There was so little with which he had any emotional ties – everything could easily be replaced. All he knew was that he would never come back to this house and its memories.

Brad arrived at his mother's nursing home in the late afternoon. He had called Lorraine's number four times but received no reply. He decided he would try once more before he left. He didn't know why he wanted to see her; he was not infatuated or in love with her, but he couldn't shake off the memory of how gentle he had felt towards her, how good it had been to hold her in his arms.

459

Mrs Thorburn was seated by the windows overlooking the elegant gardens. The nursing home was ludicrously expensive, with two or three nursing staff to every resident. She was reading *Vogue*, the arthritic hands with their perfectly manicured nails gliding over the pages, pausing to tap a particular photograph and then ripping off a yellow sticker from a pad and carefully applying it to a page. She still bought lavish clothes – sometimes an entire collection – which were delivered to the home.

Brad watched her for a few more minutes. Everything about her was immaculate: her wig, false eyelashes and pale powdered skin drawn tightly over the high cheekbones. The many face-lifts had given her a surreal look so she could, at a distance, be taken for a thirty-year-old woman; only at close-up did one see the stretched, taut, ageing skin. He called her name softly as he approached and bent to kiss her cheek. As always she averted her face.

'Watch out for my hair, darling.'

He drew up a chair, sitting to one side. She shut the magazine and held it out as if to an unseen butler. Brad took it and pushed it into the side of her wheelchair.

'How are you?'

'Dreadful. How do you expect me to be?'

Her perfect lips, dark crimson, with smears across her over-large, over-white false teeth, grimaced in a sneering smile. 'I hear you're selling the house? I always hated it. Will we get a good price?'

'I should think so.'

'Where are you going to live?'

'South of France.'

'Always loved Cannes but it's not what it used to be. Your father took me there often in the early days but we had problems with the staff, probably because he was fucking them.'

Brad smiled at the way she dropped in the word 'fucking' as if to shock, but he was used to it. She could swear better

460

than any man he'd ever met and he felt something akin to fondness for her, which surprised him. She suddenly pointed one frail, red-nailed finger to the gardens. 'They're putting in a new border and a fountain. I just hope it's not some awful cherub pissing. I hate those little penises spurting water. I'm always surprised how many people choose them, very distasteful, nasty things, penises – uncircumcised ones in particular. I made sure you were circumcised – much more attractive, especially if you're being sucked off.' She gave a shrill laugh, and placed her hands over her lips like a naughty schoolgirl, her diamonds glinting in the sunlight.

'Do you remember that big topaz ring? It had diamonds all round it, very large, set in platinum,' he said quietly, surprised at even bringing the subject up.

'Hard to forget. Your father would always give me something extravagant when he was screwing somebody else. The more expensive it was the higher the chance of it being a close friend. The topaz was good quality and they were rose diamonds, excellent carat. Why do you ask?'

'No reason.'

'Ah, my darling, there's always a reason. I suppose it was one of the items Steven stole or sold or whatever they wish to call it. Well, it was a beautiful ring but too ostentatious for my taste.' She turned to face Brad, her eyes even at eighty still china blue.

'Why did he have so many other women? My father. It's always struck me as odd. You must have loved each other at one time?'

'Love never came into it, sweetheart.' He wanted to hold her clawlike hand but she was turning to one of the other wealthy inmates, waving like royalty. 'That was why he hated me so much and tried to hurt me in every way possible. He hated me because I could not find him attractive. I married him for his money. I told him but I don't think he believed me.'

'Is that true?'

She turned back to face him, her blue eyes like ice chips. 'What do you think?'

'I don't know and I have to go.' He stood up. She waved again across the elegant room and murmured that it was tea-time. 'Will you write to Steven?' he asked.

'He's dead to me. I can't bring myself to write or make any contact. He does not exist. I've already changed my will. You'll get everything.'

He touched her shoulder. 'I'll write, and then, as soon as I'm settled, you'll come visit me.'

'That would be very pleasant, dear.' Both knew the other was lying; there would be no visits. There was no antagonism or reprimand in her bright eyes. She held out her hand and he kissed it gently. How often had he smelt that sweet floral perfume? How many times had he as a child wanted this woman to hold him and kiss him? He felt it even now: he wanted some sign that she cared for him. But she gave none, dismissing him by withdrawing her hand.

He walked away across the polished wood floor, then turned back, half hoping she would still be watching him. But she was already flicking through the pages of *Vogue* again, positioning a yellow sticker on a long cream evening gown worn by a doe-eyed model.

She hadn't worn an evening gown for more than thirty years but she hadn't wept for much longer. Tears ruined her make-up, made her false eyelashes unstick. It had taken many long years of practice not to weep. She could recall the last time she had cried herself to exhaustion. It had been when she had found her husband in bed with her closest friend. The two of them naked, moaning with orgasmic pleasure. She had never had an orgasm in her entire life; she was frigid; she was, as her husband had called her, the 'Ice Maiden'. Only little Steven had broken through to her heart. Only Steven had known how to love her, seemed to know intuitively the fear she had of allowing herself to be

462

loved. He had known how to kiss her without pawing or fumbling. Only Steven knew how delicate she was – and now even he had betrayed her. He had been as brutal as every man she had ever encountered. Sitting trapped in her wheelchair, she remembered his slim, delicate body, his sweet, tender kisses, his perfect circumcised penis that she had loved to kiss awake and then to rub his semen over her skin, because it was better than any expensive creams. They had discussed its therapeutic powers endlessly, lying together in her overheated bedroom. She had never believed that what they were doing was wrong – it was only natural. She bore no blame for what he had sub-sequently done: that was nothing to do with her. The women were whores, just like the bitches her husband had brought home. They had meant nothing to her, and she refused to feel any remorse for the women her beloved son had killed. She started to sing softly to herself, snatches of a song she'd sung in a chorus someplace a long time ago.

If I say I love you, do you mind,
If I shower you with kisses, if I tell you, honey . . . this is . . .'

but she could no longer recall all the lyrics.

Steven Janklow was being led from his neatly made bed in the white-walled room. He liked night time. Every night on the way to the bathroom with his warder, he passed a window. He always stopped in his tracks when he saw his reflection in his white cotton institution gown. 'Oh, hello, darling,' he whispered, before he was led into the bathroom. He never spoke to anyone else, only to the image in the dark window-pane, but he was always smiling. He seemed happy and contented. Often singing the same few lines from some half-remembered song.

'If I say I love you, do you mind,
If I shower you with kisses . . .'

Brad Thorburn returned to France. He made one last attempt to contact Lorraine but received no reply. 'If I say I love you, do you mind . . .'

Rosie and Lorraine had worked hard all week. They had bought some cheap office furniture, a bookcase and filing cabinets. They had arranged for the phone to be connected and delivery of a word processor. Lorraine dropped by the gym to see Hector and explained that she was taking over the office next door. The close proximity of the gym would make it very convenient for workouts.

They did not hire a sign painter as no good agency wants their work broadcast. They were to keep a low profile and advertise in newspapers and magazines. Lorraine would require a licence and a permit to carry a weapon but she felt she should give Bickerstaff a few weeks before she asked a favour. She'd left the number and the address in case he wanted to talk to her but he hadn't called.

She and Rosie were surveying their handiwork when there was a rap on the door. Lorraine turned. 'I thought you were doing Europe.'

Rooney took off his hat. 'The wife still is. I was called back for the Craig Lyall business.'

She tilted her head on one side and he gave an odd, rueful smile.

'Okay, I'm lying. I called Josh to see what was happening and, well, in case they needed me I thought I should come back.'

'Do they?' she asked, wanting to give him a hug but deciding against it. Rooney was not the kind of man you hugged often.

'Got the bum's rush. They're all very pleased with

themselves and now there's no nasty smears about the Art Mathews suicide, which makes the FBI happier.'

He edged further into the new office and looked around. 'You won't get a licence, you know,' he said flatly.

She shrugged. A lot of agencies were working without one.

'Won't get the good clients. You won't even get a weapon licence.'

'I'll take it day by day, Bill.'

He sniffed and looked around, twisting his hat. 'You got my home number?' he asked. He had something on his mind but was too embarrassed to come out with it so he merely shrugged his shoulders. 'I might go and have a curry. I don't suppose you're in the mood for a vindaloo?'

'Not right now, but thanks for the offer.' She let him plod all the way to the door before she called his name. 'Bill . . .'

He turned, plonking his hat on. 'Yep?'

She walked slowly towards him, arms folded. 'I know you're retired and looking forward to sitting back and enjoying a life of leisure, but I was just wondering . . .'

He couldn't hide it: his face lit up as he looked at her expectantly.

'Well, as you said, I couldn't get an investigator's licence or a weapon permit. I've only got my driving licence thanks to you. What would you say to helping me out – not full time, I wouldn't ask that of you, maybe just a couple days a week?'

She let him do a lot of frowning and head scratching but then he smiled. 'I'll make the licence application today. I've got a lot of contacts – we could make a go of it.'

She put out her hand and he shook it and then he pulled her towards him. The big man that nobody dared hug clasped her tightly, his voice was hoarse with emotion. 'Always said you were one of the best. I'm proud you pulled yourself back up. I'm proud of you, Lorraine.'

Rosie watched him walk off before she snapped, 'I thought I was your partner!'

'You are. We need him, Rosie, he's got his retirement bonus, he's got contacts. It's all to do with contacts and he'll be a good front man.' She put her arm around her fat friend's shoulders. 'I'm feeling good, Rosie, positive. How about you?'

Rosie was as tickled as old Rooney had been. Lorraine had this ability to draw you to her, make you want to please her – kill her at times too – but more than that, you felt if she was happy then you were part of that happiness.

'I'm feeling good, partner. I know we'll make a go of it, I just know it.'

Rosie and Lorraine went on to an AA meeting. They both went regularly twice a week. Jake was waiting for them to join him. He was the greeter at the door as they took their places in front of the small informal platform. This meeting was important because Lorraine was going to share her story. Rosie glowed with pride. She herself was not ready yet to stand up and be counted, as Jake called it, but she was closer than she'd ever been before and she felt she owed it to her friend Lorraine. Rosie had a future. It wouldn't all be plain sailing, she knew that – she was no fool – but at least she was in a far better position than she had ever dreamed possible. She was thankful that she'd taken that crazy chance on the strange skinny woman minus a front tooth because they'd both come through. To see Lorraine sitting up there, elegant, strong and vital, made the long, hard journey they'd travelled together worth every minute.

Jake took out a big square handkerchief. He couldn't stop himself: Lorraine was making him cry, not because of what she was saying but because, like Rosie, he was so proud of her, and it was hard for him to believe that the wretched creature Rosie had brought back from the institution was now facing the demon head on. She had fought it, and almost been beaten, but now he was sure she was on her way to recovery. You could almost feel her energy, her optimism.

'My name is Lorraine and I'm alcoholic. Eight years ago, I was a police lieutenant. I was also a drunk. I committed a terrible injustice. I mistakenly took a young boy's life because I was drunk. There is no excuse. Nothing will ever take away the guilt I felt, still feel, will always feel.' Lorraine continued the story of her life, how she had lost her children and her husband, how she had sunk into prostitution, how she had fallen downwards to every kind of depravity simply to earn enough money to drink herself into oblivion. She talked about meeting Rosie, about her introduction to Jake, how she came to be there, and lastly that she had opened up a private investigation agency and was hoping she would make a success of it. She then thanked everyone for listening to her story.

'I don't want oblivion any more, I want my life, I want to live my life and I want to live it sober. I will always be indebted to AA and to my friends. At last I feel more at peace with myself and with God.'

Don't miss the next compulsive thriller in the Lorraine Page series

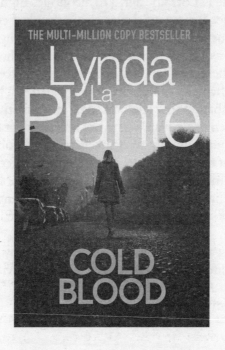

THE MULTI-MILLION COPY BESTSELLER

Lynda La Plante

COLD BLOOD

Keep reading to enjoy an extract now …

SIMON &
SCHUSTER

CHAPTER 1

ANNA LOUISE Caley remained beneath the shower for a full half-hour, scrubbing herself clean, making sure every inch of her perfect body was cleansed. She could blank what she had done from her mind – that was easy – but it was the abuse she inflicted on her body that worried her, and she examined herself with care, pleased to see that there was no bruise or other mark to show what she had done the night before.

With just a soft white towel swathed around her, she re-examined herself, checking and patting her flesh until she was satisfied, then oiled and powdered her body and got dressed. White tennis socks, white cotton panties, white tennis dress and, lastly, pristine white tennis shoes. She laced them up, then chose one of a row of professional-standard racquets and unzipped the cover, tapping the taut strings with the flat of her hand before she slipped the cover back on. She checked her hair, putting on a white stretch head-band to keep her long blonde hair back from her face.

Anna Louise left nothing out of place in her room, placing the towel she had used in the laundry basket along with the previous night's soiled clothes. She liked the fact that she was not like a normal teenager, prided herself on being meticulously neat, and she slowly appraised her immaculate room before she headed for

1

the tennis court. She passed through the kitchen, still empty at 6.30 in the morning, before any of the domestic staff had begun to prepare breakfast, and went outside, where a gardener was already turning on the sprinklers and sweeping up any dead leaf that might have fallen during the night. He did not look up, however, as Anna Louise headed for the changing room where the tennis balls were kept, picked up a large basket of them, then made her way to the court. First she examined the net, making sure it was precisely the correct height, then fed the balls into an automatic delivery machine and set the dial for speed and direction. She carefully removed her racquet from its cover and switched on the ball machine, ready to begin to play against it – against herself. She stood on the service line, her weight thrown on to the balls of her feet, poised and ready for the first ball to shoot out, then began to practise her double-handed backhand. She was a precise player, fast, meticulous and very powerful, and she slammed ball after ball up the court until she was sweating with exertion, each stroke accompanied by a low grunt of satisfaction.

Her concentration lapsed for a moment and she missed the next ball, which struck her hard in the chest. Someone was laughing, and she recognized both the laugh and the accompanying soft, low giggle.

The balls continued to pop out of the machine, but Anna Louise ignored them now and walked off the court towards the summer-house, through the shrubbery, where she knew her approach could be neither seen nor heard.

Some time later, the machine fired out its last few balls, but now Anna Louise was slashing furiously at them, sending them crashing around the court as Tilda Brown,

2

her closest friend, opened the court gate. Tilda was as blonde and as pretty as Anna Louise and dressed in a similar white tennis dress, but Anna Louise didn't stop playing even for a moment to acknowledge her.

'Hi, Anna!' Tilda called. 'Sorry I'm late, I've got a terrible headache. Maybe I won't play this morning, I feel real bad,' she continued, pulling a face.

Anna Louise made no reply, but switched off the machine and picked up the basket to begin collecting the stray balls. Tilda, still complaining of a headache, balanced some balls on her racquet and carried them across to the basket to tip them inside.

'Did you hear what I said? I don't feel like playing.'

Anna Louise smiled.

'Ahh, but I've been waiting for you. I want to show you my backhand, it's really progressed.'

'It was always good,' Tilda replied.

'Yes, but now it's better,' Anna Louise said nonchalantly.

'Maybe later!' Tilda carried the basket over and tipped the balls into the machine. 'I'll refill it for you.'

Anna Louise stood on the service line, bouncing a ball up and down on her racquet, then suddenly took aim. The ball slammed into Tilda's back, making her turn round, gasping. The blow had hurt so much she could hardly speak, and the next ball hit her so hard in the stomach that she staggered backwards, winded.

'Stop it, Anna, STOP IT, THAT HURT . . . YOU HURT ME.'

Anna Louise moved closer. 'Get Polar to kiss it better . . .'

Tilda was scared and tearful; her belly ached, while her back felt as if it was burning, and Anna Louise was bouncing another ball, ready to aim at her again. Tilda ducked for cover as the third ball came towards her.

'What are you doing? STOP IT!' she screamed.

Anna Louise grinned as she picked up a fourth ball.

'You can't get away from me, Tilda Brown.' She was now throwing the ball up in the air as if to serve. Tilda moved further back and bumped into the ball machine, hitting the switch with her arm. The machine began to pump the balls more rapidly towards Anna Louise, who laughed as she swung her racquet, forehand and backhand in perfect unison, every ball viciously directed at the cowering Tilda, who screamed, running this way and that to avoid the swift hail of tennis balls, until she squatted sobbing behind the net.

Even behind the safety of the net, balls slammed into her arms and legs through the mesh, Anna Louise first taking aim at Tilda's body, but then at her face.

'Stop it, please stop it,' sobbed Tilda, looking up to see Anna Louise standing over her.

'You stay away from him, Tilda, he's mine. I see you with him again and I'll make you sorry, I'll hurt you more than any tennis ball, I'll hurt you so bad, Tilda Brown, you're gonna wish you were dead . . .'

Tilda was crying like a baby, terrified as much by Anna Louise's verbal threats as by her violence, and she sobbed with relief when she recognized the figure coming towards them. Anna Louise saw him too, and gave Tilda a final quick, hard blow on the side of the head, then lowered the racquet, smiling sweetly, her whole manner altered.

'Hi, honey,' Robert Caley smiled to his daughter, then looked towards the weeping Tilda. 'What's happened, Tilda?'

Anna Louise linked her arm through her father's. 'It was my fault, you know that serve o' mine, Papa, poor little Tilda here got right in the way of it . . . and you got to take some of the blame for coachin' me to serve so hard, but I didn't mean to hit her, I guess she just isn't up to my standard.'

Robert Caley had one arm around his daughter as he reached out to Tilda with concern. 'You all right, sweetheart?'

Tilda wouldn't look into his eyes, but held her hand to her head feeling the lump where Anna Louise had hit her. 'I want to go home, Mr Caley, today,' she said in a low, but firm voice.

'She is just bein' silly 'cos she lost the game,' Anna Louise said petulantly. She tried to keep hold of her father's arm to stop him following Tilda, but he pulled free of her, and she was infuriated to see him help Tilda to the gates and walk her back to the house. She smashed the racquet against the tarmacked court, then examined it, afraid she had damaged one of her favourites. Long strands of Tilda's hair were caught between the strings.

Tilda had packed, and refused to say anything else to Anna Louise through her locked bedroom door other than that she was going home at once. Anna Louise tried to cajole her, saying she was sorry, that she hadn't meant to be nasty, but Tilda refused to unlock the door. Now Anna Louise was worried about what Tilda might say to her mother, and was beginning to think that perhaps the sooner she left the better.

'Fine, you leave, Tilda Brown, I don't care,' she said angrily, but she was worried enough to decide to go and sit with her mother. Tilda would certainly want to say goodbye to her, and more than likely would tell tales. Anna Louise tapped on the door of her mother's suite and waited; it was often locked in the mornings as Elizabeth Caley hated being seen without her warpaint, even by her own daughter. Anna Louise knocked again, then walked in: all the curtains were drawn and the room was in darkness. She called out to her mother, but receiving no reply wondered if Elizabeth was still sleeping or, worse, had gone downstairs and would see Tilda. She hurried through her mother's sitting room towards her bedroom.

'Mama,' she whispered, then pressed her ear to the door, listening. 'Are you awake Mama? It's me, it's Anna Louise.'

She eased the bedroom door open and peeked inside, adjusting her eyes to the darkness of the room, then called out softly again, but saw that the bed covers had been drawn back. Her mother was known to fly into an even worse rage if she was woken from sleep than if she was surprised without makeup. She suffered from severe insomnia and her sleep was precious, if rarely natural.

Anna Louise looked across to the bathroom door and heard the soft sounds of bath-water running. She was about to leave when she noticed the low, flickering light of a candle on her mother's bedside table. The candle was sputtering, and she crossed the room to check it out, not expecting to find anything else.

The gris-gris had been consecrated, because it was positioned on top of a worn black Bible, a small white cotton sack of salt to the left and a tiny green bottle of water to the right. Above the Bible a blue candle, representing the element of fire, guttered in its candle-stick; below the book was a square of sweet-smelling incense, the symbol for air. Anna Louise felt the hairs on the back of her neck prickle when she opened the gris-gris bag and looked at the contents, unaware of their meaning and of what it meant to have seen and touched a consecrated gris-gris. Fascinated, she picked up the old Bible and opened the fly-leaf: in old-fashioned scrolled handwriting whose ink had faded from black to brown

6

there was an inscription to Elizabeth Seal – her mother's maiden name. Anna Louise carefully replaced the book, flicking through the tissue-thin pages to try to make sure it was in the same position she had discovered it.

Back in her own room, she sniffed her fingers and decided they smelt musty, so she filled her wash-hand basin with hot water and soaped her hands clean. She was just drying them when she heard her mother calling for her and returned to the suite.

'Tilda wants to go home today,' Elizabeth said, toying with a silver spoon on her breakfast tray. 'But that's silly as we're all leaving tomorrow.'

Anna Louise sat on the edge of her mother's bed, noticing that the bedside table had been cleared. 'Oh, we had an argument, we'll make it up.' She was anxious to change the subject, so asked with concern, 'How you feeling today?'

'I'm just fine, honey. Now you go and talk to your friend, it's stupid for her to go if we're all going to New Orleans tomorrow.'

'Okay, I'll make up with her. Do you want me to take your tray?'

'Mmmm, I'll sleep a while maybe, I had a bad night. Kiss kiss?'

Anna Louise leaned over to plant a kiss on her mother's cheek and then carried the breakfast tray out of the room and closed the door behind her.

Tilda had already left by the time Anna Louise returned her mother's tray to the kitchen. Anna Louise was unconcerned: she'd make it up to her, buy her something expensive. She wandered into the kitchen where Berenice, the housekeeper, had just baked a tray of fresh blueberry muffins, and began picking at one with her fingers, remembering the strange, musty smell from the Bible she had seen upstairs.

7

'Tilda told me somethin' weird, something she'd seen . . .' she began casually, still picking at the muffin's crispy top.

Berenice was emptying the dishwasher, not paying too much attention to her employers' daughter, only half-listening as she went back and forth stacking the clean dishes in the cupboards. She poured a glass of milk for Anna Louise and set it beside her.

'Miss Tilda sure was upset about somethin', crying her eyes out. We thought maybe she'd had bad news.' She continued putting the clean crockery away.

'What does it mean if you got a Bible, a blue candle and funny little bags of salt and incense, you know, like those gris-gris bags they sell back home?'

The cupboard door banged shut.

'You don't wanna know, Miss Anna Louise, an' you stop pickin' at each muffin. You want one, then you take one.'

'What does it mean?'

The housekeeper was replacing the cutlery in its drawer now, buffing each knife and fork quickly with a clean cloth before she put it away.

'Well, it depends on which way the cross is placed on the Bible.'

'Ah, so you do know what it means?'

'All I know is, if you and Miss Tilda are playing around, then you stop and don't be foolish. That's voodoo, and nobody ought to play games with things they don't understand because evil has a way of getting inside you, like a big black snake. It sits in your belly and you never know when it's gonna uncoil and spit . . . and if you touch another person's gris-gris, then you got bad trouble.'

Anna Louise broke off a large piece of muffin and

stuffed it into her mouth. 'You don't believe in all that mumbo-jumbo, do you?'

She took a gulp of milk, swallowing it the wrong way, and started coughing and spluttering as the muffin lodged in the back of her throat. She gasped, her eyes watering and her cheeks turning bright red. She couldn't breathe – it felt as if she was being choked, and Berenice had to hit her hard in the middle of her back as she retched and clung on to the edge of the table before at last she coughed the mouthful of food up, heaving for breath.

The housekeeper fetched some paper kitchen towel to wipe up the mess.

'You see, what did I say about that snake? It just come and hissed an' spat right now, almost chokin' you, so you hear me right and don't go meddlin'.' But when she turned back Anna Louise was gone, so she went out into the hall, catching sight of the girl as she ran helter-skelter up the stairs.

'Are you all right, Miss Anna Louise?'

Anna Louise looked down and then leaned over the bannister rail, whispering, 'It was in my mama's room. It wasn't Tilda that saw it but me!'

She laughed suddenly and continued running up the stairs, not seeing the fear on Berenice's face as she slipped her hand inside her uniform dress to feel for her own gris-gris. It was safely tucked into her underslip, on her left-hand side, beneath her heart.

Berenice returned to the kitchen: that silly spoilt child had no notion of what went on in the house, and she hoped to God she never would. She cleaned up the mess from the table, and finished putting the dishes away, then tipped all the freshly made blueberry muffins into the trash. She would make a fresh batch, just in case a drop of the snake's venom that had hissed from Anna Louise Caley had touched them: there were some chances that just weren't worth taking.

The following afternoon, accompanied by her parents, Anna Louise flew from Los Angeles to New Orleans. It was 15 February, and on 16 February, Anna Louise was officially reported as missing. Police in both Los Angeles and New Orleans attempted to trace her, and when they failed to do so, her parents brought in private investigators.

The weeks became months – no body and no ransom note were ever discovered, and even with top investigation agencies on the case, no clue as to the whereabouts of the missing girl, or her body, ever came to light. After nine months the disappearance of Anna Louise Caley was no longer news, and she had to all intents and purposes become just another statistic, another photograph on the missing persons files.

Eleven months passed, and with no new information, Anna Louise's distraught parents faced the possibility that she might have been murdered. By this time, more than fifteen investigation agencies had been involved with the case, the Mississippi had been dragged and helicopters had searched the swamplands of Louisiana. Agnews Investigations, along with three other less well-known agencies, were still retained on the enquiry: the Caleys had paid out millions of dollars but the expenditure had yielded no motive, no suspect, no result. All the grieving parents were left with was an aching period of waiting, while they longed for a sign that their beautiful Anna Louise was still alive.

All the PI agencies involved had made a lot of money, and some had even traded information with one another, but the Anna Louise Caley bonanza was coming to an end. Pickings were getting slim for private investigators – it was a tough business in which contacts and recommendations by word of mouth were a necessity, as Page Investigations, a small PI company, had found out the hard way. Even getting a foothold on the lowest rung of such a competitive ladder had proved impossible, and the attempt had been financially crippling for Lorraine Page: now, her agency was virtually bankrupt.

Even though she was a former police lieutenant, her own case history as an alcoholic and an officer who had shot dead an unarmed boy while drunk on duty meant that instead of being welcomed into the PI fraternity, she was being frozen out – just as she had been kicked out of the LAPD. The hardest part was explaining to Rosie, the assistant whom Lorraine jokingly called her partner, and who was also a recovering alcoholic, that they were going under. Dear Rosie, who still hoped, Rosie who still maintained that business would pick up – but there had never been any business. There was nothing to pick up from: it had all been a gamble, a dream even, but now it was over.

Lorraine had the phone cupped in her hand, half-listening to the call, half-wondering whether tonight would be the night she would tell Rosie – she knew she would have to do it soon. She listened, interjecting twice how sorry she was as the man's deep rumbling voice made incoherent references to his wife's passing.

Rosie, a plump woman with a kind, open face, was reading her star signs, a cup of coffee and two orange chocolate cup cakes beside her. She had flicked a glance at Lorraine when the phone had jangled through the silent office and sighed when she had heard Lorraine's over-cheerful 'Hi, Bill, how ya doing?'

Rosie had been trying a new diet: proteins one meal,

11

carbohydrates the next, with fruit forty minutes either before or after each meal, and no fats or fried food. She had stuck to it for a month and felt better for losing a few pounds, but today she was indulging in a binge of chocolate cup cakes, hating herself with each bite. Still, it was just one of those days – she couldn't face another chicken breast without crisp golden skin or French fries, or another salad without dressing, and a whole month with no fresh crusty bread spread thickly with peanut butter had been excruciating.

At last Lorraine was able to replace the receiver. 'That was Bill Rooney,' she murmured, lighting a cigarette. 'His wife died.'

'I didn't know he had a wife,' Rosie said, lowering her magazine.

'I don't think he did,' Lorraine said as she counted the butt-ends in her ashtray. She sighed and leaned back in her chair. By turning her head a fraction she could just make out the cheap sign printed in fake gold leaf on the outer office door – 'Page Investigations Agency'. There was a stack of calling cards on her desk with the same inscription. It was a farce.

'Well, the end of yet another over-active sleuthing day.' Rosie chomped on her cup cake, staring at the free digital alarm clock she got from ordering some non-stick pans. It was almost six. Unaware of the smear of chocolate over her right cheek, she looked over at Lorraine, watching her as she inhaled deeply on her thirtieth or so cigarette of the day. Her eyes were staring vacantly across the small white painted office. Rosie hated it when she did those vacant stares. Sometimes her silences could last over an hour and Rosie could never tell what her partner was thinking. She hoped this was not going to turn into one of Lorraine's moods. 'You should cut down,' she said with her mouth full.

'So should you,' Lorraine retorted, looking at the trash can filled with empty silver foil cup cake moulds.

'I don't smoke, so it's expected to crave sugar. That's half of what alcoholism is about too, you know, sugar craving.'

Lorraine pushed her second-hand typist's chair back from her empty desk. 'Is it? Well, well, isn't that interesting. And just what are hamburgers and fries, are they a craving too?'

'For chrissakes, don't start having a go at me! You and your brown rice and your vitamins make me wanna throw up.'

'Might do you some good!'

Rosie now pushed her large ass back in her catalogue sale of the month office chair. 'Right, that is it.'

'Yep, I guess it is, Rosie.'

It was hard to explain how each day Lorraine felt more isolated, because in physical terms she wasn't: Rosie and big Bill Rooney were always there. It wasn't that she didn't have anyone to talk to, interact with – it just felt that way. Her mind seemed to be atrophying and she felt drained, lethargic; sometimes she wanted to weep, out of a deepening feeling of utter loneliness, or was it loveless-ness? Whatever it was, it was having a more and more destructive effect on her, and she felt its undertow sucking her down.

Lorraine flicked the old venetian blind that didn't quite fit the windows. She gave a sly look at her plump room-mate as she stubbed out her cigarette. She didn't even live in a place of her own, but was sharing Rosie's small apartment in a run-down district off Orange Grove. She was thirty-seven years old; almost six of those years had been lost in a sea of drugs and alcohol addiction, and sometimes, especially at times like this afternoon, she felt it was all a waste of time; in reality she was never

13

going to get back into the only business she knew or had known when she had been a cop.

The two women had met when Lorraine had been recuperating from a near-fatal hit-and-run accident. It wasn't the vehicle that had almost killed her, but her drinking and self-abuse. Now she had been sober and attempting to get her life organized for nearly two years. As an ex-lieutenant attached to the Pasadena Homicide Squad, she had experience not only in the field but as a detective, and she had been a very good one. 'Had' being the operative word: after drinking took over her life it had cost her the husband she had loved and the two daughters she had adored.

'What you thinking about?' Rosie asked, pretending to be immersed in her magazine.

'Nothing,' Lorraine answered, but she quite obviously was. She wondered if she should attempt another reconciliation with her kids. Yet as always whenever she thought about them, she decided they were better off without her intruding on their new life, a life she had not been a part of for too many years. Added to that, her ex-husband had remarried and her daughters called his new wife 'Mother'. They didn't even want to see her.

Rosie pored over her magazine again. Lorraine's long sighs made her aware that something was coming, but she said nothing, flicking over the pages to a new diet that guaranteed you could lose weight with ease if you sent off for their special-priced 'slimming drinks'. But as she'd attempted most diets, including slimming drinks, and none had worked, she flicked over to a knitting pattern.

'This is a farce, you know it and I know it. I mean, I

dunno what else we can do. How many more adverts can we afford to run, if we don't drum up any customers by the end of the week?'

Here it comes, thought Rosie, scowling. 'You've said that every week.' She hated it when Lorraine started on this tactic, partly because she knew everything she said was true but also because it made her afraid. Afraid Lorraine would leave, afraid that without Lorraine she would go back on the booze, afraid Lorraine would too.

'Got to face reality.' Lorraine prodded her empty cigarette carton, hoping she'd overlooked a stray one. But it wasn't to be, so she looked over the stubs in her ashtray again.

'Yes, I know, I know, and I hear what you are sayin', but at the same time we got to stick at it. Everyone knows any new business takes time to lift off, even Bill Rooney told us that.'

Lorraine appeared not to be listening as she rummaged in her purse and started to check her loose change.

'I mean, we could get a case in tomorrow that'd make everything you just said obsolete,' Rosie said a little too cheerfully.

'What?' Lorraine asked challengingly.

'Obsolete,' Rosie repeated flatly.

'Really? Well, you've been saying that for the past month and we've not had so much as a telephone call. And if you want to check the diary out, we are hardly likely to get some case off the street that'd pay for your cup cakes and my cigarettes, never mind the rent on this place and your apartment, so straighten out, Rosie. Shit, I need a cigarette.'

Lorraine crossed to the hooks by the toilet closet. She yanked down her raincoat.

15

'Maybe the rain'll stop soon.'

Lorraine pulled on her raincoat. 'Oh yeah, so it's all gonna be okay if the sun shines, is it?'

'Maybe.'

'You're a dumb optimist.'

'What?'

'Optimist, Rosie. Even if the sun cracked the paving stones that's not gonna help us. Two stray dogs, a missing senile grandfather, a two-week stint in a department store to cover for their in-house detective's vacation, five car traces, four warrants and a woman suspecting her husband of having an affair with his secretary, and as the wife was your size and his secretary looked like Julia Roberts, it didn't take us long to investigate, and that . . . that is it, Rosie, that's been all there's been for the past nine months.'

'You always gotta get personal. If you look on the good side, you've been sober nine months more, so have I come to think about it, so my guess is we'll make it. This is just a bad patch.'

Lorraine clenched her teeth. 'No, it isn't, Rosie, it's just a fact. We are flat broke and searching my ashtray for dog-ends is not exactly what I had planned for the future. We might as well admit it, face it, before we get any deeper in debt.'

'But we are facing it,' Rosie said stubbornly.

Lorraine closed her eyes as if talking to a child, her voice sounding annoyingly over-patient. 'No, we are not. Fact is this whole idea was shit, and to be honest I am not feeling like patting myself on the back 'cos I remained sober. Truth is, right now I feel like tying one hell of a load on and the only thing stoppin' me is that I have no money.'

'Never stopped you before,' snapped back Rosie.

Lorraine's eyes were like cold chips of ice. 'What's

16

that supposed to mean? What are you suggesting, Rosie? Come on, spit it out, are you saying I go out and screw a few guys to keep this place open? That what you think I should do?'

Rosie blushed and turned away. She loathed Lorraine when she was like this, she could get so cold, so unapproachable, so downright nasty. But unlike the times they'd bickered about the agency before, there wasn't another sarcastic retort forthcoming, just an ominous silence.

Lorraine was staring at herself in the small mirror glued to the back of the door. Her hair needed a cut and new highlights. She leaned closer, frowning, as she checked the scar running from her left eye down to midway of her cheekbone; that needed to be fixed but plastic surgery cost. She stepped back, giving herself a critical appraisal. Considering the punishment her body and insides had taken from all the abuse, her skin looked remarkably clear, but there were fine lines at the sides of her eyes and they were getting deeper. Either way, she didn't like what she saw, and kicked the door closed.

Lorraine picked up her gym bag and flicked off the main overhead light switch. Her shadow etched across the main office wall as she reached for her purse. Caught in the half-light from the lit-up screen on Rosie's word processor, Lorraine's chiselled features never ceased to make Rosie's heart lurch. She obviously didn't see herself as Rosie did, because she was still a very attractive woman. Perhaps not as ethereal as Rosie thought, but for her age, and considering what she had been through, Lorraine Page was still a looker. The stronger she had become physically over the past twenty-one months, the more her natural beauty shone through. Lorraine's strict diet, her almost obsessive work-outs at the gymnasium, had proved that a woman who lost six years drinking herself into oblivion, who had become a hopeless, scrawny, sickly alcoholic when she and the overweight Rosie had first met, could now pass for an athlete. The only thing ex-Lieutenant Lorraine Page could not recapture was her career, and her husband and two daughters. She never spoke of them, either to Rosie or at AA meetings, whereas Rosie spilled many tears about wanting to be reunited with her son.

Rosie now took a long deep sigh; maybe, as she herself had half-suggested, the failure of their business would send Lorraine back to the bottle, back to a life in the gutters. Rosie was therefore totally unprepared for what Lorraine had to say as she hovered by the main office door, about to leave.

Lorraine swung the door slightly with her foot. 'I meant to tell you, the department store have offered me a full-time job as their store detective. Remember the job I took over for two weeks? Well, apparently she had one hell of a holiday and came back pregnant.'

'What?'

'So, we close up at the end of the week and at least I'll have enough for the rent on the apartment.'

'What about Page Investigations?' Rosie asked as the tears started.

'Like I said, it's over, end of the week we close up shop.'

'What about me?'

Lorraine wouldn't look at her friend, still tap-tapping the door with the toe of her shoe. 'Well, I guess you got to go out into the big world, Rosie, and get a job. Shouldn't be too tough, you can use a word processor and . . .'

Rosie turned away, her eyes brimming, and Lorraine felt awful. She went over and slipped her arm around her friend's shoulders.

'I'm sorry, sometimes I say things and they come out all the wrong way. What I am trying to say is – you got a life, Rosie, and maybe I have too, not just doing what we're doing, okay?'

Rosie nodded and felt in her pocket for a paper tissue. Lorraine hesitated, knowing that to stay with Rosie would only involve going over old ground, but was saved by the ring of the phone. Rosie snatched up the receiver, hoping against all hope that the call would mean a job, but didn't even get out 'Page Investigations'. It didn't matter anyway – it was only her sponsor, Jake, wondering if she'd be at AA that evening. By the time Rosie had replied that she would, Lorraine had gone.

'You okay, Rosie?' Jake's friendly rasping voice enquired.

'Nope, we're shutting up shop. Can I see you tonight before the meeting?'

Jake agreed and Rosie replaced the phone, feeling the tears welling up again. Was it ever going to end? Did she have a life of her own, as Lorraine had said? Did she hell, as without Lorraine, Rosie knew she was hopeless – sure, she could use a word processor, but she didn't have enough confidence to go out alone into the big wide world. That was the difference between them – Rosie needed Lorraine, and without her, the world scared the shit out of her. Or maybe it wasn't the world, just her own weakness and low self-esteem. Just seeing the empty cup cake carton made her want to weep – she couldn't even stick to a diet! How could she cope without Lorraine? By having a drink, that would be how, and that realization made her want to weep even more. She badly needed to go to that meeting.

*

ACKNOWLEDGEMENTS

I sincerely thank Suzanne Baboneau, Gill Coleridge, Esther Newberg, Patty Detroit, the real Lorraine Page whose name I borrowed, Hazel Orme, Clare Ledingham and Liz Thorburn. To everyone at the Pasadena Police Station and Sheriff's Office, thank you for your time and expertise. But above all my thanks to a very admirable lady who brought me the story of her life.